...but Lyse's horse, shoved violently sideways, lost its balance as more of the path broke away. The whinnying animal toppled over and fell down the slope, hurling its rider into the air. To Lyse everything seemed to happen slowly but inexorably, even the piercing scream issuing slowly from her own throat...

She landed hard on her back and slid down the scree of the slope, becoming tangled in some small shrubs which slowed her but did not hold her, Lyse continued a further helpless, horrible tumble and slide

Breathless and sobbing, she frantically clawed at the slope with nothing to grab onto to stop her careening plunge toward the edge of the overhang and thin air. She was all gouging fingernails and clawing, bleeding hands and a horrified heart about to burst with fright.

Suddenly, with a leafy swish, another bush finally jolted her to a stop. From below she heard the horse's high scream as it plunged through thin brush and shot over the slope's edge. She wept without hope, for the bush holding her trembled violently, and she heard branches cracking and felt then the terrifying meaning of the phrase 'alone with one's fate'.

Shaking with fear she opened one eye, as if opening both would overload her fragile platform. She had crashed a wide hole in the small-leafed tangle of shrubbery that surrounded her. Nevertheless, she managed to raise her head to look all the way up to the path, for over the roar of the rapids below she heard someone shouting her name...

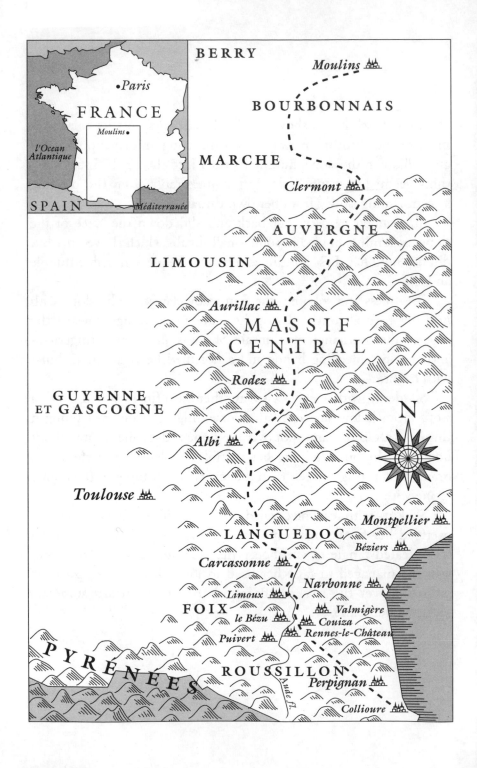

FIRE, BURN!

also by Mallory Dorn Hart

Published by John James

A Glass Full of Stars

Published by Simon & Schuster (Pocket Books)

Jasmine on the Wind
Defy the Sun

FIRE, BURN!

MALLORY DORN HART

JJ COMPANY NEW YORK

This adventure novel is a work of fiction that includes some historical events of 12th and 16th century France, and features some characters based on actual personages from these periods. All characters in this novel are fictitious and any resemblance to actual individuals, living or dead, other than those clearly in the public domain, is entirely coincidental.

Map on Page 2 drawn by Craig Jordan, after a 16th century map of France by the Flemish cartographer Abraham Ortelius.

First Printing 2002

©2001 Mallory Dorn Hart. All Rights Reserved.

Library of Congress Catalog Number 2001132624
ISBN 0-9675915-1-1

Published by John James Company
New York, NY

Printed in the United States of America

Prelude

"Heaven defend us, look up there!" the young woman gasped, jabbing the fellow riding before her. "But we've had no advance message!"

Above them a file of armed riders riveted their attention, coursing along the crest of the hill streaming the white Bourbon flag and dramatically silhouetted against the lowering sun. The two dawdlers on the road below immediately and frantically kicked up the pace of the one horse they were sharing.

"Can we make St. Piteu before my uncle does?" Lyse-Magdalene cried into the wind, her red kerchief fluttering against her face.

"Not unless this animal can fly," responded the stolid youth handling the horse, having ridden after the defector and chased her down, then swung her up into the saddle as she grasped his arm and jumped—a trick of timing they'd practiced since adolescence. "This is what comes of always running away, *ma princesse*, and now when you're seen in those peasant clothes your foolish game of disappearing will be found out."

"No it won't, not if we can make the postern gate so I can slip through the kitchen door," Lyse panted. "Anyway, my uncle Charles never receives until he is refreshed from his trip. And I don't run away, you impertinent!" Nevertheless she gave a guilty glance down at the sturdy field shoes she always borrowed to slip out of the gates and clomp the road blessedly on her own, to one nearby village or another, away from the routine of her dutiful, monotonous life before she was missed and Germain dispatched to find her. "I just need to see more of the world than the house's high walls where he keeps me like a prisoner."

Germain had no patience today for Lyse-Magdalene whining over her fate. "A very spoiled prisoner indeed" he clipped out. "The duke supplies you and your little household with every need and luxury."

"Except my freedom." She coughed as the pace jolted her. She didn't know why her life had to be so circumscribed that she must live far from any court, subtly being watched every minute, for no one ever answered that question except with a shrug. So she feared in her heart that her beloved uncle was ashamed of her because of her dead father's disgrace and the distressing, random visions she suffered occasionally. But she always shrunk from disturbing her august guardian with questions or complaints during his short visits; she ached to please him.

Germain kicked insistently at the horse's flanks as they galloped on. "You are barely eighteen, lady. 'Tis obvious he is trying to guard you and keep you chaste until you marry."

His passenger hated that subject. She leaned back harder against him as the path slanted down and their pace increased. "Pah, I told you, I could never, ever marry. Who would accept an orphan daughter of a traitor, with not a sou of dowry or bit of land to bring with her and who has never even been to the royal court?"

"Nevertheless, you are a Bourbon..."

"A well-hidden Bourbon, isn't that true? I don't fool myself. Money is money and a woman is invisible unless she has some. And if the duke gives me to some ugly, horrid creature who just wants a young girl I will swallow poison."

"You'll do nothing of the sort," Germain muttered at her. Yet he worried for her anyway. He had looked after her since they were little children together, he the son of the commoner *Intendant* who ran her solitary estate and she the noble orphan girl who sometimes had puzzling spells. He himself was content with his little room and his work, he was happy learning to follow in his father's footsteps. But her governess had filled her head with classics and romantic legends and now she was chaffing to burst the tight boundaries of her life.

Nevertheless, the girl truly loved her august uncle Charles, her only relative, and she was always sweet and affable and eager to please him when he visited. Getting her back home and in her own clothes before Bourbon learned of today's rebellious escapade was important.

Germain plunged the horse onto a ragged shortcut through a patch of woods behind the manor house. "I think we'll make the postern gate in time," he declared, endeavouring as usual to calm her. "But I'll wager right now Madame de Dunois is turning purple..."

Red was more the word for Madame de Dunois, as the governess, hands on her narrow hips and glaring angrily, caught sight of Lyse scurrying up the servant's stair as the duke's dusty party was dismounting in the courtyard.

Her charge was becoming harder to control every day.

Chapter 1

It was past the night hour of eleven when Elinor de Dunois was summoned to the duke's chamber. She sketched a quick bow to her employer, the plume on her flat, pearl-edged hat bobbing, and, full of concern, she blurted out, "My lord, what is happening between you and the king's mother? My friend drops maddening hints in her last two letters of grievous relations between the royal mother, Madame Louise, and you. I sense some evil."

The countess' worry, in fact, had been heightened by Bourbon's precipitous arrival that midday and immediate retirement to his rooms, where he had been occupied with his lieutenants arriving at St. Piteu from all directions; a strange event, for Bourbon's infrequent visits to his ward, Lyse-Magdalene, was usually just himself, his valet and a few guards.

Confused by this sudden invasion, she and her charge Lyse-Magdalene, had earlier shrunk into the background before the parade of frowning confederates striding to the duke's rooms, but at this moment his chamber was lit by guttering candles and occupied only by him.

Charles de Bourbon laid down his pen atop the sheaf of papers he had been signing and ran a hand through his shoulder-length brown hair to refocus his attention on her. "Whatever your friend hinted at is true, Madame," he answered his usually open, boyish features drawn by tension. "The loud whispers have spread all over France and surely England and Spain too by this time. My poor wife Suzanne was hardly in her grave when Louise de Savoie offered herself to me in marriage, believing the head of the house of Bourbon would be delighted with a sour, greedy woman many years his senior, with the lumpy face of a peasant."

He rose and straightened tired shoulders. "She even claims to have favorably influenced her son in my appointment as Constable of France. Just because she loved me, of course." His voice dripped sarcasm. Madame Louise loved nothing but the crown on Francois' head.

Elinor made one of her birdlike jitters. "So much I knew, and that no one in France has blamed you for running from that woman's yoke. It takes no wizard to see Louise de Savoie's fat outline behind every insult you have suffered since you refused her, but now–there seems even worse?" She had not missed the new grooves running between nose and mouth on the ordinarily youthful face; they were not reassuring.

Bourbon settled by leaning back against the table acting as his desk. His thumb unconsciously rubbed at the jeweled pommel of the dagger he still wore at his waist, although he had doffed his fitted doublet and ebony boots and donned a loose jacket over his shirt and breeches. "Well. You may have the worst in a short sentence. Louise de Savoie now has a suit before the Parlement claiming as hers the entire Bourbon inheritance, both that which I had from my wife and my own Montpensier lands as well. She claims that her kinship of first cousin to Suzanne is closer than mine as husband."

The governess' thin hand, adorned with gold rings, flew to her mouth. "*Mais non!*" she gasped.

"*Mais oui,*" he mocked her bitterly. "A complete farce, she traces a ridiculous path two hundred fifty years back to Jean, the first Bourbon, to substantiate her claim. If this amuses you, Madame, save your laughter, for the king himself stands behind this madwoman as an easy way of sequestering my title and possessions to his branch of our common house. Even more, the scurrilous suit even acts to divest my old mother-in-law, the duchesse Anne, of her Bourbon dower rights."

"Oh! That ingrate! The duchess Anne actually reared that woman and made for her that brilliant match with the *comte* d'Angouleme whose son would one day be named king! Oh, monseigneur, I cannot speak. I fear for you, and my heart bleeds for Madame Anne who has already suffered so with the loss of Suzanne."

The duke paused a moment in respect for de Dunois' stunned expression. The governess was sister to his closest ally, the marquis de Joyeuse, yet where Joyeuse was stocky and bluff she was thin and birdlike. But the woman was learned, and deeply loyal, and he depended heavily upon her when it came to Lyse-Magdalene.

He went on, "My mother-in-law, despite her sixty-one years and fragile health is not to be trifled with. She insists there is going to be only one possible outcome for me in this trumped-up lawsuit supported by the king: the loss of all my possessions. This scurrilous victory they will follow up with more false charges against me, then there will be a hollow trial and the inevitable march to the headsman." His gaze flickered, as if for an instant to shut out the reality of Francois' complicity, formerly a constant friend through the years.

He squeezed the bridge of his nose. "The tragedy is, Madame, I have finally come to agree with her."

De Dunois collapsed into a nearby chair. "*Dieu me sauve*," she whispered, patting at her heart. "How is this possible?"

Charles stared right through her, sorting over in his mind for the thousandth time the swift events, the betrayals, the options remaining, and he chose to admit to her, "The situation is deadly enough that I may, perhaps, pick one other road that has been offered which would tempt the saints themselves. But first I ride with my partisans to Paris at daybreak tomorrow to consult my lawyers and appear in my own behalf before the *Parlement*. After all, the outcome of this wild attack still remains to be seen."

The governess stared back at him. She did not miss the implication of what he meant by 'another road'. It was called treason.

Charles de Bourbon's distinguished and successful military services to France, carried out with the reckless, *condottiere* bravery inherited from his Italian mother's family, had early been honored by Francois the First with the Bourbon's appointment as High Constable and Commander of the Royal Forces, the greatest honor the king could bestow. All France was impressed by Bourbon's victories through the years, and dazzled by the pomp of his rich establishments crammed with commandeered art.

Perhaps it was no real wonder, so it crossed the governess' thoughts, that in spite of the king's own popularity with his subjects, he had begun to writhe with jealousy of this acclaimed hero. She sensed Bourbon's torment over his monarch's unthinkable rejection, but she was also no fool: without the kiss of the reigning king, no amount of gold or popular adoration secured a man's honors to him, even a Bourbon's.

The duke's eyes blinked into focus again and he forced their talk to another important subject. "Madame, what leads you to believe that Lyse-Magdalene is 'seeing back' more clearly? Now is the time when what information she could tell us could mean the very survival of the house of Bourbon. And—of our special confreres, Madame Elinor." He raised an eyebrow significantly.

De Dunois determinedly threw off her shock and rose, features drawn taut, a wiry warrior girding for the siege, her hat plume a-tremble. "Monseigneur, let me repeat what recently happened exactly. We were sitting in the south hall here, for the daylight is so fine there for sewing. It was a windy day and one of the standards flying from the roof ripped loose from some of its moorings. It billowed down before the chamber's windows and I rose to find a servant to draw it up again, when I noted on Mademoiselle

Lyse's face that staring, distant expression, with her eyes wide and unfocused, which we have both seen.

"I stopped in my tracks so as not to distract her. Most often she has merely a blink of her eyelids and the memory is gone. But lately, as she matures, as you have described it happening to her mother, the visions last longer; it was half a minute that she stared so."

Bourbon walked to peer from the dark window, his back half-turned, but listening with absorption.

The comtesse de Dunois clasped her thin hands in fervid recollection. "Finally the girl blinked and stirred, and from where she sat looked up at me in puzzlement. 'Madame,' she croaked, 'does that billowing ensign at the window have upon it a great rosy cross?' I drew in my breath sharply and asked her, 'What sort of cross?' and she answered 'A fat, blood-red cross with splayed arms.' Then she rose up and seemed to float over to the window from where she announced, in disappointment I thought, 'Ah, But I can see for myself there is only chevrons and lions-rampant, the Bourbon insignia. And yet—oh Madame, I saw it there all by itself, a scarlet cross, puffing out against that white ground like—like an emblem on a cloak.'

"Immediately I took her by the arms to keep her in concentration. 'When you saw it, what did you think? What entered your mind?' I fear I almost shook her."

The duke turned fully to face his minion.

"My lord, the girl answered that she had felt very sad, very heartsick. She hung her head for a second, then said slowly, in a shaky voice, 'There is more', and my heart jumped. 'It has great importance to me, that blood cross. It holds an answer...'

"But on muttering this she yanked herself away from my grip, suddenly declaring in a more normal tone that she would find someone to rehang the fallen banner. But she wore that false smile she uses to cover the confusion that grips her when she remembers disorienting things, and she ran from the chamber.

"Me, I sat down again, overwhelmed, for, as I could help it, no one had ever told this young lady of the splayed cross. And I knew, from her mother's history that the girl's real trial was surely beginning, and that she finally might soon give us much to think on."

Bourbon snorted, of a dual mind. Although feeling encouraged by this pregnant tidbit, he also held his niece in much affection. "'Tis almost a great pity, this weird business of ancient memories. I dread to think Lyse-Magdalene might end up violent and mad, like my poor sister Jeanne."

The governess' fingers played nervously with the ring of keys at her waist, which she carried as chatelaine of the small country manor. She knew her employer was never a cruel man so she hastened to reassure him, "The young lady is different than her mother, as I have observed to you before, she is more contained and stronger in her will than her delicate looks would have you believe. If her memories come clear they will not frighten her as much. She is capable of understanding that they are neither her own reality nor the fearful work of Beelzebub to gain her soul."

But Charles was suffering momentary guilt for manipulating his niece. He muttered around a bitten thumbnail, "My sister mumbled and fell incoherent and screamed of fire often during that whole year. She died shrieking of flames consuming her, as if she could actually feel acute pain from those ghostly memories."

"The poor princess died of an ordinary, creeping, consuming fever, brought on by eating sour apples," the countess stated dryly. "You know the Bourbons are prone to fevers." Anxious to help him regain his balance, she summoned up her narrow smile. "Monseigneur, I assure you Lyse-Magdalene is very little concerned by flames, she even carelessly ventures too close to a wood fire sometimes. Mayhap those memories that tortured her mother will not be hers at all, mayhap she is plunged into a different time."

The duke recovered himself. "Madame, I will pray so, and that she is seeing the right time for our needs. Her vision of the rosy cross gives me hope we are much closer to our goal. Be you very alert."

Shrugging out an aching shoulder, Bourbon said as he ushered the governess toward the door, "Elinor, my star has come under a deadly shadow, which is why I am instructing you to move your household to my Moulins stronghold in the next month. There I can better provide for Lyse's safety from those who might know our purpose with her and would take advantage of my loss of strength—you know the faction I mean. Also the marriage contract I mentioned to you in my last letter will be realized there as part of my design for controlling and protecting her. In the event of my very long absence."

The very exclusive bond between the two gave Charles every confidence that Elinor de Dunois would do what was needed, but he still cautioned her, "Keep her always in your sight and record everything. Right now my niece may be all we have of secret advantage in this political turmoil."

"My lord, she has become very curious about my intense interest in her 'flashes' as she calls it—impatient and resentful at times because I answer so vaguely. As you know, she is bright, she has easily absorbed the arduous studies

I have put her to; it is hard to hold off her curiosity. She is no longer a child, and sometimes she balks because of this."

The duke was aware enough of his ward's metamorphosis into a young adult, but he gave the governess only a diffident shrug for her complaint, assuming she was turning a little pout into a rebellion, exaggerated by her middle-aged, female crankiness. The Lyse he knew was a malleable creature, unassuming and sweet.

"Then tell her just as much as will keep her cooperative, I trust your instinct to know where to stop. She is too young, too uninformed to be given full knowledge, in case later she might descend into irresponsible actions and madness, as did my sister. We can tolerate no exposure."

Madame de Dunois' agreement set the small plume in her cap bobbing again, even though she realized that the *duc* de Bourbon didn't know his niece as she did, who had lived with the girl for twelve years. Lyse-Magdalene Marie de Bourbon-Tonnière was nowhere near as docile as he believed, but de Dunois had truly come to love the child she had raised, a girl who was often as genuinely sweet as a honey sop, so it helped nothing to dwell on the maid's human faults.

Charles was still unsettled. "But how long will it take to get the results we seek from her, that is the bitter question. And in our emergency do we dare push the daughter as we tried to do with the mother?" He gnawed on his lip in gloomy indecision, and the woman he addressed realized the heaviness of heart that was overshadowing his usual brash confidence.

Nevertheless his mood suddenly shifted upward and he smiled at her, gently ushering her toward the door again. "Courage, Madame, for the perfect God will help us prevail. I know it is late, but wake the girl from her slumber and send her in to me now."

To the apprehensive governess the duke's clearing face was a relief, like a light shining out from a dark window, perhaps a signal that said not all was lost no matter how things looked. "Immediately, monseigneur," she responded and skittered through the door he had courteously opened for her.

Lyse, in night shift and enveloping stole and rubbing her eyes, hastened after the duke's valet through the darkened rooms of the house. Intimidated by the heavy traffic of his gentlemen that day, she had feared that this visit to St. Piteu he would have no time to see her, to talk and ride the countryside with her as usual, or play at quoits or cards, happy to be with her a few days—for the great duke's sons had died in infancy and he was childless.

The valet shoved open the carved bedchamber door and Lyse hurried in, first bowing respectfully to her uncle who was propped against pillows on his bed, then obeying the wave of his hand to run giggling and plop herself down to sit on the bed. He'd never required ceremony between them.

Charles enjoyed a laugh at his niece's youthful exuberance. Taking her hand he teased her a bit about how his duckling had grown into a beauty he could hardly recognize, then asked after her studies in music and the Greek classics, and then inquired kindly after the health of her enormous pet cat. He also related a few tidbits of unimportant but amusing news from the royal court.

And then, abruptly, he brought up what was foremost on his mind. Her marriage.

Taken aback, Lyse leaned towards him, careless of how the stole gaped away from the neckline of her nightshift. "Uncle! Marry? But why? And why now?"

"Be less naive, *ma popette.* You are already eighteen and should be betrothed." He noted her unprepared surprise and reached to toy soothingly with a rod-straight strand of gold-red hair that fell on her shoulder. "I can't keep you to myself forever. It is my duty to provide you with a husband and I have been too neglectful, so I must do it now, especially since His Majesty rages over the Hapsburg triumphs in the northern Italian states. As constable of France the devil needn't spit in my ear to warn me I am soon to be entangled in another long Piedmont war. Ergo I must take care of all unfinished business, including you."

Lyse, trying hard to handle this sudden reality, drew her pale, hair-fine eyebrows together in a frown, but only faintly so it did not mirror her real, rebellious thoughts. Here she was, out of love for him keeping him from what she had burst out to Nurse even this morning as the bleary factotum brushed out her hair, whining to the old lady of her ache to see people, the royal court, at least some of the world. Here she was, unwilling to give her dear guardian one moment's trouble with her, always acting docile and agreeable, and here he was, precipitously marrying her off! To be shipped away *le bon Dieu* knows where!

He had never before even hinted at any potential bridegroom who would be interested in a female with no lands, houses or money, no matter her mother had been a lofty Bourbon. Oh, she was well aware she was at an age for marriage, even two years ago peering fascinated from her window at a village boy dumping firewood in the courtyard, lifting and bending in his smudged, sleeveless jerkin so that the muscles in his big arms bunched and knotted, even though she'd always been repelled by his pimpled face. And then she'd noticed that the youngest guard in the manor's tiny garrison had firm, round haunches and broad shoulders. And that the black hosen of the *intendant's* son, Germain, with whom she'd been raised, outlined knotty legs which once had been as slim as hers.

She had surreptitiously studied the few younger men in the household, with the way their contours differed from hers, and peeked with a grin at the guards below as they held their cods to urinate lusty streams into a corner of the courtyard. She began to muse how it would feel to see, to touch a bare male body, perhaps one as graceful and beautiful as the marble Jesu expired in his mother's lap, a wondrous sculpture copied from a famous one in Italy and recently installed by the duke's generosity in the village church. She was once taken there just to admire it, and she was fascinated to study the long, strong form, the leg muscles, the tendoned arms, the flat, lean chest and narrow hips –always careful to exhibit a pious look to appease de Dunois and Nurse.

Then there was her weekly bath before the fire in her chamber. She'd learned to trickle water down the pear-shaped breasts so recently filled out on her chest, growing pleased and excited by the sensation it caused, finally sliding under the water to remove her stiffened nipples from Nurse's suspicious gaze. And even her uncle, at his advanced age of thirty-one, on his last visit could not keep his gaze from the square, low-cut bodice of her gown which finally swelled out properly.

And then there was that wanton vision, the longest one yet, which, for shame, she had never recounted to de Dunois.

But in spite that she owed Bourbon all acquiescence, his sudden intent to marry her off soon, as if he were washing his hands of her, caused a turmoil in her heart, so she pressed a finger to his lips as if to erase the word he had spoken. "I pray you, uncle, you are taking my breath away. I have so little knowledge of the w-world, of gentlemen, of s-society..." Lyse stammered.

Charles de Bourbon's velvet gaze, which easily heated up many a court lady, took in the purity of his ward's gaze, then dropped a moment to her white shoulders, sweet bosom, the slimly-rounded hips outlined by the big stole she clutched, and the fact that the wench forgot she was no longer a child to loll on his bed. How she looked at him, he thought, a guileless lambkin with her wide, pale blue eyes under the barely visible russet brows, so good, so trusting, so ignorant in her hero worship of him. Surely no man in history had been forced to so difficult a duty as to remember that this nubile maid, completely at his beck and command, was his blood niece. Seduction was not unknown when powerful men had control of a poor, young relative with few prospects. The girl had no idea how much she owed to the commendable self-control of her guardian, the glittering constable of France. His forlorn little princess had been born of a stupid father who lost everything including his life in an ill-advised revolt against the Valois branch of the Bourbons–in essence, against Francois the First, ruler of France. Nevertheless, Charles had taken in his sister, the stricken widow, along with her little girl and female baby, and few servants, and quietly installed them in St. Piteu, a remote dependence several days ride from his huge castles in the Bourbonnais.

The baby had died first, and then the tortured, mad mother a year later, when Lyse was seven. Nevertheless, Charles continued to maintain his orphaned niece, no question of shunting her off to a convent, and he had asked the governess already appointed, Madame de Dunois, to stay on and raise her. Back when the little girl was five she had already begun showing signs of the eerie 'seeing back'. memories of past events of which the victim knew nothing other wise, an eerie ability which had secretly afflicted one or two Bourbon women every century. At first Charles' interest in this was merely curiosity and idle pursuit of knowledge, but now his interest had become desperation for her to 'remember' the key to a special search. What gave him hope was that so far the girl was not as distressed over the mysterious jolts of memory and fragmented visions which had finally driven her mother into insanity. He firmly believed the solution to his present dilemma was locked in the past.

Bourbon shoved himself upright on the bed and tented stiff fingers against grim lips to signal his seriousness, he had no time to coddle the girl. "Niece, know that the king has grown wrongly jealous of my popularity with the people, and that his small-minded suspicions have been fanned up into hot flames by his vindictive mother, Louise de Savoie, and his sister, Marguerite d'Alencon. He has shown unprecedented hostility against me recently, me, Charles de Bourbon, his once beloved friend, both boy and man. The terrible fact is, he is openly aiming to destroy me."

Her eyes had widened to their greatest extent. "Oh, my uncle! But how do you know this?"

"Too many slights and mortifications have occurred: usurping my right as constable, ignoring my demands to be repaid the huge sum of personal funds I spent in the Italian campaigns and not from lack of gold in his Treasury, not heeding my military advice and in fact sacrificing military opportunities just to contradict and humiliate me. Many, many in the past two years...*Peste*, how many sleepless dawns I have passed wondering how to heal this breach with him, and all over a popular acclaim which I have never sought!" Dramatically Charles kissed his fingers to the sky to swear, "So God hear my truth!"

He stared down a moment, then he gripped his arms against his chest, as if armoring his heart from any more bitter arrows, but not before Lyse had glimpsed the wounded pride, the bitter hurt he was suffering over such undeserved wrongs. She was shocked and confused, he had always come to visit her in affable and confident mood, never so distressed, nor told his affairs to her in so unvarnished a manner.

Charles continued with an angry shrug. "Rulers are like hot turnips, my little innocent, they may feed you well but they burn off your fingers. My friends believe the king has been made very wary by the example of the prostrate Italian peninsula, so badly cut up and bleeding from its own proud, warring nobility that it has become easy prey for foreign invasion. It is suspected Francois' hidden agenda is to form a new France—not one led traditionally by powerful lords such as myself in a confederation with the Crown, but a nation held by weaker, vassal nobility heavily dependent on the throne.

Lyse absorbed this. Then she said slowly, "And so because you are the lord most admired by the people and your peers, the king uses you to demonstrate that he can control even the highest and strongest of his nobles."

Charles threw her a quick glance. She was smarter than he thought. But he hesitated to tell her the worst: if the royal mother won her contrived lawsuit against him, if Francois' power pushed the royal judges to rule in Louise' favor, it would cut him down to penury. He saw danger to her visions to fill his ward's young head with this dire possibility. She represented now a desperate gamble. What she needed was time, and protection from certain dangerous factions she knew nothing about, closer protection than he might be able to provide soon.

This meant the right husband, and he was already collaborating with the man, an excellent choice in spite the awkward fact that he was already married, except that his wife was mortally ill. Lyse-Magdalene would sign the betrothal contract, which had to be kept secret until the man was finally widowed, for she would never say her guardian nay in anything. Even so, Charles wisely had a carrot to dangle in front of her; she was quite naive compared to most young women her age.

But Lyse was plucking nervously at the fringe of her stole. "Oh please, uncle, I want to stay with you still." Emboldened by the sudden complications she begged, "Not here, but at Moulins, your palace in the Bourbonnais. You promised that when I was seventeen I could leave St. Piteu and join your great household, that I could have fashionable gowns, even dance at the royal court, and now I am eighteen." A tiny moan of frustration escaped her lips before she could grab it.

She had played right into his hands, but Bourbon was touched, for he knew she was lonely, his charming ward, his mysteriously possessed possession. Her look of gentle accusation was so sweet he leaned forward to seize the opportunity for generosity.

"Aha, sweet Lyse, and so you will do these things, for you will sign the betrothal papers at Moulin! A chamber has been made ready for you at the château and my admirable mother-in-law, the dowager duchess Anne, will welcome you. Madame de Dunois tells me you are suitably prepared for society, and you will capture the heart of my entire establishment, my wager on it."

He reached to give her finger an affectionate tweak, but such joy had leaped into her light blue eyes that Charles was impelled to fold his own hands warmly over the slim hands she had clasped in delight. Radiant, she cried, "Oh my lord, I am so happy!" On impulse, moved by her delight, he rose onto his knees on the bed and hugged her. His fond smile turned wry behind her back. Thirty-one was not so old, his body was strong, his handsome features still held their boyish lines, his hair had not one thread of gray. Yet her youthful excitement to be released into the hard, miserable world was making him feel as hoary and spent as a squeezed-out fruit.

He released her, swung off the bed and stood solidly to face her, staring, so that her smile finally wavered. He didn't like removing her from the obscurity of St. Piteu, but there was no help for it. He riveted her eyes with his.

"Mademoiselle, heed me. This is not a request; it is a command. If you value your very life and mine, you must never, ever, for any reason tell anyone except Madame de Dunois, your old nurse or myself, of your curious dreams and memories. Never. Not ever. For any reason. Do I make myself very clear?"

Solemnly Lyse nodded.

But Bourbon was not convinced. "When you visit the market in Coulcy, do you see the blackened stake in the square there, where *intendant* Matz tells me three heinous witches were burned in the past year? *Bon.* There is no witchcraft in this family, this we know, for these–visions–you have, bring you no other power. You are a child of the perfect God, you have been raised in His Own Name and there is only good in your heart, but when townspeople or fanatic clerics are afraid, sometimes even a lofty lineage as yours will not cow them into forgetting the use of those blackened stakes. If they suspect you, they could deem you evil-possessed; you could be condemned as a witch and killed. Do you understand my dire warning about silence?"

She nodded again, white-faced, although not quite as appalled as he imagined, for he was late with his interdiction about loose talk. She had heard it once before as a little girl, so harshly ordered of her by her moaning mother that she had always obeyed it. She was disdainful that Bourbon hadn't cautioned her to silence long ago, she might have carelessly told Germain, her close playfellow. She and the *intendant*'s son would tell each other almost everything, in between chases and spats and quiet times when they gambled at cards with twigs for money. But she'd held her tongue out of shame, and fear the boy would think her in the thrall of the Devil.

Bourbon stepped toward her and grabbed her up by the shoulders; she thought he was going to crush her. "Swear, now, that you will tell no one of this trait you have except those I alone designate."

She swallowed and answered passionately, "I swear, I swear by the Holy Blood of the Lord, uncle, and my love for you. You need never fear."

The tension in his boyish face relaxed. He saw once more only the pretty tyke whose little arms about his neck had eased the pain of the early deaths of his own children. He dropped his grip on her and patted her shoulder. "Lysette—" A nostalgic smile momentarily chased the bleakness from his brown eyes. But, clearing his throat, he continued, "Very well, I believe you. I will return home to Moulins perhaps a month or two after your arrival there. You will grow fond of the very erudite duchess Anne. Live modestly with the countess and your nurse. Seek no undue attention. Not everyone can be trusted, remember that."

But Lyse's bottom lip was caught between her teeth, for it had finally descended upon her like an avalanche of rocks, that her life as it had been, was about to be crushed. She quavered, "Monseigneur...I have this tremble in my heart that nothing will ever be the same..."

"You are simply leaving the cradle at last, and your child's fears will pass."

"I fear that you will forget me..."

"That is impossible," he told her, with more meaning that she understood. "You will always be my kinswoman, even when you marry and live afar."

This truly shook her. In a small voice she asked, "Will you tell me which gentleman you are considering for my hand?"

"I will at Moulins, I promise you. I have chosen a gentleman of good station, of course. But no more questions, I must depart at dawn tomorrow and I must try for a complete night of sleep, which seldom visits me anymore."

Lyse stared at him a moment, a slight tremor in her lower lip. Then she bowed her head in acquiescence. "You have my loyalty, uncle. I will pray that your good prevails in this terrible time."

He kneaded the sore muscles in his neck and gave a short, lamenting chuckle. "Pray loudly, *ma petite*, I shall need all the help I can get. Leave me now, I shall bid you *adieu* tomorrow."

She curtsied and backed away, then turned. Smiling, Charles watched her retreat to the door, The flickering tapers about the room, which his valet would extinguish at his call, brought up reddish-gold glints in the silken curtain of her hair which had fallen from a hasty bun to descend down her back. He felt no guilt for keeping the girl hidden all this time so her strange affliction might neither be discovered nor submerged. Lyse-Magdalene's life and difference was the burden she must carry as a result of her birth, just as he and any individual chosen for unique destiny must do.

The rich and acclaimed *duc* de Bourbon, the esteemed constable of France, feared he could not avoid the bitter future galloping towards him, but only prepare for its impact with every strength and weapon at his command, even such a leap in the dark as this young woman.

Still, now that he must pass her on to another's care, he would surely miss the charming female child he had nurtured.

Chapter 2

Bourbon's entire escort waited for him in the brightening day, alert and astride in gleaming half-armor. The azure or white insignias of his house, with three gold lilies, one halved by a slanted bar, whipped above the riders' heads in the cold wind. In their rear the pack mules bore their burdens stolidly.

Lyse stood with the household on the low, broad steps of the St. Piteu manor house and watched the dauntless Bourbon swing into his saddle in a swirl of velvet cloak, purposely left open to display the heavy gold medallion of office hanging across his etched breastplate. His velvet gauntlets were heavily embroidered, and on the ring finger of one temporarily ungloved hand flashed a large sapphire. His prancing horse, which he sat like the king he could have been, being at one remove from the present throne, displayed a gold-thread saddle rug with tassels.

The be-plumed, select gentlemen and men-at-arms who would ride in his wake were armed with sword and halberd, and some guards carried bulky shoulder muskets, for the roads were not safe.

Lyse, looking at her guardian with dazzled eyes, was bursting with pride to be this lofty hero's niece. Suppressed for the moment was the helpless anger that he had not even asked her consent to the bridegroom he had already selected, and an ominous fear of the future which had ruined her few hours of sleep.

Bourbon saluted her and Madame de Dunois with a flourish of his long-feathered beret. "Until a few months, my dear ladies," he called out in farewell, cheering both their spirits considerably with his usual jaunty, farewell grin. Then the gravel crunched away from under his horse's hooves, and the entourage behind him followed, cantering smartly out of the estate's iron gates.

That evening, after supper, Lyse-Magdalene brushed the crumbs of honey cake off her skirt and told Madame de Dunois, who was suffering her usual dyspepsia from too many onions, that she was going to the manor's tiny, detached chapel to pray for her dear uncle's safety.

Dunois' small, distressed eyes studied her, for Lyse had not made a secret of her fuming to be so suddenly dispensed into marriage with a nameless stranger, even if this was, she knew, not uncommon amongst the nobility. But a great belch suddenly seized the lady's attention, leaving Lyse to take the dip of her governess' coif for an assent and scoot away before otherwise could he said.

It may have been the *Duc* de Bourbon's dutiful niece who mounted the lantern-lit step of the chapel to pray, her head meekly bent for the benefit of the old porter-guard glancing over from the courtyard gate. But it was Lyse-Magdalene who quickly exited the chapel's rear door with her head up and filled with surreptitious excitement. The arched door opened into a dark, cloister-like little garden, and there a shadow detached itself from a corner of the surrounding wall. Lyse rushed to fall into its arms.

"I thought you would never come, my lady," the young, broad shouldered pikeman whispered in her ear, pressing her against him.

She shook back her hood and billowed her cloak playfully around the both of them. "Can you never learn patience, poor Grigoire?" she teased him. "I had to make sure my uncle would not ride back for a forgotten sword or something. But see, I am here now."

She pressed her hip into his thin flanks and felt him tremble. She enjoyed that. This was the only power she had, her ability to affect Grigoire. She lifted her head and offered him her lips. He kissed her strongly and she liked that too. She liked kissing.

In the deep shadows and the chill, starless evening, she was pleased to let the young man kiss her, and kiss her again, and reach in to fondle the upper part of her breasts, and under the cloak she deliberately rubbed her groin against his hard-as-iron spindle which could be counted on to pop up fast. Finally he jerked abruptly and twisted his mouth in a voiceless yell, and she jerked away so he wouldn't dampen her skirt.

They always stood up to do this, for she didn't allow him to go further with her, even though her body began to tremble too and there was moisture between her thighs. She knew what more they could do, however, even standing up, for he had once showed her what, in the seductive warmth and perfume of the past summer, both of them in the grip of a jug of wine she had stolen. The wine had blotted out her control, which was loosened by her certainty that standing up she could not get pregnant.

From the moment Lyse's menses had commenced, de Dunois made it clear that women who lay with men to whom they were not wed were damned to die with the suppurating pox, skin rotting and peeling away like a leper. So, the next morning after Grigoire had penetrated her, Lyse wakened with both a bad headache and terrible fright. She had prayed that the one time, well, two in the same hour, that she couldn't hold out against a good diddle—as cook's ribald daughter, her source of worldly knowledge, might put it—would not damn her forever. Besides, the dizzying, exciting feel of taking a man inside oneself, as she'd learned, also caused some pain and chafing, and blood on her next-to-best shift she blamed on her monthlies.

She'd avoided Grigoire for two months after that, but when the perfect God was good enough to keep the pox from her, she couldn't resist a now-and-then meeting with the fellow again, except with the staunch caveat that there would be no more complete sexual congress. But since there seemed to be no interdiction against kissing, or the feverish touching and petting leading up to his ultimate demonstration of how much he loved her, in her loneliness and boredom and for just plain devilment she continued to play with the young man.

She certainly loved the touching part.

Still, when they reached the great Château de Moulins she planned to discard Grigoire, because everything would be fine and new at her uncle's grand court and she could fall in love with some splendid gentleman instead of having to dally with a common pikeman.

As she cuddled with Grigoire under the dark cloak, her excitement at finally being allowed to join the world blotted out the impending betrothal Bourbon had arranged, because if she thought about it, it might occur to her that a nobleman who would agree to take a dowryless woman might be old and creaky, a toothless lecher wanting a young female. She preferred to vaguely hope that the gentleman would be something like her uncle Charles, dashing and handsome. And kind.

The journey to Moulins was uneventful. Almost.

Thunder snarled over the distant mountains, storm clouds piling up in menacing billows that bulged into the fiery sunset. Agonized, she watched from the ramparts as her love, her life rode away, and her heart twisted in torment as his white cloak flowed backwards as if reaching for her one last time. The ballooning symbol traced on it glowed blood red in a lurid finger of sun which fell across the castle's shadowed courtyard like a flaming bar.

Her knight cantered under the barbican gate, leading out her husband's son and twenty other mailed men acting as grim escort to heavy wagons shrouded in canvas and hauled by huge drawing horses. She fought back her tears of dread, for her husband at her side might notice them.

In farewell her lover had commanded her to go on with all hope. God, he had declared, would look after those in the right. Yet she trembled inwardly that the evil king who ruled their land would prevail, and she would never see her knight more, her dearest heart, never his smile, his touch, the warmth of his lips on her forehead, never again in all of life. A tiny whimper of pure anguish and pain escaped her.

Her husband took his lady by the arm to lead her back into the square tower where they kept their apartment. "Do not fear for my son," he said gruffly, mistaking the object of her concern. "They go to Bézu where they will be safe. There is no way that towering citadel can be conquered unless on the backs of eagles."

It was not the clean death of battle she so feared for her knight, but the desperate plan she had overheard him devise with his superior, an ultimate sacrifice which he could be asked to make in this long, strange struggle.

"The Roman Pope reaches everywhere," she reminded her husband grimly.

And yet her bitter words held some triumph, for she was privy to knowledge which her pacific husband was not: the cruel persecutors of her knight's order would never, never find the thing they sought, and that alone lifted her weeping heart; she would match her love's valor. Her limping, elderly companion would have chided her for the grimace of hate contorting her mouth had he seen it.

Descending through the tower, they came to their tiny, bare-walled and plain chapel, there to silently meditate together on the tragedy of evil.

Germain's blunt face swam back in Lyse's view wearing a puzzled half-smile. "*Tiens*, where did you go, *ma princesse?* You are always daydreaming."

He reined his horse away from crowding hers as their little company plodded towards Moulins along a dirt highway so worn down by centuries of pack animal trains that it had sunk an arms-length between its verges.

Ordinarily quickly shrugging away her little lapses, this time Lyse had to struggle a moment to throw off the anger and grief that were not her own. She managed to muster up a return smile that wouldn't seem vacant, but she was truly shaken by the unusually long 'seeing-back'. She felt as if she had been punched in the belly.

She twisted around in the saddle to look back, and there it was, a length of white fabric flapping in a tree, a farm wife's lost headcloth, perhaps, blown there by the wind. Madame de Dunois' creaking litter chair, with Nurse's behind it were just passing under the very limb, so it was only a few moments ago Lyse had casually looked up to see a white cloak and blood cross. Images had flooded into her head sharp as glass, words has sounded clear in her ears, overwhelming emotion had shaken her and still burned in her belly.

But still no faces. She had seen no faces, heard no names. She was captured by some fantasy of mind which seemed real to her body and soul, and yet about whom? Who did she imagine? What was happening to her, to them? And when?

She turned back to Germain, who by her strong request had been permitted to temporarily transfer with her to Moulins in the capacity of steward —not that she had much property or servants for him to look after. The level-headed Germain might be a commoner, but he was not ordinary. For the journey he had affected the pale gray robe and knotted rope belt of a Cistercian lay brother. The little chapter of cloistered monks set up near St.Piteu by an earlier Bourbon to care for a collection of Greek and Aramaic manuscripts, grateful for the youth's sturdy help about their premises, had given him the habit as a gift.

In the relaxed atmosphere of St. Piteu he wore it when it pleased him, and somehow the simple color and lines of it suited his square, plain, open face. Under the robe, however, he carried a long knife, and a cudgel was tied to his saddle.

Lyse wondered vaguely what her rational friend would make of the mental images assailing her lately, of a striking but unfamiliar red cross with arms splayed at the ends? And Bézu? Where was that? And the vindictive king? Which king? The only French king whose character Lyse knew was the present ruler of France, the elegant Francois, who, from all she had heard was liked and respected by the people.

Her temples began to throb, for she was trying to remember every detail to relate to de Dunois, as she had promised. But she worked up a chuckle anyway to soothe Germain and she covered up the incident with prattle about the new wardrobe the seamstresses at home had turned out from bolts of fine cloth her uncle had once sent to her at St. Piteu.

Germain looked straight ahead, his inner sigh matching his slight frown. No matter that his nature was practical and he'd been taught by his father how the world was arranged in levels of power and privilege, he had entertained a chaste love for the graceful young woman with the face of an angel from the time he was a stupid fourteen. His father would have beat him for being ridiculous, no matter that his father had long been visiting Madame de Dunois' bedchamber. But that was different, so the *intendant* Matz would growl. The *comtesse* was a mature widow, not an unmarried Bourbon girl whose uncle was the lofty constable of France. Did Germain long to be hanged from the nearest tree?

Therefore Germain hoped he would find maids aplenty to flirt with at Moulins to distract him from his incurable attachment to the Bourbon princess who as a little girl had trailed him about in a crinkled shift and pelted him with mud the same as he pelted her.

He glanced over to tease her as she swayed in her sidesaddle. "Somehow, *ma princesse*, I was more comfortable when you preferred rabbit hunting in the brush to wearing some strange contraption on your head."

"Pah, the new Italian berets are no stranger than that habit you prefer to an honest man's dress," she tossed at him. "You've spent so much time with the priory's herbalist these years 'tis a wonder there's not a sprig of rue twisted about your neck."

"The herbalist was not just some old hag combing the meadows for wolfbane. The man's preparations were complex and finely measured. And mostly successful. You didn't seem so unbelieving when his medicine cured your bellyaches."

She giggled at that, which gave him back his good humor. Let her become a court favorite if thus she was born to be, perhaps even forget her loyal friend, Germain Matz. Never would he judge her. She was too unique in all this world, a beautiful, neglected girl who had until now belonged all to him, and to Téodore, Dunois' page, and to cook's vulgar, lustful daughter, Renée, whose amorous adventures they had all listened to with relish as they grew up.

But once more the excitement of reaching their fabulous goal glistened in her artless eyes, and her expectant joy worked to soothe his qualms.

Chapter 3

The cold stone floor of the château's imposing church was chilling Lyse's toes right through her slippers, and her insides growled unbecomingly over a missed meal. But a throng had been hastily gathered in the nave to give thanks to God for the *duc* de Bourbon's safe arrival from Paris. One was obliged to stand and listen to the Bishop d'Autun's endless droning but Lyse could put up with the discomfort, for with the duke's homecoming to his extravagant court her life should get better: it was appalling, she had not received even one of the coveted invitations to the small, private gatherings various members of the peacock nobility held Wednesday evenings.

Still, even after more than a month in residence she was yet thrilled to be even a tiny part of Moulins, a palace crammed with paintings framed in carved, gilded wood, marble sculptures, and several libraries of priceless books plundered from Italy where it was fashionable to own such treasures. The château's splendid rooms, one opening into the next, had wonderfully painted ceilings, and entertained a constant traffic of aristocrats and their retainers, including chamberlains, equerries, pages, secretaries, men-at-arms and menials. Lyse's head swam to reckon the many hundreds of people the huge residence held.

And all this company was soon to be stretched to capacity by a visit of the king and his court in mid-May—so the heavy-bodied Duchess Anne had announced to them with a barely disguised *moué* as they sat stiffly before her fire during their initial meeting.

But even thinking of that first meeting with the august lady made Lyse's cheeks heat up with embarrassment, for ten minutes into the conversation the duchess had exclaimed in an astonished, plummy voice. "Why Madame de Dunois! I know you to be an educated woman. I cannot believe a female child in your care has not been taught to read, neither in French nor Latin! Why, the young noblewomen in the school I instituted here are expected to be knowledgeable in many disciplines, not the least of which is reading, and writing in a fine hand."

It had seemed from some of the duchess' probing questions that she knew little about this penniless Bourbon female of disgraced parentage her son-in-law had chosen to segregate leagues away. But an abashed de Dunois nevertheless summoned her dignity to explain that they meticulously followed the orders of the duke, who felt that since his beloved sister could not read or write, so would it be a sign of love and respect for the daughter not to surpass her.

It was a very weak story to cover the truth: from the moment Bourbon's sister Jeanne had learned to read as a young woman, the 'seeing-back' assailed her more often and with more intensity, finally bringing actual physical pain and terror. This may not have been caused by the many diverse scrolls and books she had pored over, but those involved thought it might, and Bourbon did not want to risk Lyse-Magdalene if such negative result could be avoided. His niece was not taught to read.

The duchess gave up: she had more important things to resolve. That Charles had also cautioned her to see the girl was not invited to any small parties where she might make friends, and wouldn't explain why, was another puzzle that would have to wait.

The stone floor of the church seemed to be getting colder. Elinor de Dunois poked a sharp elbow into Lyse's ribs. "We must kneel now, girl, for prayer," she hissed. "Do pay attention!" and again there was that curious hint of apprehension her voice had adopted in this church.

Lyse obediently sank to her knees, held up a helping hand to steady her governess, and bowed her head. But as soon as they rose again, to the sweet-acrid perfume of incense and the deep chanting of white-robed friars in the choir stalls, her mind wandered away once more. Her eyes roamed over the Gothic vaulting and then the numerous niches packed with gem-encrusted bronze saints, paintings, ivory reliquaries, crystal candlesticks, all glimmering from the light of hundreds of tapers. And over the bronze alter hung a stunning piece of art, a great, ebony crucifix with a tortured, ivory Christ hanging flexed-kneed on it, bleeding ruby drops from hands and side, and weeping crystal tears.

From the first time Lyse had walked through its tall, bronze doors she was struck by how totally different this ducal church was from their little chapel at St. Piteu–and not just in the matter of its rich appointments.

No, the stone chapel where Lyse had always prayed had a small, sculpted image of a warmly smiling Jesus Christ Blessing the Multitudes, not dying in agony on the Cross. Nor were there any statues of saints or apostles to revere.

The few painted panels hung on the whitewashed walls had offered figures from the Bible, Adam and Eve in the Garden, Job and Isaiah, and Holy Mary and Mary Magdelene with the Saviour as a very young man. There was a painting of a serene Last Supper too, but no depictions at all in the St. Piteu chapel of the fateful events past that sad meal. And no crucifixes.

Mass was said at St. Piteu's little chapel once a week by a priest from the nearby priory and was as simple as the surroundings, and only a certain few reverent songs were sung by the gathered household. Lyse had soon discovered that in the château's church she could hardly bear to look up at the suffering figure on the Cross, it gave her the shivers and a feeling of doom, as did the carved rendering of a broken St. Catherine on the wheel, her eyes bulging heavenward, or the painting of naked St. Sebastian pierced full of arrows and dripping with gore, or the stained-glass Roman soldier burying his sword into the fainting Saviour's side.

Rather, in her old chapel there had been a small tableau of Jesus raising the dead Lazarus, and both were smiling sweetly. Devotions, and they were only on Sunday night, had surely been gentler at St. Piteu.

Madame's elbow dug her in the ribs again. The assembly knelt down on their pillows for the third time and the choir of Dominicans, white robes spangled with jewel-tones from the stained-glass windows of the apse, offered up another polyphonic Latin *Te Deum*. But now the constable of France and the gentlemen who rode with him stood forward from the crowd to receive the blessings intoned by the mitred prelate, "*O Seigneur de Puissance...*"

Lyse was nowhere near the chancel but still had a good line of sight. She was startled that her uncle, still in his travelling clothes, did not look at all well, deep fatigue etching his face and dark smudges under his eyes. Lyse hoped he would spare her a private minute the next day, before the festive dinner in his honor, although she was sure there were hundreds of people waiting to see him.

The duke had several supercilious nephews, her cousins in fact, who had rudely shown her no interest, and he had also an older niece, but she was married and lived in Saxony, so Lyse's close relationship to Bourbon should give her some advantage in the contest for his time.

Her eyes wandered over the other newly arrived cavaliers kneeling at now with Bourbon at the side of the altar steps, bare-headed, with cloaks flung back from their dusty gear. Madame de Dunois had earlier proudly pointed out her grizzled-haired brother, the *marquis* de Joyeuse, amongst them.

With the signal to rise, the congregation came off its knees with sighs, groans, and loud rustling. Standing again and helping de Dunois up, Lyse again wiggled her cold toes in their stylish but delicate slippers, and daydreamed. But her wandering gaze suddenly stopped on a tall fellow now a few steps behind her uncle who must have been standing off to the side before.

Her lips parted in sudden shock.

She had never seen the man before but she found herself staring in recognition at his bronzed face and high cheekbones and the narrow, dark beard just hugging his jawline. What she could catch of her breath stuck in her throat, and she felt the blood drain from her face and her heart skip. And for no reason at all that she could imagine.

She had no idea in this world who the cavalier was, but his wide shoulders were taking up room among the constable's closest confidants. And over her uncle's head he was now directing a cool, brooding stare right at her. Or so it seemed. The dowager-duchess' ladies stood further forward; Lyse realised she wasn't close enough to the apse to be singled out so easily.

She gave a convulsive little shiver; her breath rushed back to her and her pulse calmed. Standing there astonished over her reaction to a total stranger – 'Blackbeard' she quickly named him in her mind–she decided he must be a foreigner, for although facial hair was creeping into fashion among the young gallants, not many French gentlemen had adopted the new style yet.

Blackbeard turned his head to focus on the purple-robed bishop now holding up a golden chalice, and in profile she could see the implacable set of his jaw. He had a hard mien, similar to the many career mercenaries flooding her uncle's court, although this man was obviously one of Bourbon's own coterie.

She was certain Blackbeard had never accompanied Bourbon to St. Piteu. So why her drastic reaction to the sight of him?

Madame turned to glare at her for her inattention and quickly Lyse bowed her head for the ensuing prayer, still trying to decipher what had happened. Well, perhaps he had been at St. Piteu years back, when she was a child, for a vague sense of recognition still nagged at her. But so did the certainty that such a fellow would not be easily forgotten, even by a young girl.

Feeling normal once more, she cautiously raised her eyes to the iron profile again, and behold, the bold fellow was slyly smiling. Not at her, she could see now, but beyond the bishop, at the flirtatious Mademoiselle de Coucy, a saucy brunette with rosy cheeks and a dimpled chin, a girl who always looked right through Lyse as if she didn't exist.

Well, maybe I don't exist was Lyse' disgruntled conjecture, for she had received no invitations to any small suppers or gaming parties where she could make friends rather than just nodding acquaintances. The ladies she encountered at the milling, heavily attended plays and evening poetry readings were either uppish, disinterested, or too shy to extend themselves. But there was at least one person she could count as friend, the witty *vicomte* de Lugny, who had been delightfully admiring and attentive to her, although Madame de Dunois always warned that gallants were fickle.

Her governess had tried to soothe her feelings over her unpopularity by noting that such things as friendship took time. But Lyse didn't feel better. She needed the proper introduction, not just arriving at the château unannounced and unheralded, with only a tiny household. She needed to be seen at her uncle's side so everyone would realise her true standing.

Madame de Dunois poked her in the ribs again; her side was getting sore. The bishop finally concluded his praises and prayers for the health and serenity of their beloved lord, the constable of France, and all those he loved, and Lyse bowed her head and mumbled the string of *Deus facits* along with everyone else. But by now the spring's last cold spell was swiftly climbing up her legs, in spite of her woollen chemise and heavy gown. *Dieu*, where was the real spring, she wondered crankily.

As she and de Dunois left the church amidst the crowd on the church square, they brushed by a vendor in a felt hat who had a leaping fire in an iron cart and was threading pieces of meat on skewers to sizzle deliciously over it.

The fuel was pine faggots, and the curling, odoriferous woodsmoke assailed Lyse's nose and she halted. A remembrance flashed before her widened eyes, just a flash yet she could feel it physically, someone holding her captured from behind, arms clamped about her shoulders and waist...

The woodsmoke was choking her and she heard herself cry out, struggling against the rough arms to run forward, the heat and noise were terrible, ten paces away from her and above her the high pyres burned, flames crackling and shooting upward in terrible orange gouts — she was weeping the hot tears of grief, of frantic will. Devil's-spawn! Monsters! No, she would never give up what she knew!

Horrified and blinking fast, Lyse grabbed blindly at de Dunois' arm to steady herself, to anchor herself to reality. The governess took one look at her charge's face and rushed her away from the vendor's fire and quickly on to their quarters. Lyse suffered a pounding headache the rest of the evening.

That night Charles de Bourbon took supper in his lavish chambers with the lieutenants who had accompanied him from Paris and a dozen other key men gathered at Moulins awaiting his orders. With a crackling fire behind them they devoured fat pullets, a haunch of mutton, ham, roasted turnips and onions, and various cheeses. Invited to relax as they took their fruit brandies and shelled nuts, the men removed sword belts, undid the small, standing ruffles at the necks of their shirts and stretched out their legs. But the expressions they buried in their cups were somber.

France's *Parlement*, supine under the royal boot, had nevertheless voted to stall the case as to who had the right to the Bourbon possessions. Prior to this vote, in essence not to summarily throw the claim out as worthless, Charles had clung to pretense, and he remained for weeks at the royal court with the faint hope that *Parlement* would courageously deny the Valois their greed. His rivals delighted in his painful position and openly anticipated the downfall of the First Gentleman of the Land. But the majority of his partisans, although numerous, did not dare show him open sympathy before the king. The exceptions were the brave men who now itched to follow discussion and argument with some decisions.

In his deepest heart Charles was certain what would be the ruinous outcome of Francois' onslaught when *Parlement* met again. Reluctantly, during his stop at St. Piteu and after, he had begun formulating plans for revenge.

His trump card was France's enemies: the countries that for thirty years had battled France's inheritance claims to various parts of Italy by waging bitter war against her. No matter their ever-changing alliances, Europe's various armies had rampaged for decades throughout disputed Italy, slipping and sliding their way through rivers of blood and decimated countryside.

His mind reviewed swiftly that land meant power, even small parcels of it, and for millennia the approved occupation of Europe's gentlemen was waging war to obtain land. Thus wars were run by the nobility, fueled by their dependant subjects and serfs, and sustained by professional brigades of mercenaries who made their living fighting for whoever paid them. War was practised from early spring to mid-fall, and from dawn to dark—except on Sundays. In the winter's bad weather, when supply routes were impassable and food was exhausted, the honorable occupation of war became inconvenient, and it was shut down for repairs. Unlucky besiegers who had been held from victory too long often folded their tents and went home for the winter, swallowing their losses.

For decades the ownership of the southern Kingdom of Naples and of various northern Italian provinces see-sawed back and forth between France, England, Spain, Milan, Venice, and the Holy Roman Empire. Even the Borgia Pope, and Pope Julius II after him, had sent armies to attack the Italian principalities they coveted for the church.

Finally, after years, the Swiss tramped over the Alps from Italy and into France itself, besieging Dijon and Burgundy, rich areas, both of which were dramatically saved by the brilliant defence tactics of the young commander, Charles de Bourbon, along with his army. As the Swiss were shoved out of France there occurred the bloody battle of Marignano, which presented another splendid victory for Charles de Bourbon.

When Francois de Valois had gained the French throne in 1515, he brashly challenged the king of Spain for the crown of the Holy Roman Empire—which was neither holy nor Roman, but a confederation of rich German princedoms. Because of the dynastic marriages of Europe, the Spanish monarch's grandfather had been the renowned Maximillian I, emperor of the Holy Roman Empire and a Hapsburg, and the German confederation preferred a ruler of Hapsburg blood to lead them rather than the French. Thus was born an undying enmity between the ruler of France and the newly-elected Emperor Maximillian of these wealthy principalities.

Both kings energetically courted an alliance with Henry VIII of England, for these three monarchs, all in their prime, represented the main military power of Europe. But because of jealousy and dislike between Francois and Henry, it was the new Emperor, the king of Spain, who finally won a treaty of mutual interest with England.

A league of European nations formed behind Germany and England to pry France from Italy forever, yet this ambition was often thwarted by Francois and his powerful armies, troops under the astute generalship of Charles de Bourbon, now appointed constable of France. During the years of these violent Italian clashes many of Europe's most illustrious young nobility, including Bourbon's younger brother, were slaughtered on the battlefields. Nevertheless the duke's fame as a brilliant military figure spread far and wide, and was everywhere applauded.

But a year ago, after Francois' mother had sprung her suit to gain all the Bourbon holdings, and previous secret reports received about Francois' growing enmity towards Charles de Bourbon, the intrigued Holy Roman Emperor, presently residing in Madrid with his court, twice sent clandestine ambassadors to Bourbon to boldly offer him an option. Among the inducements to the duke to switch sides was the emperor's prestigious promise of the hand of his sister Eléanor, who once had been the Queen of Portugal.

Such a prime alliance was heady temptation, but Bourbon had refused it firmly both times. Until now.

Now he reiterated this offer to his companions as they sat at his table, his gaze travelling from one to the other of the men he trusted, some peers of the realm, some lords of his vassal domains, a few less exalted but fine officers, all representing only a fraction of others silently outraged by the king's astounding strike against the Bourbons.

Each man's sombre expression told Bourbon the same thing: they felt there was going to be no choice left for him but to turn traitor and join the foreign confederacy against François, and to aid in the Valois' defeat at the Hapsburg's hands.

The *marquis* de Joyeuse, bulky shoulders tensely set, offered his blunt confirmation of this into the heavy silence. "Monseigneur, rebellion on your part remains the only answer. The nation will see you not as a traitor but as a liberator, fighting the chaotic reign of an unjust king who is slave to every fleeting passion. I say you, join with the emperor."

In spite of such drastic remedy there were courageous 'ayes' all around the table.

La Clayette, swarthy captain-general of Bourbon's personal forces, seconded the idea. "My lord, who better to lead a rebellion against the great legal abuses in this country and improve the people's condition than the hero of Marignano himself! And who better to claim the throne of France at our victory!"

In nervous protest, Charles was rapping softly against the chair arm with his knuckles, not that he did not agree with them, but that the idea of turning against Francois hurt him desperately. He lifted his cup and gulped down his strong brandy before he spoke to change the focus somewhat.

"A word more, gentlemen, of our present condition. 'Tis hard to believe that Francois has initiated this friendly visit to Moulins merely to take present stock of holdings he believes will soon be his. I am informed he knows of the Spanish ambassadors' visits to Moulins, as furtive as they were. Therefore he must surely suspect what furies could be unleashed against him by his vindictive actions towards me. Perhaps—perhaps this visit shows a softening of his position?"

His aide, Saint-Bonnet, had a long, sorrowful face above a lanky frame. He answered such wishful thinking: "My lord, he dares not shrink back from his course now, it is too late. It would own he was wrong in the first place to allow his mother's despicable lawsuit. I am convinced the king will uphold his royal authority at all costs, for that is the very point of this proposed illegal seizure of the Bourbon territories. And eventually he will find a way to murder you."

"You are too close in birth to the throne, *mon connétable*. He needs to break you, and he has been at it subtly since Marignano," morosely insisted the *comte* de Valentinois for the tenth time.

"Not once have I been ambitious for his throne," the duke rapped out, although they all knew this. Charles' angry brown eyes travelled over his good friends again, men willing to commit the highest offence of treason for his cause: staunch Joyeuse, cautious Saint-Bonnet, the wily Aynard de Prie, Valentinous, count of Beaujolais, and La Clayette, a fierce and loyal officer. Also the two Norman Matignon brothers, and ten other brave officers who had followed him through every campaign.

And then there was Ferrante di Gonzaga, a mercenary who had made the hard winter journey over the Alps to reach him in Paris, brother of the duke of Mantua and Charles' close cousin. The big Italian, a three-time campaigner for the French under Bourbon, a man of strength and fierce loyalty not devoted to light chatter, had contact with a large force of arms in Italy's Piedmont who would follow him even against the French should he want it. However, his indispensability to Charles at this point was for other reasons.

Charles scowled around at his confederates, "But the problem with rebellion, Messieurs, is money. The clever Hapsburg is not merely negotiating for my distinguished person—" his tone was sardonic, "—but this distinguished person before you is expected to arrive with heavy coffers. It is one thing to consider exile from one's country with finances enough to pay a strong army to eventually return you home. Francois has already blocked access to all my Paris and Bourges bankers, and I am sure has seized what remaining gold we could not transport here from Paris. There is no time to sell off properties and who would even buy them in this legal limbo?"

The duke upended his glass again and held it out for La Clayette to pour more brandy into it from a crystal decanter. He hoped it would help the persistent hotness and fatigue bedevilling him. For days Charles had been feeling much below par, sickish and feverish, so that the unusual royal visit loomed to him as an ordeal. Francois would certainly continue, in every subtle manner, to diminish his host in the eyes of both courts; and if the viper mother, Louise, had the gall to join him, she must be received with a vestige of courtesy—duty that would sicken the poor Duchesse Anne, and strain him. At least the visit was planned for a short one, for the king had made clear his intent to reach Lyons by mid-May.

Charles saw his men staring at him, waiting for some direction. The great Bourbon, constable of France, master of a thousand life-and-death choices in war, still could not stomach that switching allegiances was the only path open to fight back. Even his old mother-in-law, in desperation to save the house of Bourbon from disappearing, had counseled him: yes, accept the Hapsburg alliance and the advantageous foreign marriage, strike back! "It is what every prince has done under deadly threat from his liege, what the dukes of Burgundy, Brittany and even my own royal father did while he was still Dauphin!" railed the grand lady, her voice hoarse with emotion. "They took their allegiances to powerful rulers elsewhere, and they lived to come back to France in triumph!"

Bitter tears had stood in her faded eyes.

Charles shifted fitfully in his seat; the fire on the hearth was much too hot. "My faithful friends, hear me. I will not make an absolute decision, not yet. I wish to see what this royal visit may or may not bring."

His bleary gaze caught the piercing green stare of his cousin, Gonzaga, and for a moment their eyes locked in a silent, personal communication.

Now the Italian broke his silence, speaking in a confident baritone. "My lord, will you consider this: since Francois is possibly aware of your most recent contact with the emperor, perhaps he intends to surprise you with arrest!" The Mantuan's French was fluent, without accent. As a youth this nephew of Charles's mother, Chiara di Gonzaga, had spent eight years in the Bourbon-Montpensier household, instructed by the same tutors, getting into the same scrapes, showing off in the same sports and tournaments of arms, as his older cousin, Charles.

"Ah, he could attempt that, Don Ferrante. But not likely in my own domain, and certainly not here at fortified Moulins where I have three thousand men under arms. He is not stupid."

Joyeuse mused, "Still, it would serve us better if we could devise some way to limit his insults by limiting his access to you."

Charles rubbed at his hot brow with a velvet-covered arm. The pear brandy had started up a nausea in the pit of his stomach. His bones and joints ached. "*Le Diable!* It may be limited anyway, if this damned affliction doesn't leave me," he muttered, and accepted the goblet of cool water Saint-Bonnet pressed into his hand.

But Joyeuse, riveted by a half-formed thought, considered Gonzaga's complaint. "'Tis an idea!" he murmured.

The *marquis* heaved his bulk up, his heavy chin jutting forward as he stared with concern at his leader. "You need rest, mon *duc*, we should leave you now, if you will so permit. With sleep we will all be fresher tomorrow to plan a solid strategy."

There were tentative nods of agreement. They all realised how hard Charles had been hit by the king's treachery, but he had never been a despondent sort, even when his forces had been outnumbered and seemingly overwhelmed he had lent them all courage with his unflagging spirit, and they had pulled through. Now the man to whom their personal fortunes, their very lives were pledged, and who was seldom tired, advanced no objection against Joyeuse' suggestion. He nodded glumly, slumping in his chair.

Joyeuse put a firm, steadying, loyal hand on the duke's shoulder as he and the other prepared to depart the chamber.

The constable's niece rose early the next morning, too happy and too excited to sleep. There was a festive, welcoming dinner at an hour past noon to attend and she'd had a message that immediately before dinner her uncle would summon her for a private talk. The best way to help time pass was by enjoying her usual morning fast canter escorted by Germain–the one activity she was allowed where Madame de Dunois wasn't able to accompany her.

She had a green riding costume–the same color gentlemen wore when they hunted stag–and although its flowing, velour skirt and loose-backed, fur-edged jacket were not very new, the verdant shade went gloriously with golden-red hair and a wind-pinked complexion. She topped her neat chignon with a flat, green hat, newly perked with a floaty ostrich plume which Madame had brought her from one of the dozens of merchants displaying wares in the château's outer court. Velvet riding gauntlets shielded her hands from the reins.

Germain always met her with the horses in a certain part of the stable-yard, an unpaved rectangle huge enough to accommodate eight hundred animals in long buildings, with quarters above for the army of hostlers and grooms; an area always milling with the activity of humans and beasts, this morning being no exception.

Eager for her ride, Lyse hurried forward, dodging careless attendants and picking her way around piles of horse droppings. But as she came close to the rendezvous, voices grabbed her attention and she glanced up from watching where she was stepping to see a shocking tableau–Germain, grabbed up by the doublet and being furiously shaken at the end of two long arms, his compact form half-lifted off the ground as if he had the weight of a feather.

The man assaulting her friend was the one she'd noticed the evening before in church, 'Blackbeard.' She saw Germain's poor head snap back and forth as if it would come off under the furious assault, his shorter arms fruitlessly flailing to defend himself. A frightened groom hunched nearby, holding the reins of a huge charger, and several grinning hostlers stood about enjoying the spectacle.

A squeal of outrage escaped her and she launched herself at a run, reaching the pair of them and slamming the big bully on the back with her doubled fists as hard as she could.

"Stop that this instant!" she cried, "Put him down. He is my steward and you have no right to beat him!"

The dark head snapped about and suddenly two green eyes blazed down emerald fire at her. "Who the damnation are you? This vermin dared to mount my horse. Dared! Without permission. No one touches this horse except me or my squire. I'll break his dirty neck for him."

Lyse darted to the woozy Germain and tried unsuccessfully to yank him from Blackbeard's grip. "Oh no you will not, you villain! He is of my household and only I have the right of reprimand. He is an honest man. I am sure there is some innocent explanation."

"You think so? Then let us hear it." For good measure Blackbeard gave the gasping Germain another violent shake, rattling his teeth. "Speak, *figlio di putano*, were you trying to steal this animal?"

"Steal!" Lyse shrieked in outrage. "My steward does not steal." She ran at the glowering man and with all her might banged both her fists on his arm to make him let go of Germain's strained doublet. "You let him go, you big, stupid oaf, how can he talk if you're throttling him?"

The green eyes flared, Blackbeard did not welcome insults. He glared at her, but his fingers opened and Germain staggered loose.

Germain coughed wretchedly to catch his breath and finally wheezed, "I beg– I beg your pardon, Monsieur, I meant no harm at all. The stallion is such a magnificent animal, I merely came closer to admire him when you dismounted and left. I wanted only one moment's sensation of what it meant to sit such a great, beautiful beast, just another moment and I would have slid off and departed–"

But the angry stare under the winged, black brows swivelled now to pinion the hapless groom. "Where is my own squire, dog?"

"Seeing to the shoeing of your black gelding, Monsieur," the fellow quavered.

"You scoundrel! So you thought it was fine as a silk rose to let anyone up on the prize animal left in your charge to be cooled down and fed? You scum! I ought to break your bones."

"Monsieur, I beg to confess, I coaxed him with a coin for it," Germain bravely intervened. "I did not plan to ride the horse. Just to sit astride a moment. There was no harm done."

"No there wasn't, because I came back for something forgotten in the saddle bag. Should I ever see your face around this horse again, varlet, I shall mash it into pulp."

Lyse could not bear to see Germain humiliated by the great brute hulking over him. "See here, you are making a great smell over a tiny liberty. My steward has received your violent message and will obey it. You have my word."

Blackbeard now stopped to insolently look her up and down, brows drawn into a fierce line, and in the midst of everything she was ridiculously aware of the several rubbed spots in the velvet of her skirt.

"Your word!" he erupted, unmistakably insinuating how worthless he thought that guarantee.

Her cheeks burned. She faced up to him, and although she was of good height the shoulders of his doublet were fashionably exaggerated and he made her feel like a mouse broaching a mountain. But the insult had intensified her temper. "My parole is as good as yours, anytime. A hundredfold better, I'll wager. How dare you treat me so rudely, you churl! Now let us pass or I will call the castle guard. The incident is over," she declared with angry hauteur. "And I want my morning ride."

He stared down at her a moment, jaw clenched, and a shaft of sunlight underlined a puckered white scar just below his left eye. He mumbled something scurrilous under his breath, then turned to the hapless groom. "Take my horse back to the stall. Now. I'll deal with you later." As the giant charger was lead off Blackbeard returned his riled, sardonic attention to Lyse and growled, "Who would dream of preventing your morning exercise, my lady? Believe me, not I, even though you are too free with your puny blows. Count yourself lucky I do not strike women."

Abruptly he turned on his heel, and shoving aside some of the onlookers, strode off.

"I wouldn't wager a sou on that either!" Lyse yelled after him, to the motley audience's mirth. "*Espèce de cochon!*" she bounced off his retreating back, "Pig!"

"What a dreadful man!" she huffed to Germain as they walked towards the mounting step where a stable boy patiently held their horses.

Germain answered miserably, "But the gentleman was correct, *ma princesse*. I had no right to sit on his horse, and in his saddle." He was embarrassed and avoided her ruffled gaze.

"Gentleman? I doubt it," Lyse flounced, still incensed. "A gentleman would never lose his temper so, and speak so roughly to a lady. I should have told him who I am, the churl. But whatever came over you to do such a thing, Germain? You know how these cavaliers hold their steeds in reverence."

"I've never seen such a charger as that great beast, a beauty, a chestnut body but with a bright auburn mane and tail, and over seven hands high, with eyes a pale brown and rolling with intelligence. I suppose I was envious," he admitted and glanced at her, then away again. Suddenly he confided, as they used to do, "Sometimes I wished—when I was younger I often daydreamed about being a knight, suited up in polished armor, with it known far and wide that my sword and lance were the terror of my enemies."

She was startled. "*Tiens*, I never knew that. You always seemed quite content to be you."

"I was, mostly. At St. Piteu. That's why I don't like it here."

"Oh Germain, do you wish to leave me already?"

He saw that had upset her and hastened a reassurance. "No, *ma princesse*, I swear I will not. I'm just a country fellow. I'll get used to all this commotion."

She mounted the three wooden steps and as he steadied her dependable hackney horse she sat into the lady's saddle and hooked one leg about its horn, then settled her skirt. Germain swung up onto his own horse and they threaded their way through the hurly-burly of others coming and going, heading for the east drawbridge along which a flood of morning sunlight offered them a golden path.

But Lyse's irritation still lightly gripped her. She lectured herself, See how lovely the day is, already warmer and the trees have begun to flower overnight, and your dear uncle Charles has come home. A few minutes of nastiness with a crude bully mustn't ruin your mood. You should never have lost your composure like that, anyhow. You are supposed to be a lady of refinement. Madame de Dunois would have been aghast— But picturing this reaction caused Lyse to grin. Anyhow, she had rather enjoyed flinging that last epithet at the scabrous bully.

As they cantered away from the château on the hard-packed dirt road, she threw Germain a conspiratorial smile to pick up his self-respect, for no male could like being so mauled about, especially Germain, who was proud of his strength. "You know what I would love? To try that trick again that we do, where I am afoot and you ride up and hook me under the arm and swing me up on the saddle with you?"

He rubbed his spiky hair and smiled. "That was a child's trick, not a lady's."

"*Merde*, we did it not even three months ago when you caught me trying to get away from St. Piteu, for we didn't even know my uncle was arriving shortly at the house."

"So, that sport will please you? *Eh bien*, but we'll have to find a meadow out of sight of the road. And truly, you ought not to curse..." But he was pleased too, for they both knew it took strength and timing to swing her up safe and sound.

As they rode past already furrowed fields looking for a meadow, Lyse thought about Germain's fantasy of being a knight, and felt sad for him because it was an impossible dream to realise. His dream was never as feasible as the unprincipled idea that had lately grabbed her mind, jabbing at her every time she reported a flash of memory to the eager de Dunois. With boldness, her own flight of fancy could surely be accomplished a thousand times quicker than his.

Chapter 4

Halfway back to the chamber he shared with La Clayette, where his servant had his breakfast waiting, Ferrante di Gonzaga barked out a laugh. He took the stairs two at a time, his choler dissipated—gotten out and forgotten, the way he always erased unimportant things. But it was tickling him to pleasure that female's vexation as she threw herself at him like an avenging harpy. Fortunately he hadn't missed that she was most attractive under all that wrath.

The baggage; he could still feel her fists pounding his forearm. She'd cared to hear no excuses, she'd faced him up, quivering that he dared touch her minion, her eyes lancing pale blue outrage. Ferrante damned himself for a fool that he had not learned her name, for actually that was the way he liked women, peppery, lively, a challenge to a man even in bed. He could find precious few women at the French courts to match the zest of Italy's ladies.

Diavolo, the game was in the hunt, no? A sly fox would find delectable dovecotes to be raided, even in France.

Seating himself at table, he was still smiling as he tucked his napkin under his chin and picked up his fork to attack the fine fried tripe prepared by the *duc's* own kitchen and kept warm by his long-time valet, Collini. A fork of course. No barbarous eating with the fingers as many French gentry still did.

Well, even in this great collection of people he'd come across her again, the coppery-tressed fury below, and she might be the perfect one to add some lightness to the difficult days ahead. Keeping up a semblance of normalcy during the royal visit was the best protection Bourbon and all of them had against misstep.

The truth was there wasn't much lightness in his own grudging consent to Charles' proposal of betrothal with a landless female, even if she was a Bourbon and reported by her uncle to be beautiful, sweet, demure, obedient, and soft-natured. Hah! How cloying! The way Charles had painted her he sounded like a besotted lover, and the woman much too wonderful.

He couldn't grasp the reason for Charles' startling request at first, to marry the niece to more easily protect her from Bourbon's enemies. But the detailed, strange story the duke then offered—leading up to an unusual young woman with memory of the past, perhaps of an incredible treasure, and who must not fall into the wrong hands—that was the truth, there was no doubt. Charles was not at all joking about the necessity of the betrothal, even if he, Ferrante, was already married.

With a huge knife Ferrante cut a loaf of white bread against his chest, then slapped sweet butter and a hunk of cheese on the slice and wolfed it down. Considering what he now knew of the Bourbon woman's history, he was far from honored to be drawing water from that well. Sourly he considered that two was a number he wasn't fond of, and this would be a second marriage to an impaired woman he was forced to accept from a deep sense of duty.

Duty? When he was a strapping fifteen years old his father had ordered him, a third son, home to Mantua from living with the Bourbons in France, and with a bullying will cast him into a hateful alliance. His frantic objections were overruled, the duke thundering at him that the honor of marriage to the second of the Sforza daughters, even though she was badly crippled, would bring him a solid living in dowry and possessions. In any case, the doctors reported the poor invalid was often in pain, and that unfortunately she was doomed to die young.

So the marriage took place in Milan when he was sixteen and the bride twenty. The first promise had proven true; his income from lands and rents had been tripled. But the second had not even now occurred: it was nine years later and Aliesa, partially paralyzed now and bedridden—but always crabbed, tart-tongued and scolding—was still alive. But very barely so, as her mother's last letter had informed him when it reached him in Paris in April, begging him to return home.

Ferrante scarcely knew Aliesa. She was small, dark, her hair was thin and lifeless, and her mouth drooped petulantly, although she might have been comely enough in the face had it not been so grooved with pain. At first, even though repulsed by her skinny body and withered arm and leg, he had pitied her enough to gather his courage, close his eyes and give her the humpery for which she burned. But, young and angry, he could not sustain this, each time he invaded her he lived in dread she'd give him a child as tragically crippled and snuffling as she. The unreasonable woman pounced on his absence from her bed as if it were the cause of her illness, and thereafter derided and rejected anything else he did to be kind.

They had made their establishment at Trina, a small estate near Mantua which he had inherited from a grandfather. Finally, restless and miserable, unable to live with her or even look at her, he had fled a few years later and spent the next years on the battlefields, building a reputation as a clever, dauntless captain of mercenary forces, a *condottiere*.

Alternately, for his name and family was his *passe-port*, he could also be found swaggering and gambling at the courts of Italy and France, where his usual recipe for recovery from streaks of debauchery and womanizing consisted of drawing lessons. He did this so that he could better study and understand architecture, a discipline that fascinated him.

But Aliesa was the devil on his tail, always, always. He had been forced to marry her, he disliked her intensely, he could not bring himself to live with her spite and curses and groans, or view the limbs worse twisted every year in spite of her doctors. He pitied her for her misfortune, but he could not abide her or waste his young life with her. Yet she was his wife in the eyes of God and the church.

Somewhere underneath his swaggering bearing he was often in battle with his bad conscience about Aliesa. Mortification often jabbed his heart, a pain worse than sharp pebbles unremoved from a boot.

And now came this new call to marital duty, from a fealty even greater than family, a fealty involving certain grave and secret vows he had taken in a special clan, and represented in the person of Charles de Bourbon, who, fearing for his niece had now drafted him as a sort of legal guardian for her.

Hoisting his cup by both handles, Ferrante drained the hot cider. He cracked several walnuts under an impatient boot heel, scooped up the broken results and picked at them. He was already twenty-five. Once death had put an end to Aliesa's suffering, marrying a mealy-mouthed 'peculiar' with weird visions was not the future he'd been planning, for he was growing tired of the blood and stink of war, and the drinking, gambling and women in between. A hearth he could happily return to now and then, a healthy wife and strong children were what were missing.

His mouth went grim under the thin arch of moustache that ran into his jaw-hugging beard, for such normal marriage would certainly be missing in the unappetising new alliance he was caught in. Unreasonably, it was Aliesa he now wanted to curse at, for her mortal illness, soon to end, had only made him available for this new misery.

Bourbon had no miniature painting to prove his niece was a 'beauty' and Ferrante had known two of the duke's sisters, who were not by half as handsome as he. What's more, the distracted Charles seemed not to understand that the colorless temperament and boring meekness he so acclaimed as bait were not at all beguiling to the chosen bridegroom.

Ferrante snorted, wiping his mouth and tossing down the cloth. Even sight unseen he already had no use for the Bourbon woman, for if not crippled in limb, to him she was just as damaged by her eerie ability, which might be a form of madness one day to blossom horribly. Hah! Is this what the smirking minions of Satan had decreed for him? Was he to produce either crippled heirs or mad ones? And spend his life avoiding his home?

But he was bound by very special, secret ties and a stringent oath, to oblige Charles de Bourbon. Caught like a rat in a trap.

He sat scowling a moment at the crumbs and nutshells on the table as Collini filled his glass. His oldest brother, now Duke Federico of Mantua, had inherited their father's title and wealth. His second brother had been given a cardinal's hat at fourteen. But Ferrante had been early chosen by his half-French grandfather to inherit an ancient secret so vital, so overwhelming, that Ferrante could refuse no duty in its service. And in this service, he and Charles de Bourbon shared infinitely more than worldly battle scars and affection. They shared a fearsome obligation.

But he was merely a man, did he not deserve legitimate children to be the rightful heirs to his possession and fortune, and the perpetuators of his essence? Well, the Bourbon woman was at least sound of limb and body. Making heirs with her would heavily depend upon how strange she was, or could become as she grew older.

He shoved back his chair so that it almost fell over and unrolled himself as his servant hurried forward to clear the plates. He was to greet the bent-neck 'peculiar' today, he had been notified, an hour before dinner, in the *duc*'s private cabinet.

Ferrante di Gonzaga decided he would dress in black to meet the damsel, although black was a sombre color not very popular in France. But that's how he felt. Chastened and somber.

On the writing table of the dark-panelled ducal study there was a carved monkey of wizened face, painted red coat and a crystal orb in its paws, absorbed in studying the glowing Saracen carpet covering most of the room. Behind the table the constable of France regarded Lyse-Magdalene de Bourbon-Tonnière over the rim of his gold goblet, even in his sick condition charmed by the woman seated before him.

She was beautiful, more poised than he remembered, her head balanced proudly on her slim neck, her hair knotted up in a fashionable chignon, with frizzy little curls about her face—no more bouncing maid with silken hair flowing loose, whose dazzled eyes opened wide at his gifts when he visited St. Piteu.

Those eyes, the first thing one noticed, a limpid, light blue shining with sincerity under thin, russet brows, with long lashes which sometimes descended because she was shy. The surprise of her delicate beauty, however, was her rosy, pouty mouth, with a voluptuously indented bottom lip.

This delicious mouth always had a sweet smile for him, and often her whole, mobile face lit up, a surprise gift.

She was dressed in her best for the occasion, in a tight-sleeved, shiny, brown satin gown embroidered with gold leaves, its square neckline cut low to display the swell of her bosom. A russet velvet hat worn well back on her center-parted hair rose like a half-moon around her head and the pearl drops Bourbon had just presented to her gleamed creamily from her ears.

A delicious young creature, Lyse-Magdalene, in spite she was a bit tall. His cousin Ferrante would have to be stone blind not to appreciate her.

The duke knew her 'seeing-back' had been longer and more focused recently; de Dunois, excited by them, especially the one which offered an incredible name, had entrusted her account to a special courier for Paris. Now he was certain his instinct was right; this unlikely female could find him the key to his desperate search. But when? That was the agonizing question. When! And how could she be hurried to the needed revelation?

Lyse, upset at the sight of Bourbon's sunken face and the hot hand which had caressed her cheek in greeting, had banished all thoughts of complaining about social neglect. But immediately as she was seated on a cushioned stool opposite him, he brought up the betrothal. She began to feel faint because the situation was finally upon her, and it unfolded worse than she'd expected. Ten minutes later, when her uncle finished speaking, she sat rigidly, not touching the fruit liqueur he'd offered her in a stemmed, green glass.

He repeated, "But it is a triumphant match for you, Lyse-Magdalene!

Under the circumstances, *n'est-ce pas?* A noble Italian family of wealth and power, a gentleman of refinement, honorable and brave. What more could you require?"

Her eyes lifted miserably and she said softly, "Please, uncle, to stay in France."

He tried to be patient. "Don Ferrante di Gonzaga was my own mother's nephew, so if she, Chiara di Gonzaga, came with pride and honor to make her life as a Bourbon in France, you can go with a husband to Italy, *ma petite Lysette.*" He tried to make this point with kindness, although the girl had no choice anyway—even had she been aware that his mother had selfishly spent more time visiting her sisters in Italy than with her husband and children in France. "Besides, remember this is a secret contract, the gentleman is still married and his wife may live a year or two more. Although this marriage is a foregone conclusion, there is still plenty of time for you to enjoy the amusements of Moulins and the sweet Bourbonnais countryside."

In spite of the fever draining him, Bourbon noticed the scant hope she'd harbored vanish from her face like a disappearing light. But he continued, "As I have bid her, Madame de Dunois tells me you have now been informed of the hateful legal contest I am plunged into by the king's mother. On the outcome of this process rests the fate of the great house of Bourbon. A negative verdict for me would be disastrous. By setting up this marriage I am securing your very future, Mademoiselle, so do not disdain it."

He watched her indented lower lip quiver. She was silent a moment, then the placidity of facial expression to which he was accustomed wavered like a pool shivered by a stone and surprisingly tautened into something like resolve.

With a brave straightening of her shoulders she said, "Monseigneur, I beg you do not mistake my great love for you, but I believe you protect me not just because I am your niece but because of the strange visions in my head. Why, uncle? What are these illusions, what meaning might they have for you? I ask you to tell me now, since we will be far separated one day. You must allow me to understand this affliction which you insist is not devil-possession, but which I fear terribly."

He stared at her with some surprise. Suddenly there was a collected young woman before him demanding information, rather than the naive girl he had nurtured.

But she jumped up, darted to his armchair and dropped to her knees in a rustle of brocaded skirts, urgently grasping his silk-clad knee with her hands. "Monseigneur, I beg you take me into your confidence, for I am your blood and will never betray you. As your niece and your ward, I love you. Please, my uncle."

The trusting eyes looking up in appeal started swift memories for Charles: the curtain of straight, silken hair that used to engulf him as he swung the young girl onto her horse, the sweetness of the pretty poppet playing with the gold chain about his neck, charming snippets of memory of this only child God had allowed him to raise thus far, melding with the alluring scent of the grown Lyse's skin as he hugged her on his last visit. In spite of his debilitation, the duke had to shut his eyes a second to stop in its track a lewd train of thought.

But she was right; it was time, for time was running out for them all. He removed her fingers from his knee and rose, leading her to a window where they could look out on Moulins budding gardens, awakened to spring by unseasonable warm weather. "You do not have visions, you have memories, somehow passed to you by an ancestor. You are remembering, we believe, the past of two centuries ago, what we call 'seeing-back.' In other ages so did other female Bourbons have memories, different from yours, even your own mother, as you know." In the duke's feverish stare there was an impatient need for her to understand fast. "What you may learn through your seeing-back is urgently important to me and to future Bourbons as well, because I am seeking something valuable that has been lost. You must remember the key to its location."

"What something?"

He drew a kerchief from the padded sleeve of his surcoat to swipe away the sweat beading his brow, although it was cool by the window. His eyes were filled with an unnatural shine. "I cannot tell you because I fear to direct your vision, which I carelessly did several times with your mother. It was a bad mistake. Instead of leading her along it seemed to increase just one vision, the violent one which drove her mad."

Pale-lipped, Lyse murmured, "The fires she screamed of?"

"Her seeing-back was blocked to one recollection, an ancestress being burned at the stake. Only a memory, but somehow, horribly, she felt the dreadful pain throughout her own body.

"An ancestress—burned as a witch?"

"No! Not at all! You must believe me. I forbid any more talk of such damnation!"

"But is that my fate, to suffer and go mad?"

"No. You seem not to remember the same things, and your visions are pure, we have worked to see they are not rising from any suggestion. We try to keep your rational mind clear of any knowledge remotely touching on the information I need, or on the Razès."

Lyse grasped at the straw. "The Razès? What is that?"

A strong expression of self-disgust crossed the still-handsome but exhausted face. "*Malédictions*, that was nothing. You will rid your mind of it. Swear to me!"

She retreated, intimidated by the violence of his reaction, and she nodded, placing her hand on her heart as oath. "But uncle, who do you mean by 'we'?" she went on doggedly.

"Your governess and old nurse are aware that your seeing-back is important to me: Madame de Dunois reports to me all that you tell her. What may seem disconnected nonsense to you has meaning to us."

His strength ebbing, Bourbon moved to a chair and flopped into it. He reached out to grab one of her hands in both of his. "Lysette, if you love me, if you wish to be of the greatest aid to me in this dangerous time, accept this betrothal so I may not be concerned for your safety."

"And how shall I explain to this gentleman my sometimes absent stare?"

"You need not. He knows all about it."

Her jaw dropped. "But—you said it was a secret of the family!"

"Your future husband is my mother's nephew as I told you, family enough. And there are other more important reasons why he knows. You can lean on him."

She studied his face and her voice held mild sarcasm. "It seems he knows more than I do. Dear uncle, at least what is that peculiar crimson cross always in my mind, or the couple in that gloomy keep in the mountains? Oh, how incredibly real they seemed to me. When they happen these—memories—take over my complete consciousness."

Bourbon ordered tonelessly, "Ask no more questions." He wiped his face again.

"But—"

"No more!" he commanded, in harsh finality. He got up and walked to his table, turning his back on her.

So Lyse left that subject alone, but she was not yet finished. One night, when a particularly bad dyspepsia attack convinced Madame de Dunois she was dying, the lady had clutched at her heart and gasped out to her charge, "I dread to leave you alone, *ma fillette*, in the event God calls me to him. So you must ask your dear uncle to do a certain thing—" And the lady described what.

Smoothing out her brow to look more helpless, Lyse stepped around to face Bourbon, kneeling at his knee again. "Dear uncle, I bow to your wishes, and I will do all that I can to serve you. But in return I ask a favor." At his wary nod she hesitated, fearful, then pushed ahead. "A purse of one thousand gold écus for my own private keeping and not to be mentioned to my husband-to-be."

The duke appeared startled, for Lyse knew she had never had an interest in money more than a few coins for sweets or ribbons, or fabric for clothing as she grew up.

"But I just told you I have settled on you a generous dowry of thirty thousand écus to see you married as a Bourbon, Mademoiselle, plus to you the ownership of St. Piteu and sums to pay the wages of de Dunois and the old nurse. That should be sufficient."

"Oh indeed, I am infinitely grateful for your largesse, you fairly took my breath away when you told me of St. Piteu. But when I marry, the dowry considerations are bestowed upon my husband, including the jointure income from St. Piteu. Please, my lord, I wish the thousand écus I beg just for myself. Not that my husband would not be generous," she hastened to deflect his frown. "But for an–an urgency, a danger. I swear not to use it for anything less."

He opened his mouth to pooh-pooh this, but she added tremulously, eyes wide, "The thought of eventually being taken to Italy where I might know no one frightens me terribly".

Bourbon scratched at his neck, considering. Her worth to him, if she finally succeeded with a timely 'seeing-back' answer to a riddle, was enormous. One thousand écus was a respectable amount, especially now, but hardly a large sum to him who had lost ten times that on the turn of a card. There was no question Gonzaga would shelter and provide for her, for in spite of Ferrante's neglect of his spiteful, crippled wife, Charles knew him for a basically decent man. Still, the world was a bedlam place, and should something go badly wrong a secret resource might help this young woman, and throw off a benefit to him as well. It was little enough she asked. And so he nodded.

"Done!"

"Oh, uncle! And one more *petite, petite service?* The fellow who accompanied me here, you know him, the *intendant* Matz's son, is due to return to St. Piteu very shortly, along with the few pikemen who were my escort. Could I not retain him in my service? He already acts as squire to we three females, he sometimes reads from Madame's books to me, with her permission and choice, he is very useful, and I count him as a friend. My only one, in fact."

He sat straighter. "Just a friend, Lyse-Magdalene?" he asked watchfully. The duke had dealt his whole life with the clever prevaricators abounding in the royal court; reading faces was one of his talents. Maidens not strictly guarded were prone to temptation, but her shocked expression convinced him she told the truth.

"Heavens, Monseigneur! Of course, just friends. We were brought up together. He is like a brother."

Bourbon thought cynically, And I am your uncle, but I could happily climb into your bed were it not a sin. Nevertheless, to keep her cooperative, he nodded his consent again. "*Eh bien*, a train of three is little enough for a French *princesse*," he conceded.

He smiled at her grateful, bowed head, stood and lifted her up to kiss her on both cheeks and forehead, then stared blearily into those guileless eyes. "The house of Bourbon is under attack. We must link hands, Lyse-

Magdalene, and never let go our grip."

"Never, uncle dear, never," she promised fervently and he could see she was much moved by his need of her loyalty.

There was a soft scratch on the door and a secretary entered. "My lord, *Signore le Visconti di Trina* is awaiting your pleasure."

"Ah, here is Don Ferrante, your intended," Bourbon said in a soft, voice, gazing steadily at his niece who met his stare with a small smile of her own meant to be reassuring, and then submissively bowed her head.

A pliant child, for the most part.

"Let him come," the duke ordered.

When Lyse raised her eyes her fate was standing before her like a wall—in black boots, striped thigh breeches, a black brocade doublet displaying a small white collar, and a short burgundy surcoat with great, puffed sleeves. Aggressively parting the doublet at the bottom was a fashionable codpiece, a stuffed and embroidered fabric imitation of the erect male member jutting up. The hand taking off his flat, feathered beret wore a heavy gold ring on the middle finger. And a gold earring ornamented one ear. A posturing bravo indeed.

She gawked, there had to be some mistake.

She could not believe her uncle would join her to this bearded brute, whose sharp green eyes stared at her a moment in startled recognition before he remembered to make a sweeping bow. "Mademoiselle de Bourbon-Tonnière, I am deeply honored," the viscount of Trina murmured in a rich baritone, and bent his dark head to kiss the hand she finally remembered to offer.

Her uncle smoothly presented them to each other as his trusted secretary entered bearing a leather folder from which parchment documents protruded. And on the clerk's heels came the *marquis* de Joyeuse, to act as second witness.

Lyse swallowed twice, for her throat had dried up. In the past months, strolling through Moulins' salons and galleries with de Dunois, she'd played a game with herself, wondering how she would react if her intended husband were this fat count, or that bow-legged man, or that doddering one, various gentlemen casually encountered as they wandered around. She even wondered if the duke might have chosen the debonair but lower-echelon de Lugny, who'd excited her by boldly demanding, out of earshot but not out of sight of her governess, how they might meet privately, and she'd spent some hours trying to figure that out.

It should have been almost anyone but this great smiter of unarmed commoners. Her cheeks burned with dismay and she kept her eyes down to hide her distress. Still, she'd have to raise her eyes when the man spoke to her directly.

He didn't however. He addressed his first remarks to Bourbon, making the various and expected comments on her pulchritude, voicing assurance that the establishment she would one day preside over near Mantua would match in every way her beauty and refinement, and so forth and on. Then, still not looking at the subject of all this, he asked Bourbon, "Does Mademoiselle perhaps know our tongue, the language of Dante's divine Beatrice, who I might swear she resembles?"

"Why don't you ask her for yourself? My niece does speak, you know." Bourbon chuckled. He was amused. He'd never seen Ferrante in so oblique a social dance with a woman.

But Lyse raised her eyes to forestall the man. "I don't speak Italian," she said curtly.

Gonzaga's polite smile definitely did not reach his green gaze. "No matter, Mademoiselle, your eyes speak for you and such lovely orbs as yours may command every service." Then, having passed the expected compliments, his voice dropped. There was an uneasy silence, until, constrained to rescue courtesy, he continued, "What amusements do you favor, Mademoiselle? Early morning riding?"

"Yes."

"And the hunt, I presume?"

"Yes."

"Hawking?"

"No, I've not been taught"

"We shall have to remedy that. Many ladies enjoy flying a bird."

Silence.

Non-plussed, Bourbon looked from one to the other. Ferrante was uncommonly stilted. Lyse-Magdalene was practically tongue-tied. A young woman, of course, would be shy at her betrothal to a stranger. But Ferrante? He'd seen the practiced Mantuan gallant charm the most skittish beauty from her shell.

He offered, "My niece plays the lute quite nicely. She enjoys music."

"Ah?" A winged eyebrow went up. "Perhaps you will play for me one evening, Mademoiselle?" Ferrante asked.

"Yes." Her bare retort was very close to rude.

Ferrante pushed himself to inquire her reaction to the Château de Moulins, having heard she came from a quiet estate. She finally cleared her throat, remembering her promise of cooperation to her uncle, and complimented him on his fluent French. He said briefly he had spent almost half his life in France.

Silence.

They both sat opposite Bourbon at his writing table, Lyse with hands in lap and eyes downcast, the Mantuan uncomfortable and increasingly gruff. The constable of France was confounded. They were both handsome people, fairly well matched; he had expected them to be delighted with each other. But he himself was suffering; he was feeling sick as a cur and with patience as short. He glanced over at Joyeuse, who shrugged. So Bourbon nodded to the secretary who pushed forward a gold inkpot and two plumed quills and commence unsheathing his documents. "*Eh, bien,* we might as well go forward at this point," Bourbon announced, and both his listeners' faces turned to stone.

The secretary read aloud the short betrothal agreement, Ferrante nodded and signed three copies, then Lyse, pale and quiet, laboriously wrote her name, then Joyeuse, who had been leaning against the mantle observing, stirred himself to sign as witness. The duke and the secretary quickly signed as well. It was done. Two months after the death of the invalid Aliesa, the widower would announce his betrothal to the French princess Lyse-Magdalene de Bourbon-Tonnière. Eight months later, or whatever decent bereavement period circumstances allowed, they would marry. Or if there were trouble, they would marry as quickly as possible, to empower Ferrante's protection of her.

Lyse sneaked a look at the married man who was to be her future husband. Between the furrow under his eye, which was actually a long scar, and the barbarous gold circlet pierced through one earlobe, she imagined he looked like one of ancient Aleric's Huns. Surely he acted like one, not only for the brute way he had treated Germain, but especially in the heartless way he anticipated his wife's death. She realized she was being shifted from one man's prison to another.

Don Ferrante drew a folded square of suede from his doublet and placed it before her. "A small earnest of my faith, lady, although its brilliance fades before your own lustrous beauty," he rumbled out the formula.

She glanced for guidance at Bourbon, whose face, beneath a flush on the cheeks, was the color of ashes, but Charles merely managed a weak smile. She then unwrapped the square to stare at a fine emerald set in a round, gold pendant encircled with small diamonds. The deeply verdant stone flashed green fire in the light from the double candelabra on the writing table, and the diamonds glittered. It was a most lovely piece. Her betrothed picked it up by its long, gold chain and handily slipped it over her head.

She had never owned any such splendiferous jewelry before. Dazedly, she touched the pendant as it lay cool on her bosom. "It is most beautiful, Monsieur. I thank you," she mumbled.

But the symbol of engagement nestled on her bosom caused the significance of the occasion to strike her fully. She had just been signed over, via legal contract and tender, to the fuming bravo who had almost killed her best friend that morning over nothing. True, she had promised her beleaguered uncle, had sworn to him solemnly to behave in his interests. But in this particular service she felt diminished, just an inanimate object being passed from hand to hand. Terribly conflicted, she suffered a deafening ringing in her ears.

Claiming dizziness, which was no lie, she begged to be excused, and Joyeuse gallantly offered his arm to accompany her to the adjoining chamber where his sister would take charge of her. Lyse made quick, unsteady bows to the men, muttered a stammered apology, and wretchedly fled.

As soon as the door closed Ferrante glared accusingly at his host. "What is wrong with her? She seemed close to fainting. Am I that gruesome?"

"Of course not. She is shy, overwhelmed, minus a mother to lean on at such a momentous step in her life."

"She barely said a word to me."

"She needs to know you better. Lyse-Magdalene is a quiet, submissive sort."

"Hah! You think that? That's not what I saw this morning when she believed I was bullying her minion. She attacked me like a singed cat, fists and claws at the ready, and screaming the curses of a scullery maid."

"Come, Ferrante, you must be mistaken. Not this lady. It was someone else."

"It was she. There'd scarcely be two with that falsely seraphic face. I fear that women were always able to take you in, cousin."

Having some latitude to be bemused now that one problem had been shifted, Charles sat back in his chair and managed a smirk as an objection. The valet entered with a carafe of fresh wine and a dish of dried figs and pears, and poured two goblets. "Yes," Charles told him, "she mentioned the incident to me briefly, although she didn't know who you were. Well, I promise you such temperament is not her ordinary way."

"You mistake me, for that is a pity. I prefer some animation to the limp doll that was here today—although not such vitriol as I heard this morning."

"Ah, she happens to be attached to that fellow you chastised, Germain Matz, son of one of my *intendants*. They were children together. You know women: attack one of their cubs..."

"He was insolent. I merely gave him a good shaking. I suppose your niece's imitation of a mute just now means she is still angry?"

"A bit of time is required, and gallantry from you. She has been very sheltered.

But don't you agree she is an entrancing woman?"

Such leading question did bring up a glitter of appreciation in Gonzaga's green eyes, which he dampened with an ungallant response. "The face and form might do. But she surely needs more balance in temperament."

Seeing the duke's jaw tighten at the criticism and remembering Bourbon's lyrical description of her character, Ferrant thought darkly that this admittedly beautiful woman possibly had a claim to his cousin's heart far beyond her valuable ability, or his duty of guardianship. To make up for such ugly suspicion which peculiarly shocked him, he lightened his manner.

"You needn't worry, my lord, I will not mistreat her. You know that."

Nodding, Bourbon got up and pressed a goblet of his finest Anjou wine into the Italian's fist, taking one for himself. "A display of temper by Lyse-Magdalene is hard for me to believe," he admitted, "but she is your province now, cousin. I have my hands full with other matters. Make of her what you will to please you, only do not block her ability. She is one of my defences against overwhelming misfortune, she is a wild gamble but I have usually been a lucky wagerer. Sit near me at the banquet later, and so will Lyse-Magdalene. I'm sure you will find her less bashful."

But the unsteady ducal hand on the wine glass caused Ferrante to peer acutely at Bourbon, who had been suffering for several days. "How goes the fever, Charles? Do your doctors prescribe?"

"Everything from hourly leeching to cold cider-vinegar rubs, to forcing potions of unspeakable horror down my gullet." Bourbon mopped his forehead again, pulling his head into his shoulders like a sick turtle, and tugged at the damp shirt ruffle that stuck to his neck. "But as long as this misery draining my strength grows no hotter, I can manage."

Lines of concern deepened around his listener's mouth. "You should be in your bed, Charles—"

Bourbon sighed disgustedly, and wet his dry lips again from the goblet. "I agree," he muttered. "I will retire immediately after the banquet and concentrate on regaining my health."

But he knew he was not quite finished for that day, for hours later it was from his bed, under a light satin coverlet and bedcurtains pushed back on their rods, that Bourbon again addressed his summoned council.

"Gentlemen, I give you my plan for the present. As you can see, I have sought my couch tonight and I intend not to leave it again for a fortnight. I want the king to believe that I am very ill, for a man so stricken can be little threat to anyone. Francois will then depart here lulled as to my intentions, and thus I shall remain unmolested. On the royal court's departure I will send for the new ambassador from the Hapsburg emperor, who awaits in Clermont, and at that point I will have decided my course of action."

His men nodded unhappily, aware that time was slipping away before an inevitable arrest, but forced by his sickness to agree to this two more weeks of hanging back.

"Be normal in your actions and words, and take care how you contact Messieurs de Pompérant and Severalt when they arrive with the royal court, so no suspicion accrues to them. We can turn this perverse royal visit to our advantage; it is going to buy us time to put our plans in place."

Joyeuse added, "De Pompérant reports little anyway, from his dispatches. The king takes only de Brissac and Admiral Bonnivet into his confidence on this ugly matter with you." He shrugged, then gave voice to the same ominous conjecture Gonzaga had made that afternoon. "My lord, 'tis altogether possible he is truly coming here to detain you..."

"I say no," the duke broke in, "The always genteel Francois would not abuse the hospitality of a sick man. His temper may be inconsistent but his honor is not."

"His 'honor' is robbing you of your birthright," came Joyeuse' blunt reply. "But La Clayette and I have been conferring with your guard officers and in any case we will be on the alert."

Saint-Bonnet worried, "It poses a grave risk, all the same, this visit."

"Francois has given us no choice in the matter. He will arrive."

Uneasily, Gonzaga brought up to Bourbon another problem. "'Tis a given that all the weasel Lorraines will be with him, basking in his favor and licking their chops. Claude de Guise would love to stoke his own blazing dreams of a dukedom with Bourbon bones."

Charles rolled up the sleeves of his silk night-shirt, slumped against his heaped-up pillows and fanned himself with one of the documents scattered on his bed. He was too miserably hot to hear of blazing dreams; his temples pounded, his vision blurred. He murmured, almost to himself, "Ah, but the head Lorraine, the *comte* de Guise, dreams of much, much more than that..." His voice trailed off when he saw all eyes centered on him and he clamped his lips tight on uttering any more. Finally he was able to continue, "Yes, it will be wise to be alert as much to the Lorraines as to the Valois. Francois in his arrogance does not bother to cloak his moves, but the Lorraines will act with their customary stealth."

Armand de Prie asked in puzzlement, "I don't quite understand. Since what ever poison de Guise may have poured into Francois' mind against you has already done its dirty work, what further covert move do you expect from him, monseigneur?"

"Lyse-Magdalene, of course," Joyeuse blurted out without thinking, talking only to Bourbon. Heads went around in startled inquiry.

But Bourbon was too ill to quickly realize the indiscretion of Joyeuse's remark and answered hazily, "Yes, they are too shrewd not to be at least dimly aware of her." But, in the next beat he shook some of his torpor and repaired the slip by glossing it over for the rest. "It is a small, inter-family matter, my sirs, a minor irritation caused by my older sister's betrothal agreement years past which caused some bad blood."

"No marriage arrangements go smoothly," Valentinois said sagely.

Bourbon grabbed his wine cup from a bedside table and drained it, causing two hectic patches to bloom and spread on his pale cheeks. His anxious followers remained to confer with him a while further until the watchful Saint-Bonnet suggested an end to the night. Grateful, the bleary duke concurred and dismissed them all then except for his loyal doctor, who had brought a potion to reduce the fever and help him sleep through the night.

His valets were clearing the bed of papers and fussing about to make him comfortable, when, as he had signaled to them, Joyeuse and Gonzaga slipped back into the room. The servants and the doctor obeyed his croaked order to get out, and the meeting continued, limited now to only these special companions.

An upset Joyeuse apologized profusely for his previous gaffe, which fortunately seemed to have been contained, but muttered, "I never liked the idea of bringing the girl here in the first place."

"It was necessary. I thought her too vulnerable alone, even in the obscurity of St. Piteu, and I was hoping to speed up her task. How could I have foreseen the court would travel here? But Francois and his spying cohorts will remain only a fortnight. We can discreetly remove her to Chantelle for that time."

Bourbon closed his eyes a moment and shook his head, trying to clear away the fogginess but only making his headache worse. But remnants of the indulgent uncle he'd been still clung and he continued, addressing Gonzaga. "Ferrante, I know my poor niece will be overwrought not to see the king. She has been very excited about the visit, I'm told, and might make some fuss to be deprived of her maiden's dream. But I am certain she will go to Chantelle without problem if we allow her at least to observe the royal entry into Moulins from afar. There can be no danger in that."

Ferrante fingered his earring, looking unconvinced, but then decided this was no time to argue, and nodded. "I will spirit her away from here immediately after the entry, during all the arrival commotion. Joyeuse would be missed if he absented himself for a few days, but not me."

This was agreeable to Charles. "It is an easy ride to Chantelle. Deliver my niece and her retainers there, settle them and return here for the rest of the festivities. Take a complement of men to remain with the women as safeguard."

"Your pardon, my lord, but if de Guise is looking for her she won't be hard to find at Chantelle," Joyeuse warned.

"*If* he is seeking her. He may well have lost interest and we are being morbid. This is just a precaution, with Chantelle quickly accessible to us. Moreover I keep messenger pigeons there."

Gonzaga said nothing; he suspected that Bourbon was not thinking clearly, but the duke was stubborn and time, as usual, was short. It would be done the duke's way.

Bourbon, still uneasy with his cousin's luke-warm reaction to his charming newly-betrothed, scolded, "And you might spend the hours you stay at Chantelle worming yourself into the better graces of your future wife. She seemed still wary of you at this evening's banquet."

"It is that damned, foolish incident with her squire," Ferrante growled. "I just can't seem to get her to realize what a fine, gentle fellow I am." He guffawed through his wry grin and the other two laughed with him.

The duke upended the sleeping draught the doctor had left and settled wearily further into his pillows, wiping his forehead with the linen sheet. He related that an informant had ridden day and night from where the great royal train was camped on their way to Moulins to bring his employer rapid information. "At least we know the matriarch Louise is not traveling with them; that would have killed my mother-in-law. But 'tis my strong guess that this royal interlope upon Moulins will pass uneventful, nothing more serious than someone's broken pate in the championship tourney-of-arms our knights have planned. So we shall innocently fête the king and his lords and ladies with all the hospitality for which Moulins is famous. We will dandle them dizzy with pleasure until they continue on to Lyons."

He snorted a sigh and stared up at the ceiling glumly as if what to do might be written there. "But afterwards Francois, my false friend of so many years, will want to extract his due from me, and I must...I will be ready to move on it." This necessity seemed to overwhelm him in his weak state; he was burning up but yanked up the sheet as if it were a shield and ordered them, "Joyeuse, my good friend, convene everyone in the morning once more. I've still some thoughts to work out. And send in my doctors again, for I will saw off their cods if they do not deliver me from this suck-wart fever!" His sunken eyes closed, giving in to the illness.

His good Joyeuse stood hands on hips and regarded the flushed, waxy-faced duke lying supine on the bed. He grunted, "You'll not have to do much acting, monseigneur, to make Francois believe you are very, very sick."

Outside the duke's apartments Gonzaga pulled the *marquis* into a shadowed corner of one of the rooms. "I think the king certainly comes here to take inventory of what will soon be all his, providing he has intimidated and paid *Parlement* enough. It wouldn't be past him..."

Joyeuse was weary himself: it had been an extremely long day. But Gonzaga had seemed unusually disgruntled at their meetings, for lack of assurance he supposed. "Well, if you see his clerks walking about scribbling down every artwork in their ledgers then it will be time for the duke to flee, suffering or not," he yawned. He lightly punched the younger man on his arm, then saluted him goodnight and walked off towards his own bed.

Chapter 5

Excited riders galloped into Moulins to report the royal procession sighted on the river: the king and half his entourage traveling south from Orleans, having commandeered every available barge and boat there for themselves, their retainers and their horses. The remaining huge train of lesser lights, servants and baggage, were struggling two days behind them by bad road.

But Lyse was weeping in her chamber, her face crumpled, her nose reddening. She grabbed the missive from her uncle from Madame's hand, crumpled it up and hurled in a corner. "I won't go!" she wailed, "it is not fair!"

Madame de Dunois, informed earlier of the need to take Lyse away, had already quelled her own disappointment. "Tut, *ma fillette,* it is only for a fortnight."

"But I want to be presented to the king!" Lyse cried. "I have saved my best gown for the occasion. And there will be hordes of new people and plays and ballets and dancing every night. And great and splendid tournaments, with the finest champions in all France riding in the lists, so said the duchess, and I've never even seen a little tourney! I won't go!"

De Dunois sighed. "Well, you must. As always, the duke is to be obeyed, and for your own sake."

"But what does he mean, 'for my safety'?" Lyse snuffled loudly, devastated. "Does he think the ruler of all France is going to threaten *me*, a person of no consequence he's never heard of?" She dropped down on the bed, flung her arms around one of the fat posts and wept afresh. "Oh, it is so unjust, so cruel. Have I not had enough of separation from the world?"

Elinor patted the quaking shoulder, suffering for her charge, so young and eager, who should be enjoying all the roses life had to offer and was instead kept in the shadows. But the conscientious de Dunois had her special duty. And so, all unwittingly, did Mademoiselle de Bourbon-Tonnière.

"It's all that huge foreigner's fault!" Lyse cried.

"He's not a real foreigner, he was raised in France."

"He was born in Mantua, wasn't he? That is a foreigner to me!" Lyse insisted spitefully. "He, he is causing all this—" she moaned, pounding on the coverlet.

For ten minutes more the sympathetic governess tried to coax and cajole her charge, reminding her of her duty to obey and bringing her a cotton kerchief to dry her tears. Finally, losing all patience, she gave the girl a hard pinch on the arm and waxed stern. "You are acting like a mewling infant and I'll not have it! Must I remind you again you have no way of living except by your uncle's good will? You know enough now to understand his concern for you. He does not wish you in the eye of the royal court, and that is that!"

"But why?" Lyse screeched, outraged by the truth that she had no control over her life. Then, the next instant, her swollen eyes quickly widened in a blank stare, for the white plaster walls around her were moving, intensifying and metamorphosing into heavy stone, and there were black and white tiles gleaming through the polished wood floors.

"No! Oh God help me, I cannot give him away," she pleaded, falling to her knees and desperately clasping the portly man about his shins, hugging her wet cheek to the embroidered silk of the churchman's chausable. "For the love of Christ I beg you, do not make me."

"You must! "From above her came the sepulchral voice, one without pity. "It is your duty."

Full of anguish, Lyse blinked hard again, only to find herself in the midst of a whine to de Dunois, "Listen, I have never so much as peeped to anyone about my visions, why should I do so now?" The justified question hung on the air a second but suddenly Lyse was exultant inside, for it seemed the instantaneous wrench back from past to present had occurred this time with not even a jerk of her head to mark the intensity of the intrusion, or give it away to de Dunois.

"Ah, but it is not just for the usual reasons of secrecy," the Governess retorted impatiently, and regretted it the next moment. Joyeuse had cautioned her not to alarm the young woman. In eighteen years the Members of the powerful house of Lorraine had made no move toward Lyse, as once they had toward her mother. Creating fear in the girl could fog her precarious recall. Adroitly de Dunois repaired her slip. "'Tis that monseigneur believes the excitement of the royal court may be too much, that it would inhibit your remembrances."

Another jolt, and a continuing flash of memory streaked its way through Lyse's head...

...sightless, milky eyes looking down at her. A satin stole over purple robes. A sepulchral voice offering no escape: "The sacrifice will save many lives, poor child, hundreds of them—"

"What do I care for them," she keened. "It is he who matters to me. Oh Seigneur, take this cup from me!"

"What is it?" de Dunois asked her charge uncertainly, not having seen the usual seeing-back signals she recognized.

Lyse blinked, for in this instant her governess had been staring at her, and noticed her twinge of shock. *Merde.* If she couldn't control her expressions she would never control her life. Later, she'd report the visions, not now. She smoothed the agitation from her face, and tried rationality. "Nothing at all, Madame. If only you could tell me what you think I *might* remember, then I could concentrate, I could *will* myself to 'see-back' to what you want and report the details."

But de Dunois answered, "It doesn't happen that way. Believe me." There was no time left. The governess hauled her charge off the bed. "I must see immediately to the packing and send Germain to ready our little party for departure. Nurse must bathe your eyes in chamomile, they are ugly and red, and your nose too. I'll wager we're going to hear the royal trumpets from the town's barge landing any moment. Ah, *ma petite*, do you wish to be blotch-faced when your impressive betrothed, Don Ferrante, comes to fetch you to the ramparts to view the arrival?" She forced a chuckle to lighten Lyse's gloom.

In truth, the governess reflected she was glad enough to share her burden with Gonzaga now. The man reminded her of her brother, a man of action rather than of honeyed words. And the Gonzagas were a powerful, respected family, Mantua a rich city. It would be exciting to someday accompany Lyse-Magdalene there. She was not too old, perhaps she too could find a suitable Italian husband and make her own life again.

But Lyse had pulled a face at the mention of her betrothed, and her governess clucked at such childishness. "*Écoutes*, we are not to depart for Chantelle until nightfall anyway. Why don't you don your new sapphire silk gown to see the king arrive, it is so very becoming to you?"

But Lyse was not to be consoled. "A new gown, merely to stand in the wet weather on one of the far battlements where few might see me? What a waste."

"But Don Ferrante will see you."

"Don Ferrante may see me in my ordinary gown, and *tant pis*, too bad! That way I will be all ready for him to sneak me out of Moulins as furtively as those village bare-behinds used to be spirited in and out of the monastery near St. Piteu. At least those women had no reason to feel humiliated."

With an expletive, Madame de Dunois threw up her hands and hurried away to raise Nurse, who kept a jar of soothing chamomile lotion for Lyse's eyes, a recipe from the monks' apothecary which Germain had learned and freshly prepared for them a week ago.

Even though the weather was depressingly grey, the road up from the river was thickly lined with excited townspeople whose wild cheers of *'Vive le Roi'* penetrated the château's walls and wafted to the roof of a high, interior tower being used as a viewing point by a small group of people, including those from St. Piteu. The procession was not yet in sight from this spot.

The huge castle was brilliant with celebration. Great swags of cloth-of-gold and silver billowed from all the château's battlements, and a riot of flags and pennons flew from every roof. Suspended from the outer walls were monumental tapestries depicting Caesar being received in Rome with his victorious troops, and these blatant flatteries were bordered with rippling drapes embroidered with Francois' bold symbol, a crowned salamander encircled by fire and looking back toward its tail. Many of the Bourbon courtiers waited along the road and main drawbridge for the procession to wend its way through the town below, but many had climbed up to throng every forward battlement for a better view of the royal *entrée*.

Don Ferrante, however, had taken his little group to a less popular inner tower, province of a handful of clerks and third secretaries and cooks, and Lyse had everything to do to contain her anger.

She was, no question, being hidden away, the way a family concealed a drooling idiot, and she might have been in the farthest reach of Cathay for all the detail she could make out from where they were so poorly stationed. *Boudin de Diable!* She did not understand the reason for such inordinate caution, and nobody was telling the complete why. Her mind, bouncing between various lurid surmises had given her a slight headache, and this was making her peevish.

Ferrante, invigorated by almost a week of breaking lances in practice jousting engagements, as well as sundry hearty amusements at night, was doing his best to be engaging, but a glance here and there at Lyse to see only a sulky, turned-down mouth kept bringing up unfortunate comparisons with his wife. So he stationed himself behind her, marveling at how differently she conducted herself in her uncle's presence, as a maiden so sweet and smiling and demure it was enough to make one retch, yet her true face, the one she showed to him, was ill-tempered and ungracious.

She was a beauty, yes, but petulant and spoiled. He'd learned there was no use remarking on this to Charles, who refused to believe it. Ah, what did it matter anyhow, when Duty had sealed his fate?

For the first time in his life Ferrante rankled at the heavy burden of the secret knowledge given to him which bound him to help Bourbon, whereas always he'd felt chosen and proud to be selected over both his older brothers. So he stood in back of the 'weird one,' as he'd come to think of this female who could remember her ancestor's lives, the better not to see her moping face. He had no patience for her tantrums.

He ignored the presence on the tower of her stolid man, Germain, and the wheezy old nurse who was tipsily past her usefulness to anyone, but he was happy for the company of her governess, the countess de Dunois, Joyeuse's sister, who, bound by the same obligation as he, had received him most cordially. She could make his dealings with the resentful Bourbon-Tonnière much easier.

At last the vanguard of the long procession snaked up from the town and appeared like a rainbow through the pearly-grey wisps of fog drifting over the distant road. So vivid against the sullen day were the flying, colorful flags and the gorgeous garb of the jaunty riders passing under a hastily-erected triumphal arch, it was as if the sun actually shone down on them.

Trumpets blared and drums rattled, but their bright proclamation was muffled by the cottony, saturated air. The advancing, multi-hued ranks of banners and flags, the clop of a thousand hooves, the jingling of myriad harnesses seemed only a far-away echo dulled through the drifting layer of fog. Yet Lyse could not tear her eyes away from the oncoming panoply magically advancing from the grey overcast.

A large Bourbon guard of honor cantered through the arch first, followed by the royal company of prize Swiss pikemen in striped costume. Just behind them, flanked by noblemen on each side and riding a black charger draped with red-gold brocade, appeared without doubt *le Roi* Francois Premier, and as Lyse gripped the damp stone of the tower's battlement she imagined an aureole shimmered all around the tall, imposing figure of France's lavish ruler.

The flat beret on his dark head was plumed and bejeweled, he wore a deep blue surcoat with massive puffed sleeves, skinny, slashed breeches, and boots above the knee. A cuirass of etched gold and silver gleamed out from beneath his surcoat, and large gems flashed on his gloved fingers. He rode majestically, with one hand on hip, a tall, strong form. At his steed's sides trotted a pair of huge, shaggy hunting dogs.

But at Lyse's distance his exact features were a blur, she had only the impression of a long face, smiling and determined.

Don Ferrante rumbled from behind her, "On His Majesty's right you see Admiral Bonnivet, his chancellor and favorite advisor and no friend of the Bourbons; on his left, with the white hair, the Grand Master of Falcons; next to him the Grand Seneschal. The ranks behind, riding under various insignia, are high officials and nobility from the princely houses, along with their sons and squires, and various important foreign ambassadors."

He had moved in closer trying to make out faces, and in spite of the fascinating pageant unrolling in the distance, Lyse was suddenly very aware of his presence behind her, as if the great furnace necessary to fuel such a man was warming her back. "You seem quite familiar with the French court," she remarked dryly.

"I have spent a certain amount of time with the French court as a member of your uncle's train."

"I see." What she did see just then was that the man she was betrothed to had a disconcertingly strong presence; he was causing a sort of prickling on the back of her neck.

"After that group rides the king's personal bodyguard, picked and honored gentlemen attached to him at all times."

"*Tiens*, there must be more than two hundred of them," Elinor de Dunois trilled, happy to once more have some view of the world.

Lyse was straining forward across the battlement to try to make out more. Gonzaga drew a small leather pouch from the purse hanging at his trim waist, undid it and took out a little metal tube. He touched Lyse on the shoulder, then put the object her hand and said, "This is a rare, ancient device of lenses used by Persian jewelers to engrave gems. It was traded during the last Crusade in the Holy Land three hundred years ago to Don Lorenzo de Gonzaga, and kept by my family as a curiosity. Close one eye, put this end to the other eye, and see what you can see."

She threw him a suspicious look but did as he suggested, and then gasped. She took the tube away, staring, and then tried it again. "*Bon Mère*, why it makes things clearer, like spectacles—or larger, perhaps. I can tell faces..." she marveled, "Oh, la–!"

"'Tis a toy that has the peculiar property of bringing distant objects a little closer."

Used to the little novelty's trick, Ferrante made little fuss over it, so he was surprised as the young woman suddenly whirled around and looked up at him with a great, incredulous smile, and for the startled *condottiere* it seemed that the grey day had suddenly become luminous, beaming from artless blue eyes that suddenly held all the world's delight.

"Why, Monsieur, what a wonder!" she cried, with sincere joy.

He stared down at her and for a moment the radiant beauty of her face took his breath away. He managed a smile.

But she whirled back, screwing up an eye and peering again through the squat tube. She pushed away de Dunois' demanding hand and concentrated. "His Majesty has a very long, pointed nose," she observed with relish, "although it suits his face, which is strong and quite handsome."

The Mantuan grunted. "That is the Valois nose, very good for ferreting out lootable artworks and money and any nubile maidens the passing countryside might harbor." Ferrante di Gonzaga was not one for reverence.

"And I see His Majesty also wears a beard, a short one–like yours." She looked up at him again, wonderingly.

"Except I have nurtured mine longer," he said. "Last winter Francois was clean-shaven. In high spirits, he spent Christmas at his favorite palace of Amboise, on the Loire. He challenged one of his courtiers and his minions who had a home nearby to defend their château in a snowball fight, and so the defenders laid in a huge supply of snowballs and eggs and rotten apples. The king and his men, successfully hurling their own snowballs and eggs, were soon pushing at the château's doors and someone above snatched a burning chunk of wood from the hearth and threw it out a window. It bounced and hit the king on the side of his face, making a serious wound. Yet he allowed no investigation as to who launched such a deadly missile."

De Dunois added, obviously impressed, "My friend wrote to me at the time that the king publicly insisted that if he indulged in tomfoolery he must take his chances with accidents."

"The beard is to cover the scar that resulted," Ferrante continued.

"Is that why you wear such a one? Do you have a scar, Signore?" Lyse asked, snippy again.

His lips curled into a sardonic smile. "I do, several. One you can see, under my eye. The rest are on my heart, Mademoiselle, and one engraved on an unmentionable place."

Lyse stiffened, not caring to go further into that. She turned to again stare at the king, who had now been met at the arch by a formal delegation on the *duc*'s behalf, led by a resplendent de Joyeuse. She handed the tube over to her governess, who was jittering impatiently to see her brother.

"His Majesty sounds a most gallant man," Lyse remarked.

"He is brave," Ferrante admitted, with a shrug.

"But restless, so I hear," de Dunois chimed in as she gave Lyse back the tube, the pleasure of seeing her brother make the king a many-flourished bow lighting her narrow face. "I hear Paris makes him feel cooped up, with its crowds and smells and mud, so that he travels around the kingdom constantly, to the royal châteaux, or to visit courtiers or various cities, and he insists that every man, woman and child of his court accompany him. Why, even back in Louis Twelfth's demanding service, when my husband was alive, we had time to breathe between court journeys, at least it seemed to me."

"He travels to keep the royal finger on the country's pulse, Madame," Ferrante observed dryly, "and the throne firmly under the royal rear."

But Lyse was still staring out. "What a lengthy procession. Some of it must still be at the town."

Ferrante's baritone responded from behind her. "I am told this will be only a small train, perhaps four thousand. For Francois' triumphal *entrées* into the big cities, where the burghers literally bankrupt themselves to make elaborate welcome receptions, your king is followed by a royal train of eighteen thousand and more!"

"*Ma foi!*" Lyse breathed, stunned, momentarily reverting back to the girl at St. Piteu, to whom the village's procession of sixty worshipers behind a reliquary holding a fingernail of St. Piteu was large.

Behind her Ferrante's mouth twitched at her incredulous gasp.

Putting the tube to his eye, he went on pointing out important court members as they rode onto the drawbridge. Then his dark brows hauled together and he passed her the tube. "Do you see, Mademoiselle, to the left, the noble with a large sweep of feathers in his hat, riding under a green and gold banner? That man is Claude, the *comte* de Guise, a member of the princely house of Lorraine. And on either side are two of his three brothers —the cardinal of Lorraine, who is also bishop of Albi, and Louis, the *vicomte* de Marques."

Lyse looked up at him inquiringly, wondering why he singled out these courtiers, but Gonzaga's green eyes were staring over her head. Then he continued, "De Guise and his brothers hold large French land patents, but some consider them foreigners, still in thrall to Lorraine, which is an independent duchy ruled by the their eldest brother. Francois is not enamored of any of them, especially the count de Guise, but he gives them honors for political insurance. In fact, there are rumors that a dukedom will be conferred upon de Guise before fall. It is in your interest, though, to know that they claim descent from the old French Merovingian kings, and that they argue this gives them precedence in the hierarchy of nobles over the Bourbon princes."

Staring through the tube Lyse observed, "But he looks a fair, mild man, Monsieur de Guise, his face is tranquil and he smiles pleasantly, not the sort who would or could wrest my uncle's position from him with such fanciful pretensions."

"Looks deceive. He is calculating and avaricious. And he is married to a lady of the Vendome-Bourbon branch, which roots his issue strongly in France and even makes him a distant relative of yours by marriage."

She remarked caustically, "I doubt he will ever feel the necessity to come and claim me as such."

"One never knows," was the offhand answer, and she supposed he was joking.

Madame de Dunois took the tube from her and quivered with excitement. "Ah, look, there on that buff hackney rides Queen Claude, along with the king's beloved sister and all their ladies behind, hundreds upon hundreds of them, oh, what a sight, oh, just look at the sleeves of their gowns, how wide and turned back the ladies are wearing them in Paris, look at their hats, the trimming, oh!"

For the next ten minutes the two women and Nurse, pummelled out of her daily stupor by Lyse's excited taps on her arm, passed the little tube of lenses back and forth and exclaimed in female detail over the long train of proud, bejeweled ladies, riding in litters or sitting hackney horses. This left Ferrante free to see if he could spot, unaided at this distance, his favorite court amusement, the flamboyant Madame de Rougerie.

At last the entire train of arrivals had passed under the arch, across the drawbridge and through the outer court, and the noise and milling and excitement grew loud below their tower, the duke's equerries darting about disentangling backed up lines of dismounting gentles and ladies' litters, and scurrying attendants trying to find their bawling masters. The château portal where the royal party itself had been escorted could not be seen from their tower, and out of the roiling clouds a true drizzle had started up, so Ferrante indicated they should descend.

Unhappiness erased the high excitement on Lyse's face.

Ferrante ignored it. He ordered Germain, "Without fail, see the horses and baggage wagon brought around to the north gate tonight, where we will meet you when the church bells peal seven, a dark enough time in this weather. See you keep your mouth shut about it."

"*Oui*, Monsieur," Germain answered, blank-faced.

Germain was baffled about what was going on, but he was also distressed over the few words he had said that morning–by chance *before* Madame de Dunois had come hurrying back to the stableyard, for she had forgotten to caution secrecy over the orders she'd given him to extract their horses and baggage wagons from the sheds before the *entrée* tangled things up.

"We are going elsewhere for a fortnight," was all she had told him at first. "See that we are ready to depart tonight."

So when the smitten viscount de Lugny happened to pass by the side court and recognized Lyse's mount tethered under a shelter along with a baggage wagon and mules, all alarmed he approached Germain, who was supervising. "Tell me, *mon homme*, it can't be that Mademoiselle de Bourbon-Tonnière is leaving Moulins right now? Even before His Majesty arrives? Why, I would be devastated not to have her company at all the festivities." The man's eyebrows crawled up his high forehead.

Germain knew Lyse favored this gentleman, a witty and attentive one who made her laugh, and this sat well with him, her loyal friend. So he had eased the courtier's disappointment by assuring him she was leaving that evening only for a fortnight, and she would definitely return. Some urgent family matter–he had shrugged casually, since he was bereft of any real information, even of destination.

It was only a quarter hour after this innocent indiscretion that a dithered de Dunois hurried back to add that absolutely no one was to be advised of their departure from Moulins, or when and from what gate they were leaving.

Well, he hadn't said much, knowing little anyway. And de Lugny wasn't courting Lyse seriously enough to want to drag her off her horse and refuse to let her go.

Germain snaked a finger under his damp hat to scratch his head. Ever since they had come to Moulins, Lyse had complained she felt as if a semi-transparent shroud had been dropped over her for some reason, for she was not led forward in the crowded court as a member of the Bourbon family would be. And now, she suffers this sudden, mysterious removal to points unknown, soon after the duke's return and just before the gala events of a royal visit?

It was very strange.

Germain was aware that the volatile Don Ferrante, whom Lyse had morosely confided to him she'd been ordered to marry at some future time, now had control over her life, curse the luck. Since the incident over the charger, the Mantuan's sharp glance mostly slid over Germain as if he hardly existed. But Germain understood that if he wanted to remain with his *princesse*, he must seem as indistinct as a shadow to the *condottiere* who carried out her uncle's wishes. So he accepted orders and said little.

He felt in his bones that Lyse-Magdalene, who had never seemed of much consequence to her family before this, was going to need a true and loyal champion in future.

Chapter 6

Francois Premier, jovial and unrumpled by the ten-day journey, wandered amiably among the lavish buffets of food and drink laid out on long tables in the Great Hall, accompanied by Queen Claude as well as his current strutting mistress, and followed by members of his intimate coterie. The *comte* Claude de Guise trailed casually behind, nibbling on a dainty fried pasty—but his gaze not quite as casually marked the members of Bourbon's court for who they were.

Francois, once restored by the hearty tidbits, requested escort to the ducal chambers to console his suffering constable. De Guise was tapped to accompany him, along with some others of the royal coterie, and the king took his personal confessor along, an archbishop, to offer spiritual comfort to the sick one.

But twenty minutes later de Guise was back in the Great Hall, which was still milling with people. He rounded up his brothers, then herded them quickly to the small chambers his valet had wrangled for them, for yammering, churning crowds made the hollows under his eyes ache. Hanging back, his brother Louis grabbed some roast fowl from a heaping salver, wrapping it in a napkin for private gnawing.

The five Lorraine brothers hardly resembled each other, except that three amongst them carried the family's light coloring and blue eyes. Claude's already thinning, bowl-cut hair and vanishing lips were ordinary in the family. Louis, *vicomte* de Marques, a greasy blond and square-jawed, scowled at the world out of a face heavily scarred by a bout with smallpox. But Jean, the next oldest to Claude, and an august churchman, had spent a childhood squirming under the cruelty of family humor, for he was short, portly, with olive skin and beetling black brows—"just like *Maman's* confessor?" the others had ragged the boy as he ran weeping to bury his head in his grim mother's lap.

Ferri, the youngest, was as slim and almond-eyed as the sleek hounds he bred with such care, but he had not arrived at Moulins yet, being detained by a mission for their oldest brother, Antony, now the ruling lord of the northern principality of Lorraine.

"That was a fast visit to monseigneur de Bourbon, my brother," the skull-capped Jean observed as he defiantly drew a square of sweet bread from his pocket, defiant because the fastidious Claude never had much patience for food.

The count de Guise leaned back in his chair, distracted in thought, absently holding a glass of spiced wine in one ringed hand and a small piece of cheese skewered on a knife in the other. He answered, "There was little reason for the king to stay long with Bourbon, and the air in a sickroom is dangerous. The man appears very, very ill–a flux, a tertiary fever–" He shrugged. "He could be dying."

"He could be faking. It would give him more time to enlist aide to foil the decision of *Parlement* when it goes against him," Louis growled, dragging a chair up to the table and depositing his bird.

Claude quietly sipped his wine, his voice as mild as his expression.

"Charles de Bourbon is not faking, unless some sorcerer has miraculously wasted his face and hollowed out his eyes and produced the hot forehead which almost burned the king's hand."

"Good riddance to him then, I say, a low and fitting end for a man who strutted as if all France was his private domain," Louis concluded, busily disjointing the roasted pullet half.

The cardinal shook his head. "A great pity should the man escape in death the humbling he so richly deserves."

"*Tiens*, he will not escape, please Your Eminence. One way or the other, Francois' mother, Madame Louise de Savoie, will send him to hell."

"Did he recognize His Majesty?"

"Yes, but he could hardly speak. Tears fell down his face as he raised up a hot and trembling hand, and Francois, ever gallant, took it in both of his. Very touching. In a whisper Bourbon assured us of the hospitality of his château, and begged forgiveness for his debility. His partisans, Joyeuse, St. Bonnet, the rest of them, all looked most grave over his condition."

"Perhaps, but I would not put it past that posturer to have taken some potion or other to produce his symptoms."

"Goodness, dear brother Louis, you are a cynic. The king is satisfied Bourbon is truly suffering and helpless, but nevertheless, when we depart he will leave a secret watch here to see the constable stays in his bed and doesn't decamp to a healthier climate."

A familiar argument then broke out between the cardinal and de Marques as to whether Charles de Bourbon, a popular hero, was incurring too much public sympathy battling the loss of his entire patents noble, and further, should already have been imprisoned by the king on any sort of pretext. Had he been held at the Château de Vincennes inside the Paris walls, and not allowed to reach his own domains, his support might have eroded by now.

Bored with the dispute because it was apparent Francois had no need to play such out-and-out villain when the prize was assuredly his, Claude broke in, speaking past his spring-clogged nose to report to them the casual information de Lugny had whispered to him after more important news, for Monsieur de Lugny had been his conduit for news from the Bourbon court for some time.

So he threw onto the table the informative morsel about Jeanne de Bourbon's barely known daughter suddenly appearing at Moulins and looked around at them for comment.

Louis licked his fingers with gusto. "*Merde,* I don't know," he grunted, "it strikes me that if some Bourbon females like that one can go back to the past, crop up insane, or were truly witches as suspected, they would already have led the family to the prize. Or at least wound up subject to serious interrogation by Holy Mother Church." He picked up the chicken leg and his strong teeth began to rip at it, although his narrow blue eyes remained on his brother. He demanded around the mouthful, "Have you ever thought those hoary rumors could just be some ancient troubadour's drunken imagination?"

"But they aren't. You were only a boy years ago when Bourbon's widowed sister was so precipitously removed from her dwelling place that we lost track of her. Finally we learned that she had died raving, overcome by whatever demons whisper lost knowledge into female Bourbon ears from one generation to the next."

"Bah! She merely went mad, I remember father said so. A streak of insanity descending through the blood, nothing more."

"Yes, dear brother, but over a century ago, in the year 1420, this family 'streak of insanity' as you insist, sent Guy de Bourbon south to Roussillon, where he recovered a part of the Cathar treasury which no one else had been able to locate in long years of searching. No one—including some of our own illustrious forebears."

De Marques was a good fighting man, he was brave and stubborn and would not give way. But he was not imaginative. "Bah, a fiction, I tell you, never proven, born of old jealousies of the expanding Bourbon power."

De Guise's mild blue stare hardened. "There are things you do not understand, Louis."

De Marques jumped on this with irritation. "Then explain them finally, *mon frère.*" He tossed the gnawed bone into a glazed bowl one of their servants had provided on the table. "Me, I'm drag-arse weary of hearing about what I don't know."

Claude turned his gaze to the swarthy Jean, for whom, at age ten, their father had obtained the Bishopric of Metz, and who was now cardinal de Lorraine, and archbishop of Reims. This unordained churchman had benefices all over France, including five great abbeys; his money chests overflowed with the returns from all of these sinecures.

Most pertinent to the present discussion, he was also bishop of the southwestern city of Albi, which in the far past had been infamous as the seat of a heretical Christian sect known as Cathars.

The cardinal had taken a seat in the window embrasure, and seemed to be moodily studying the rain from under his heavy brows, his hands hidden in the wide sleeves of his crimson wool robe. He had removed his round-brimmed hat, leaving a small red skullcap atop his mussed hair.

Claude sarcastically demanded of the churchman, "Re-educate this lout, Your Eminence. Maybe a bit of it will stick to his brain this time."

But the prelate shook his head impatiently at Claude's baiting of the unclever Louis, for those two had never liked each other; Claude irritated with Louis' plodding thinking, and Louis aware enough to be resentful of this. "Ah, he already knows about the *Cathari* from our father," the churchman grumbled. Then, because de Guise's unblinking stare was boring into him, he saw fit to add, "But I am always happy for the chance to tell again what an offense to God they were."

Claude relaxed in his seat and sipped his wine.

"The Cathars, my dear viscount, were a large group of anti-Christs who appeared in the eleventh century of Our Lord and swiftly multiplied in the southern regions of this country—in cities like Agen, Toulouse, Albi—and indeed, in parts of Italy and Germany too. They called themselves Christians, but they believed fervently in two Gods—one good Deity administering over Heaven, and one evil but equally powerful Lord, who administered over the earth, which these people deemed was the true Hell.

"It was their central belief that Christ's Kingdom of God in heaven made war constantly with the Satan of this earth. Humans were actually fallen angels, imprisoned by Satan in human bodies, but each soul so punished by being on earth nevertheless had left its spirit with the good God in heaven. A bizarre duality, a separated soul and a spirit, do you see?

"To the benighted Cathars, whose main religious rite was to say the Lord's Prayer together, salvation came only through the reunion of the soul here and the spirit above, and this could only be accomplished by the individual alone, through a humble life of asceticism and prayer."

Louis' grimace squeezed his large pockmarks. "My dear Cardinal, our Franciscan or Cistercian friars practice such worldly renunciation, yet we do not abominate them."

The cardinal glared into his brother's insouciance, although he knew Louis, at heart, was devoted to the church. "In those times the Holy Orders of priests and brothers we revere had not yet been founded, and when they were, were founded in Christ. For the worst of the Cathari abominations was that they abjured the Godhood of Jesus, holding he was not Son of God, but only God's human messenger, a prophet. They believed not in the baptism of children, or in the mediation of the saints and Apostles for us. And the Cross, the symbol of Our Lord's ultimate sacrifice? They abhorred it!" Jean shuddered at the very thought of such blasphemy and shook his head.

But he continued. "Intimates of the Devil they were, the Cathars, many residing in northern France, in Italy, even in Slav countries. But more than forty thousand of them lived in Languedoc alone by the time the blessed Pope Innocent III ordered a Holy Crusade to fall upon them, to kill them everywhere and stamp out their heresy. This blessed task was begun in 1208, and was a work of many years. In France 'twas named the Albigensian Crusade."

Claude took over, hugging his elbows to him as if to restrain any words about Louis' sluggish wits. "The Holy Office, which was newly established then, needed decades to root out the Cathar poison, for the heretics hid, or armed themselves and fought back strongly.

"Many of them were powerful knights with fortified mountain strongholds and hard to dislodge. Some, terrible to admit or understand, were Catholic churchmen, secretly affiliated with the heresy and giving it aid. But finally the very last cur of a Cathar leader was burned and his unrepentant soul cast into hell."

Claude leaned forward to deliver his real message. "And this damned last heretic took to hell with him the secret of what the Languedoc Cathars had done with their considerable treasury."

He leaned back to nibble the cheese off his knife, an incongruously mild action amidst the inflammatory subject.

Finally, he continued. "Their congregations were rich, Louis. Those who became their priests, both men and women, called themselves *parfaits*, 'perfects', and gave everything they owned to their 'church'. Their many thousands of fanatic communicants were tithed heavily as well, and large numbers were able to make lavish bequests at death.

"Yet when their last castle, a stronghold in Languedoc named Montségur, was captured in the year 1244 of our Lord, there was still no sign of what had become of the great chests of riches these heinous ones had amassed."

But Louis still scoffed, "How would outsiders know there had ever been great wealth?" He wiped his greasy fingers on a linen napkin. " 'Tis all rumors, so I've always felt, no substance."

"There were witnesses," Claude insisted. "Prisoners escaped from Cathar clutches in Montségur, men of honor who swore to seeing, just before one nightfall, great caskets secretly taken down the walls above a deep, sheer drop which the Catholic besiegers of the mountain mistakenly thought needed no watching. It had to be the Cathars' accumulated treasury, but whatever it was those doomed creatures of the Devil were spiriting away, it vanished forever."

"*Merde!* That happened two hundred seventy years before today," Louis exclaimed. "And not a splitting trace of any such treasure since."

"Admitted. And yes, there have been avid searchers for this treasure, centuries of them, prodding and digging and burrowing through league upon league of dark, wild hills and the caves and tunnels and deep ravines that foot the Pyrénées, in that part of Languedoc along the Aude River which is called the Razès. Yet for all that, only once has there been a believable report of success.

"And that report came in the year fourteen hundred and sixty, confessed by a repentant sinner on his deathbed. Forty years before, the dying man had been a member of a secret party led unerringly to a buried cavern in Languedoc by Guy de Bourbon. Then it suddenly happened that around 1450 the house of Bourbon's influence at Charles VII's court grew more powerful and prominent than it had ever been. Somehow that Bourbon had found a way to make massive money loans to the Crown, which financed France's victory over the English after one hundred years of fighting."

Louis shrugged, not overawed. "Luck. Good fortune. Accident. A story from skewed old records."

Jean levered up his bulk from the window seat and launched forward to pound the table against Louis' stubbornness.

"No! You know the truth as well as I. You were shown the old documents, for it was to our ancestor, the third prince of Lorraine, that the dying man swore that Guy de Bourbon had recovered an old chest full to the brim with gold and jewels. Preparing to face his Maker, the man broke his oath of secrecy and told about the Bourbon witch-girl who heard voices and had led her father almost by the hand to the buried entrance of a cavern. As a proof, this poor and dying knight opened his hand to show Lorraine a heavy five-sided golden medallion in the shape of a pentagram which he had filched from that cavern. Such a pentagram was a symbol revered by the Cathars as represent- ing wisdom and knowledge."

But Louis picked his teeth around a sneer. "And so the ancestral gentle- men of Lorraine and now the eminent Claude de Guise of France have spent all these years spying to discover which living Bourbon females might also be possessed of Satan!"

"Through the centuries there *have* been two we are sure of," Claude retorted. "In spite they were held from view, neither seemed to have had the power of the early diviner, or the sorcery to locate the remainder of the Cathar chests. The dying knight told the duke de Lorraine that Guy de Bourbon found only one chest. The reports of ancient witnesses, which our dear brother Cardinal here traced years ago in church records, mention five great coffers lowered down the wall. Alas, early searches were so unsuccessful that interest died years ago, and few remember any more.

"But our family always kept the information gained from that dying knight to itself. Now, at this crucial point in the Valois' reign, I insist it is worth some effort to find a treasure of gold enormous enough to turn our special ambitions into reality."

The cardinal leaned to lightly flick Louis on the ear with thumb and third finger, earning himself a glare of fury as the man jerked his head. "Eh, Louis? What say you, do you wish eventually be brother to the king of France?" he asked with heavy jocularity.

Claude de Guise's expression went iron hard at the stupidly unguarded remark, for the servants clattering in the next room to set up their masters' lodgings had very big ears indeed.

There were times when the cardinal's lumbering and Louis' bad temper made de Guise reluctant to trust them with anything sensitive. Only young Ferri, of all of de Guise's brothers, and in spite of the fellow's vices, directed his life with the deft mind he respected. Ferri was guileful, quick-witted and discreet, traits which made him valuable to de Guise's ambitions, and the count wished he were at Moulins now rather then the other two. Ferri was good at picking out important undercurrents from the ocean of gossip that engulfed French courts.

Louis blew out his lips. "*Boudin de chien,* so why do we not send an expedition south to look for this cache ourselves, then?"

"Where? The territory is large and difficult and has been combed over for generations. And the Cathar poison had spread like disease–into Italy, Germany, Spain. Men who could engineer the silent removal of weighty chests down a great, sheer drop in the dark of night, had ways to get them through the Christian siege army at Montségur and finally transport them elsewhere, even out of France. They worked with the black powers of darkness, do you forget?"

All three brothers fervently crossed themselves.

Louis was a man of confrontation, of war and battle, and lacking these, a master of murderous tournament competition to relieve his tedium. He had no patience to follow convoluted intrigue. He always felt himself outmanoeuvred by Claude, who owned the political power in the family and whose devious but successful machinations awed him, and by Jean, who, nevertheless, allowed him to share in the dissolute squandering of the church wealth that had brought the cardinal his fame as a patron of arts and antiquities.

Always cynical of any circumstance not a frontal attack, Louis demanded, "So, what is the point of all this conjecture?"

Claude responded, "The point is, I feel we have fortunately stumbled across a person who could be one of those 'hidden' Bourbon seers, for de Lugny reports that the young woman just arrived here seemed almost forgotten by society. Why would that be? She is of the blood, after all, and beautiful, so de Lugny swears, a daughter of a princely house who should be exploited for advantageous connection, surely.

"Yet this offspring of the Bourbon the Lorraines have always known to be 'peculiar', her mother Jeanne–this girl was held most obscurely until now when she comes to view at Moulins when Charles' realm is flying apart. One must believe he would keep what is of special value immediately under his eye. And then, just as suddenly, he deems it safer to hurriedly remove her from Moulins, according to de Lugny's offhand remark? Why? Because of the royal court's arrival! Ah–and with the Lorraines in attendance!" A smile crept across the thin lips.

An attractive thought brightened Louis' coarse visage. "*Eh bien.* So we kidnap the bitch and threaten her with the thumb screw, and squeeze out what she might know of this ancient gold. Easily done."

But the interested light in his eyes shriveled under Claude's look of pure disgust, and Louis' stomach clenched in resentment.

Jean caressed the jeweled crucifix on his portly bosom. "Ah, my good brother, if you torture a devil's confidant for information the creature may tell you what you want to hear, but in such a way that if you pursue it devilkins will cause you a fatal accident, a rock fall on your head, a hunter's arrow through your eyes, a bridge collapse under your feet, *Domine secoramus.*"

Claude cleared his throat softly. "We do not need to use force nor consider kidnap yet, expedients which once failed our father with Jeanne de Bourbon. No. Now that we have a clue to Bourbon's hopes, the path of stealth and cunning in this sudden opportunity could yield everything. We have only to watch and follow like silent shadows, and where the female may lead Charles de Bourbon, if his fever abates, she will also lead us."

"What's the bitch's name?"

"Lyse-Magdalene de Bourbon-Tonnière."

The Cardinal sat down heavily in the high-back x-chair his valet had previously readied for him, a tasseled velvet pillow comforting his backside. "Tonniére? Wasn't that the stupid rebellion leader who died in Vincennes years ago?" he rumbled. "Quite fitting for such a fool, an aberrant daughter."

"But maybe Bourbon has already profited from this woman's witchcraft and found the treasure. How do we know?" Louis asked.

De Guise put down his glass carefully. He leaned his forearms on the table and stared at Louis intently. "Because were such a huge horde of gold available to him he would have already bought the vote of all three hundred members of *Parlement* in the royal mother's lawsuit. Look at him, this glorious hero of Marignano and First Prince of the Blood—for all the wealth he already has, he is a conquered man, dying with fever, unable to resist the power of the throne sequestering his lands and seizing his coffers, and finally reducing him to poverty. No, he has not found his miracle. But if it exists it would save him, and he believes that and therefore so do I. De Lugny thinks they intend to take this Bourbon-Tonnière woman away from Moulins this very night. It would help us to know where. From now on, to always know where!"

"So, what good? She's not going to shout her divinations from the battlements of wherever they take her."

"Ah. But I have some ideas on this matter. I wish to wait for Ferri to arrive before discussing it. Meanwhile, I ask you to work with de Lugny to have this lady followed when she does leave Moulins. Followed only! And watched." Claude's tone was sharp. "I merely need to know where she is at all times."

In an attempt to seem just as crafty, Louis' eyes narrowed. "Not ten minutes ago you said there was much I didn't know, even though I learned almost all of what you've repeated from the same source as you, our father." His glance shifted from the nobleman to the churchman, both older brothers who had an alliance of mutual greed that sometimes seemed to shut him out. "So what do you hold back?"

There was only surprise on the cardinal's swarthy face. "Why naught, dear Louis. Are you not our brother? We know the thoughts we express here between ourselves will not go beyond this room. Why should we hide something?"

Claude's dry smile was placating. "Saying that you didn't know was merely a figure of speech on my part. It signified nothing. You know what we know. But with your good offices presently, we will learn more. Will it help us to watch this woman who may solve an old mystery?" He shrugged. "Possibly. Will our effort to foil any secret quest of his condemn the *duc* de Bourbon to his humiliating destiny and clear my own political path? It well could. In Francois' eyes destroying Bourbon could elevate the position and influence of everyone in our house. It's a road which must be explored."

Louis stood up, shoving back his chair with an abrupt noise on the bare parquet floor, for Claude's servants had not yet laid the rugs which were part of the household effects nobles traveled with to furnish the empty chambers offered guests. He moved his shoulders hulkingly, mollified, for the moment, into cooperating. "I'll be at it then, since de Lugny thinks she'll leave tonight. This palace is huge, it must have four or five drawbridge portals in various directions, t'would be hard to watch them all. A bribe to one of the grooms in the stables might do it the easy way. I'll see to it..."

He nodded and headed to the door with his rolling gait, tightening the buckle of his swordbelt as he went. A hail from the count de Guise stopped him with a hand on the latch.

"Louis! Give de Lugny no information. He is paid well enough merely to report and to ask no questions. Watch your words."

"Of course. Do you think I'm dim-witted?"

De Marques slammed the door behind him. The richly-dressed Claude de Guise in his embroidered violet doublet, and the red-capped cardinal de Lorraine looked at each other with thin smiles, but the prelate's oily forehead was creased.

De Guise shrugged to soothe the prelate. "Peace, Your Eminence. Louis has his uses. But Ferri will be here soon."

Germain's conscience was battering him over the improvident remark he had made that morning to the Monsieur de Lugny. He struggled between the safety of saying nothing and the humiliation of going to Gonzaga with a confession. Upset, he absented himself from the rowdy turmoil in the vaults below the château where the army of visiting retainers were being fed, and hung about in the stableyard by his party's horses, which were sheltered from the gentle rain by a shed roof. His presence at least allowed the groom assigned to watch them go get his meal.

Sitting on a mounting step, he stared glumly out at the tethered rows of patient, canvas-blanketed beasts, heads drooping in the rain because there was no more room in the huge stables. Germain had never seen such a congregation of four-legged creatures together, and there were many hundreds more, including baggage animals, in open corrals outside the walls.

His eyes were resting on the horses, but his head mulled over the mystery of where Bourbon was ordering them to go—and why. Most of all, why? Why was Mademoiselle de Bourbon-Tonnière being excluded from the king's visit? And why needed she to leave at night and in secret? Why was this swaggering Italian intimate of Bourbon's, Gonzaga, suddenly betrothed to Lyse and appointed leader to their little household?

And why had he himself not worn his protective, cowled robe, for the drizzle was seeping wetly through his doublet and drooping his felt hat.

How could he *not* go to Gonzaga with the confession of his slip? If something happened to harm Lyse-Magdalene, God forbid it, he would be responsible. Frustration gnawed at Germain's insides; he hated the devil-begotten Gonzaga, who would surely humiliate him again.

So the two cloaked men approaching were almost upon him before he looked up and saw them. He scrambled to his feet, recognizing that one was the viscount de Lugny. The other, whose face was marred by pockmarks, he did not know, nor did de Lugny identify him.

De Lugny smiled as he ducked in under the shed roof. "Greetings, my man. *Peste!* Such bad weather for a royal *entrée*. It truly compounds the arrival confusion," he observed easily. "We've been to see our horses fed, for sometimes in such a throng some animals are missed. Not all equerries are as solicitous as you of a master's mounts."

Germain looked from one to the other. "*Oui,* Monsieur," he finally answered, wondering what the man wanted.

"Have you a long distance to travel tonight?" de Lugny casually asked. "In such inclement weather?"

This time Germain wouldn't tell him what distance even if he knew, so he responded obliquely, "Monsieur, any way is a long way in the wet."

"Ah, how wise you are. Well, I have a problem, *mon ami,* which I might put before you. I have tried to see Mademoiselle de Bourbon-Tonniére, but her ever-present companion, Madame de Dunois, insists she is resting until supper and can see no one. I should like to give the lady a small token of my esteem to take on her journey. To insure she not forget me, eh?" He winked. "But I want to place it into her own hands. By which of the many portals will your party leave tonight, so I may await there and offer my farewells— unimpeded by the usual closed doors and gorgon guardians? You understand?"

Not so unusual a request for a lovelorn suitor, and under de Lugny's friendly manner Germain would ordinarily have thought nothing of saying through which gate they would head out—but not now.

He took a quick glance at the stranger with the pitted face. The man held his chin low, so that he stared up from under his brows, a cold light in his narrow blue eyes. As amiably as de Lugny presented himself, this fellow, in contrast, gave Germain prickles at the back of his neck.

So he lied smoothly, "The east portal, toward the town, Monsieur."

But he had spewed it out too fast. The stranger's head came up, alert to the lie, his pursed, pale lips the only smooth skin on his ruined face.

"Fast? Why, you go towards Burgundy," de Lugny prattled on. "But I would say that road in not good enough for safety at night, 'tis narrow and plagued with holes and tree roots. What could be the hurry, not to wait until daylight?"

An innocent question, at any other time. "My lady does not care to ride in the hot sun," Germain improvised, covering up his own ignorance. But he did not miss the pocked man's sarcastic glance at the heavy, weeping sky.

Lyse's nervous hackney stomped restlessly and Germain turned toward the horse, glad to cut the conversation. The stranger, however, had more to ask, and stepped forward to eclipse de Lugny.

"Only four of you go?" he rasped, for he had counted the riding animals and the litter chairs. His narrow stare met Germain's wary gaze head on.

"Perhaps, more or less, I don't know," Germain said with a shrug, hoping to make it clear to both men that ambiguous answers was all they would get. He noticed that de Lugny seemed annoyed with the stranger's blunt interference.

"By the way, what is your name, good man?" de Lugny drawled quickly.

"Germain Matz, Monsieur."

"Have you been in Mademoiselle's service long?"

"A pleasant duty never seems long, Monsieur."

De Lugny winked. "Your mistress and I are very amicable friends, she has great regard for me, do you understand, *mon ami?* Dare I say the word—'love'?"

He could say even more that that, was the smarmy insinuation in de Lugny's tone, and this immediately caused Germain's opinion of him to plummet. His Bourbon princess was no more in love with this peacock than with a pig's ear.

"She would be upset to know, Matz, that your memory may have faltered in speaking to me and that I waited in vain at the east portal to wish her Godspeed. And a speedy return home from–ah–?"

The *intendant* Matz had always drilled into his son to be respectful to his betters, and Germain had always been so. It went against his grain to lie to a gentleman, but he sensed he was entangled with more than he could handle. So he pulled off his hat with an obsequious bob of the head and earnestly repeated, "Yes, Monsieur, the east gate, Monsieur, at nine o'clock," ignoring the rest of the man's question. "That is the route Mademoiselle takes."

De Lugny recognized no more was forthcoming. He opened the purse on his belt, found a coin and smilingly pressed it into Germain's hand. "Thank you, Matz. You have been an arrow to the bow of Eros this day."

The eager suitor made a gesture to his narrow-eyed companion, and the man, who seemed to want to press Germain closer with questions, reluctantly gave up. The two strode away hunch-shouldered into the drizzle, earning a curious glance from the groom who was returning to his post.

"Bernard! Bernard!" she screamed, bolting upright, eyes wild, "Le bon Dieu t'emmenera par la main! God take you by the hand!"

Nurse shuffled in quickly from her tiny, adjoining room. "What, what, *mon enfant?* Who shall God lead by the hand?"

Lyse was sitting up rigid in her armchair by the window where she had slumped despondently, and then fallen into a light sleep. "Too late, too late," she moaned to no one, hugging herself and rocking back and forth, "he is dead. No fire-quenching deluge of rain will bring him back. O Bernard, dear soul, you have killed my heart!"

Nurse leaned over her but did not touch her. The old woman lowered her wrinkled face close to Lyse and insisted, "Bernard who, *ma petite,* who is Bernard? Ah, why are you trembling, are you cold? What has happened?"

Lyse's eyes traveled vacantly to the window where the wind-driven rain pattered so hard against the small panes that it had awakened her. "You see, God has sent the rain to put out the murdering fires. But it is too late, they are all gone. I paid the garroter two gold pieces to strangle Bernard at his stake so my beloved would not feel the flames. He is dead. All that lives of him is through me. I, I have the key." She paused, the color bled from her cheeks. Nurse hovered, breathing noisily. Lyse's nostrils flared, she still stared unseeing into empty space. "I tell you, they will never get what they want!" she raved.

Nurse's trembling fingers flew to her own throat. The old woman hissed,

"His name. Bernard of what?"

The dainty, copper-hued head turned towards her. "Why, Bernard de la Motte," Lyse said in a suddenly conversational tone, as if the woman should know. Then she blinked several times.

With a grunt, Nurse stepped back from her. But Lyse, having of a sudden returned to her senses, whimpered abjectly. She grabbed the old woman's hand and whispered, "*Sainte Vierge!* That n-name just fell from my lips. But who is he?"

"No matter for now. What else, then, comes to your memory?" Nurse croaked.

"Rain. I was dreaming about rain. And just as I came to my senses I remembered that the heavens opened as the flames leaped up around the stake where the priests had tied this man Bernard—and the other dear, brave victims—" She was panting. She whimpered again. "Too late."

Nurse's bleary eyes had opened quite wide.

"I thought it was tears on my cheeks, at first, but it was rain. I was screaming out and would have fallen to my knees on the stones of the square but for the people pressed all around me. I wept, because God's sign was too late, I could see Bernard's head lolling forward at a strange angle. And—and—" She frowned, trying to haul back the fading strands of her vision.

"Yes, yes—"

"And behind him was a great building with a cross on its belltower. But it seemed more a grim fortress than a church, so heavy of masonry, with slits of windows up way too high..."

"And what else?" Nurse pressed, having gotten over her first shock.

"The—the man. He had dark hair, this unfortunate Bernard. Long, to his shoulders." Lyse still felt like weeping.

"Yes, yes, but you howled, 'they shall not get find what they want!' What meant you by that?"

Lyse's pale brows were knit. She was beginning to feel unwell. "I don't know. But—but I think I did know, for a tiny moment. It seemed clear in my head for a flash. Now—it's gone. Fled. I am sorry, *nou-nou.*" Helplessly she looked up, drowned in confusion.

Lyse's use of her childhood name for her nurse brought pity to the woman's face, who gave her a wrinkle-lipped, reassuring smile and stroked her face. "*Mon enfant,* I must go now and fetch Madame de Dunois, so you can relate to her all of this before it leaves you."

It had occurred to the old woman who had cleaned and fed and dressed both this girl and her mother as children, that Lyse-Magdalene had taken the shock of her detailed recall tonight with more steadiness and less fear than ever.

So Nurse felt vindicated. She'd been right. Lyse-Magdalene was not her mother Jeanne, *grace à Dieu,* she was stronger. She squinted at the young woman slumped again in the chair, her profile limned against the window in the afternoon's grey light.

"You won't be afraid, now, to be by yourself a few minutes, eh?"

"How strange, Nurse, so much seemed to fill my head this time. And yet I understood, even through it, that such 'seeing-back' could not suck me in, did I not let it! I went along and did not fight to emerge, for in a part of my mind I finally knew that I am me, in the here and now, and that I can fight off any ghosts in the long run. Whatever ancestress of mine sits in my head, I am stronger."

Overcome by this, Nurse backed away. "'Tis true, my child, memories cannot harm you."

"But who was that Bernard de la Motte who met such a sad, terrible end?"

Nurse's expression closed down; she chomped her almost toothless gums. "I could not say."

"I believe she loved him," Lyse said, bemused. "He loved her too, and he had trusted me...her." She glanced at the awed old lady. "You see, I said her, not me. She loved him. Whoever this woman was." Lyse's voice turned up a bit, it was a tentative question.

But Nurse hurried out and shuffled as fast as she could toward the Great Hall, where Elinor de Dunois had gone to search among the visitors for her friend and correspondent, Madame Rioux.

It was not Nurse's place to go to monseigneur le *duc,* but she would if she couldn't find the governess. Her sunken chest pumped in and out with the momentousness of her news, and she didn't even think of first finding the flask of strong medicinal spirits Germain had wheedled for her from the monastery before they left St. Piteu. It was almost gone anyway.

Lyse snapped out of her remoteness the moment the door closed on her old nursemaid. She felt triumph again that panic had not smote her so deeply this time, nor the dark fear that the memory flashes meant her mind was giving way, or that evil was grappling for her. The poor woman in her memory who wept so hard for her executed lover was not evil, for evil could not love so desperately.

And although she couldn't tell how long the vivid hallucinations lasted, she knew this one was the longest, and certainly the first to provide a name!

She was getting better at keeping these recollections from instantly fading away from her, but she wondered if she should be glad of that. The emotional toll on her was great: the suffering and the execution of Bernard, whose face she still had not seen, had actually torn her heart, as if he were her own lover. There was still a residual grief within her that was keeping her pinned in her chair. She seemed to pay an exhausting price for these jolting glimpses of the past.

Then she sat up straight. The man was executed by fire? But why had that happened? Only the damned, the heretics, the criminals and dirty Jews died in the flames. Surely he was none of those, this long-dead love of her long-dead forebear. Then who was he? She suddenly recalled Nurse's face on hearing her drag out the name Bernard de la Motte from her mind's recesses, and she was sure now that the old woman and her governess knew who the man was. And her uncle as well. Maybe even Blackbeard knew.

Since God had created women the weaker vessel on this earth, females were circumscribed and directed in whatever they did, even those with money and property. But Lyse believed her thoughts, her memories, were absolutely hers, and not to be used by others as if God had given her no human soul. She was not witless and inanimate, like the bones ancient seers threw out for augury. She could think of only one way to pry out the knowledge they were keeping from her. Obstruction. Dost want answers to your mysterious searching? Make me equal in information with you, then.

Militantly, a vengeful pout on her lips, she mused on that startling word 'equal' for a moment. Of course, no question, as a female, she was certainly not equal to her uncle, or to the Italian nobleman to whom she was betrothed. But why should Madame de Dunois and even old Nurse lord it over her? She outranked them.

Whatever message they plumbed her memory for, it was her only commodity to trade for this 'equalness'. She hoped she would recognize the actual 'key' they sought if it came, for that was her lever.

Germain gave the two cloaked men time to re-enter the château, then followed, heightened concern for the welfare of Lyse-Magdalene making his course clear.

One of the palace's harried major-domos, officious in surcoat and doublet of Bourbon blue and white, looked in the ledger he carried and gave him the complicated directions to Gonzaga's chamber. Once there, the Mantuan's equerry, a sinister-looking fellow loitering outside the door, went in to announce him.

But the door didn't close all the way. Germain could hear Don Ferrante's annoyed rumble, then a little slap on abundant flesh and a woman's peal of high laughter. He heard the clunk of the wooden rings as bedcurtains opened and were jerked closed again.

When the equerry finally beckoned him, he found the irritated *condottiere* with bare chest over hastily donned breeches, although it was only four in the afternoon.

Gonzaga yanked him into the muffled space of the deep window embrasure. Scowling, the Italian kept his voice low. "This better be as important as you say, Matz. You have rudely interrupted my prayers. Speak quiet and swiftly—"

Germain obeyed. Facing the green-eyed glower with stoic courage, he told of his earlier slip with de Lugny, and of the courtier's attempts to pry information from him minutes ago, and of the other unidentified man, whom he'd never seen before.

Pulled to serious attention, Gonzaga said, "So this de Lugny is a member of the duke's own court who has danced about your mistress previously? And the nameless one then? At least what did he look like?"

"Of middle height, Monsieur, and light coloring. Eyes small and blue, and a skin most ravaged by the pox."

Gonzaga tensed. "Did he speak? What sort of voice?"

"He wished to know how many were riding with my mistress, which I did not say. His voice? Like the scrape of a rasp on wood."

Gonzaga drove one fist into the other palm, "*Porca miseria!* I knew Moulins was not the place for her. Much too exposed."

Exposed to what, Germain ached to ask, but didn't dare. "But I insisted she would leave at nine this very night from the east portal and I am sure they are misled," he repeated, anxious that his original damage be repaired.

"Next time hold your tongue in the first place, *imbécile!*" Gonzaga growled in disgust. "Now we shall have to make certain other arrangements. You did well not to ignore this, Matz. But since only I know our destination, the trick is to see we are not followed there."

Thoroughly alarmed by now, Germain offered, "If there is any danger, Monsieur, perhaps I could mount guard at Mademoiselle's door before we leave?"

"Already done," Gonzaga replied, "today, during the court's arrival. Discreetly. And you will have other things to attend to within the half-hour." He padded from the embrasure on bare feet, pulling Germain with him, flipped a look of deep regret at the closed bedcurtains, and sighed. "Wait, Matz. I shall dress immediately and then you will come with me. The duke must be consulted—"

His equerry rapped on the door, then slipped in. "A page arrives from monseigneur de Bourbon, Signore. He requests your presence in his chamber immediately, without fail."

"*Morbleu*. Lucco, respond that I shall arrive in three minutes, right behind his page." Gonzaga scooped up some crumpled clothing from the floor where they had been dropped. "Marco!" he bawled, and a shaggy head, somewhat reminiscent of the equerry's popped from behind a screen. "Where the damnation are you? Get me a fresh shirt. Now!"

"*Si, si*, Signore!" the valet cried, skittering out from the screen to attack a creaky trunk.

"*Mais, comme tu es un espèce de chien!* You dog!" came a woman's high and angry curse from behind the bedcurtains.

Tugging at his little earring, Gonzaga shrugged with regret and winked broadly at Germain, who stolidly kept his impassive air.

Chapter 7

Joyeuse admitted Ferrante into the stuffy ducal chamber which was lit by candles, for on physicians orders the windows were shuttered to keep out miasma from the damp afternoon air.

Charles de Bourbon rested limply against his pillows, his sunken eyes shut, his nightdress fallen open at the neck. A doctor in black cap and robe sat on a stool at the damask-curtained bedside counting the ducal pulse, and at the physician's side stood Elinor de Dunois, rigid as a heron on one leg.

Approaching with Joyeuse across the great expanse of Turkish carpet, Ferrante ventured from the corner of his mouth, "*Merde,* he doesn't look any better."

"But he is," the *marquis* whispered back. "The physician says his temperature has dropped. What you see now are the fine ministrations of the artist who paints backdrops for the troupe of actors the duchesse has hired to entertain the guests. And monseigneur has proved to be an able mime. For the king's visit an hour ago, with the help of a bilious green dab here, a little graveyard grey there, *voilà,* a dying man."

The duke moved his lips, for he'd heard. "But unfortunately, this moil of heat still rising from me is not painted on."

"Hot bags of salt under the blankets kept him sweating heavily during the visit," Joyeuse added, as they stopped by the bed.

"Most of which sticky flood was natural too," the duke muttered further. His eyelids snapped open. "Ho, Don Ferrante, I have striking news."

"And so do I, cousin. But first, was His Majesty very impressed?"

Bourbon struggled further up on his pillows, helped by the doctor, and Ferrante observed by carefully looking past the cosmetics that the man's eyes seemed much less bleary, his manner a little more alert.

"I am sure of it. Of course, afterward, he very solicitously sent up his own doctors to me, but we had removed the salt bags in the meanwhile. No matter, I still had a fever they could mark, although, *Deo gratias,* it is passing."

"Deo gratias," Bourbon's trusted doctor echoed into his beard as he reverently laid the ducal wrist back on the velvet coverlet. A low word from his patient and he hurriedly packed his case, bowed, and hied himself out.

Ferrante dropped down in the physician's place, riding the stool like a horse. "My lord, our friend de Guise does have interest in Lyse-Magdalene and has been made aware of Lyse-Magdalene's presence here and our immediate plans for her. It seems his brother, de Marques, along with one of your courtiers, one Robert de Lugny, pressed Matz to say by which portal Mademoiselle would leave, and at what hour tonight. Matz endeavoured to lead them wrong, but in any case I can arrange to rid us of any trackers." He shook back a dark lock from his forehead. "'Tis my strong opinion that if people are actively searching for a woman who one moment is at Moulins, and the next moment gone, they would logically look next at nearby Chantelle. The Lorraine's show of interest must change our plans, from precaution to active evasion."

Charles thought a moment. "You are right, but for more reasons than this new one." His eyes in their exaggerated sunken circles held a small glow of triumph, and he extended a ringed hand toward Joyeuse's sister. "Come here, Madame. Repeat for Signore di Gonzaga the incredible memory which has just overtaken my niece."

So de Dunois did so, nervously but meticulously, exactly as Nurse had reported the event to her, and she finished her account with the same guarded triumph of expression as her employer, narrow chin doubled and hands clasped in satisfaction over her stomach.

Ferrante reacted with a low whistle. "Bernard de la Motte!"

"We couldn't have hoped for a better connection to our goal, unless it was Jacques de Molay himself. Do you see? My niece's memories are becoming stronger, more detailed and more accurate every day!" Vindication strengthened Bourbon's voice. "She is more comprehensible than my poor sister, who could never endure or rationally describe her memories at all."

"It seems to me," interjected Joyeuse, "that their memories are totally different. Both ladies cry of fires, but Jeanne suffered as horribly as if she herself were burning, while Lyse-Magdalene grieves for someone else. Her viewpoint is different, which could be vital to adding up what she tells us."

De Dunois spoke up with repressed excitement. "Messieurs, I insist even more strongly now that between mother and daughter we have been dealing with separate incidents, incidents perhaps centuries apart. Now that Lyse-Magdalene has mentioned a man whose history and fate are recorded, we can tie her 'seeing-back' to an exact date and place.

"We know Bernard de la Motte died at the stake in Albi, in March of the year thirteen hundred and fourteen, the very year that interests us, and the girl gave even a partial description of the fortress-like Cathedral there. But can we forget that one hundred years before there were others in Languedoc who were cruelly condemned to death by fire, many of them women. Perhaps the dying agonies of one of these were the dreadful misfortune of poor Madame Jeanne to remember."

Although a shadow drifted over Bourbon's face at the mention of his dead sister's agonies, he concurred. "It stands to reason you must be correct. Yes, with my niece we are luckier in several respects, so to tarry now in our mission is to court interference. Now we must push, we must focus the girl more swiftly upon retrieving the answers we seek–pray God, without destroying her by it."

"I agree, my lord," de Joyeuse growled. "Time dwindles. We must act to accelerate her memories if we can."

"I agree too," Ferrante nodded, "especially now with de Guise sniffing around."

Bourbon's dry smile with its hover of mischief softened his haggard face. "It is well that you agree with us, signore, for 'tis you whom I elect to escort your betrothed southward to the Razès, to settle her there and do anything you and de Dunois can to sharpen her visions and produce our ultimate answer."

Ferrante recoiled, the stool leg coming down with a thump. "What, cousin, do you send *me* on this nursemaid mission?" he objected. "But I was expecting to come with you!"

"Use your head, Ferrante. My closest intimates are not so many that Joyeuse' absence from my side would not be noted with suspicion. But you, cousin, have interests in Italy which might legitimately call you away from France for a length of time, at least this is what we can say." Bourbon saw the flare of bitter disappointment in the green eyes, and how the big shoulders moved unhappily, so he broadened his appeal. "But who else can handle this, Ferrante? Not Madame Elinor by herself, at this juncture. Lyse-Magdalene is a child no longer, she needs a greater control–which I cannot provide now."

The moisture of breaking fever gleamed on his forehead, plastering the locks on his brow, and the smile had faded. "As your commander, I can give you an order, but I am hoping just for love of me you will consent. Think for a moment: our burden is staggering. Without the huge horde of gold I seek the house of Bourbon may be at an end, and carry down with it to doom many of our staunchest allies..."

With a stare that spoke a great deal, the sick man made a strange gesture, two right fingers swiftly to his brow, to his lips, then pressed to his heart.

"...and even, possibly, collapse the ancient service we are sworn to," he warned, his voice turned hollow. The fervent speech had used up Bourbon's forced energy; he fell back on his pillows, his breathing shallow. "I am placing a great weight of expectation on your back, Ferrante. But you will not fail, this I know."

Ferrante studied the constable of France in his habitual way, head tilted back and frowning down his nose. The doctors may say Charles de Bourbon was recovering but the sick man before him couldn't lift a feather yet, much less flee a vindictive king if such was soon the necessity. Staring steadily into the unwavering demand in Bourbon's eyes, he understood just how bitterly his cousin was dependent on this chancy scheme to succeed, now that the main Bourbon fortune was being decimated through seizure. As well, he understood his own deep affection for this noble kinsman whose birthright was being subsumed; and he well knew the rigid outlines of his own duty.

So, with a deep sigh, a shrug and nod, he relented. "I have a strong back, Charles," he gave in.

Neither man smiled, but there was mutual alliance in their glance. Nevertheless, Ferrante demanded, "But will you make me a promise, monseigneur? For love of me? That if a battle for control of France's throne is finally joined, wherever and whenever it is, you summon me forth to join you. My *métier* is not nursemaid."

"Well do I know that, cousin. My word, then, that unless circumstances are completely impossible, I shall bring you to my side. But think a bit of the extra good of your service, Ferrante. You will have an unusual opportunity to become acquainted with this damsel who will someday belong to you and grace your house and give you children. You'll see. You will find her disarming, once she is less unsettled. She is sweet, and she can be truly diverting."

Ferrante strongly doubted any of that about Bourbon's lady-of-the-deceptive-coloration, but he held his tongue. His acceptance of his obligations made it pointless to disagree.

De Joyeuse, seized by doubt, scratched at his neck. "My lord, we deal with the Lorraines. If Chantelle is the first place they'd look, the Razès will be the second place de Guise will think of. It might be a dangerous mistake to be so obvious."

"Nevertheless, to immerse Lyse-Magdalene in those surroundings is a chance we absolutely must take if we wish to unlock the memories we need. But Languedoc is a Bourbon territory, we've a measure of friends down there; Don Ferrante will know how to take advantage of their protection."

The Mantuan remarked to Joyeuse, "Don't you recall, *marquis*, that old *dicton* about hiding something in plain sight to secure it? I have been in the lower valley of the Aude River once before, and I remarked that which you also know, that unidentified parties of strangers in the area are immediately suspect. Unless the Lorraines or their minions intend to fly over the foothills, we can expect ample warning of any group traveling below Carcassone from any direction. We will protect her."

Joyeuse' weather-beaten visage remained dubious, but he slowly nodded his head in acquiescence anyway. "You're right, I suppose. But Ferrante, reside, then, at Puivert, my fine château there in the Razès valley. You will be the welcome guests of my dear wife, who devotes herself to our ten children and to continuing Puivert's ancient engagement with the arts. That lady, I tell you, shelters half of the country's beggar musicians and starvling scribes under my roof. But at least at Puivert you will not yawn with boredom of an evening."

Bourbon struggled up on his pillows again to sip from a cup of water de Dunois had poured for him. He objected, "Grammercy on my cousin's part, good Joyeuse, but if we do this thing, we do it fully. Ferrante will settle my niece and her companions at Rennes-le-Château. Of course, they may visit Puivert now and then, for a few days, I could hardly deny them that relief—"

But both men now were staring at their feverish leader.

"You would put her under the auspices of La Dame?" Joyeuse grunted in surprise.

Hard lines had pressed themselves on either side of Bourbon's mouth. "Yes. I must. That woman can use her cunning to push my niece's recall forward. And Ferrante's presence will act as a balance."

De Joyeuse folded his arms. "Charles. Lora de Voisin is not your best friend."

"She is nobody's friend. But she will bow to my orders and not hamper my desires. I will send my fastest courier south with word to Rennes-le-Château immediately. So leave tonight, Ferrante, as you planned, for the less Lyse-Magdalene is seen here the less she will be missed by our guests. The courier will wait for your arrival at Rennes before he returns to me, so I'll know you've gotten through safely. Joyeuse, furnish him a map for traveling."

The *marquis* nodded.

His sister chirped staunchly, "Mademoiselle and I are all prepared to leave, my lord. Don Ferrante, just give us your signal."

Ferrante rumbled, "I'll need a small company of guards."

Bourbon answered, "Send La Clayette to me. He will furnish you fifteen of my best men and a purse for their keep. And summon in my chief secretary; I will prepare a letter for you to the Voisins."

"Monseigneur, how will I know where to get word to you, should you leave Moulins?" They both knew, with muted sorrow, that eventually Bourbon would have to leave Moulins.

Bourbon sighed, dipped fingers into the enameled Venetian-glass drinking cup on his table and patted the cool water on his neck. "Momentarily, there is no way, but go and make ready. I know where you will be, so I shall try to keep couriers arriving there periodically, until I have some base."

Elinor De Dunois slipped in front of the men. "Monseigneur, Mademoiselle Lyse-Magdalene is anxious to bid you goodbye in a personal audience, even though she yet thinks we will return in a fortnight. She is deeply concerned over your health."

Charles closed his eyes a moment then said, "No. Tell my ward I am recovering, but that I will not see anyone. Even those I love. She will be unhappy to go so far away from me, thus I think it is best that she have no chance to try and reverse my decision."

He stared into Ferrante's gaze: "If she becomes difficult, cousin, you have my permission to give her whatever knowledge you think will hasten her remembering and make her cooperative. You have my confidence and my prayers. The Lord grant you success." The open smile, so seldom seen now, flitted over his face. "Believe me, my great warrior, I envy you her."

He missed the stoic irony behind Gonzaga's answering smile. But Ferrante wished to God he did not have to leave his leader's side, ill and beset by evil as the man was, and so deep was the bond he felt. When they were very young and practicing at jousting at Louis Twelfth's court at St. Germain, Ferrante had foolishly left up the visor of his helmet. He would never forget how Charles had vaulted off his horse and raced to where he lay with his face gushing blood and his arm broken, unseated by the unnecessarily violent slam by an older youth, a more experienced tilter cruelly eager to wound. He remembered the spasm of deep grief that twisted the handsome face looking down at him when Charles thought his younger cousin's eye was out and he was dying. Ferrante cherished the memory of that deeply bereft expression, even though he had seen it through a barely-focused consciousness, for it was one of the few times in his childhood he knew he was loved.

His mother, Isabelle d'Este, a beauty envied for her glittering, artistic court, had never time for him, her third son. Ferrante's aunt Chiara de Bourbon, who, with her husband, had reared and educated him in France, was more affectionate, but often absent on extended visits to Italy. Besides Charles, the Bourbon siblings were either girls or little, so since he had always been both tall and mature for his age, he and Charles were each other's family, each the other's bulwark, and sometimes each other's source of irritation, as between most brothers.

At fifteen, when Ferrante's father summoned him home to Mantua, Charles, already married, dashed tears from his eyes as he said a final farewell to a cousin grown a head taller than he did, and they exchanged vows of eternal fealty. In later years there were reunions too, joyous and boisterous ones when the rulers under whose banners they fought happened to join forces during the incessant wars in northern Italy.

So, when Ferrante finally fled his miserable marriage, as well as his guilty envy of his older brother's ducal power, there was no question but that he would attach the proud Gonzaga standard to the victorious arms of the Bourbon constable of France. Further, the incredible secret that had been separately passed to both of them, as keepers of their families' unique obligations, drew them even closer.

This winter Ferrante had cut short his yearly duty trip to Mantua and hastened back to Charles, outraged to learn the political contortions relentlessly forcing the *duc* de Bourbon into a corner, and possibly into prison. He was ready to grab his sword and slice up a few of Bourbon's enemies, including that old *putana,* Louise de Savoie. His soul's need was to ride at the constable's back with de Joyeuse and Pompérant and Armand de Prie, and not to be shunted off on this visionary quest.

But his duty, at Charles behest and order, was clear; he throttled his disgust and shouldered it.

He took the hand the sick man held out, noting how clammy it felt, careful to use only half his strength to squeeze it. "I will find the cache you seek, cousin," he vowed, "however it must be done." For further assurance, he placed two fingers against his brow, his lips, and then against his heart. "The Lord help you to health, monseigneur, and keep you safely in his sight."

"Never fear, we will ride together again, Don Ferrante."

Time was running away. With a bow Ferrante withdrew backward a pace, then whirled and strode out, slapping on his flat bonnet, his mind already focusing on what he must do.

He found Germain and La Clayette in the anteroom. He gave the one some special instructions to carry out, and left with the other towards Moulins' guardroom.

The *marquis* de Joyeuse and Madame de Dunois took leave of the *duc* de Bourbon a few moments after, both making in farewell the curious fingers-to-temple-to-lips-to-heart gesture.

In spite of thousands of people under the roofs of the great château and several ways to reach each wing, yet returning from the guardroom by a narrow corridor bridging two ells of the castle, Ferrante and La Clayette chanced to cross paths with Louis de Marques.

After perfunctory nods as befit gentlemen, it was Ferrante's intent to stride on, but de Marques barred his way.

"Well, Gonzaga! It has been a long time. One heard in Paris that you had left France and gone home to Mantua after St. Barthelme's Feast." Louis' bland tone nowhere matched the vindictiveness in his eyes.

"It seems I've returned," Ferrante replied curtly, and he stared down his nose at a man he'd be happy to see in hell.

Louis, a little shorter than he, but solid as a rock, stared back. "Ah, but of course you would want to be at monseigneur de Bourbon's bedside in his unfortunate illness. Loyalty in distress as well as in triumph, eh?" The tight smile hid none of his ill-will. He forestalled Ferrante's move to go around him by quickly adding, "You intend to enter the master tournament, certainly? The king announced in Paris the transfer of his Crown of Roses tourney from Amboise to here, to be held in the middle of the month. It will draw the best lances in France to Moulins."

"The best is already standing here, Monsieur," Ferrante growled.

He knew what de Marques craved, a chance to regain the honor he had lost against Ferrante's own lance in the famous "Field of Gold" tourneys before the collected courts of France and England. In fact, Ferrante craved that too, another crack at dumping the vicious Lorraine on his arse, and by luck running the lance accidentally through the helmet's visor and into the wolfish brain. He imagined that the scar under his own eye was throbbing.

"Do you enter the Crown of Roses, Monsieur?" La Clayette suavely joined the conversation.

"Without a doubt. So, shall we cross lances once more, Don Ferrante?" de Marques persisted. "Will you finally defend your ancient victory? Or are we never to be found in the same lists again?" The implication of avoidance was as clear as a flung gauntlet.

A muscle twitched in Ferrante's jaw, he would have relished the chance of having at de Marques again. But he had no choice now but to lie. With a brief, icy bow he said, "The pleasure of defeating you once more will be all mine, de Marques. The perfume of roses pleases me mightily. So does the smell of gold." For each of the lucky thirteen roses in the champion's wreath, the king presented a heavy purse.

Louis stepped aside, one hand on his velvet-covered breast in mock respect. "Such sweet scents of roses and gold a man may also detect from a distance —even as he is carried off the field broken upon his shield. In war, that is, of course. Our tourneys are only mock havoc, *n'est-ce pas,* Signore?" Louis' eyes, like blue shards of ice in his pocked face, showed the aggressiveness towards the Mantuan as they'd always displayed since youth, when he spied the young Italian welcomed into the embrace of the maiden who had turned aside his own suit.

But Ferrante discontinued the exchange. "Your servant, Monsieur," he muttered coldly and shouldered past, followed by la Clayette, whose hand had rested by habit on the pommel of his sword during the animosity-filled encounter.

Ferrante grunted in the officer's ear, for other courtiers fared through the passage about them, "The damn vulture. I was hoping to slip away from Moulins with my absence not immediately apparent, but de Marques and I know each other well and he'll never believe he frightened me away from the competitions. He and De Guise will connect my disappearance with Lyse-Magdalene's."

"But 'tis known your wife is very ill in Italy—"

"'Tis also known I don't give a clipped sou for that," Ferrante replied. "I've been wondering if my plan for leaving here is unnecessarily complicated. Now I'm sure the ruse I've devised is right."

Curious, La Clayette ventured, "De Marques seems to hold a very personal grudge against you. One he wouldn't mind discharging with violence."

"The rancor is mutual and of many years standing. He gave me this scar under my eye and almost blinded me when I was a boastful stripling who stole his place in a lady's bed. We have battled back and forth in many lists, but at the "Field of Gold" I unseated him in a crashing sprawl before the kings of France and England. And thus I stood champion for France, Gonzaga, an Italian. He was deeply humiliated, as I meant him to be. *Voilà,* no love is lost. But circumstance has not brought us together in a tourney since." Ferrante muttered, "I would give a bag of gold to sit the *crottin* on his arse again..."

At the far end of the dressed-stone passage Louis turned to see both of Bourbon's partisans disappear through a Tudor-arched doorway into a new section of the château. There was no expression on his frozen face, but he was flexing the strong fingers of his right hand and his hate-filled thoughts as he stared could have themselves pierced the Italian's back: "Stinking grand-spawn of a Lombard merchant! Neither roses or gold, nor even life for you. This time Louis de Marques' lance will shatter your skull."

In the dark, still hour before dawn, Ferrante responded to an appeal from Madame de Dunois by striding into Lyse-Magdalene's chamber determined to take no nonsense from the cause of all his problems.

At his orders, Germain, along with Nurse in her litter, the cook and the maidservant had ridden out of the north portal hours before, the women heavily muffled against the drizzle, with the maidservant wearing Lyse's bright green velvet cloak. The lumbering baggage carts creaked after them and they were accompanied by the St. Piteu guards. That was the decoy group. Now it was their turn to depart.

"I can't get her to quit her bed," the governess huffed after admitting him. "From the moment Germain brought in the habits and vanished, and I told her she must put one on, and that Germain would not be riding with us, she has refused to follow instructions. In fact, now she is refusing to depart Moulins altogether."

The black-bearded jaw jutted.

Chewing her lip and feeling disloyal, de Dunois followed the Mantuan's broad back towards the bed.

Ferrante jerked back the partially-closed curtain to reveal his grim charge sitting with legs drawn up under her skirt, although fully clothed in a traveling gown, a small coif, and a chiffon veil which hid her hair. She was a study in stubborn outrage, mouth set, thin russet brows puckering the white skin of her forehead into angry furrows.

"And so much for her sweet, disarming nature," Ferrante reflected with irony. The girl had taken the ends of the fringed sash looped about her waist and knotted them strongly about a bedpost to emphasize her resistance to departure, a device so patently silly Ferrante almost wanted to laugh.

Curbing himself, he tried to stay calm. "What is this, Mademoiselle? You refuse to obey your uncle's will?"

Her eyes were narrowed. "The last I saw of the duke de Bourbon he bade me go to Chantelle for a fortnight, along with my little household. He would not say why, but he most certainly did not say I must wear a monk's habit and depart before cocks-crow, like a scoundrel in the night, and be kept from farewells to my few acquaintances, and leave without Germain or my baggage or even my poor, old Nurse." Her voice rose in distress.

"Nevertheless, lady, that is what he means for you to do. Quickly, and in the manner I direct."

"How so, Monsieur? My poor uncle is so very ill that I am not even allowed to go to him. He may be raving, he may be unconscious. How do I know he has given such commands?"

In spite of Ferrante's impatience with this unruly female, the question was reasonable. "Because if you don't trust me, monseigneur de Bourbon's kinsman and friend, and the gentleman to whom he has promised you in marriage, you surely trust your governess who loves you, Madame de Dunois. She was present at the duke's bedside when he made his wishes very clear concerning you."

"*Mais oui,* she was there, you were there, maybe even Germain, my own squire, was there," Lyse flared. "Everyone but me. I am his niece and I am to be transported from Moulins as unknowing of my fate as a sack of groats. Well, I will not go. Not until someone declares the why and what and where-fore of all the machinations controlling the life of this helpless woman." She gave an angry wave at Germain's grey habit, flung on the bed. "Why should I wear that in order to leave the castle? Is my own traveling costume not good enough? And where, then, are we going, if not Chantelle?"

Blue sparks flew from her eyes but what they couldn't know was that Lyse was stunned herself with her own temerity in challenging them.

De Dunois hustled up and picked apart with nervous hands the knot in the sash tying Lyse to the bedpost. "Oh hush, Lysette, you are being foolish."

Lyse pushed her away. "No I am not, I am a grown woman and I am being treated like an imbecile. *Bien sûr,* I have always been so handled. But as a woman grown and now betrothed–" She lanced an unfriendly glare at Ferrante, "–it is time I know all the reasons for my state."

Ferrante was acutely conscious of the minutes passing, for his hasty plans to avoid trackers involved the fortunate coincidence of a large party which was leaving Moulins just before dawn. He took over from de Dunois, roughly unknotting the sash around Lyse's waist, rudely shoving her in the bargain as she struggled. "There is no time for this. Stand up and don your cleric's robe. The horses are ready and waiting and so is the assemblage we are leaving with."

For the first time it registered with Lyse that the Mantuan was enveloped in the brown, rope-tied robe of a Franciscan friar, his dark hair gathered into a tight brown cap and covered by a string-tied hat with a curled brim. Unsure from the callous way her uncle had abandoned her to this great bully, and frightened by her own boldness, Lyse locked her arms around the bedpost, and pressed her face into the carving. "No," she balked. "I shall not budge until I know why and where, and you may go to perdition! "

"*Mon Dieu!*" came Madame's shocked gasp.

Looking up, Lyse saw the glittering green eyes move toward her, and the scar beneath one was puckering white.

"What, do you think I relish shepherding a bad-tempered wench across France in this scratchy disguise, when I'd much prefer to stand back to back with my cousin Bourbon against the calumny heaped on him? But I have orders too. Lady, I can truss you up and gag you and throw you on a horse like the sack of groats you mentioned, and none would prevent me, with the duke's signed and sealed order tucked in my doublet." He patted the coarse robe at the approximate spot. "I can do it and believe me, I will, Mademoiselle. You have one second to make up your mind to leave on your own two feet."

A silky strand of copper hair had escaped from her veil to spiral innocently at the base of her smooth throat. In spite of Ferrante's temper with her insolence the stray lock recalled to him her youth and helplessness. But this drop of pity didn't change his threat.

The cutting glare in the young woman's eyes displayed none of the docility her uncle insisted was there. But, conversely, her balking at their manipulations showed an intelligence he had not paid attention to before. She was primary to all they were attempting, after all, so as he stared at the upset young woman, he couldn't see why she must be so completely insulated from their purpose. So far the memories coming upon her seemed to hold no harm for her, and she would have to know something anyway when they reached the Razés.

"Mademoiselle, if you willingly cooperate, I will tell you some of what you want to know as soon as we have traveled three days from here," he bribed her. "You have my absolute promise."

"No, now!" she defied him.

Ferrante ran out of patience. He blew out his breath and with a sharp tug easily broke her hold on the bedpost. Grasping her arm he rumbled, "Half a second left for you to get up and move on your own." And then a mean grin began to spread across his bronzed face.

This threatened Lyse more than his wrath. She thought, "The dog! He is enjoying bullying me, but he will adore even more gagging and tying me up against my struggles." Desperately, she glanced at de Dunois for support, but no help there, the woman was shaking her head disapprovingly at such disobedient behaviour.

She looked back at Blackbeard, whose smile gleamed white, eager for the job of subduing her. *Merde.* She didn't relish having that great bully put his hands on her. She really had no choice but to trust the promise he had just made.

"Just leave hold of me," she said, jerking her arm away. "Three days and you will tell me all? I hope you mean to keep your word?"

The wolfish smile hardened, his face lowered close to hers. "Do not dare insult my integrity, Mademoiselle. Men have been carved up for that. A Gonzaga never says what he doesn't mean." He straightened up abruptly, grabbed the grey robe off the bed and tossed it in her lap. "Put this on quickly. Pull the hood deeply over your head, and hitch your skirt so it does not peek from the closures or below. Madame Elinor, the same for you. Hurry!"

Both robes were big for the women, they had to haul them up over the knotted rope belts not to trip on the hems.

Ferrante herded them to the door, instructing, "Follow me and keep your heads down, faces and hands hidden meekly. Don't ever speak to anyone. You are brothers under an oath of silence."

"But from whom are we hiding in these smelly habits?" Lyse cried, still avid to know what was going on.

"In three days, I told you. Now come along."

"My clothes chests—"

"On their way to Chantelle. Your precious Germain will bring them to you. Eventually."

She turned back. "But my bed—" she objected, reaching out toward the familiar couch being left behind.

"Unimportant, you'll find another. Or sleep on the ground like any mendicant monk," he chuckled.

He opened the door, explaining as he gave her a slight push forward, "It turns out that Madame la Duchesse Anne has provided shelter and food for a party of religious pilgrims returning from Rome to Bourges. They are leaving before dawn after saying their offices in the church, and to prevent too much indulgence at the court festivities. We join them."

"What? We are going north to Bourges?" came Lyse's muffled confusion, and she tilted her head back to see from under the deep hood.

He didn't answer, merely hunched into his own cowl, pushed her head down again and herded them forward quickly. He nodded to the Bourbon guard who had been stationed discreetly in a cross corridor, and who then followed behind them at a distance.

Festivities! Even as Gonzaga had said the word, Lyse's memory—her own this time—of the sounds of earlier revelry, returned to gall her. The music, the leaping voices and mirth, the bursts of laughter at capering jesters and mimes had echoed seductively up into her room from the Great Hall and its surrounding chambers until well past midnight, draining Lyse's heart of all charity toward this duty into which she was forced.

She thought of how excited she had been about mingling with the royal court and Their Majesties, at last; about the lavish new gown meant to stand her out as a Bourbon amongst the duchesse's ladies, the marvelous smells from the kitchens which had been cooking and roasting and baking day and night, about the elegant young gentlemen she'd watched arrive from the tower, the wine she'd meant to drink, the compliments she'd hope to receive, the dancing, the flirting she'd meant to do. She had not been observing the joyful amusements of the damsels of the Bourbon court for nothing.

Her chagrin went deep. Bitter tears welled in her eyes about it as she kept moving towards departing Moulins. She tried to dash them away, for if she cried her nose would run and she had nothing to wipe it on but the wide, rough sleeve. It turned out she had to do that anyway.

Ferrante, remembering the same gala sounds of merriment from the Great Hall, saw her furtive dab at her eyes but said nothing. He understood her frustration, for he'd had to stay away from the Great Hall too, including his sometime paramour who was so especially entertaining.

It wasn't so much leaving the lascivious Madame de Rougierie, even in mid-fuck, or not getting even one succulent mouthful of the huge boars the hunters brought in yesterday to roast with juniper berries; or a sip of the Greek wine he'd heard would be poured out from golden ewers by toga-clad nymphs, or a chance to gain back some of his gold from the card-cheating Milanese ambassador. But the Razès—it was so miserably removed from everything important in the world, the politics, the wars, the intrigues, the gambling, the celebratory shattering of a tourney lance against a solid adversary, even a sweaty game of racquet tennis.

He was every bit as disgruntled as she, even more so because in his deepest heart he believed their quest would produce nothing. Nevertheless, getting this damsel to find a vast treasure, if it existed, was a job that had to be attempted.

From a close-by chamber the clink of coins and the raucous sounds of merry, all-night card playing carried to his ears, then faded as they padded down the narrow, spiral steps of a stone stairwell lit by guttering candles in sconces.

The large party of more than one hundred religious from different orders, plus a few wealthy, devout bourgeois, was already gathered for departure in the barrel-vaulted gallery adjacent to the stables, the members filing through a door and into the dark drizzle to find their mounts. The majority were tonsured brothers in brown robes like Ferrante's, but some wore grey habits, and some were Dominicans in stained white. Black-robed chaplains milled among them, and there were a few nuns in white coifs and blue cloaks, riding their mules side-saddle.

Clerks, appointed by accompanying abbots who were distinguished by their round-brimmed hats and white horses, took charge of bringing order to the procession. Up ahead, on donkeys, would ride linkmen holding up lanterns and brass crosses on poles. In the rear harried novices and lay servants were to manage the piled baggage carts. Alongside the middle of the main group would trot a sparse number of mounted, hired soldiers.

One of the official clerics rode by and glanced down to nod briefly at Ferrante, whose height and broad shoulders stood him out of the confusion of habits.

Ferrante's two companions stood huddled together watching the procession form until they saw coming towards them a fellow leading their own horses and a pack mule. It turned out to be the curly-mopped valet Marco Collini, humbly dressed and in a damp felt hat. "Well timed," his master grunted to the servant's shy appreciation.

Lyse gratefully rubbed the familiar white blaze on her hackney's nose, then jumped to hear Gonzaga's baritone close to her ear. "There were no extra nun's robes to be gotten, so I hope you can easily ride astride—brother," he rumbled. "If not, it doesn't matter, just hang on. Many of these monks are fumbling riders anyhow."

With her hand already on the saddle horn, Lyse raised her head enough so he could see, under the hood, the disdain in her eyes. "I can ride lady's saddle, or astride, or no saddle, or any way you please!" she retorted low, but forcefully.

Marco came forward and bent, lacing the fingers of his hands to offer a lift. "A step up, ah, brother?"

"*Merci, mais non*," she rebuffed him, and grasping the horn, one foot in the wide stirrup, she handily swung herself up on the mare. She sneaked a glance toward Gonzaga to see if he was impressed, but he seemed to have turned away to boost Madame de Dunois.

With a flustered squeak, the governess landed awkwardly astride her mount. Spotting Lyse grinning at her from the depths of the grey hood, she made a peremptory sign for her charge to lower her head, although so far in the noisy mount-up no one had paid them one bit of attention.

As they turned their steeds to join the procession, it occurred to Lyse that Gonzaga's auburn-maned charger was missing, the horse he so treasured. Of course, no simple friar would own a horse like that. Maybe an archbishop or cardinal. But would Gonzaga leave such an animal behind? She couldn't see the Mantuan's face, but he was mounted on his black gelding. Well, she was without Germain and Nurse, and he was without his precious beast. She shrugged mentally. So they were even.

Shortly after the château's tower bell tolled four of the morning, the finally organized party filed out under the thick west barbican, the four interlopers surrounded fore and aft in the chilly drizzle by the pilgrims. Some were muttering prayers for safe passage as their steeds clomped over the drawbridge, some were half-asleep, some still munched the rosemary-scented bread and little meat pies from the royal reception the duchess had specially sent out for their departure.

To Lyse's whispered concern about the road, Ferrante had answered that so large a company, with some hired mercenaries, had little to fear by traveling in the dark before dawn, except their horses tumbling into a ditch or stepping into a hole and breaking a leg.

The column plodded and creaked on doggedly in the thinning dark, behind the linkmen's snapping torches. Even before another damp and dreary dawn finally shed its grey light into the sky ahead, Lyse, who'd been too agitated at Moulins to sleep, let her head droop in a doze.

Chapter 8

By noon they had crossed two roads heading south, one being the main route to Clermont they might have taken, but nevertheless they continued west with the pilgrims. The rain had stopped and the fickle weather had shifted wildly; a hot sun had been beating down for hours, turning damp garments and the countryside to steam.

At a market town where the conjuncture of four roads was marked by two gruesomely tenanted gibbets, the company halted to stretch stiff legs and eat dinner, some at the long tables of an inn, others drawing meagre portions from knapsacks. They filled leather water bottles at the fountain and sat hunched on its broad rim, commiserating with each other for having to leave the celebration for His Majesty.

The four who had joined them at Moulins sat apart on a low stone wall, sharing a flask of wine and some food Marco had bought at the nearby caravansery. Giddy from aggravation and the unseasonable heat, Lyse imagined they must look like rumpled, featherless chickens perched on a rail–including a big rooster. She realized she had dozed in the saddle between the little villages they'd clopped through, for she didn't feel sleepy any more, just sore in the thighs.

She leaned over to their leader to announce snippily, "It is impossibly hot. I am perspiring. Everyone's throwing his or her hoods back. We'll look passing strange all wrapped up like this."

Ferrante peered past the jumble of market day stalls and villagers as well as he could, focusing on the road back the way they had come. "No matter," he answered calmly, "we part company with this holy parade soon. We are merely waiting for Lucco to catch up." He glanced at her and caught her unspoken question. "Lucco Collini, my equerry, brother to my valet here. The Collinis hail from Mantua too, which makes them men of exceptional ability in their chosen work and retainers of unquestioned loyalty." He grinned over at Marco, who shyly hung his tousled head.

But Lyse couldn't care less about his servants. Her legs ached, her back was tired, the coarse robe was growing heavier by the minute. And she had another problem, she realized, looking over to where her governess sat slumped in a state of collapse, muscles knotted from hours in the saddle–and probably with the same bodily problem. Well, he had dragged them here, let him solve it. They weren't peasants, after all. On the trip from St. Piteu, for instance, a portable stool and pot had accompanied them in the sleeping wagon.

"What are we supposed to do, Monsieur, Madame and I, for need of a pipi?"

She caught a gleam of white teeth from within his hood. "There must be some latrines behind the hostel there–brother. Do you require I take you by the hand?"

De Dunois heard and levered herself up, thinking Ferrante di Gonzaga could be a little politer to the girl, in spite of her childish performance last night. "*Merci,* we can handle the matter, Don Ferrante," she sniffed, and with surprising strength for an exhausted little woman commenced steering her charge across the square to the yard behind the inn.

Waiting on a long line for access to the stinking, overflowing privies when, not for the first time was Lyse envious of the ease with which men relieved themselves anywhere, against any handy corner or tree.

Head humbly down, her thoughts were far from humble as she began to review her 'Plan', for if her peremptory overseer thought she was simply going to ride after him like a sheep after a Judas goat, he was *bien fou.* In three days, she had figured, they would be no more than forty leagues from Moulins at the slow pace of the pilgrims. Then, if he kept his promise, and depending on what he told her, she would either comply with her uncle's orders, or escape and flee back either to Moulins to throw herself upon the mercy of the Duchess Anne, or to St. Piteu, where surely he must have sent Germain, Nurse and the servants.

She was grateful to Bourbon; he had not forgotten to deliver her the purse she'd requested, so she could now hire a sturdy peasant to protect her, and she could inquire of villagers for devious routes to foil any pursuit. Every day she grew more resentful of being an ignorant puppet in everyone's hands and became more enamored of her burgeoning spirit.

She hadn't much idea on how she might initially escape Don Ferrante, but she'd manage. Now, for instance, he was over there watching the road from his perch on the wall, and there was a gate to this noisome back area; she could slip away and find a place to hide, if she wanted to. So it shouldn't be hard to decamp eventually, especially at night when her governess would be so wretched from riding she would sleep like a rock.

She and de Dunois were just reapproaching their party when Gonzaga abruptly stood up. Following his gaze Lyse saw a decently-dressed but rascally-looking horseman enter the square, conspicuous for the great charger that carried him, even though the dual-toned coloring of the horse was partially concealed by a long drapery of patterned wool furnishings. The rider's sharp glance about finally located them. He threaded his way toward them and, with a leer, swung off the horse.

Gonzaga, squinting from his hood, nodded a welcome. "Ho, Lucco! *E verro?*" he questioned in an undertone.

Lucco grinned evilly. "*E verro,* Signore. *Uno.*" He ran his finger across his throat, with a squinching sound.

Shocked, Lyse could see that the Gonzaga was well pleased.

"Good. You will ride well behind us. Keep alert." Ferrante ordered. He was feeling parboiled himself in the unseasonable heat; glancing at Lyse and de Dunois all he could see of them were sweat-glistened chins and drooping shoulders. "Courage, Mesdames, now we'll depart this group to join with a route south, but by roundabout way not to attract anyone's attention."

Leading their horses, they soon reached the town walls where they remounted and rode out past the heavy, iron-bound gates. Lucco hung back, following far enough behind that he was often not visible.

The stony way meandering between farmsteads was sometimes blocked by flocks of sheep, but it was not much traveled, either, and after a weary time of riding they dismounted to draw some cold water from a well. Ferrante consulted a parchment map he took from a saddle roll, and nodded to himself.

Lyse surmised that wherever they were going they were getting there, but she thought she might not make it, for the lack of air under her hood and the sweat tricklingly down between her breasts was terrible. Defiantly she pushed the hood partially back. The Italian watched her, and then said mildly, "I think we can discard these habits now," and proceeded to step out of his.

With great relief, Lyse peeled herself out of her robe, and then walked over to help de Dunois.

Ferrante saw the middle-aged woman stagger slightly and strode over to brace her as the robe puddled at her feet. "Forgive this necessary hardship, Madame. Just another two hours or so and the journey will become less painful, I promise you," he encouraged her, although the little woman gave him a despairing look. This easy courtesy, the courtliness of giving his hand to Madame de Dunois, surprised Lyse. But she still considered him a brute.

Marco threw the habits into a river they crossed to save their one laden baggage mule their weight. Ferrante had reclaimed his big charger, and a little refreshed, they rode on.

The resulting coolness without the habit helped Lyse's disposition, even though riding astride now displayed her cerise stockings. She glanced at the man who was now her new keeper, as he rode along beside her. He had emerged from his monk's robe dressed in a simple doublet and deep blue breeches which met the top of his knee boots, a sword belt buckled at his waist, but without his stylish codpiece or huge sleeves. The sardonic thought crossed her mind that not even plain clothes could turn this bearded, ear-ringed, imposing man into someone ordinary.

Finally bored with the crawling hours, she tried conversation. She nodded at her escort's arch-necked horse. "Does that huge beast have a name?"

"*Mais oui*. He is called 'Bucephalus.'"

"The name of Alexander of Macedonia's warhorse."

His look was curious. "I am happy to know you are familiar with classical history, Mademoiselle."

What, did he think she was an ignorant peasant? "My education has not been entirely neglected," she sniffed. "Yes, and I am acquainted with our own far past, our Carolingian kings, and the Merovingians," she added airily, showing off, but abruptly stopped right there, for Madame de Dunois' history had never gone beyond those very early kings with her, except in barest out-line. Unwilling to display any ignorance, she quickly changed the subject. "Might I at least ask where we will stop tonight, Don Ferrante? As a matter of curiosity?"

He drew his parchment from his saddle roll and frowned at it, control-ling the horse with his knees. "If all goes on schedule, we will attempt to reach Brecie before sundown, more than twenty-five leagues distant from Moulins, very good for our roundabout first day."

"If all *what* goes on schedule?"

He glanced behind them along the straight, flat road, then squinted more casually up at the bright sun. "In somewhat more than an hour you will see."

"But where are we eventually going?" She took a stab that he might blurt something out.

He cocked an annoyed black brow at her. "Hah! Do you forget our bargain so soon? In three days, Mademoiselle. Three days."

Well, she hadn't thought the knave would oblige her. But the dusty road through fields and farms was so monotonous, it had been worth a try. She fell into a pouting silence.

They were approaching a swath of forest verdure, squeezed between the terra cotta earth and the faded blue sky, where another road intersected theirs, and at this juncture there was an old hostelry set back from a sapling fence: a half-timbered farmhouse, with chickens and geese pecking and honking on the road. And white sheets a-flap on a line.

She gasped–

–a billowing of white cloak marked with the blood-red cross of martyrs, retreating from her, seen through her hot and bitter tears–

Lyse blinked hard and breathed out sharply, and except for the usual slight nausea, the memory invading her head instantly vanished. Control! She was beginning to master the 'seeing-back', and silently she exulted. No one had even glanced at her suspiciously just then.

They entered the inn yard where a farm boy slouched towards them to take the horses. One of the new-fangled 'coaches' stood unhitched before the open door of the place, a tall vehicle on four ungainly wheels, hardly more than a pitched-roof box set to bounce on leather straps. But to de Dunois, who had limbs and a back screaming in pain, it seemed like a wheeled canvas and leather heaven.

Out of the inn's rude doors stepped two men wearing breastplates, and the olive-skinned one smiled and raised a hand in greeting. "*Bienvenue,* Don Ferrante, you have made better time than we expected. Pray come sample the local brew, cold from the host's deep well."

Ferrante swung off his horse and wiped the sweat from his face with his sleeve. "Something cool for the ladies too, and some food. Then we ride. I want to reach Montmarault before dark. Lucco Collini, my equerry, is trailing us, so do you watch for him." He grinned. "He has a villainous face."

He turned and held up his arms to Lyse. "Come, Mademoiselle, refresh yourself. Life will be easier from now on." Seeing her perplexed gaze following Tournel as he strode over to help de Dunois dismount, Ferrante volunteered some information. "These are Bourbon men waiting here, lady, fifteen of your uncle's private guard, who will ride with us from now on."

"But what are they doing out here?" Lyse thought she would never get used to such astonishments.

"I sent them ahead of us yesterday, by a faster route. They've been waiting for us."

"You sent Germain on one road and these men on another, and we traveled another, impersonating pilgrims. Your man Lucco rides behind as if looking out for someone. Signore di Gonzaga, I demand to know who, or what are we running from?"

He raised his arms again and squinted up at her stubbornly, a lock of dark hair fallen on his forehead, his faint, mocking smile closed on any answers. Even in her exasperation Lyse noticed his mouth, wide and strong, the lips quite sensitively formed for a bravo. An impatient moan escaped her. "Yes, yes, I know. In three days," she croaked out of her dry throat.

She swung a leg off the saddle and he clasped his hands about her waist and lightly deposited her on the ground. She discovered she had landed too uncomfortably close to him, but to step back was to bump into the horse. Their eyes held fast for a few heartbeats; she couldn't drag her gaze away from the green stare, which seemed to want to penetrate her brain—to fathom her memories, perhaps, which she didn't intend to give up so easily now, oh no.

With murmured thanks, and with a tilt to her nose, she brushed past him to enter the seedy caravansery, which at least offered shade.

Lyse-Magdalene de Bourbon-Tournière was familiar with her sins of impropriety, so it didn't surprise her that she'd been aware of the broad shoulders she'd grasped and the muscular thighs outlined by Gonzaga's tight breeches. In spite of everything, the Mantuan had a physical appeal one couldn't ignore, no doubt about that.

And no doubt that his temper was vile, his character both overbearing and scoundrelly—to sign a marriage contract before his poor wife was even dead—and his close-cropped black beard rough-looking.

So, *tant pis,* she wasn't going to please him by ordering some barley water to quench her thirst. She wanted a mug of strong country beer like they made at St. Piteu.

With his usual semi-scowl, Ferrante watched the slim, retreating back of his charge. He couldn't fathom this female. All he'd done days ago was to shake her minion a second, the fellow wasn't even hurt! And yet she was still surly toward him. She was treating him like a fire-breathing dragon, in spite of the expensive pendant he'd given her in promise-of-marriage, a jewel which he'd carried all the way from Paris. Ungrateful little bitch. So where was this sweet, demure, affectionate girl Bourbon had known and promised, one who might have appreciated what he was doing for her uncle, and for her?

Or was she already showing signs of mental unbalance?

Madame de Dunois staggered past on the arm of Tournel, paler than ever. "Ah, Signore, would that that travel coach there were for me," she sighed.

He made a good-humored bow. "But indeed it is, *Comtesse,* and my regrets for the necessary discomfort you've suffered. The coach, which also brings two ladies' saddles, was slipped into a group of merchant's wagons leaving Moulins and driven to the other end of the town. After Sergeant Tournel and his men left the château—a simple patrol to any interested eyes—they recovered the coach and brought it along. *Voilà*, you and the demoiselle may continue in comfort."

Elinor brightened up instantly, beaming at him for his consideration. From the grin he gave her through the frame of a clipped beard, their leader was obviously buoyed up at the success of his hasty plans to remove them unnoticed from Moulins.

Wincing as she walked forward, now leaning on Gonzaga's arm, de Dunois quavered, "I don't suppose this tawdry hostel would have any cool, spiced wine? *Eh bien,* a foaming mug of country beer would certainly do instead."

The much bigger party, including Tournel's halberd-equipped men, now continued south, finally joining the main road, not stopping evenings until they reached some accommodation. The second morning after they joined the main route south, Gonzaga informed them that Lucco had arrived during the night, and evidently with good news, so they deduced, for the Mantuan's scowl was almost erased.

The weather turning cooler, they often cantered along, making good time. Because of their impressive number of guards, more than once they were yielded the right-of-way by lumbering hay ricks, flocks of sheep, and carts of early produce going to market, although as they traveled through the Bourbon-loyal province of Auvergne, Lyse grew miffed again. She couldn't understand why her party flew neither flag nor pennant to identify her as a Bourbon, and why Gonzaga shortened her name to just Mademoiselle Tonnière at the hostelries. But it was a waste of her breath asking questions.

By the third night they had reached Clermont, the last center which could be called a true city for the next two hundred twenty leagues. De Dunois mentioned this, for she had made this trip years before.

"Two hundred twenty leagues! Are we riding into the Mediterranean sea, then?"

"Near it. And further," was her governess' ambiguous answer.

"Then we're going to Spain."

The woman ignored Lyse's probing and bustled about the decently clean chamber they'd rented for the night at Clermont's best hostelry, laying out the few toiletries they'd brought, precious Marseilles soap, powder, a perfumed unguent to keep the skin supple. The governess sighed with relief. "Here, at least, they will bring us baths and send a maidservant to wash our hair. We must take advantage of the quality of this inn, there won't be many like it until Carcassonne."

Aha! Lyse's mind pounced on the crumb of information. She knew some geography. The city of Carcassonne was in the Languedoc, west of Avignon where the French popes had once resided. She was elated to have even this smidgin of knowledge.

And this was the third night of their travels and she was determined to find out the whole story—or implement her escape back to Moulins.

"Madame, I would like to ask Don Ferrante to sup with us tonight. Would you convey the invitation?"

"In fact, I was just going to suggest such an arrangement," de Dunois said. She looked at Lyse sharply. "My dear, have you had anymore flashes of memory? Do you think the traveling has repressed the 'seeing-back'?"

"No, nothing has happened," Lyse answered, leaving out the second's flash three days ago she'd been able to turn off. "And who knows why?" she answered the second part of the question. "But you are aware of what Signore Gonzaga promised for tonight? I will hold him to it."

Although she had been riding beside Gonzaga for several days, he took more of an interest in the countryside than her, turning his head to gaze at this and that as they rode through pasturelands studded with strange, volcanic mounts. One would think he'd care to know more about the woman he'd contracted to wed, even just to pass the time. Behind them the Collini brothers argued in Italian, her governess was nodding in her jouncing coach, and the guards bantered with each other. But she was cast into silence, because her companion was ungracious.

Lyse hated silence, she liked to talk, so that afternoon she ventured in a especially courteous tone, "Perhaps you would tell me something of Mantua, Monsieur, to pass the time? When my uncle visited St. Piteu, he vividly described the elegance of the noble houses of Florence and Milan and Mantua, and especially he dwelled on your mother, Isabella d'Este, with her brilliant court of philosophers, poets and musicians—" Genuinely interested and eager to know, she had gazed at him encouragingly.

But Ferrante, startled out of a reverie, looked away from her fresh young beauty and the copper hair coiled neatly below the little coif. He squinted his green eyes into the distance. "Ah yes, the dowager-*Duquessa,* my dear mother—" His tone was flat. But they were interrupted by Tournel, who rode up to report one of the coach wheels a little wobbly, and after Ferrante returned from inspecting it—when they stopped for the night a mallet would pound the axle in—he stubbornly changed the subject by asking Lyse of her life at St. Piteu. Nevertheless, already she had gotten the sense that the son was not very fond of his admired mother. And this disdainer of women was the husband her uncle had chosen for her?

That evening, diligently stroking a brush through her silky hair, she had no need to decide what to wear, she'd been allowed in her small bundle only one other outfit, a white bodice and skirt of plain blue serge. She dressed in it now, then decided just to tie her loose hair back with a ribbon, for it was tiresome to do more and Madame was not handy with the frizzing iron that made the little curls in front even if they'd had one.

The two women had ordered from the innkeep a veritable feast, including stewed hare, mutton pie, roasted turnips, and almond pudding. Ferrante arrived on the hour, his blue doublet and feathered tam brushed clean of dust, and he brought to the table a jug of the host's best wine. Famished since their noon meal, hours before, the three of them fell to, passing bowls and platters, licking fingers, tearing bread, smacking lips and murmuring praises for the first decent food they'd been served in days.

Finally, the wine gone, but fizzy cider still available, they sat back contentedly. De Dunois' eyes darted from the girl to the man. She was nervous against what was coming; her habit of years, limiting the girl's knowledge to keep her recall clear of suggestion, was hard to break. Smiling weakly, she tried to fend off the inevitable. "I wonder how the roast was braised to arrive at that piquante flavor? Do you think it was cloves?"

But Lyse stared directly at the Mantuan and demanded coolly, "It is the third night, Monsieur. So where are we going? And why?"

He answered as bluntly, "South to the Razès, a district below Carcassonne on the Aude River."

Her lips parted. "Below Carcassonne? Why, that is close to the Pyrénées mountains, and close to Spain."

He nodded. "I see this good lady has taught you proper geography."

"But—but where? What specific place?"

"Rennes-le-Château, a little village atop a foothill, above the town of Couiza."

"Couiza?" she repeated the peculiar name. "That doesn't sound French."

"Some names and words down there are from Occitan, the ancient *langue d'oc,* a mixture of French and Catalan, although, as a Frenchwoman you'd have trouble understanding it."

Lyse glanced at both her companions, their expressions similar, serious but wary. A stab of reluctance to leave the protection of innocence drove through her, and her pride in her bravery wobbled. But to turn back to ignorance was to become a Lot's wife, a pillar of salt, heedless, eyeless, and mute, while others shaved away her substance to use her gift.

She took a breath and plowed forward. "Pray, I want to know, why are we running to this obscure place on a mountain? What does it all mean?"

Ferrante had to admire her courage in insisting on the truth. Even though he was going to tell her only what was necessary, he didn't quite know where to start.

Unwittingly, she helped him by doggedly demanding, "What is that splayed red cross I remember so often now?"

Ferrante began pacing the tiled floor to avoid Madame de Dunois' worried gaze. "Very well, Mademoiselle. I don't believe you have been told of the Knights-Templar?"

At the shake of her head, he continued. "The splayed, blood-red cross on a white ground was the symbol of a famous religious brotherhood, the 'Order of the Poor Knights of Christ and the Temple of Solomon'. It was a religious brotherhood founded by nine French knights about the year eleven hundred and ten, an order of gentlemen warrior monks and their underlings, pledged to protect all Christians on pilgrimage to the Holy Land. The Order's first Priory, or Preceptory as they called it, was built in Jerusalem, on the foundations of an ancient temple, hence came their popular name, the Order of the Knights-Templar. They owed allegiance only to the Pope, otherwise they were totally independent of any other civil or religious authority."

"Was this not unusual?" Lyse questioned, hanging on every word.

"Hah, unusual indeed, as was everything else about the swift-growing Order. Many of the highest nobility took the Templar vows—for religious fervor or sometimes other reasons—although it meant signing over most of their wealth and possessions to the Order. The Templars, in truth, were basically men of war, hard fighters, although in the beginning they were sworn to poverty, chastity and obedience like any other religious group. But they soon grew arrogant in their manner and too zealous in their mission of combat for Christ. Some centuries ago there were certain foreign military campaigns called Crusades. Do you know of them?"

Lyse was enthralled. "Barely. Just that there were three or four occasions when the lords of Europe sent armies to the East to secure the Holy Land for Christianity and to expel the Saracen non-believers from Jerusalem." She shrugged. That succinct description was all she knew.

Ferrante ceased pacing and linked his hands behind his back to stand before her. "*Eh bien,* during these wars the Knights-Templar became re-nowned for their military successes in the Holy Land, and most especially during the Second Crusade, a bitter campaign which was otherwise bungled by an alliance of Christian rulers. So, with its booty-filled victories, the Order grew hugely in its possessions, in money, castles, and land, and these were not only in Palestine, which they called 'Outremer.'

"They also owned great estates and strong preceptories in France, England, Spain, and in other lands. They were a power everywhere and their Grand-Masters sat on the right hand of kings. Rumors flew that they even had special influence with the Saracens and the Jews, for in decades of living in the Levant many Templars spoke fluent Arabic and were deeply versed in Muslim ways."

Wide-eyed, Lyse leaned forward. "So the man of the rosy cross, the person I seem to remember as my–my ancestress' love, this Bernard de la Motte, was a Knight-Templar? But you said they were monks, with vows of chastity. How could he–"

De Dunois said quickly, "Well, things were different than in our own modern time, those were chivalrous days of romance, when love often flowered from a distance..."

But Ferrante, impatient with such coyness, dropped into his seat again, which creaked, and added, "If you wish to be so naive about the ways of fighting men under such vows, you may believe Madam's sweet fable, Mademoiselle. Love God and the Saviour they did, but those knights were of the world, unsequestered. Your de la Motte was important among them and recorded in letters as a man of integrity. He would be impressive and attractive to a woman, even to a married one."

Lyse felt the blush rising on her cheeks, and felt silly for it. *She* was not the married woman.

"The Order lasted two hundred years, in which time it grew stupendously rich, even commanding its own fleet of eighteen merchant vessels, and so strong that its ranks were feared as the most disciplined army in Europe. So, in the Order's last generations, it attracted men much more interested in its military and political aspects than in its religious base."

"But who was Bernard de la Motte?" Lyse persisted.

The scar under Gonzaga's eye puckered a bit. "A member of a leading family of Languedoc, a region whence many important Knights-Templar had derived. But most importantly, he was a 'seneschal,' an assistant to the last Grand-Master of the Order, Jacques de Molay, and to its Treasurer."

"And–who was I? No, not I," Lyse hastened to add, for it was surely a sin to believe another soul could be reborn in her body, "but my forebear, many, many times removed?"

He contemplated her again, entertaining some remark but thinking better of it. Instead his looked appealed to de Dunois, who, now the die was cast, had calmed somewhat. Carefully, the governess took up the tale. "We are not sure who you are recalling, *ma Lysette*. Daughters of families sometimes married more than once, families branched and branched again, records were accidentally lost or burned. Only one female over a hundred year ago, Mathilde, the little daughter of Robert de Bourbon, is inscribed in the Bourbon's secret annals as capturing more than just fleeting and jumbled memories of times before her own life. And now there is you–so we hope."

But Lyse wasn't satisfied. Hope? "Hope what?" she flared. "What do you look to gain through this unhinging affliction that has separated me from the normal life of a high-born woman?"

Ferrante stared at her again, shrugged, and gave her the answer. "A vast, lost treasure. The equivalent of twenty million gold écus in portable coin, along with coffers of jewels, and precious plate, enough to assure your uncle the military and political means to regain his domains and wealth, should your King tear them from him."

Lyse fell back in her chair, the breath leaving her. Her only measure of twenty million écus was that the fine manor of St. Piteu with its sixty hectares of producing land was worth perhaps five hundred pieces of gold, as the duke had indicated. A treasure of twenty million? An unimaginable amount! A torch flared blindingly in the dark landscape of her mind as she finally understood the role thrust upon her.

"Le bon Dieu me sauve!" she cried in horror. "You rely on me to remember where is this lost treasure? But what if I cannot? What if I am not able to?"

The Mantuan's green stare did not waver. "Mademoiselle, we do not want–we hope. No blame, no censure will come to you if your memories do not lead you to it."

"Nothing but disgrace in the eyes of people I love! But I cannot even control when and what I remember."

"Understood. Just concentrate when it occurs, and try not to lose details. Even some small thing could be a signpost."

Lyse's mind skittered around, looking for purchase. She bit her lip. "But–do we know what brought this Templar, Bernard de la Motte to grief? Has he anything to do with the treasure? He seems to have been burned at the stake, if my memories are true. But when did such tragedy happen?" From the corner of her eye she spied Madame de Dunois wringing her hands.

But Ferrante went on calmly enough. "The Order of the Knights-Templar is extinct, now. In thirteen hundred five the Pope Clément, fearing its strength, abolished it everywhere, but the king of France, called Philipe le Bel, coveted its wealth and lands, and joined the Pope by villainously prosecuting the French Templars as heretics. It is a long, ugly story, but fascinating. At any rate, the French Templars managed to hide their Treasury and their military ships, and these have never been found."

Lyse felt her heartbeat quicken, for she was able to hook up one of her visions to this. "*Tiens*, I sometimes remember de la Motte leaving a castle in the face of an approaching thunderstorm, riding with other men as escort to a great, shrouded conveyance. Could this freight have been that great, lost Treasury?" Her excitement rose even as she quailed about how much depended on her in her uncle's plans.

De Dunois said, "Yes, yes, we believe so, and it has stirred us up mightily. Especially since the lady–the one you remember–in your subsequent memories agonized over a vital knowledge she refused to give up."

"You think that the Templar she wept for told her where the Treasury had been hidden?"

"You will have to tell us that," the Mantuan drawled.

"*Merde*." Lyse said under her breath, overwhelmed. She heaved a sigh. "Who else, then, knows of this Templar treasure?"

"Many people. And for centuries. Most are convinced that the horde had been spirited from Paris down to Languedoc for eventual transportation elsewhere, and that this latter part was never accomplished. There have been unsuccessful trenches and holes dug all over the Razès, because that was where the last of the Templars found refuge before they were finally taken. The redoubt in the mountains where they held out a long time was called Le Bézu."

"Oh! Madame, I asked you about that!" Lyse cried to de Dunois.

"Yes, Lyse-Magdalene, so you did. Your mention of Le Bézu is one of the reasons we are taking you down there now, where certain things might prod your memory much further."

Their astonishing answers to her questions were ricocheting about Lyse's head, but she would sort them out later. It was important to continue on while these two were finally willing to part with information. Now she caught up to her governess' statement.

"*One* of the reasons? Then what are some others? Such as, why did we leave Moulins so hastily and in such stealth? Who besides my uncle would care where I went? Please, it is fair that I should know everything that is happening to me, you owe me that!"

Ferrante noted, as her shock wore off and she realized her own importance, that her tone had grown confident again, and Bourbon's words, 'docile and submissive' echoed like witless laughter in his mind, for he realized that behind that ethereal face dwelled a lively intelligence, and he believed it could occur to her that she might hold the reins in this quest. But it was worth giving some illusion of power in order to enlist her goodwill in the use of her weird ability.

"Very well, if you insist. The Bourbons are not alone in thinking you could locate the Templar Treasury; one other strong family in particular pays attention to you, having knowledge of the female Bourbons' ability to 'see-back'. It is the Lorraines. They are why you, and your mother before you, were kept away from their sight, for they have never given up on the Treasury, or been above kidnap and painful persuasion to gain their ends."

Lyse was incredulous. "The Lord *Duc* Antoine de Lorraine, a reigning prince, would kidnap me?"

"Not Antoine de Lorraine, but his crafty brothers in France, the cardinal de Lorraine, the *vicomte* de Marques, and the most dangerous and powerful of them, the man I pointed out to you during the *entrée*, a naturalized Frenchman sometimes riding under the double-barred cross of Lorraine, the *comte* de Guise. He is a hard man, he is calculating and greedy, and your uncle suspects him of ambitions so vaulting they would take some millions of écus to achieve. Do you begin to understand?"

He continued, "At Moulins your man Matz discovered de Marques sniffing around for information about you and so we decided to spirit you away from danger, using Matz' lie about the road you would take and the dressed-up servants as bait. But de Guise is crafty, we suspected he had agents lurking at *all* the portals, and so, as a precaution, we posed as monks and left mingled with that group to avoid being followed. Even though they couldn't be sure you were amongst the pilgrims, the fact is, we were followed. But Lucco took care of that."

Lyse made a weak motion across her throat, mimicking how Lucco's finger had made a slash across his throat. "*Mon Dieu!* But would that not give away what direction we took, if their man is found with his throat cut?"

His green eyes were a-glint with the pleasure of a hunter. "My Lucco is an artist, he has a way with these things. He uses that motion merely to mean the man is dead. Actually he broke the rascal's neck and then made it look as if the horse tripped—"

"I doubt that would fool me," she sniffed, to hide her distaste for such violence.

"It was the best we could do on short notice, my lady. And from that road to Bourges we could have taken crosspaths in any direction along the way, or gone to Bourges, or past it. Without the fellow's witness, they will have to guess."

With a sudden whimper, Lyse put her hands over her ears and squeezed her eyes shut. She felt as if fingers were around her throat cutting off her breath, her life had turned so extreme. Memories hundreds of years old, a Treasury, enemies, murder, it was too much.

Ferrante shook his head at de Dunois to keep the woman in her seat. He came around the table and pulled Lyse's hands from her face, roughly drawing her to her feet as well.

"Attend to me, Lyse-Magdalene de Bourbon-Tonniére. Your uncle Charles is in grave danger, even of his life, from a vindictive and jealous king who orders a weak Parlement to ignore the law. Bourbon may be forced into precipitous escape from France to avoid arrest, with only what money and gems he can carry on his flight. He is a warrior, he will return in force to fight such injustice, but he will need to pay troops and buy arms and bribe allies in what may be a long war. If he is to overthrow Francois and regain his eminence and lands, he will need a great, new fortune to help him."

He was holding Lyse by the arms, his deep concern for Bourbon obvious in his eyes, making her wonder if somewhere Blackbeard had a heart after all.

"There are some foreign sources of funds for him, but they entail hampering entanglements. You are the real key to Charles de Bourbon's ability to return to France. Do you love him?"

"Yes, I do, I love him very much," Lyse said softly. She had always adored the splendiferous grand constable from the time she was a tot; he was her protector, her only family, her dream of a father.

There was a tiny change in Gonzaga's gaze; some of the warmth faded. But he continued intently, "*Eh bien,* then cooperate with us."

She glanced over at her governess' strained face, then back at him. He felt her slowly relax and released her arms.

"Very well, Signore. What do you wish me to do?"

"Nothing different. Go along as before. But report to us every single scrap of remembrance that isn't part of your very own life. It is our hope that living at Rennes-le-Château, in the heart of the Razès, will stimulate your 'seeing-back' into releasing more detailed information about the Treasury."

The whole scheme was so chancy, it seemed to Lyse, so dependent on the unintelligible bits and ragged visions that came to her, it already seemed doomed. "But it could take years for me to remember anything significant."

"That is in God's hands. We can only help you to concentrate. And keep you out of the grasp of the Lorraines."

For her it was imprisonment again, no matter how she wished to help her uncle Charles. Momentarily yielding again to infantile disgruntlement, she turned her back and flounced away from him. "At St. Piteu my only dream was to live at court, my uncle's or the King's. And now I might grow grey and old a month's ride away from either one and still not succeed in this momentous task. No, it isn't fair!"

He came around to face her, his eyes were like hard emeralds again. "You're a long age away from being old and grey, Mademoiselle. In any event, when we are finished here, Mantua has a brilliant and lively court, enough to please you. You will see. When the time comes."

Yet, for all the placating promises, she discerned a chilly withdrawal in his voice, a peculiar retreat from where they had almost joined hands as seekers and plotters after the same prize. It had always been clear he did not like her that well, the man to whom she was promised in marriage, but never why he did not—besides that incident with Germain which he should have been gentleman enough to forget.

He concluded, "You are tired, ladies, I will leave you now to your rest, for we continue the journey tomorrow just after dawn."

He had come to supper with a small volume under his arm, which he now picked up from the table and proffered to Lyse. "I know you have other questions. I brought this along for you from your uncle's collection, a history of the Knights-Templar, translated from the contemporary account of an Italian scholar. You will understand more as you read it."

With thanks for the supper and a polite bow to both, he took his leave, but Madame de Dunois followed him out of the chamber for a private word.

Alone, Lyse turned the leaves of the soft-leather bound book, her eyes strained as she stared down, as if she could force them to make meaning of the heavy black print crowding the pages, and feeling more debased than ever by her inability to read.

Outside, Madame de Dunois asked Gonzaga, "That is all we will tell her?"

"That is all she needs to know. Why dilute her focus?"

"I agree. Even with what we said, I still worry we may have changed something in her head. The seeing-back is so unstable."

"The risk was required. And approved by the duke. Just remain watchful."

She nodded, turned to re-enter the chamber she shared with her charge, then turned back. "She is young, Signore, and does not know how to hide her disappointments. But in the end, Lyse-Magdalene has many good qualities, not the least of which is intelligence and humor. And she can be sweet."

"So I've been told. Charles de Bourbon seems most greatly enamored of her."

Elinor stiffened, having heard darkness creep into his voice, and an unwelcome thought jolted her. *Nom de Dieu,* the beautiful, adoring child, Lyse-Magdalene, had been so much in Bourbon's power, could it be this one thinks that Charles seduced and bedded the girl and he harbors jealousy? Or deep anger? Or does he consider her a compromised strumpet?

Although one day the man would know his bride a virgin, the governess felt a pang of hurt for the poor young woman. Many marriages between nobility began only with respect to sustain them, which, with luck, grew into kind regard. Sometimes even love. This well-born *condottiere* had been chosen as Lyse-Magdalene's future, but already he carried a worm of suspicion against her. And what could be said, by herself or any other, that would not make his suspicion even worse, until he had his own proof of the young woman's innocence?

She took her leave with an abrupt nod for him and re-entered the bedchamber.

Chapter 9

Seven difficult days later they were skirting the mountains of the Massif Central and heading south. When at last they came through the foothills and reached Aurillac, Gonzaga announced that the hardest part of the long journey was over: the route towards Carcassonne was now straight and fair, as shown on his map.

Their exhausted relief was short lived.

Two mornings later, coming through a pass at the village of Puylois, they stood frowning at the edge of a rushing river that slammed its wild, white spray against the remains of the piers of the completely collapsed stone bridge that had carried their road.

A passing local with a maul over his shoulder volunteered, "Oc, 'tis the highest water we've seen, t'worst spring runoff give us fifty years, so me old uncle says." He guffawed, meanly amused at the travelers' dilemma. "Can't fix t'bridge 'til the river level goes down and she calms."

"It could take months to rebuild that bridge. So where are travelers to cross?" Ferrante demanded.

Eyeing the troop of guards behind the big knight, the peasant thought he'd best answer straight. "Aye, so ye can go up the gorge or down; at Moens where the river, she narrows, a high bar makes a shallow that's easily forded. At Festiral, down t'river, there's a ferry can withstand a strong, high water current. Well, most o' the time, eh? Either way, 'tis eight leagues in distance to a crossing. Either way, theren't no road in the gorge but it mounts up and then down again all the way. Or ye can return twenty-five leagues to St. Clyme and make a way around."

Little Puylois was situated on a natural landing, but otherwise the river had carved a rugged, narrow channel through the cliffs of white-grey rock on either side, one of the precipitous gorges that sliced across France below the Massif Central. From the muddy edge of the wild river where the north-south road had been severed by the broken bridge, Ferrante could see to right and left part of the alternative routes the peasant mentioned; they were squeezed and rocky in either direction.

He gestured at Lyse and de Dunois peering from the coach. "We have ladies here. Which route would give less discomfort?"

"No one better than t'other, save to go back twenty-five leagues and then around. But I be told that folks, they prefer the shallows to the ferry, for he sometimes sink and all aboard drownded." The fellow crossed his breast a few times and made an 'O' of his mouth. Then, squinting at the coach, he scratched his head. "Eh, Monsieur, I don't know about that strange cart with a roof, I never seen the like. The paths be hardly wider than it, and rough. Best ye leave t'contraption 'til the bridge be fixed." A foxy gleam crept into the man's eyes.

Anyone could see Madame de Dunois' alarm as she contemplated having to make the rest of the trip on horseback.

Ferrante reassured her. "We will not abandon the coach, Madame. But I feel we must hurry on forward, so just for these hard eight leagues you'll go on horse, for safety's sake."

Tournel mentioned one of his guards who happened to have been raised in similar earth-slashed country, so after conferring with them both, Ferrante decided crossing at the high bar was more prudent than chancing the ferry.

The path right along the river was easy for the first several leagues, but then it petered out and continued upward as a rough incline cut into the side of the cliff. Ferrante rode first on the narrow trail, for two could not ride abreast, then Lyse, then de Dunois hanging onto her saddle horn nervously, then their escort. The coach brought up the rear, its horse led by a man on foot. The river, tumbling some way below, twisted and curved, and so did the path as it climbed up and up. Finally the path reached the rim of the gorge and leveled, and they could draw easier breath as they moved along.

"Oh, *Ciel*, are we finished now with that?" the governess called out, not relaxing her iron clutch on the sidesaddle grip. "I was so young when I made this journey once, it hardly seemed so onerous. But neither was there a bridge washed away."

"A pity, Madame, for we still have to go down there again to cross the river, you know," Lyse teased. She felt impatience with the timidity of the old, for she herself was a good rider and she thought the narrow road cut into the curves and juts of the gorge walls very exciting, more fun than riding all day between farms and forest with little to view but country people at their chores.

Lyse could see Blackbeard in profile. He was frowning as he studied the composition of the narrow path they rode, which was not hard rock or compacted earth, but scrabble that slipped under the animal's hoofs. The cliff bearing their trail sloped down on one side very steeply, with bare slide areas amidst patches of scrub foliage, ending in a sheer dropoff hanging high above the river. As their path left the rim once more because of an uncrossable crevasse and slanted down, Gonzaga slowed their pace. The horses had to pick their way over a detritus of stones and pebbles, and step over breaks where the edge of the path had been hit by debris rolling from above.

As they spiralled down, the thin patches of foliage on the slope sometimes hid the wilding river from their view, but never dampened the continual roar of rapids, tumultuous in the gorge far below.

The animals' hooves sent stones tumbling down as the party threaded their way slowly down the corkscrew path, all of them intent upon their mounts' footing, never looking back and up—or they might have glimpsed another rider peering over the cliff edge at them.

Lyse's horse made a slight stumble on a loose rock, her breath caught in her throat and it occurred to her going down wasn't as jolly as going up.

She glanced at the path's edge and down beyond it to where the slope became an overhang. Her horse, hugging the cliff wall on one side, had no more than a short arm's length between his flank and the edge, and the poor pack animals with their wide burdens barely fit. Behind, for some unknown reason, de Dunois' mount was crowding into hers. She could feel that her own high-strung horse was nervous, and leaned forward to pat the animal's cheek from time to time. But they could meet another party coming toward them and then what would happen, who would have to back up? Perspiration broke out on her upper lip.

Ferrante, astride his sleek gelding, turned about in his saddle to check his party and noted that Lyse's initial exhilaration had been extinguished by the hard descent, although she was nowhere as tense as her governess behind her.

Actually he was furious with the spiteful peasant who had directed them on this precipitous route, and disgusted with himself for not being prudent enough to take the women on the slower but surer way, back twenty-five leagues and around the gorge. Nevertheless, the nod he gave his charge was easy, designed to be encouraging, and she even smiled back with pert bravado.

But the petrified de Dunois, joggling and leaning back against her steed's forward pitch, moaned, "Oh, I wish this was over. These are horses, after all, not mountain goats."

Sorry now for her earlier teasing, Lyse called back, "Courage, Madame, the beasts are very sure-footed, nevertheless."

"Merciful God, but I—"

And then it happened, in an instant, a weakened section of path falling away beneath de Dunois' horses' front hoof, the horse lurched forward into the rear of Lyse's mount and then, panic-stricken, reared up, whinnying and pawing and spilling his screeching rider backwards, almost under the hooves of Tournel's mount.

But Lyse's horse, shoved violently sideways, lost its balance and its two rear hooves went over the edge. It scrabbled frantically for purchase and more of the path broke away. Failing to balance, the whole, whinnying animal toppled over and fell into a tumble down the slope.

To his fright-paralyzed rider everything seemed to happen very slowly, but inexorably. She felt the unbalancing blow to her horse's rear, she heard the shriek behind her, there was a deep shout from before her, and then a scream issued slowly from her own throat. And as languidly as if in a summer dream her horse tilted and parted from her, she drifted out of the saddle and into the sky, the sky, the sky which could not, would not hold her up.

Slowly then she twisted around and down, down to land hard on her back, breath knocked out, to go sliding down the scree of the slope–and get tangled up, her dress, her limbs, in some small shrubs which slowed her but did not hold her, but disgorged her into a further helpless, horrible tumble and slide–

And suddenly everything turned real again and fast, and Lyse heard herself screaming, frantically clawing at the slope with nothing to grab onto to stop her careening plunge toward the edge of the overhang and thin air. Her whole being consisted of gouging fingernails and clawing hands and a horrified heart about to burst.

Suddenly, with a leafy swish, she jolted to a stop, but she heard below her a crash and then an animal's high scream as the falling horse plunged through a thin barrier of brush and shot over the slope edge. Her eyes were squinched shut, her breath was knocked out of her, her face was scratched and slapped by the tough scrub edging the overhang which had caught her almost upright, but her foot had found a purchase and her desperate hands had grabbed some narrow branches. Her fall was stopped.

She sobbed wildly and the brush holding her trembled.

Shaking with fear she opened one eye, as if opening both would overload her fragile platform. She had crashed a wide hole in the small-leafed tangle of shrubbery that surrounded her. Slowly she raised her head to look up, for over the roar of the rapids she heard someone calling her.

The trail she'd fallen from was so narrow she could see much of what transpired above. Several of the guards had slipped past the horses and were involved with something on the ground. And Gonzaga was kneeling at the edge and calling to her, Tournel behind him. Numbly she stared up, not sure she was alive, but frighteningly aware that somewhere under her feet the branches which grew out from the cliff were slender and bending. They were going to break.

Not daring to breathe, she glanced down past her booted foot and discovered to her added fright that the vegetation was thin enough to present a good view below. Past the scrub there was nothing but air between her and the white-foamed river far under her, which had already savaged and drowned her poor horse. Her numb brain worked on it. Down below there, only separated from her by an uncaring, fragile tangle of branches and roots, was death.

She felt the true meaning, then, of the word 'alone' as she clung to the cliffside and she knew she was going to die. Her life, a story hardly just begun, was over. She began to whimper a prayer, the only one she'd been required to memorize, the 'Our Father.'

Helpless tears leaked from her eyes. Moaning, she looked up again and saw the guard captain had produced a rope and was passing it quickly and expertly under Gonzaga's arms. Blackbeard was coming down to get her. Poised to slip over the edge, he cupped his hands about his mouth and yelled down over the river's noise, "Lyse, hold on! Don't move! I'm coming for you. Hold on!"

Lyse turned her face against the prickly leaves and tried to control her panting sobs. They were going to pull her up. She was not doomed to follow her horse after all, plunging to a cold, wet death. She would live, live to help her uncle's cause, to primp and preen and dance at the royal court, and to someday become wife and mother and chatelaine of her own domicile.

She heard the loose scree pattering down about her and looked up. They were lowering her rescuer down the sharp slope, three men paying out the rope while Gonzaga slid down using what finger and toe-holds he could find in the crumbly rock. She had rolled and tumbled a long way and Gonzaga seemed to descend so slowly, but her panicked heartbeat slowed a little. She was all right. In a moment he would lock his strong arms around her and they would both be pulled to safety.

More debris, loosened by his descent, bombarded her and she ducked her head. From the path she heard someone shout, "Mademoiselle, don't look down!"

The warning was too late. The sun had moved across the sky a little and now the sheer drop and the river, spiked with tumbled boulders, stood out below in sharper relief, and to her terrified mind the flood seemed a foaming, roaring mouth baring its rocky fangs and eager for her to drop down its gullet.

The limb under her foot creaked and gave a little, for a wind had sprung up which made the branches sway, and her heart jumped into her throat again. The nausea of fear grabbed her and burst upwards, and she vomited sickly into the bush, causing the limb to creak and tremble even more.

Panic returned and her fingers clung with an iron grip to the slender branches sustaining her, oh hurry, hurry...

"Lyse-Magdalene! Reach up!"

She opened her eyes and just above her head and a little to one side dangled Gonzaga, one hand grasping the rope, the other straining down to her.

"Lyse! The rope is not long enough," he yelled, to be heard over the river's racket. "But raise your left arm, I'll grab your wrist and pull you up to me. They will haul us both up. Reach up!"

Let go? Grasp the bush with only one shaking hand while the river roared below her feet with its waiting, rocky teeth? No. No. She began to tremble. She was going to die. She heard herself sobbing. "No. I can't!"

His boot scraped along the rock, looking for any support. But his voice was matter-of-fact. "Of course you can. Just loose the hold of your left hand and reach up to me, I'm only a half-arm's length short of you. Your other hand will keep you steady while I get a grip on you. Don't be afraid, I won't let you fall."

Fall? Totally addled by hysteria, Lyse thought, "so why shouldn't he let her fall? Then he wouldn't have to keep his word to marry her, which her uncle had surely forced him into. And then he could put an honorable end to all the tiresome months which might be needed in the Razès, and jauntily don his heavy armor once again to fight at Bourbon's side. No one would suspect he deliberately let her fall."

"No!" she cried out wildly. "I'm afraid! I can't!"

"You can! You must!" The wind buffeted both of them and he tried to hold his position. "That bush may not bear your weight if the wind blows stronger. Lyse, You cannot stay there. Trust me!"

"You'll drop me! That is how you'll easy rid yourself of me, your hated burden—" she wailed out, eyes squeezed shut, nose running, frozen against the brush-covered slope, "you'll let me go!"

Shock silenced Gonzaga a moment as he stared down at the top of her head which he could almost touch.

Desperate to get her to cooperate, he no longer felt the hairy rope eating into his palm, his ribs, trying to cut him in half. He struggled to keep his tone controlled. "Lyse! How can you think that? It is not true! I beg you, trust me. Give me your left hand." Another gust of wind ruffled the brush and he fought not to swing away.

"You'll let me go, I know it! You hate me! I'll fall!" she cried.

Blackbeard lost his temper. "Listen, you stupid, hysterical wench! Use your brains! You are your uncle's darling. If I do not love you, I dearly love him and I would never hurt him through you, never. So reach up, I say, before it is too late!"

The limb bearing Lyse's weight creaked and gave a little more, and she shrieked out in fear.

She had no choice. Using all her will she got her stiff fingers to uncurl. Pressing herself to the cliff, she raised a trembling arm as high as she could, looking up at his darkened, tense face. She heard him grunt as he strained to close the gap, and then his hand closed about her wrist like a vise.

"I've got you! Now let go with the other hand, I'll hold you steady. You'll have to clamber up the bush a little to get yourself clear." He glared into her terror. "Do it!"

She didn't care anymore. She lifted one foot a little and found a toehold on another thin limb. With a gasp she unlocked her right hand and grabbed at a higher branch which bent almost double; she grabbed a handful of small branches and was able to boost herself only a small length, but enough to get her shoulders clear of the brush.

"Good. Now, pull at your skirt if you can, to see it's not badly caught."

Pull? With what? She was in God's hands, now only God and His miraculous Angels could save her. But she disengaged one foot and felt with it as best she could; her torn skirt did not seem seriously snagged.

"Lyse. I'm going to pull you just free of the bush. Then try to drag yourself up against me. I'll help you."

Speechless, sand-throated, she nodded. She was in God's hands.

Gonzaga looked up at the anxious faces above and cried, "Haul away! Slowly!"

Lyse felt herself tugged, then towed, and it was impossible to keep her only handhold. She let go, and in a moment she was clear of the brush, supported only by the unrelenting grip on her wrist, which was pulling her arm right out of its socket. The lifting stopped. Now her feet and fingers scrabbled desperately at the sloped rock, and by miracle one toe found a deep niche and her seeking hand found above a gnarled root to grasp, relieving her screaming arm of some of her weight.

Her hat was gone, her hair had come loose in the fall. Panting again, she shook it out of her eyes to look up at the clench-jawed face above her. He braced himself almost sideways to the steeply-pitched slope, his eyes squinting in the bright sun. "Climb, Lyse! I've got you. Come up where you can grab my waist or shoulder. I won't let go until you've got strong hold of me."

She dreaded to budge, she was fighting not to picture in her cringing mind the chasm of air beneath her, she couldn't move, she couldn't. But her arm was going to be ripped out of her body this way. She had no choice. Her right foot found a tiny purchase and she was able to inch up, then dared to move her left foot and inched further, her face scraping against the gritty rock. Now she would have to let go of the comforting root, it was too low.

She heard him grunt encouragement, for now she would have to depend on her toes to hold her, and his grip. She had come up to his knee. With a gasp she let go of the root and snatched at an embedded stone jutting out above her, and it held. She searched with one foot and then the other, and she was slithering up his thigh to his hips; her arm which he was grasping was bent at the elbow, finally, and the pain in it slackened. Or it had gone numb.

"Very good, Mademoiselle, you are a fine mountaineer," her rescuer rumbled, with a crooked grin. "Now I shall put your left arm about my waist, but without releasing your wrist. Get your fingers into my belt, it's strong, and when you have it tight, then release your other hand and put your arm about my neck, I'll brace my leg so you can step up on my knee, if necessary." The gust of wind that flattened them against the rock almost caused her to lose one toehold and she whimpered in panic.

"Move! Now, before your strength slackens!" he commanded.

He drew the arm he gripped around him. Her fingers were slowly slipping from the jutting stone above her, but she grabbed at his leather belt and hooked her fingers into it like a limpet. The vise-like pressure on her left wrist disappeared, but with terror she realized that now only her own grasp on his belt and on the stone was between her and a fatal fall.

He stretched his freed hand along toward where she was clutching the jutting stone. "Give me your other hand, now, and we shall be pulled up," he ordered, shaking the sweat and the dark hair from his eyes.

It would mean a second of no grip but the one she had on his belt and her weak toeholds. "I can't!" she cried.

"You must trust me! Move slowly and you will not fall. I promise you!"

Like an automaton she did what he said. She stared up into his eyes fixedly, pressed her spread-eagled body into his, and let go of the stone. Above her head she slowly moved that arm towards him. Suddenly she became very dizzy, a buzzing started in her ears. She felt herself sway outward, and again time seemed to slow like poured honey, so slow, and even her panicked heart was hammering slowly, and she opened her mouth slowly to shriek.

Then Gonzaga's hard grip was encircling her forearm and he jerked her back against him so that she lost her toeholds but was able to frantically lock her arm about his neck. He let go to grip her strongly around the waist as she dangled against him. She felt his roped chest rise and fall, heard him panting hard in her ear.

"Haul away, *mes amis!*" he yelled up. "*Doucement!*" And he gave her waist a squeeze of triumph.

Yank by yank they were pulled up the slope towards the narrow trail, Gonzaga's body shielding Lyse from the worst of the scraping and bumping. She had both arms about his neck now. She heard his grunts and curses as projecting rubble jabbed at him and small stones dislodged by the rope bombarded their heads. Above, the tense voices of their escort came down to her, "Easy, easy—don't jerk them..."

Then there were hands under Gonzaga's armpits and she and her rescuer were pulled over the crumbly edge of the path and into a cluster of legs, human and animal, for the end of the rope had been looped as insurance over the saddle pommel of a sturdy horse. Backing up, the men stood her up on her wobbly legs.

The Mantuan, freed from the rope, got to his feet too and with overflowing gratitude and wrenching sobs, she fell into his arms. He held her in a tight hug, patting her back, smoothing down her hair, murmuring comforts until she stopped shaking. Finally she could stand on her own, she wiped her eyes on the back of her sleeve and looked tremulously into his somber green gaze.

"Anything badly amiss with you?" he asked.

She moved her left shoulder and arm and winced. "This arm is very painful and my ribs are sore. Otherwise I'm alive, Signore," she whispered from a sand throat. Her fingers were rasped raw, the nails dirty and broken. She lifted her hand to brush the hair from her forehead, but then brought her broken-nailed fingers forward to stare at the sticky blood on them.

Gonzaga grabbed the handkerchief his equerry offered, lifted her chin and swabbed carefully at her brow. "It's nothing, just a small cut. Your face is scratched; you've probably got abrasions and plenty of bruises all over. Indeed, you gave us a scare, Lyse-Magdalene, but God kept your spirit yet in his hands and you are alive and unharmed. So we must go on."

Lucco handed him a flask which he handed to her with an order to drink, then watched with interest as she hardly coughed over the big swig of brandy. He took a long pull himself.

She stared at his dirt-streaked face, at the ruined blue doublet torn from rubbing against the scree and dark where sweat had soaked through, at his bloody knuckles and ripped hosen, and quavered, "You saved my life."

He smiled. "That blessed scrub bush saved your life. I merely relieved it of you."

"Nevertheless, I will find some way to show my gratitude. I thought I was going to die," she confessed. Now she remembered with deep embarrassment the lunatic accusation she'd made in her extremity: that he wouldn't mind letting her fall. "Signore di Gonzaga, I beg you forget the stupid words which terror put in my mouth."

He again pressed the kerchief against the cut on her forehead.

"Forgiven," he rumbled, but said it as gently as he was ministering to her.

Enjoying the moment's sweetness, she swayed, leaning against his strength and he steadied her. It occurred to her that her face must be as dirty as his, and tear-streaked besides, her hair tangled, her dress ripped and bedraggled, a frightful sight, needing help. Which caused her finally to think of her governess, de Dunois, and she instantly reproached herself that in her wracked relief to be alive, Blackbeard's embrace had eclipsed the lady who had cared for her so long.

"Madame de Dunois–?" she queried, then gasped, for looking past Gonzaga she saw the poor woman lying unconscious on the path by a large crimson splatter staining both the ground and her broken, gabled hood, the lax face chalk white below the cloth they had torn from her underskirt to bandage her bloody head. The governess looked almost peaceful amidst the kneeling men working over her. Lyse followed Ferrante, edging along the narrow path to finally bend over the wounded woman.

A guard said, "She has broken her forearm, Monsieur, but I have splinted it with a dagger case until we reach a town with a surgeon. The gash in her scalp that causes the blood is not deep, but it may need cauterizing. That is all we can tell of what harm the lady has suffered."

"You've done well. But we will have to submit her to being carried on horseback, for I trust the width of the coach less than ever on this infernal path."

"But what if she has an internal injury?" Lyse worried.

"We do what we can. It won't be long, we have almost covered the eight leagues. You will ride tandem with me until we get you another mount."

They wrapped the limp de Dunois in a blanket Marco managed to worm out of one of the saddle packs, then lifted her up into the saddle of a burly guard who supported her against his chest with one arm. Lyse was likewise seated before di Gonzaga. Everyone mounted up and they rode slowly on, downward.

From far above them on a switchback of the path, the man who had intermittently peeked over the edge, withdrew his head.

At last the Bourbon riders reached the river bank where the heightened noise of the tumbling torrent assailed them. Ferrante felt Lyse stiffen against him, but he did not blame her, for this wild water had almost received her in its deadly clasp.

He imagined for a moment the girl's lovely face, delicate as a white rose, her eyes, the luscious mouth, all closed and drained in death, plundered of her grace and promise, and a muscle in his jaw jumped angrily. How could she think he would want to kill her!

Because he had shown her little warmth so far? Pah, not true, she was only a woman, this person leaning against his chest, it would have been beneath his dignity to have treated her badly because she was a peculiar. Or even for the possible true sin in her past. He recalled the remnants of terror in her eyes when she thanked him for her life, back there on the path, and of her apology to him, said in so shamed and sweet a voice that perhaps he'd had a glimpse of the person her uncle Charles thought she was.

He resolved to be more kind to the young woman; *diavolo*, after all, she was bound into the situation just as he was. He should not let his flinching from her aberrant mind make their task harder.

She shifted her weight lightly against him to keep from slipping, and he admitted to himself she was nice to hold, just the right size. He liked holding her. Then, like a shying horse, he backed away from this. 'Well, why wouldn't holding her be pleasant?' he thought, reverting to sour form, remembering the truncated assignation with his lady-love at Moulins. "I haven't had the pleasure of female company in a month. Lack of love-making thins the blood, they say, so a healthy man looks to find it anywhere."

Eh buono, but not with her!

She was a woman strange in the mind, and—so his crude and jealous thoughts whirled on—maybe already bedded by her uncle in a repugnant relationship. For a moment Ferrante hated himself to suspect his good cousin Bourbon of incest, but such license wasn't at all unknown and absolute power over a beauty so eager to please her keeper could easily corrupt a man, even the exemplary duke.

Hah!

At Moens they crossed the high sandbar uneventfully, the rushing river so blocked by the natural barrier that it streamed swiftly across at a depth barely reaching the horses' shins. They rested in the village while a smith stretched and nailed two cowhides over poles to make a litter for Madame de Dunois, and a farmer sold them, at an outrageous sum, two donkeys and hitches to carry it. The next town had an animal surgeon in a dirty leather apron who set the unconscious governess' arm and cauterized her wound, and who tended Gonzaga's lacerated back and gave Lyse a powder for the pain of her pulled shoulder, and salve for the scrapes on her face and the sore bruises all over her body.

A goodwife brought them cool goat's milk, bread and cheese as they sat wearily in the shade of a great linden tree in the village square. Lyse caught Ferrante staring at the angry purple marks his fingers had imprinted on her wrist. He raised his gaze to hers. "I'm sorry for that," he said.

"Forgiven, Signore," she breathed, accentuating the phrase, for he's said the same to her on the trail, and for a moment they were smiling into each other's eyes without prejudice.

"How does she do?" Gonzaga called out, striding into the small chamber at the inn outside Lalac, making it smaller by his presence.

Lyse sat at the stricken woman's bedside. She had been acting nurse for three days on the road in spite of her sore body, scorning the Mantuan's order to travel in the coach, but riding her new mount at the side of the litter, never leaving the unconscious woman a moment unless somebody spelled her.

De Dunois' arm was strapped between wood strips and bundled against her chest. But even though the surgeon had closed up the scalp gash and felt no break in her skull, she would not wake up. Her fever had receded, more helped by Germain's fever-reducing powder which Lyse had discovered in de Dunois' pack than the one the animal healer had given them.

Lyse had had a moment of sad contemplation over the packet of labeled nostrums she had found in de Dunois' belongings, deeply missing Germain and his sympathetic support, feeling unsure and forsaken without her governess' guidance. Sorrowfully, now, she eyed the prone, still form on the bed, the lumpy bandage over the woman's scalp wound covered with a white cotton cap with long strings tied under the narrow chin.

"How does she?" she sighed. "There's been no change at all, I fear. But at least she's not vomiting up, or her belly swollen." Such signs would indicate internal damage, the doctor had said. "She will swallow the broth I feed her, but she shows no other consciousness, she does not hear my voice. Oh,

Monsieur, why won't she wake up, my poor Madame de Dunois?"

Ferrante studied the patient's slack face. "She took a hard blow to the head. Sometimes that results only in a bump and a headache, but sometimes it brings a sleep like death which can last a day or a year. I've seen men carted from the battlefield unscathed and breathing, but dead in the brain."

A tear trickled down past Lyse's nose. She had never imagined her governess would ever leave her, and surely not to expire in this tragic way. No, she would not entertain that idea, she was sending up prayers to God many times a day to save the lady. Wiping away the tear she mechanically reached for the hooped needlework which for both women had filled the hours before bed every night on this long journey.

Ferrante thought his charge too wan. "Have you supped, Mademoiselle? You must eat."

"A little. Marco brought me some meat and bread."

"How is your shoulder? "

"Oh, better I think for the ointment your Marco massaged into it for me."

Ferrante was startled. "Marco did? When was this?"

"Earlier. He has very gentle hands."

"So do I," Ferrante grumbled to himself, suddenly grudging that the servant, by his lowly status, had access to a specially pleasant task the master did not. "*Eh buoni,* he has obviously taken great liking to you."

She threw him a wondering glance for his suddenly grumpy tone.

He plopped down in another chair. He was aware he often gave the impression he was anxious to be somewhere else except around her, but now he was content to simply sit in the sick room and watched her for a while as she bent her head, her fingers dextrously wielding the embroidery needle. The light from fat candles in iron brackets on the wall made lustrous her copper hair.

Finally he said, "You are very good at that."

"I hate it. Needlework sorely irks me. But there's nothing else to do."

Through the days since the accident, little by little, the bumptious tone he was familiar with had come back into her voice. He shrugged. "No one forces you to sew. But have you read the book I brought for you on the Knights-Templar?"

She kept her head bent over the hoops and wouldn't look up. "No."

He was irritated. "*Tiens,* and why not? Surely now you should have some interest in the subject, and reading is certainly more absorbing than sewing."

"I know it," came the muttered response.

Frowning, he slapped his palm on his knee in disbelief. "Mademoiselle de

Bourbon-Tonnière, I most certainly do not understand you."

"You may call me Lyse-Magdalene," she said stiffly.

But he would not be deflected, having taken that privilege now and then anyway. "Of all people, you should be eager to learn the history of those who come to your memory unbidden. It shouldn't be a strain on your intelligence to peruse a small book."

Her head came up, eyes flashing in self-defence. "There is nothing wrong with my intelligence, Monsieur. I am as intelligent as–as you. But I–" Flushing deeply, she caught her runaway tongue.

"But what? You have candles, and the evenings after we halt are long enough for a half hour's study. I should think you'd feel responsible to learn all you could about the Templars." Ferrante scolded her as if she were a child because he was disappointed. He had begun thinking of her as more curious and interested in the world, not just a simple, rustic girl knowing more ways to skin a hare than her cook.

"But I can't read!" The painful confession burst out of the young woman before she could stop it. "Madame was ordered not to teach me to read. Or to write. I can only form the letters that are my name." Once her secret spilled out, the stubborn turbulence in the limpid blue eyes shattered into humiliation, and she hung her head again, bursting into unnerved tears.

He strode over to loom over her, his fists resting on his hips. "*Sang de Dieu,* you are not literate? That is passing strange for a woman of your high rank."

"My uncle had his reasons which were obeyed," she snuffled defiantly through her sobs. "He did not wish to contaminate my memories with learned knowledge, for that had done great harm to my mother, so I was educated with only what was carefully culled and read to me. But now I feel–I swear that I would not be hurt by learning, because I can separate what I learn from what memory may reveal to me. I'm sure of it!" She began to keen.

"Stop blubbering," he ordered impatiently, pulling a kerchief from his sleeve and pushing it into her hand. "Right now." With his half-scowl in place he rubbed at the back of his neck and contemplated her situation.

Lyse dried her eyes with dispatch, mortified, and dared a look up. Although she felt diminished in front of this rogue, the surprise was she was glad he was scowling at her for her lack of literacy. Maybe he'd be willing to find her a teacher.

The *Duchesse* Anne had remarked, in discussing the school for females she supported, that formerly men cared little for educated women, fearing opposition if a wife was accomplished. But the modern gentleman was beginning to appreciate a woman with whom he could discuss the world's events and the decisions in life he must make; the modern gentleman was learning to approve of women in the ranks of thinkers, for example the king's sister, Marguerite, soon to be Queen of Navarre, who wrote excellent treatises on various subjects.

The duchess maintained it was not enough for an aristocratic woman to grace her husband's arm and birth his children, or even excel as chatelaine of her household. She must also appreciate and foster the finer things of the spirit, music, art, poesie, drama; she must piously read her bible, but also with a passion for its literary beauty, and write letters of wit and eloquence and decent spelling. She must surely be able to check the steward's account ledgers in case of a life where a husband was so often absent.

If Lyse's betrothed was rude in ridiculing that she could not read, at least he felt literacy was necessary to a lady. Lyse had not thought a swaggerer whose main business was battle would care a fig about a woman's accomplishments, other than in the bedchamber.

The Mantuan lifted a jaundiced eyebrow, having come to a decision. "Very well, if you feel so strongly over your lack that it makes you wail, we'll rectify it. And so, in the absence of Madame de Dunois' service or objections, I will teach you to read. And then to write."

Her mouth hung open. "You will? When?"

"We'll start tonight. And pass a few hours of study every night of our trip." He rubbed at his neck again and stared down at her. "But—we will need a book to act a primer, although not the Templar history, which I prefer you to save until you are a little proficient."

"You have a book, the one you are always reading."

This made him laugh to think of it, and pull on his little earring. "'Tis a treatise on architecture, Grecian, Roman, studies up to the buildings of our own recent past. Much too scholarly for our purpose."

But she was curious. "I thought you were of the military caste. Why are you reading about architecture? Do you intend to build a church? Or a castle? Can you not hire men already versed in such things?"

"Of course. But it intrigues me, the whole science. Haven't you ever wondered what is holding up those soaring, pointed arches and heavy, ornamented walls, why do they not collapse, and how does the human brain reason out the plan for these remarkable buildings and domes and spires?"

She looked at him in wonder. "No. I have marveled at them, those I have seen, but not about how they are constructed."

"Well, it is an engrossing *métier*, architecture, but it requires some knowledge of physics and mathematics to understand."

"I thought armies were more your interest."

He frowned at her. "And so? A man of inquiring mind can have more than one interest, can he not? Anyhow, that book I'm reading won't solve your problem."

The thought entered Lyse's mind that the man was turning out to be quite fascinating, a person of more parts than she had imagined. But she petulantly damped out this admiration; it could change nothing between them. She offered: "I have a small Psaltery but its lines I know by heart."

"No, we should not use a familiar tome. From my own experience I know one learns faster and deeper when one is curious as to where the story goes." He rubbed a thumb against his lower lip speculatively, and suddenly he gave her a satisfied shrug. "The only other book I have with me is a collection of tales by the renowned Boccaccio, a favorite of mine." The green eyes glinted a challenge under the dark brows. "But they are bawdy."

She wanted to laugh with disdain that he should believe bawdy would discomfort her, she who had sat about with Germain and the little page Téodore and cackled with them at the cook's daughter's instructive, salacious gossip, and savored the page's graphic reports from peering through bed-chamber keyholes. But she made her smile sweet innocence itself. "Whatever you set me to, Monsieur. You are the teacher."

"I hope you prove to be a swift pupil. I've not much patience," he growled.

"I have never disappointed a teacher. Of any subject," she murmured, her manner as virginal and baby blue-eyed as could be.

But Ferrante, somehow feeling off-balance, could swear he heard a double-entendre in the remark, and the suspicion he stifled rose closer to the surface.

The bones rose sharp in de Dunois' shuttered face, the shadows lay purple under her eyes, but the unconscious woman automatically swallowed the puréed potages Lyse had chivvied the landlords of their accommodations into providing, nourishment which sustained the invalid during the eight days longer they traveled toward the Aude Valley. But she did not wake up.

The Mantuan and his charge sat together every evening just beyond her bedside and labored over his brass-clasped volume of fourteenth-century stories in French translation, famous tales that had been the scandalous delight of every court for two hundred years.

But Lyse had almost taught herself how to read at St. Piteu, she admitted, drawing back then from the actual achievement because such disobedience was not in her nature. So now she easily followed his pointing finger–"This is an 'a,' an 'n,' a 'd,' this word of three letters is 'and.' So, with an 'h' as you see here," he flipped the pages forward, "'hand,' and here–'l'–'land.'"

The pupil concentrated mightily and repeated the letters and sounds after him, and at his order hunted for similar words in the text. Sometimes, when she'd found a particularly long word he'd asked for, she looked up with so touchingly radiant a mixture of delight and awe with her accomplishment and gratitude to him, that the teacher turned his eyes away not to be dazzled.

For his part, surprised with how quickly she learned and remembered, he deliberately gave her hard words to find on the page just in order to receive so charming a reward.

They needed to lean close together to share the book and the light. Her earnest attention to the print never wavered, but Ferrante often quietly raised his eyes from the page to study the flawless velvet skin stretched over the bridge of her nose and catching the glimmer of the candlelight, and to inhale from her the scent of the perfumed soap, a parting gift from Bourbon, with which she had washed her face and hands.

He swung off his saddle at day's end looking forward to the evenings, not so much because she was a gratifying student, but because he was actually enjoying her company and the gentle diversion of teaching her–except the times he gazed at her pouty mouth and then had to quash a quick desire to bite that indented underlip.

Eight days later they had ridden through two thunderstorms, but found shelter at a hospitable Dominican friary where the herbalist administered de Dunois a steaming, stinking drink he proclaimed would soon cure her, which it did not. And where, as well as praying for her sick governess in their chapel, Lyse did take communion, for de Dunois had urged her always to do so in unfamiliar churches, even though the cleric who read the service in the privacy of their little chapel at St. Piteu had not offered it. Which was odd. He must have been very lazy, Lyse had come to think.

They skirted both the city of Albi because it was a bishopric of the cardinal de Lorraine, and Carcassonne, leaving it unseen behind its old, encircling walls. The next day, by riding along the Aude River, they would finally enter the Razès. The three-week trip was nearly over.

Lyse's quick mind and determination, and the Italian's able tutoring had worked a miracle: she could read sentences, slowly but correctly, although still sounding out some words. Delighted, she practiced her reading every minute she was not in the saddle or tending to Madame de Dunois. She began to read well enough to giggle in private at Boccaccio's rollicking tale of Ser Ceporello, although its eroticism provoked her into heightened awareness of the big, broad-shouldered *condottiere* who patiently taught her, of necessity sitting close to her in their small circle of light.

She had to admit to herself that Blackbeard was handsome in a rough-hewn way, that in spite of his brusque manner his audacious stride and occasional broad grin were attractive, and even his usual semi-scowl was intriguing. She realized that teaching her to read was generous of him, for it meant hours spent in a boring task when he could have been enjoying his tome on architecture or drinking with the guards.

Primed by the lively stories she was reading, she sneaked a glance at him now and then as they rode along, studying his hard profile and reluctantly wondering what it might be like to smooth her hand along his strong neck and shoulders.

Lyse's first glimpse of the low purple mountains edging the lush Aude River valley made her heart jump, for several times through the years she had 'seen-back' to country just like this. The mountains were gird with leafy foliage at their bases, but their peaks reared up just naked granite, atop which the broken ruins of old fortresses jutted stark into the blue sky.

Nothing human moved in those ruins; Ferrante said most paths to the hard-to-reach summits had been destroyed. On those deserted heights only wild goats nosed amongst the silent, jagged walls, walls whose stones gleamed white as bleached bones in the harsh sunlight.

Below, the roadside trees rustled pleasantly in the soft wind as the party from Moulins passed, the birds called and twittered, there came on the breeze the peaceful voices of peasants in their fields and herders on the road. Yet somehow, in strange opposition, a profound silence seemed to drift down from the sad, brooding ruins above them, somehow wrapping about them.

Lyse noticed Ferrante, expression subdued, twisting in his saddle to stare up at the shattered fortress-castles, an expression that mirrored the strange, melancholy feeling she was experiencing. Again the man surprised her. She would have thought a *condottiere* quite habituated to the sight of blasted castles, for wasn't producing them part of his trade?

She just couldn't explain the unease that crept through her as they cantered toward their destination, for the rolling countryside was a smiling one in the warm sun, and the villages they passed were ordinary, sleepy huddles of small dwellings with red tile roofs.

In her discomfort she turned for a reassuring peek at the faithful escort cantering along behind Madame's litter, and the men seemed in normal spirits, and there was only eagerness to be finished with the journey on their weathered faces. Then why did she think Blackbeard looked disturbed? And why was she fighting nervousness not fully caused by their imminent arrival at an unfamiliar place where she must live for who knew how long?

So she took a chance Ferrante di Gonzaga would think her even more strange than she believed he already did. "*Monsieur*, do you—ah, I mean, why do I have such a strange feeling since we have come into the Aude valley? As if..." She had to first unlock her unwilling voice to take the plunge, "...as if there is a suffocating stillness over the land, although 'tis plain that these rolling fields of indigo-tinted plants, whatever they are, are pretty, and the people we meet are pleasant, quite normal. Still—even these people..? I seem to sense a certain hidden silence just beneath their skins."

For once his eyes met hers sincerely, without wariness of her mental balance. "You are perceptive, Mademoiselle. I know what you mean. 'Tis almost like a soundless keening in the air, to remind us that this dulcet land was often the scene of terrible violence. The truth is, from the time of the Visigoths there have been great slaughters hereabouts."

Lyse's gaze lifted to a stark ruin on a rocky tor ahead of them. "Yes, but even around peaceful St. Piteu we discovered old arrow heads and maces and rotted leather shields half buried in the meadows from dire, ancient battle," she protested. "Here—there is something else—something especially pitiful to me in the sight of these battered remains."

He stared up at the near-distant ruins as they passed them. "That stronghold up there was Pomas, the home of an old Cathar family called de Cabaret."

"Cathar? What is that? And what happened to that family?" He turned a piercing gaze on her, obviously weighing something for that moment, but finally answered, "Not now. I will tell you of them when we have settled in at Rennes-le-Château. It is a long tale of people with a deviant theology, who defied the True Church."

"Heretics?" She almost whispered the dread word.

"In a manner of speaking," he nodded, and then cut off the subject by turning to command the guard captain to send a rider ahead to find them lodgings in Limoux.

When he turned back he had withdrawn so firmly into himself that, although she started to speak several times with the insistent questions buzzing about her head, his rigid expression made her think better of it, certain he wouldn't answer anyway.

Chapter 10

Lyse planned to surprise her reading tutor their last night on the road, having passed the time as they traveled reviewing over and over in her mind the look and spelling of many new words. Gonzaga had grown so agreeable and easy-mannered in teaching her that she sometimes had to remind herself that she was merely a burden which Charles de Bourbon had shifted upon him, and not a damsel that pleased his heart. But she thought she could impress him with her prowess.

After lighting some extra candles on the rude table of their passable accommodations, the Mantuan cast her a glittering-green glance and a sly half smile and chose a new story for her to read aloud from *The Decameron*.

"So, my lady—this is the tale of an innocent and silly village girl named Alibech who thought to be pious by wandering alone in the wilderness, looking for a holy man to teach her how to serve God. Soon she comes by this young hermit called Rustico who, in spite of his prayers, is tempted by her beauty—so tempted that he tries to think how he might take her virginity under the pretext of serving God. *Eh bien*, read on from here, Mademoiselle."

Obediently, running her finger along the lines, Lyse started out, interested to learn the rest of the ribald tale. The account went on to say that the clever Rustico made a long speech to Alibech showing her how the Devil was the most powerful enemy of the Lord God. And that God needed people to help him put Satan back in Hell whence he often escaped. When the naive girl asked how this was done, Rustico took off all his clothes and told her to do the same, then he caused her to kneel in prayer opposite him, but the glory of her naked body made the hermit's yearnings blaze more fiercely than ever.

Lyse hesitated right there, pink rising up in her cheeks, but, at her teacher's bland request that she go on, she continued, as even-voiced as possible. She read out loud:

" ' "Rustico, what is that thing I see sticking out before you which I do not possess?"

" 'Said the hermit, "This is the Devil you see, and oh, he is hurting me so much I can barely endure it."

" " "Oh, but how can I help you, poor soul!" Alibech cried. And with that the sly rascal tells her that Hell is located within her own body, and if she takes pity on his pain, she will allow him to stick the Devil back in Hell, and so render service both to him and to God!' "

Lyse had to struggle with mirth. She kept her eyes on the page but the fingers she pressed to her mouth couldn't stifle her titillated giggles. Cheeks burning, she stubbornly went on reading, and if she stumbled over a word here and there, Gonzaga quickly helped her. She continued:

" 'At the pious Alibech's consent, the hermit conveyed her to his bed and proceeded to instruct her in the art of incarcerating the accursed fiend. Never having put a single Devil into Hell before, the girl complained that Satan, as well as plaguing men, even contrived to hurt Hell too when he was driven back into it. But Rustico assured her it would not always be so, and to demonstrate that it wouldn't, he put the Devil back into Hell half a dozen times.' "

Helplessly Lyse just burst out laughing, the story was so ludicrous, the hermit so crafty, the girl such an imbecile! But her cheeks were fiery. She glanced up at the disrespectful teacher who had selected this story for her to read and she wanted to be mad with him, for wasn't he insulting her choosing such a naughty story, but his open, roguish grin as he laughed with her, made her even more giddy. And after all, she wasn't giving away her experience by understanding Rustico's dishonorable seduction. Any woman over thirteen secretly knew what life was about, if only by stumbling over servants in lusty embraces who thought themselves hidden.

"Go on, Mademoiselle," Gonzaga chortled, encouraging her, "I am astounded by your progress—in reading."

Proud of herself, she continued. The story went on to say that the Devil frequently escaped from Hell in the next days, and Alibech took seriously her duty to bring him under control, and in fact developed a taste for the task. The girl saw that doing God's work gave a woman great satisfaction, and she soon was insisting, 'Brother, here I came to serve God and not to waste my time. Let us put the Devil back in Hell again.' Rustico did the best he could, but her drive to please God many times a day was taking the strength out of him. 'The Devil must only be punished when he rears his head in pride,' the exhausted man moaned desperately. But the pious Alibech insisted Hell was in a great fury to receive the Devil and he had to be stuffed in!

Entranced, the reciter of this tale did not notice that she was following the page alone, that her teacher was studying her bent head, where the soft gleam of her red-gold hair, plaited into braids around her ears, was not hidden by her small coif. He was studying how long eyelashes swept her cheek as she moved her eyes along the lines, at the way her lips, although struggling with a naughty smile, carefully formed the words.

The young woman had spirit, Ferrante had to admit. She was also a shining, seductive beauty, and he chewed the inside of his lip, for he was certainly feeling like poor Rustico before the Devil met Hell. But he was not going to be caught in the coils of lust for this unstable woman.

There were, if he remembered right, comely women in this region, fair, dark-eyed charmers with the fire of nearby Catalonia in their loins. Any number would be willing to dally with a stranded warrior and turn him away from considering his peculiar charge's charms before the duty of marriage might force it.

Lyse continued reading, " 'But Alibech was an heiress and soon a young man named Neerbal came to find her, and to the great relief of Rustico, took her away and pledged to marry her. Before the wedding, the women of the village asked her how she had served God in the desert, and she told them everything, partly in words, partly in gestures. They erupted in laughter, and in fact, they may be laughing still.

" 'The women assured her, "Don't worry, Neerbal will give you plenty of help in serving the Lord!" ' "

Lyse read on to the author's conclusion. " 'And so, fine ladies, if you want God's grace, see you learn to put the Devil back in Hell, for that is much to the Lord's liking and pleasurable to all concerned!' "

She fell back in her chair in a helpless gale of laughter, eyes dancing, completely tickled. "Why, this author is surely blasphemous," she gasped at last, wiping her eyes, "although the tale is so funny."

Gonzaga was chuckling along with her, just as entertained. His expression, minus the usual semi-scowl, had opened up, he looked younger, more receptive, there was warmth in his grin.

But he remarked, "I thought you would able to appreciate its sly nuances."

The blush, which had never left her cheeks, deepened; her smile curdled at the insinuation, and she stiffened as if she'd been hit. Nevertheless, she resiliently dredged up some round-eyed innocence. "Well, there was a cook's girl at St. Piteu who somehow learned such lewd tales and recounted them to me, before I could stop her, of course. She explained them too, a little, so in my lack of worldliness I would have some idea of the vulgar joke. I paid her little attention, of course."

Her chin lifted and a hard light in her blue eyes dared him to believe otherwise.

"I see." One eyebrow raised politely. "In that case, would you like me to explain Boccaccio's story?" he asked, with a straight face.

She knew he was mocking her. Her mood fractured, she shook her head and dropped her eyes back to the book to hide her discomfiture. Frowning, she began silently to read the next tale, stubbornly following the progress of her own finger, but all the while exquisitely aware of him.

She heard him get up, then felt a slight pressure on her back as he leaned very closely over her, ostensibly to follow what she was reading. His face was disconcertingly near, almost against hers as he murmured in her ear, "I beg, don't be insulted, Mademoiselle. I only meant the choice of that wonderful and ridiculous story as a gift, to mark your fine progress in reading, and also to celebrate the last night of our journey."

But his warm breath was so suggestive in her ear that excitement shivered down her spine. All sense of what she was reading fled, although she was still staring at the book. Her finger had stopped its progress. In fact, she was barely breathing.

What she wanted terribly to do was to squirm away from him, jump up and with dignity remind him to keep the distance required of strangers, for they were not even openly betrothed. But what she did, astonishingly, propelled by a sexual force which neither her will nor dignity could withstand, was to turn her head slowly so that her lips just brushed his.

He pulled her up out of the chair and against him, and she thought she would faint as the subtle aroma of musk from him sent a flame racing though her that burned up her control and weakened her knees. His fingers forced up her chin and he took her mouth with relish, a relish that grew in intensity as he refused to let her go. Helpless in his thrall, finally she began to kiss him in return.

The hand on her back slid down to her rump, pressing her along his length, and her arms, having left off their weak push of protest, came up to encircle his neck. Lyse had kissed a few young men before and hugged, *mon Dieu*, she had done more than that once, but she had never felt her insides evaporate into a shower of floating stars, felt her reason disappear, her substance dissolve, to leave her with nothing but welcome for the ardor of the man whose mouth was burning on hers.

She thought, with faint terror, that she was melting into him. She felt, stunningly, that in his arms was exactly where she belonged.

Suddenly, and with a tremor she felt through her own body, he grunted deep in his throat and dragged his mouth from hers.

He stared at her; there was surprise and uncertainty in his stare, slowly shading close to anger, although she didn't understand that. For her part, she still stared at the lips that had pressed themselves deliciously on hers, and longed for their pressure again. She had never opened her mouth to her pike-man, but this time she almost had, and of her own volition, wanting to taste him, to savor him, to bind him. Beginning to suspect there was much between a man and woman she really had no experience of, she gazed at him in wonder, speechless for once.

But, with his semi-scowl back in place, he roughly stood her away from him. "Forgive me. That liberty was unfair," he stated with gruff formality. "I humbly beg pardon, Mademoiselle."

She stared at him, she had no idea why it was 'unfair'. All she knew was that while he was kissing her and holding her she had been transported to some astonishing level of sensation and, more astonishing, she wanted, she needed more of it. And from him. She felt caught, enmeshed in a net cast over her from nowhere, for neither the pikeman, de Lugny, nor the other gallants at Moulins had caused her mind and her body to suddenly yearn with such compulsive, greedy desire.

But she also wanted to hit him for putting her aside so suddenly, like a toy he was tired of, not caring one bit for what he had produced in her.

Ferrante saw every emotion flitting across the young woman's inexperi-enced face and damned himself for a miserable knave. He was here to oversee a desperate hope, not to seduce his cousin's ward, this female 'peculiar' of weird gifts. And especially not to let a beauteous face and form, albeit no more entrancing than others encountered in his life, shake him up with a mere kiss? But he had to admit his heart had jumped with pleasure at the touch of those soft, biteable lips, at the feel of her arms winding about his neck, at the moment he realized she was eagerly responding to him. He still felt the jolt of letting her go.

Like a boy! He was acting like a damn stripling wet behind the ears that needed to find a hidden corner to rub his cod at the merest touch of his sweet-heart's hand. Ferrante was disgusted with himself, not for the understandable arousal that drove him to embrace his charge, but for his lapse in controlling it. All he needed in his life was to embroil his emotions with a woman who might be destined to lose her grip on reality, just as her mother had!

He found another excuse to add, evenly, he hoped, for all its stiffness. "I do apologize, Mademoiselle. It was relief that ran away from me that we have completed our journey without interference." She gave him a wooden nod, but he could see she was hurt. Not knowing just where to go from there, he felt like a blithering fool. There was an awkward silence which he would have desperately wished to escape.

Instead, he bumbled on, grasping at ordinary conversation. "So. We have come at last to our goal. I expect you will be delighted to finally escape from the tortures of the saddle."

Lyse pushed her confusion inward, away from his sight, to remold herself. She blankly turned to de Dunois' motionless form on the nearby cot and managed to aver, "I will be happy to finally put my poor governess in a decent bed, where she can be properly fed and cared for, and where doctors can be consulted to rouse her. I had a dream last night that she would never wake, and when I open my eyes I was crying."

Gonzaga, too, wrenched himself back into balance. "'Tis sad, indeed. Yet, a propos of dreams, have you experienced any significant memories or visions since the accident? Since Madame is unavailable, you must report them to me."

She turned back to him, but her gaze now in place reflected only concern with his question. "In fact, Monsieur, I have not had any recall of significance these three weeks, and I am very worried over it. It would be tragic to have come this far and yet have lost my seeing-back, which is the point of all this. Madame, I think, knew of certain things, certain circumstances which seemed to bring these flashes to my mind, but she never told me what they were. I—I don't know what to do."

He reached out and gingerly patted her shoulder as a show of encouragement, and she wondered why he wanted to touch her even for a second, since he certainly regretted kissing her.

"Never mind, it is probably the stress of the trip that affects you. But it is entirely possible that the chatelaine of Rennes-le-Château can offer some methods to stimulate your memory."

"What? Does our hostess also know of my visions? And of the Treasury?"

"Let me explain that these are very old, intertwined families in the Razès, and what one knows they all do. In fact, it was from this area that the original Bourbons and their cohorts built their power. But the 'seeing-back' ability of some Bourbon women was divulged to only a very few people, so you can still count it secret."

"Then how do you know of it, Monsieur, coming from another country altogether?" she challenged him.

He avoided answering. "That, *chère demoiselle,* is another story and 'tis too late to begin it." He stretched, and circled his shoulders to relax them. "You should sleep now. We must start at dawn to reach our goal during daylight, for part of the road is not easily traveled in the dusk."

He stepped over to close the book on her table, stared at it a second, then threw her an unreadable glance. "You hardly need a teacher of reading any more," he commented.

Lyse wondered at the trace of regret she heard in his voice, but the compliment wasn't that satisfying because distance had opened between them again

"I bid you good night, Signore di Gonzaga," she responded tonelessly, suddenly feeling drained.

He stopped at the door. "Lyse-Magdalene, don't you call me by my given name, Ferrante? Or at least Don Ferrante. After all, in our situation of secret betrothal, complete formality is not necessary when we are alone."

Lyse's chin went up. "But the betrothal agreement *is* a secret, isn't it? Therefore I think it is expedient that formality be kept." She was riled that he had pushed those incredible few moments between them completely away, obliterating their fervid mutual embrace with ordinary talk as if it had never happened, simply because for him, as he had noted, it had only been ordinary relief that caused it. And now he wanted familiarity between them?

Her words had caused hard lines to form around his mouth. He shrugged. "As you wish it, Mademoiselle. So we shall leave tomorrow just as the sun comes up. Please be ready."

He nodded, bowed slightly, turned on his heel and was gone. She stood looking at the closed door in rising bewilderment. She had expected him to josh her and insist on his offer of informality and not withdraw the suggestion so quickly, in so abrupt a manner—just as he had withdrawn from the fact that they had kissed and pressed against each other and enjoyed it, no matter for what reason.

It taught her a lesson. He was a soldier, a bravo, a hard man and not at all a romantic knight of old who would fall swooning for love of her. What he did, he did, but once past it his attention was over, gone. Only the moment interested him.

That understanding, while it repelled her, still didn't explain why she felt so emptily bereft. It had only been a kiss.

Chapter 11

In early June, well before dawn of a fair day, the *duc* de Bourbon had escaped Moulins, along with his officers, and two hundred forty hand-picked cavaliers with their horses hooves muffled and thirty-thousand gold crowns divided among their saddle bags, stealthily filing through a secret tunnel leading under the south moat and then melting away into the darkness.

Several days later of circuitous riding south, Bourbon's party made the loyal castle of Herment and heard news that the Bishop of Autun had been thrown into jail. Relays of fast couriers were publishing the duke's flight from arrest throughout the land, with an incredible ten thousand gold écus offered to anyone delivering up the traitor.

Bourbon's last hope of re-establishing himself with Francois was gone; he decided to pare down his party, which was too large to escape notice. He retained eight officers and his valet, dispersing the other riders but forced to allow them to hold for him the heavy pouches of gold they carried, with a tenth of the sum to each man for his loyalty.

The new entourage of nine rode out south again, towards Spain. Cloudbursts and storms in the Central Massif mountains impeded their progress, as well as some close brushes with discovery that kept them in hiding for days. Finally they reached the holdings of another loyal sympathizer, where Charles was apprised that Languedoc's few roads and passes were so heavily patrolled by his longtime foe, the *maréchal* de Foix, that they would never get through.

The only other direction that could deliver them out of France was to the north and west, where the routes were many and they could strike for Burgundy. But they would have to pass near Lyon to do this, and the duke thought even nine men were too many to slip through Francois' alert forces and a populace greedy for the reward.

Thus only he, Pompérant and Joyeuse fled towards Burgundy, Bourbon clad humbly, huddled into an old cloak and riding third, to be taken for the servant of the other two. They almost fell into the arms of the King's men several times, and other times managed to slip away before a few citizens acted on their suspicions. They dodged and circled and retraced their route across fields and marshes, sometimes sleeping in hayricks, but at last, hungry and bedraggled, the three finally crossed into Burgundy and safety.

Burgundy, unspoken ally of the Holy Roman Empire, was full of nobility opposed to Francois, staunch sympathizers who gladly provided for all of the *duc* de Bourbon's needs. Letters were carried into France to be discreetly delivered, and soon many of the Bourbon adherents who had been dispersed at Herent, and others, a good thousand of them, joined him in Besancon, and most of his gold was returned to him. But few were yet aware of how serious was his disadvantage.

In the northeastern province of Picardy troops and artillery awaited him, and in Madrid the Emperor had a great army straining to be released. But in neutral Burgundy Bourbon was merely a fugitive, stripped of most of his wealth, vast possessions and power. He was cut off, for the moment, with nothing, with only his name and a mere thousand men to offer in the service of the planned invasion of France.

As Bourbon stood on the battlements of the Château d'Aulair, in morose contemplation of Burgundy's green hills and leagues of vineyards spreading into the distance below, Joyeuse came up behind him, fully aware of his leader's perturbed state of mind. The marquis growled softly, "In five weeks we can make Mantua, where the duke Federico will certainly furnish you enough men to see us through safely to mercenary forces awaiting you near Neufchatel."

"Those mercenaries will want to be paid, paid in gold which I do not have enough of," Bourbon grated, "nor do I have anything left against which to borrow the gold from the duke Gonzaga to keep my forces from evaporating. *Peste,* how I wish Gonzaga was at our side. Don Ferrante easily raised several companies of seasoned fighters from around Lombardy in our last campaign together, and they followed him without levy of wages until the war was over. He could do it again, were he only here."

"The man is handling a more important task," Joyeuse reminded him. "Success in his quest will free you forever from needing the riches Francois has seized. I just hope his mission resolves swiftly."

"*If* the quest has any substance at all..." Bourbon muttered, rubbing the aching back of his neck.

"Ah, don't lose faith, monseigneur, it does, I feel in my bones that it does. Meanwhile, your kin in Mantua will furnish you enough to bring us to Neufchatel, and from there we can plan anew a safe route to Spain."

"Ah, yes? Fifty bags full of gold crowns? Will he give me that huge sum, unsecured?" the duke answered glumly. "Dispatch a swift messenger to Rennes-le-Château for news from Gonzaga. Perhaps they have already achieved success there, he and my niece and la Dame."

"Or at least uncovered a strong path to it," Joyeuse quickly modified his lord's desperate hope. "After all, the time has been very short, let us remember."

But Joyeuse understood his leader's deflated confidence, he knew the soul of a soldier, how a fighter's spirit trampled almost dead in the field of devious and vicious politics would rear up again, roaring, at the clink of spurs and the slam of a helmet visor and the beat of drums. What would revive Bourbon was a fully-armored charger under him, and to either side a great phalanx of steely, mounted men in a forest of lances and plumes and flapping standards, waiting in the dawn for enough light to attack the enemy at the fall of the duke's arm with its glinting sword.

Bourbon turned to face his second in command. "Don Ferrante cannot reach us, so we must reach him with a regular dispatch of messengers. Arrange it."

"I'll send de Rogier, monseigneur, he is wily, capable of riding all night and will not ask questions."

"Good. I need to know from Gonzaga what I can count on."

"Count on God. You have done your best and He has never deserted you. He will see you, He will see us all avenged, and our purposes achieved. *All* of them." Joyeuse' emphasis on the last phrase did not escape the duke.

Both men made the strange, quick symbol upon their chests, their eyes glinting in contemplation of a higher purpose than mere vengeance upon a perfidious king.

Chapter 12

The road to Rennes-le-Château spiralled and spiralled up to a high crest; and this road was at least four horses wide—more than the width a knight needed to carry his lance horizontally on his saddle, which was the ordinary measure of roads.

Nevertheless, Lyse rode hugging the wall of the hill, away from the precipitous drop. Below them in the summer haze the tranquil village of Couiza lay along the main route through the Razès, but their path was climbing so high Lyse believed they could see all the way back to Limoux, where they'd slept, if other hills weren't in the way. Above, up the coiling road, she caught a glimpse of a tower. White-faced goats scrabbling on the slope peered down at them with stoic acceptance of their presence. A little way behind them a single peasant plodded patiently, switch in hand, leading a cow.

Rounding a turn they came on the surprise of a square stone gate built to block the road, so that unless one could fly one must either pass through its iron-bound doors or go back. But the worm-eaten portals stood open, leaning crookedly on rusted hinges, the gate a relic of ancient times when the hamlet above was a thriving commercial town safely above the busy route.

They clopped through the gate, and then past the broken foundations of vanished ramparts. A hundred paces beyond the road widened into a tiny, hilltop village, silent in the white, midday sun, its little houses crowded up against the walls of what was obviously the old château. Ferrante halted the party before the manor's portal and summoned forward a guard to knock on it with the butt of his pike.

Lyse's heart was beating fast with anticipation. It seemed to her forever before a bent-backed servitor opened and let them ride into the courtyard, but there her heart plunged.

Eh bien, what did she expect? Certainly not Moulins: the area of the whole hilltop wasn't a sixteenth as large as the land under that great palace. It was not even St. Piteu, which was small, yes, but new. But even though there was no moat, she'd expected to see a roomy domicile and there wasn't one. Just a square, old tower and one truncated residence wing, all that remained of a large château which was now just a flat rubble mass, surely looted for stone. The jagged, burned marks of ancient calamity that scarred the side of the sheared portion of château were softened by the green of old climbing vines.

Hurrying toward them across the court and squinting in the sunlight was a gentleman with wispy hair and a mild face wreathed in smiles, wearing an old silk tunic reaching to the knees of his wrinkled hosen. He approached Lyse as she was being helped to dismount.

"I spied you coming from the tower. Welcome, welcome indeed to my house, Mademoiselle. I am Robert Voisin, the *Sieur* de Rennes-le-Château, and I am honored to receive a Bourbon here, it has been so very long a time," he rejoiced in a gentle, piping voice. "And welcome to you, Signore di Gonzaga, it is good to see you once more. We prepared all your quarters, so soon as the messenger announcing your coming reached us." He and Gonzaga bowed courteously to each other. "You must forgive that my lady has gone on an errand of mercy to a sick soul in our village, but she will return soon."

Spying the litter, shaded by a makeshift awning and being unslung from the donkeys, he asked, "Why, what is this, someone ill? Could that be Madame Elinor de Dunois?" He seemed slightly lame as he slowly walked to the carrier to stare at its pale occupant. "*Le bon Dieu,* not dead, is she?"

Ferrante answered. "No, Monsieur, she hit her head and lapsed into coma, for which we had no proper treatment in our need to move on. We pray you will have an experienced physician hereabouts who will help the lady recover her senses."

"We do, we do, but we must move the lady inside quickly, out of this heat, until my wife comes. She will know what to do."

The three followed the men carrying the litter into the house. The *sieur* turned to Lyse. "And you have been the comforting nurse, my dear Mademoiselle, all through the trying trip? God will reward you for your mercy, never fear. Now enter, good gentles, enter and rest you, and a fine dinner shall be ordered up to celebrate your arrival." With a courtly gesture the old-fashioned gentleman stood back so they might pass through the door before him.

They plunged from the brilliant day into the heavy shadows and welcome coolness of a large stone Great Hall. The sun's rays struggled to pass down into the interior through the grimy glass of high, clerestory windows, unwashed for decades, but they barely lit the dust motes floating about. The stabs of illumination were supplemented by candles guttering in several standing torchieres of iron. The walls were of dark and sweating stone, unadorned, the furnishings sparse and tattered. The place was gloomy, it had a defeated air of poverty and discomfort, and Lyse's heart just sank to her boots.

There was a rancid smell from the cheap tallow candles burning, mingled with stale odors of prior meals taken in the area and the animal aroma of three shaggy, uncombed dogs that shambled up with wagging tails. On either end of the great room were tall, blackened chimney pieces, and in front of one–a charming surprise–stood a pottery urn of fresh sunflowers, whose brilliant yellow pierced the murk like the hopeful face of the sun through clouds.

Looking around at the mournful space, Lyse realized this dilapidated, fusty-smelling house was where she might, by misfortune, spend years of her life. Her stare locked desperately to the flowers' splotch of color as if they could save her. She knew Don Ferrante was watching her and that her former, expectant smile had disappeared like ice in summer. She didn't care.

Their men carried de Dunois to a chamber and transferred her to a simple bed. Lyse put water to the woman's cracked lips and wrung out a soaked cloth to cool her narrow brow. She planned to return from her own accommodations in a few minutes to strip off her governess' clothing and wash the travel dust from her face.

Her chamber was right by, but Bourbon or not, no effort had given the stone-walled room much comfort. It held a bed with a threadbare bedcover and a lumpy mattress of old, clumpy down, a rustic chair, a pitcher and basin on a stool, with a small towel, a wicker basket for dirty linen, and an earthenware chamberpot. There was an undraped window in an embrasure where one could sit on a stone ledge, but only one shutter was swung back.

Even some of the simplest amenities usually offered honored guests were missing–no lamp or candelbranch, no mirror or adornment on the walls, no table, no small rug on the uneven, ochre tile floor, no painting or hanging, not even a cross.

And Lyse's own comfortable furnishings were with Germain and the servants–somewhere!

Promising to send a servant with bathwater, and sublimely unaware of the paucity of his offerings to a longterm guest, the *sieur* de Rennes-le-Château went smilingly off to lead the Mantuan and his valet to their quarters. Ferrante turned a moment and studied Lyse's dismay from under his black brows as she stood in the middle of her barren chamber, gave her a non-committal look and strode away.

Left alone, she immediately went to pry open the other window shutter, expecting if her bad fortune held, that the window would face a kitchen court. But it did not. It overlooked a peculiar melding of flower garden and a cramped graveyard belonging to a small, old church which sat just inside the walls of the château. The garden, undisciplined and unfettered, had been planted around and in between the raised sepulchers and worn, tilted head-stones, and a delightful mélange of floral scent drifted up to her, of roses, jasmine, delphinia, marguerites, and the rainbow of sweet peas edging them. There were even some weeping fig trees for shade and ornament.

Ordinarily Lyse would have been unhappy to face a burial ground from her window, but the beds of blossoms were so vivid and fragrant she felt heartened in response. At least there was somewhere to rest her eyes that didn't make her want to groan.

The servant who came to help with the invalid, whom Lyse had unclothed, was named Marye, a moody woman of middle years in a stained apron. She easily turned the limp and naked de Dunois to bathe her and rub her back with a damp cloth, and then lifted her to put a canvas under the sheets in case of accidents.

The prone governess, with her hair smoothed under a fresh white cap from her own box, and hands folded over the light sheet that covered her, looked peaceful and remote, actually too much like a corpse in a winding sheet. With aching heart Lyse stroked the narrow face, beginning to believe she was truly alone, and would never again hear the familiar, crisp voice rap out, "Lyse-Magdalene, that is enough!"

Going back in her own chamber with Marye, she was helped to scrub away the travel stains of three weeks and wash her hair, even perfuming the tepid water with a few drops of oil of rose the servant surprisingly dug from her apron pocket. The same was mixed into an ointment appearing from another pocket and applied to Lyse's poor abraded face, which had taken sun in spite of a wide straw brim bought in a town they passed. The lumpy bed was opened and while her hair dried Lyse lay down to rest before the afternoon meal. The servant shook out and hung on pegs the few garments Lyse had been able to pack along.

Charles de Bourbon's niece was glad there was no mirror. Her body was still scattered with yellowing bruises, her heels were rough and blistered from the stout shoes she'd been wearing for three weeks, her eyes ached from days of bright sun, her palms were rough and callused from the reins, for the new gloves bought to replace those lost in the frightful fall were too thin. She had no wish to see her face, still with scrapes and scratches healing, and most surely coarsened by the sun. Surely it was no face the viscount de Lugny would sigh for now.

Life was so full of pitfalls. To make up to her for being dragged away from Moulins she'd been taught to read, she'd been given more facts about the 'purpose' directing her life, and the veil had been drawn away from certain mysterious, fascinating emotions which she'd known little about. But it was Blackbeard, unfortunately, who had casually lifted that veil for her and then as casually, and callously, dropped it back, a situation of gall and wormwood to anyone in her position, she was sure. And now this—this decayed house in a remote area called the Razès—where her days would be spent...

Despondently studying the raftered ceiling, blackened in spots from centuries of rising soot from oil lamps, she finally fell into a depressed sleep.

The table, with only long benches for seating, was laid in the Hall. The three men were waiting for her: Ferrante di Gonzaga, combed and shaven and bluff, and Tournel, the sergeant of the Bourbon guards, a man of alert eyes and booming laugh; both strapping men in sharp contrast to their frail, greying host in his old-fashioned tunic.

All three bowed respectfully as she came towards them and immediately she felt better, for she spied their appreciation of her in their eyes. She gave them all a pretty smile, but she wasn't going to especially look to see Gonzaga's assessment of her modest toilette. He and she had been very careful with each other since his lapse of being drawn to her, very stiff and polite, in fact she had ridden alongside the litter most of the way, leaving him to point out certain features of the landscape to his equerry, Lucco.

The *sieur* led her to one of the few seats in the Hall, an x-chair with a tattered pillow, just vacated by one of the dogs. "My lady has returned and is making herself ready to receive our honored guests. She'll join us any minute," he piped up, cheerily. "Meanwhile, Mademoiselle, do take some cold cider to waken your appetite, it is fine stuff, shipped from Gascony."

A varlet shuffled over to present a painted wooden tray holding a sweating stoneware mug, which Lyse accepted gratefully. She'd taken only two swallows when the dogs exploded in barks and, tails wagging furiously, ran to a tall women who had stepped from an enclosed, spiral stair embedded in one corner.

"Ah, *la voilà*," their host beamed, "the chatelaine of my house, the keeper of my hearth," he burbled in his high voice, "the most perfect lady in this valley."

"Oh, be quiet, Robert," the woman husked, "you prattle like a slit-tongued raven."

Lyse stood up, for the dame de Rennes-le-Château was a formidable figure, and she was reminded of a caravel in full sail she'd once seen painted on a map, for the woman bore down on them as if the wind was at her back, chiffon a-flutter from the crown of her grey hat. In fact, she was more than formidable, she was—Lyse ransacked her mind for a word or two—very grandly exotic.

La Dame was almost all one color, from the eccentrically-puffed silver hair rising above her face, to her grey, dark-rimmed eyes, to her argent gown of some shimmery fabric. Even her skin, olive like a gypsy, seemed to have an underlying patina of silver that gave it a faint glisten. And where her smaller and older husband was self-effacing, la Dame most certainly was not.

She and Lyse both bowed to each other simultaneously—although Lyse was of higher station—and then the hostess approached to kiss her guest on the cheek and say, "I am Lora. You are very welcome to our house, Mademoiselle de Bourbon-Tonnière." Her voice was deep for a woman, forceful. Her words were courteous, but her strange eyes held no warmth.

La Dame continued, "Monsieur de Bourbon merely wrote he was sending his niece for a long stay. He did not say she was young. She inspected Lyse coolly. "*Mon Dieu, mon enfant,* but where did you scratch your face so?"

Then, without waiting for an answer, the lady shifted her attention to the Mantuan. "Ah, my dear Don Ferrante. It has been ten years, at least." Now the coolness in the silvery-grey eyes warmed as the women boldly scrutinized her male guest, the width of shoulders, the narrow waist—her gaze widening ever so slightly at the jutting, embroidered codpiece he had facetiously re-donned for the evening, a height of fashion not prevalent in the Languedoc.

Her lips curved in a smile. "So. The gangly youth of Mantua has meta-morphosed into a man, bearded and fierce..." She stepped closer to look into his eyes, almost directly, for she was unusually tall. "And handsome," she finished in a caressing voice.

"Why the brazen old malapert," Lyse thought, "she has thrown herself practically into his arms, and right there before her husband! And just look at that swaggerer, basking in her bold admiration. His face is so bronzed one couldn't see a blush even if he were modest enough to produce one." She wisely fought down her annoyance at la Dame's behaviour, however, for it was productive of nothing, but her impression that Lora Voisin was not the most retiring of ladies grew apace.

After Tournel was introduced, the five of them settled at one end of the long table, with the master of the house at the head. The food which the listing old butler served them was simple and spare, and the conversation general, of

Moulins and the king's visit, of their trip, of the almost fatal accident, at which recounting the *sieur* patted his heart in sympathetic fear.

Then la Dame remarked, "I looked in on poor Madame de Dunois before descending. She seemed peaceful enough in Marye's care. Too peaceful. I have already sent a boy to call in several healers this very day to examine her and determine which humors are in such huge imbalance in her body as to produce the senselessness of death."

"In Rodez we found a doctor who applied cups to her back and then bled her, but it did no good. In fact, she grew weaker," Lyse reported sadly. With little gusto she took up a spoonful of her turnip soup, made without meat.

Lora gave her a sharp glance. "Of course she would, from such treatment. Here in the Razès we leave one's blood in one's body where it needs to be, and try to cure the poisons in it with herbal reliefs. We have had enough success through the centuries to believe in the efficacy of our methods."

"We?"

Lora's smile was oily and immodest. "I have some interest in the curative properties of plants. Our healers find many species abounding here which herbalists elsewhere would put hand in fire to have. Rest your mind, I have known Elinor de Dunois in health, and with God's help we shall do our utmost to restore it to her."

Ferrante asked, "Speaking of plants, I've forgotten the name of that low shrub you grow in this area that produces your famous blue dye?"

"Ah, the *pastel? Mais oui*, it must be the soil, or properties of our water, for the plant will only flourish in the Aude Valley. Good for us, eh, my husband, a cash crop easily sold at advantageous prices to dyers of blue cloth from the north, from Flanders, even Germany."

The *sieur* looked up from the pepperless stew he was smacking his lips over. "Yes, a valuable crop. And we ourselves own some pastel fields below, near the river," he added.

Lyse thought sarcastically, "But not many fields, judging from the bedraggled looks of your domicile and its few servants." She pushed around the pieces of tough hare on her plate with a stub of bread, for she found the stew undercooked and thin, but at la Dame's glance remembered to smile weakly.

Sergeant Tournel was wiping his greasy lips on a napkin as Lora turned her intense gaze on him.

"Have you brought a few soldiers to remain here, sergeant, as monseigneur de Bourbon mentioned you would? "

"Fifteen horsemen, Madame, along with weapons."

A spasm of annoyance crossed her face. "Fifteen? Well, I don't know where we shall put them."

"*Ma chère,*" her husband soothed, patting her hand.

"As you can see, this house is not large, and the stables together with grooms quarters are more ruin than not, *malheureusement.* Can we billet some in the village?"

"They must remain here at Rennes-le-Château, Madame," Ferrante interrupted.

Her eyes bored through him. "But why should we need such an army here? It is calm in this province, nothing more than a theft or two by the gypsies, or a villain despoiling a farm girl to mar our peace." Her silvery gaze shifted to Tournel again. "I can tell you, sergeant, that we have watchers in certain places from where the road through the valley can be clearly viewed. No company of more than three, except merchants' trains of donkeys, comes into the Razès without the provosts of the towns being quickly informed."

"And what good would that do you if there *were* a large, unfriendly force approaching?" Ferrante drawled. "No lord in the Aude valley keeps more than a handful of men-at-arms."

"It is the warning we are after. We would not fight back, no, not anymore, but we could successfully escape with our lives and goods."

"And then we would turn to the *comte* de Toulouse for help, he is a friend, he would send troops—" the smiling *sieur* piped, a moustache of cream on his face from a sweet dish with sliced, fresh peaches.

But Lora glared at him and said something in the strange, guttural tongue of the region. He shrugged and subsided, withdrawing like a hurt child.

Lyse had selected a luscious and juicy peach—locally grown in this southern region, la Dame had said—and cut it up, wiping her fingers daintily on a napkin before popping the pieces into her mouth. Ferrante did the same, except he picked up the fruit pieces with the two-pronged fork he carried in a leather sheath on his belt. La Dame watched him handle the implement. "I just adore the niceties of Italians," she remarked, amused.

But Lyse clung to the last conversation. "We were more than three coming from Limoux and no one approached us."

"Our sentries are hidden, of course, but I had sent notice Monsieur Voisin and I were expecting a party. In fact, we here were made aware of exactly when you entered the valley, before you even reached Limoux. And we knew just when you set out from there, at dawn."

"You must have winged runners," Ferrante rumbled.

A sly smile played on her wide mouth, the lips too big to be beautiful. She laughed softly, "*Oui,* they are light on their feet." Then her grey eyebrow raised. "Nevertheless, the question remains, why so many pikemen? I presume it has to do with the king's strong accusations against the duke?"

"News has reached you?"

"Yes, of course, and of the reward for delivering him up. We are, after all, not distant from the territory of Gaston la Foix, whose men jealously patrol our Mediterranean ports and even our borders with Spain. A company of la Foix's men came through here last week with the pronouncement. The affair is shocking."

Ferrante contemplated her untroubled expression and wondered cynically how she meant it—shocking that the king should act so dastardly to the country's hero, or that Bourbon might actually be a traitor? When Bourbon and he had made a brief visit here as youths, Lora had often ignored Bourbon, turning her back on him, responding coldly to his questions. It had something to do with his father, Charles had explained vaguely because he wasn't sure himself, a broken promise, jealousy, female spite.

Still, her understandable supposition for the presence of guards fitted the explanation he'd given the loyal Tournel for the trip and the way they'd left Moulins. He offered it again now as emphasis: the duke feared there would be reprisals by Francois against his relatives.

La Dame stared at him steadily a moment with her calculating, dark-rimmed grey eyes, then, accepting his statement for the moment, turned to address Lyse smoothly. "We are not wealthy, Mademoiselle, and little is left to this château, but we will try to make you as comfortable as possible. And you too, signore. When it is cooler, before sundown, I will acquaint you, all three, with the rest of our mountain top."

Her husband beamed and nodded his head.

"You are kind, Madame," Lyse murmured, uncomfortable under the stabbing gaze of those deep-set eyes. No question but that Lora Voisin knew of their real reason for coming to Rennes-le-Château, for Lyse could see in the woman's scrutiny something of the unflattering judgement Ferrante di Gonzaga's eyes often held, that the 'seeing-back' made her peculiar, abnormal.

Retreating at the thought, she cast her eyes down at the table's cloth, and al-lowed the conversation, reminiscences of Gonzaga's first visit, to flow around her. And after, she gave polite, quiet answers to la Dame's innocuous questions about St. Piteu.

What grew even clearer to Lyse as she added up her impressions and what she already knew, was that she was the one the entire, strange plan, Bourbon's desperate strategy, was built on. And that her time of controlling the situation was coming.

The section of an arched, open-air gallery that still remained to the château was built out from the cliff, offering an incomparable view through its arches and over its waist-high balustrade, of the nearer peaks of the Pyrénées. The arches supported a flat roof whose beamed, inside surface was still brightly painted with geometric designs, the only bit of colorful old artistry still clinging to the ancient dwelling.

Here la Dame led the Mantuan in order to speak in private and find out what memories Bourbon-Tonnière had so far dredged up. He obligingly recounted them.

She nodded. "That she recalls Bernard de la Motte so intimately is an excellent sign. It was he, as we've known, who sent word of the Treasury's whereabouts to the Scots Templars."

"But do you recognize the name 'Mélline', Madame?"

She frowned a moment, then shook her silver head. "No. There is no writing I've seen which mentions such a woman. But this means nothing, since so many records were burned or buried or lost. But 'tis exciting, a new name in the mouth of one who 'sees-back'. This Mélline, this woman who wept so for de la Motte, could certainly hold the key, for she appears to have been entrusted with something she will not give up. We must diligently massage our young lady's memory, Signore—gently, *bien sûr.*

"Charles told me Lyse-Magdalene has had instances of recall quite often in the past year, those I've described to you, each small revelation leading to a larger revelation. And Madame de Dunois had mentioned that certain circumstances could sometimes produce the recall, although she neglected to say what circumstances. Yet on our journey here the lady remembered nothing."

Trailing her hand along the smooth stone balustrade, Lora drifted down the gallery and he followed. She drawled over her shoulder in her deep voice, "There are methods I've read about that might unlock a seer, but very unpleasant ones. I understand the girl's mother went completely mad, poor soul. Monseigneur *le duc* must have pressed that poor woman unbearably." There was a slight malice in the deep voice.

Ferrante's green eyes hardened. "He did all he could to save his sister, but Jeanne de Tonnière's memory jumped back constantly to a woman being horribly consumed in a fire, and so vividly did she 'see-back' that it caused her to writhe in pain and anguish. This violent memory could not be controlled, or stopped, and it finally tortured her to death."

The tall Dame turned sharply to face him. She was very close, her mouth twisted in a sardonic smile as she stared at him with her hypnotic, beckoning eyes. "And this new Bourbon seer, her daughter? Are you in love with the pretty maiden, my dashing *condottiere*?"

"Not at all," Ferrante clipped out, trading her stare for stare. "But I was ordered responsible for both her welfare and the quick success of our venture. If we fail to revive Madame de Dunois and what she thought might produce the recall, we'll have to find another way to stimulate Lyse-Magdalene's memories. Luckily, she clings to her own present identity more strongly than her mother did."

The exotic scent of sandalwood filled his nostrils as the woman seemed to sway towards him. She murmured, "Don't fear, I promise you we'll discover a path towards the goal. And I am happy you will remain with us a while, Don Ferrante, it becomes boring on this hill with only my blithering husband. I shall have to find ways to entertain you during your sojourn so that you will stay."

The silvery drapery fluttered in the breeze about her full body, her deep-set eyes seemed to draw him in towards her smiling lips. She reminded him of those marble statues of handsome Junoesque women he had seen, and in his deprived state the seduction in her gaze might have enticed him if a shiver did not sometimes run along his spine when she turned those strange eyes on him. Sometimes he had the sensation that there was no bottom to their silver depths, that one was seeing through to a vast, spiralling firmament of stars and planets where the back of her skull ought to be.

He'd had the same feeling ten years before, only then she'd not paid him much attention. It occurred to him la Dame hadn't changed at all in ten years. Her hair had been silver then, and outside of faint grooves between nose and chin there wasn't a mark or wrinkle on her smooth, olive face.

He and Bourbon had excitedly thought, on that first trip, that she was dabbling in sorcery, but it turned out to be just herbal medicines she was mixing that sometimes gave off a stink near the tower.

But the woman was a trustworthy member of their special cause and he had no wish to anger her. Overriding the enticing scent of sandalwood looped about him, he gave her his most engaging smile of thanks and took her elbow to steer her back into the gloom of her house.

"I look forward, Madame, to whatever pastimes you devise, I am at your disposal. But meanwhile, I would like to familiarize Mademoiselle with the area—which we hoped would act as a stimulant to her memory. This very day is not too soon to begin, in the remaining daylight before sunset, if you are free. She awaits word in her chamber."

Receiving this reminder of duty with good humor, la Dame stopped and reached with an insouciant finger to rub the gold victory medallion on his chest, which had been given to him by Charles. "Ah, very well. I see you are not to be turned from your task; amusement will have to wait. Since the doctors who will attend to Madame de Dunois must come from far, I shall have some time to take you about our hilltop, all that is left of the historical Rennes-le-Château. I agree that here is the logical place to start your experiment with her memory."

He widened his smile and made a sweeping bow of thanks.

"You are too kind, Madame."

Lora threw him a mocking, sideways glance and stepped ahead of him, her words coming back in a waft of sandalwood. "But of course. I have my duty too."

Lyse was disappointed as they rode slowly about the hilltop. There was little to set Rennes-le-Château apart from any tiny village, at least that one could notice: houses and small barns along the dirt road encircling the hillcrest, a simple little church called St. Pierre, some cows and goats and chickens, a round, old watchtower standing alone on an open piece of ground. The few householders they came across bowed their heads to la Dame, greeting her in that guttural tongue of the region Lyse realized was the Occitan Gonzaga had mentioned.

Nothing nudged her memory or even interested her eye. The dreaming Rennes-le-Château baked quietly in the summer heat and Lyse was glad she had hung her sun brim within easy reach.

Their hostess's voice mellowed as she recounted the history of the ancient site, which she obviously loved.

"From the beginning of time people have lived on this mount because it was at an important path crossing and its height made it easy to defend. The Gauls, the Romans, knew it as a good place for trading. Afterward, the clans coming from the north built a highly prosperous town here, running down the flanks of the hill in three directions.

"These Visigoths converted to Christianity, and all this early history was recorded by monks. They, in turn were defeated by Clovis, a Frankish king, which is why we have Merovingian tombs in our burial ground. Later, the large town that was here was captured by the Moors from Spain, and when they retreated, the area was restored to prominence by Charlemagne."

Looking about her as they stood before St. Pierre, la Dame did not seem to see how tilted the spire was on the roof of the old building. She continued with pride in her voice.

"A fine château was built on the top of the mount and Rennes-le-Château grew famous in the eleventh century of our Lord for its culture of French and Catalan extraction, its poets and troubadours, its refined and polished court; in fact this whole valley was deemed by many the most civilized part of western Europe, impressive for its openness of mind and thought. The *comte* de Toulouse, the most powerful of our lords, was virtually a king in his own right, and allowed his territory to be tolerant of certain unorthodoxies."

Unorthodoxies. A dangerous word, always, an intriguing word to capture a wandering mind such as Lyse's, for all she saw on the plateau was the broken château, the small church, and a poor little village.

"So then, what happened here?" she asked, and saw the sparkle in the strange, silvery eyes lose some luster.

La Dame's dappled grey horse whinnied, as if he were trying to answer. She patted his neck to calm him. "The usual calamities of our world, Mademoiselle, but closer in time to our day now, and so more sorrowful to us.

"Amongst the Languedociens of the twelfth century there was a people called Cathars, industrious, pacific Christians who did not honor some of the precepts of the Church of Rome." She looked sharply at Lyse. "Shall I suppose you know of the Cathars?"

At Lyse's puzzled shake of the head, the woman's eyebrow raised over her thin smile, but she went on. "Their priests, both men and women, were celibate, and they were called *parfaits*, perfects, because they were beings of great peace and asceticism. But they were suspected of heresy, these *parfaits* and all their brethren, for their sect, albeit honoring Christ, did not follow most of the Sacraments of the Roman Catholic church. They had only one official prayer, the Pater Noster, the Our Father. And there were other deviations, more serious—"

Beyond Lyse la Dame's glance took in the Mantuan's barely perceptible shake of the head. She shifted about in her side-saddle. "In short, to fully answer your question, over the generations the Cathars grew in such numbers and wealth, their ranks included so many of the regions finest nobility, that Pope Innocent took fright and announced a crusade to wipe out the 'Albigensian heresy' as he called it, after the city of Albi where they congregated. He launched a savage war to wipe all Cathars everywhere from the earth, hounding, arresting, pursuing, executing..."

The dramatic voice deepened. "Although the Cathars fought back against the armies and greedy adventurers coming from northern France—for many of these attackers were petty nobles inspired by land and booty for the taking, rather than religious zeal–the Cathars were captured and without mercy tortured and burned at the stake.

"The remainder fled to the hilltops of the Razès, to towns such as Rennes-le-Château, which had stout double walls then, and finally in the last resort, to those now-ruined, hard-to-reach eyries you must have seen on the mountain peaks. But even those fortresses could not endure forever against huge war machines that flung boulders to shatter their walls. In reality, it took more than one hundred years before all the Cathars were finally stamped out. Stamped out," she repeated harshly.

Lyse could swear that darts of silver flew from those hypnotic eyes at such a mortal attack by the church of the King of Peace. But an unwelcome thought caught at her. "My mother screamed of being burned on a pyre, although she did not know what person she was remembering so violently. But could that person have been a Cathar? Could there have been some Bourbon ancestors of mine so misled they embraced such apostasy?" Her glance shifted between them anxiously.

Ferrante answered. "It is hard to know that, for the Cathar writings and records were cast into the flames with them, and except for the most prominent of them, their very names are lost. The Bourbons at that time, you understand, were only minor landowners, not worthy of special notice."

"But if my mother recalled so violently the anguish of a woman consumed by fire over three hundred years ago who was not a Cathar, was that executed ancestress then a murderess? Or–a witch?" In spite of the heat a shiver ran through her.

La Dame twitched her reins and they had to follow her away from the church. "Probably neither witch nor Cathar," she answered dryly as Lyse rode beside her. "Some merciful, but deluded, Catholic faithful of the region offered temporary shelter to the fleeing heretics, but when discovered, they too were executed." Her lips twitched into a faint smile as she gazed straight ahead. "There are no more Cathars, of course. If there were, the Holy Office of the Inquisition would deal firmly with them."

Then a thought occurred to her and she looked over to Gonzaga soberly. "Merchants coming down for our dye from the Lowlands and Ghent tell us news that some months ago a German monk from Wittenberg dared publicly attack the Church and the Pope on the subject of indulgences, and that the monk is now agitating for a total reformation of the Church and the Holy See, and even of the Liturgy itself. And that in Germany his ideas are appealing to the people, so that they abandon their true priests and bishops in droves. Do you think it could be, Don Ferrante, that this is a resurgence of the dread Cathars?"

"I think not, Madame. The stubborn monk Luther merely demands Christian faith be based on the scriptures alone, with great reduction of church dogma such as issuance of indulgences, for one. The problem is that there are men in France who are receiving news of this rebellion with more than mere interest..."

Since the big Italian had heard various theologians in Paris expounding on the astonishing news of clerical rebellion in Leipzig and Worms and Wittenberg, he went on to tell what more he knew of this new religious strife. La Dame listened carefully.

But Lyse was bored, she did not understand the terms they were using, the subject sounded much too complicated. She preferred the simple faith in God and Christ which she had been taught, and remembering that the High Mass at the Château de Moulins' church had seemed to her too elaborate, the incense chokingly sweet, the grandeur too distracting.

Actually she would rather hear of the Templars, in whose name she had been brought to this place, and whose secret she must discover before she could return north, and before any grief could come to her uncle, Bourbon. She had begun to read the slim volume Don Ferrante had given her on those warrior-monks, and she was going to plow ahead in it as best she could, determined to know as much of the background of her memories as did the others around her.

The way curved and they were in sight of the château again–the whole tour atop the mount would have been an easy walk. The three of them were riding abreast, here and there displacing a few grimy children from their play in the middle of the road. In his long discourse on the growing influence of the German dissenter, Luther, Ferrante's dark head was turned from Lyse and towards la Dame, who hung on his every word. They both nodded gravely at each other from time to time and Lyse noticed how the woman's intense gaze seemed to devour the man, how her lips glistened wetly, how her silvery head inclined towards him so that the wide brim of her sunhat seemed to enclose them intimately, as if Lyse weren't there.

How disgusting, a woman of that age to flirt, and a married woman too!

Well, of what age? It was hard to tell, but la Dame was surely past her thirty-fifth birthday, and to Lyse that was a crone. Well, she wasn't surprised by the Italian's indiscriminate attention to their hostess. In the saucy opinion of Renée, the cook's daughter at St. Piteu, men who spent their lives on the battlefields skewering enemies or being skewered in turn, had only one wish, to skewer whatever female on two legs came within a hand's distance of their cod.

Annoyed that she was feeling so ignored, Lyse-Magdalene didn't realize that out of the blue she was humming a little tune she'd learned from Germain, a ditty about love being fair as a spring apple blossom, and that she was humming it louder and louder until she automatically began to sing it, unaware that the startled gaze and attention of her companions had finally swung to her.

As they stepped out of a door onto the roof of the château's square tower where the Voisins kept their personal chambers, the Mantuan and la Dame halted in mid-stride, for Lyse-Magdalene had uttered a strangled cry and raced to the parapet of the wooden platform which girdled the tall, old structure. Her body was stiff as a pole and her profile rigid, its pure lines eerily lit by the setting orange sun as she stared down at the courtyard below and its closed gates.

Ferrante moved to go to her, but la Dame's hand shot out to restrain him.

Ferrante had never been present when the memories gripped Lyse-Magdalene, but he guessed that was what was occurring now. Transfixed, he watched the young woman, whose wide-open eyes did not move or blink, whose lips were parted as if in a silent gasp, who seemed not to be even breathing as she saw in her mind's eye certain people moving across the broken flagstones of the entry court that were not visible to them. Her staring rigidity both fascinated and repelled him, it was abnormal, it was a curse. Could it possibly be that the girl was actually a damned soul trapped in a febrile mind by the very Prince of Darkness?

For one moment he squinted his eyes almost shut to dislodge the unworthy thought, he truly couldn't believe that she was damned, and 'peculiar' or not, for Bourbon's sake they were lucky to have her.

The two stood rooted for several minutes, allowing the 'seeing one' her latitude. The sparkle of a tear finally ran down the girl's face, and then another, and still she did not move. La Dame's grip to restrain him was surprisingly strong on Ferrante's arm, but when a bird cheeped loudly and Lyse turned about, blinking through tears, he broke the woman's grip in an instant to go to the weeping instrument of their hope. And a good thing, for Lyse almost crumpled; he caught her by the shoulders to hold her up.

She peered at him through wet, stricken eyes. "Don't go, I beg you don't go—" she whispered in agitation.

"I'm not going anywhere, Mademoiselle," he tried to calm her.

She blinked again, strongly, focusing better. "Oh! Don Ferrante. 'Tis you.

I thought–" She cut off, but leaned more weakly against him.

"Bring her in here," la Dame ordered, and Ferrante half-carried the distressed girl back into the tower chamber, a large and incredibly cluttered room with layers of acrid odors mingled together, and they eased her into a chair.

This was their hostess's own lair. Books and old rolls of parchment were everywhere, on the big table, stacked on the floor against the walls, on the cold hearth. There was a large globe in a mahogany mount, and a stuffed fox. A jumble of bottles and beakers and jars of different, crushed ingredients, and colored liquids and unguents littered every surface, along with mixing spoons, spatulas and a small charcoal brazier. In one corner, a dishevelled bed that didn't seem to belong there.

La Dame poured some water into a horn cup and handed it to Lyse. Ferrante knelt by her chair and looked up into her pale face. "What was it? What did you remember just then?" He tried to keep avid interrogation from his voice, not wishing to frighten her.

But tears again filled the shocked eyes, eyes which recalled to him a rain-washed, blue sky.

Lyse quavered, "That lurid sunset! I have seen it before, and from that very rampart, in a memory I had of Mélline and her husband watching a party of riders depart. The minute we emerged onto the parapet I remembered again, so vividly that in an instant you and the Lady, even the Bourbon guards below watering their horses by the trough, disappeared, and I was again seeing the Knight-Templar Bernard de la Motte ride away. Through that very gate," she gasped.

Lyse looked down into Ferrante's eyes as he knelt there in a sort of silent appeal to him. "And my–Mélline's heart was breaking in two because she feared they would never meet again, she and Bernard, and she feared for his life. She cared nothing for the coffers of the Treasury he and her stepson were transporting–Oh!" With a harsh indrawn breath she caught at the word which had slipped from her. "The Templar Treasury! That is what was bulking under the canvas of that great wagon. Mélline knew that!"

La Dame stepped into her line of sight, her insistent words hammering into Lyse's brain. "And where were they taking the treasure, Mademoiselle Lyse-Magdalene? Tell us!"

Lyse struggled to dig into her mind, grimacing in concentration, but finally had to whisper, "I don't know."

The olive gypsy-face under the burst of silver hair relaxed. La Dame's smile was sardonic. "*Mais ma chère*, that is the point, is it not? To remember what was done with that huge Treasury?"

"I can't control what I remember, and it's always very short, the seeing-back," Lyse defended herself. She turned back to Ferrante as the lesser of two evils. "It was such a shock to actually be on this balcony, to be in the unknown place I had seen in my head from so far away."

"But that is a victory, it is just what we hoped would happen here," he encouraged her. "The rest will come in time."

She nodded tentatively. "But...there was something else that came into my head—that those departing riders weren't going to Le Bézu as the old man thought. Mélline knew that, even if her husband didn't. And... and, her husband's name was...Voisins?" Her voice quavered.

La Dame nodded, drawn into the drama in spite of herself. "Indeed, my husband's family has been here that long. The original Voisins, living much earlier than your visions, was given this property as reward by the general Simon de Monfort, who was the scourge of the Cathars—an ironic occurrence of which you may learn, sometime."

But Ferrante saw Lyse had retreated, her expression wooden, suffering the emotional toll the recall had wrung from her. He tried to be gentle. "Lyse-Magdalene, do you believe Mélline knew where they were really taking that freight the night they rode out from here?"

She was staring at the floor. "Everything that Bernard de la Motte knew, she knew. They were one, one breath, one heart, one life between them."

"How sentimental," la Dame husked.

"Her grief as he departed billowed up the same as his white cloak with its symbol of the blood cross, it rose in her enormous and choking, and yet she couldn't even whimper of it with her husband standing beside her." The tears slipped down again. "She loved de la Motte so desperately."

Ferrante's strong, bronzed fingers gently wiped away the tears on her smooth cheeks. "You must not weep for her, Lyse-Magdalene. The lady is long gone. She is not you."

In her head Lyse cried, "But you don't understand. I killed him. No... She killed him!" Nevertheless she was grateful for the Mantuan's sympathy. The embarrassment, the helpless, mortifying feeling of being possessed that always engulfed Lyse in recounting the uncontrollable 'seeing-back' receded under his comforting words. "But I seem to suffer Mélline's great grief whenever my memory recalls her," she told him wearily. "As if it were my own."

La Dame's rich drawl broke the connection that was forming between Lyse and her reluctant sympathizer. "*Sainte Vierge,* that is better than suffering the bodily torment of an executioner's hot pyre, like your mother. Do you not agree, Don Ferrante?"

Ferrante merely scowled at the woman for her callousness. He asked, "Lyse, do you recognize this room we are now in, perhaps? Could it have been Mélline's?"

"No, it is not familiar." Lyse gazed around again at the aromatic clutter, noticing various things for the first time, including the rows of glass jars. Then, desperately wanting to get the attention off her she remarked, "But you have a large collection of dried flowers and herbs, Madame Voisin."

"I enjoy making scents and perfumes, and luckily flowers grow in these parts most of the year." La Dame took the cup from Lyse's hand. "Come along, Mademoiselle, since you seem about recovered. There is only the outside gallery left to acquaint you with, and the doctors who should be arriving momentarily will want my attention."

They followed her fluttering robes down a spiral stair of worn stone treads and then went through a door in the hall onto the long gallery, a veranda which had been constructed centuries before to access the breathtaking view from the hilltop.

Lyse saw that they were dwarfed on their gallery by the vastness of the tinted sky around them, and the rugged, mountainous land visible in all directions. Over their heads two kestrel hawks wheeled and wheeled, calling in their high, keening whistles, and down below them goat bells clanked irregularly from the brush on the hill. Nevertheless, Lyse again felt this breathless silence over the land that she had noticed before as they had ridden along the Aude valley, as if some ill will was sucking away all the sound. Oppressive and conspiratorial, the perceived silence made one want to whisper.

They were gazing south into a wilderness of high purple mountains which jutted up ever taller as their ranks marched away to blend into the distant Pyrénées. There seemed little to view from their eyrie but nature's eternal granite and pines and piping birds, but Lyse shielded her eyes to better see, barely discernible on the edge of one distant mount, a collection of jagged shapes, like white bones jutting through the mountain's skin of rock.

"What is that?" She pointed.

"That, Mademoiselle, is Le Bézu." Glancing sidewise at her guest, la Dame paused pointedly to let the statement sink in. "It was one of the last strongholds where the remaining Knights-Templar took refuge from all over France to avoid arrest by the forces of King Phillip the Handsome. 'Tis said the Templars destroyed much of it themselves when they finally surrendered."

Lyse bit her lip. "I don't understand. Why were the Templars so persecuted?

Were they involved with the Cathar heretics? It's so mixed up." She felt angry for feeling stupid.

"Don't you know anything of the Templars either?" la Dame purred facetiously.

Ferrante hastily took over the talc. "No, Mademoiselle, it was a different time, it was a century after the last remnant of the Cathars were slain that the Knights-Templar were outlawed," he answered. "'Tis strange, but as remote as this region is from the great centers of power, it has seen much historical turmoil."

With a hidden shiver Lyse stared again at the distant Bézu, which seemed to her the loneliest of the gaunt ruins they'd seen on various peaks to either side of the river valley. "Will we go up there? Perhaps something there will speak a message to me?"

"Le Bézu is inaccessible. The Templars destroyed part of the route up, and Phillipe le Bel's forces finished it off. There have been intrepid climbers who scaled the heights and searched in the ruins, even though many fell to their deaths from the treacherous rocks. Each generation a handful of hunters reaches Bézu with pick and shovel, but nothing, neither gold nor silver has ever been found. Not one *sol*. Not even a button or buckle left behind. There is nothing there but spectres."

The three gazed for a long, bleak moment at the tragic remains of the gutted preceptory, perched on a unique ridge of rock shaped like the prow of a ship. Then Lyse emphasized in an even voice, "There never was anything to find. The Treasury never went there."

They stared at her.

But a cough sounded behind them and the shuffling varlet who had served them dinner announced the arrival of two of the doctors from Esperaza.

La Dame said, "Ah, good. I shall leave you now to attend to reviving poor Madame de Dunois. Pray be at home in my house. We all shall take supper at six in the Hall, but the *sieur* and I retire early. I'm afraid there is little of entertainment here." It was a statement, not an apology. The lady looked from one to the other of her new guests, the darkly handsome, looming Italian and the fair and virginal young woman and said with a smile full of innuendo. "You shall have to make your own."

Then the chatelaine of Rennes-le-Château parted from them as she had first arrived, a silvery, full-blown ship trailing back a wake of sandalwood scent.

"I'm not fond of that woman," Lyse muttered, allowing her irritation to show, finally.

"Hah, it's merely her way, her sarcasm. Lora Voisins won't harm you. And you can trust her implicitly."

"Anyway, I shall put my mind to reading the book on the Knights-Templar you gave me. May we talk of them when I've finished it?"

"But I can just tell you of them. It will be faster."

"No. I want to read for myself. And consider and think about what I read. I'll be swift."

He nodded, bemused, impressed again with her quick intelligence. "Your servant, Mademoiselle," he smiled.

She stood close enough that he could admire the fine-grained, satin skin over her cheekbones, and the small but lush mouth which always drew him.

She put a light hand on his sleeve, the mercurial ways of young woman-hood producing an arch glance and teasing smile. "You have turned out a fine professor, Signore. And so, since–la Dame admits there's little to do here in this gloomy manse–now might you teach me how to write?" With a chime of a laugh for her temerity she did not await an answer but made a quick curtsey and left him to return to the house, where she would probably demand entry to the sickroom, doctors or not.

But Ferrante lingered on the gallery, turning again to the impressive view, his thoughts a muddle of impatient regret, frustration with the various loyal-ties that had brought him here, doubt even now that the project was going to be worth anything, and more immediate, the realization that la Dame was right, all they had to amuse themselves atop this remote hill was each other.

Peste!

Chapter 13

Although his looks were unprepossessing, Giles Matz, overseer of St. Piteu, was not easily intimidated as he faced the two gentlemen in half armor who had burst into the house with their soldiers and arrogantly interrupted him from his supper. The *intendant* took a quick swipe at his lips, shoved the kerchief into his sleeve and answered them calmly. "I regret, Messieurs, but Mademoiselle de Bourbon-Tonnière is not here. She has been at the Château de Moulins for a number of months now."

De Marques looked at him with a cold smile. "Is that so? What's your name, *mon homme*?"

"Giles Matz, Monsieur. I am the *intendant* of this domain for the *Duc* de Bourbon."

"No longer for him, Matz. St. Piteu and its dependencies have been legally seized by the Throne, and are now royal property. Here, I present you the sequester order, signed by His Majesty." De Marques proffered a square-folded document with several official ribbons and seals dangling from it, which Matz took and scanned.

"It seems to be in order," the *intendant* agreed quietly, for he was not surprised. Everyone in the province knew the duke was being hunted as a traitor, and when Germain arrived several weeks before with the maidservant dressed in Bourbon-Tonniére's clothes, he had brought detailed news of the whole debacle. It stood to reason that the duke's land was being seized and close relatives such as his niece fleeing the country.

"Yes, perfectly in order. So you will remain at your post and operate exactly as always, except now receipts of rents and harvest are to be sent to the Royal Seneschal in Bourges. That man there," he jerked a thumb behind him at a soberly-dressed functionary with a leather portfolio, "is an auditor with the royal counting house, who will remain at St. Piteu until he has made a complete inventory of land and goods. Is this understood?"

"*Oui*, Monsieur."

"Very well. Then, in the name of His Majesty Francois Premier of France,

I demand you now bring forth Mademoiselle de Bourbon-Tonnière."

Matz's large adam's apple bobbed but he did not hesitate to answer de Marques and his companion, the *vicomte* de Lugny. "I truly regret, Monsieur, but the lady is at Moulins. She is not here."

De Marques boot heels struck the Hall floor hard as he strode over to grab the front of the *intendant's* dark doublet and yank him forward. "She was followed here from Moulins two weeks ago and my information is that no one has left the property. I wish to speak with the lady. Now."

Sweat broke out on Matz's brow, but otherwise he remained unflustered. "I simply cannot help you, Monsieur, all I know is that the lady has been residing at Moulins."

Frustrated, De Marques drew back a cocked fist to punch the stubborn *intendant* in the face, but de Lugny stepped in, softer-voiced.

"*Intendant*, the lady left Moulins recently in a party with her squire, a fellow with the same name as yours. He is reported to be here now, at St. Piteu. Call him to us, then, and do not consider lying if you wish to keep your skin in one piece."

"Ah, my son? Well, ah, you see..." Matz hesitated now, not having thought a plan would be needed to protect Germain from aggressive representatives of the king.

But a forthright voice announced "I am here, Monsieur," and Germain's sturdy form stepped from a doorway behind them as they turned. He doffed his felt hat.

De Marques gave a snort of recognition. "So there you are, you filthy liar, duping my men into a fool's goose chase. Where is your mistress?"

"In truth, I have no idea, Monsieur."

"You dare lie again? We have men watching this house and Bourbon-Tonnière has been spied every day crossing the outer court."

Germain scratched his spiky-haired head and tried to look stupid. "Eh, I don't know, Monsieur. But we have a maidservant of my mistress's height and coloring to whom she had given her cast-off clothes. Perhaps your informant saw this girl in her lady's finery. Nevertheless, Mademoiselle is not at St. Piteu. When I left Moulins with the servants, as Monseigneur le *Duc* ordered, she was not with us."

The senior Matz injected, "I beg you, Monsieur *le Comte*, if you do not believe us, feel free to search through the house, wherever you will."

De Lugny was riled with Germain. "Your behaviour is unacceptable, Matz. You lied to us about where and when your mistress was departing from

Moulins, and now we're to believe you came back here without her, she who has been missing from Moulins since that very night? And if you were merely a lure to draw off anyone wishing to follow her? Then where did she go? Where is she now?"

Germain turned out his hands and gave a slow-witted shrug. "But I don't know. See, Messieurs, I spoke to you straight at Moulins that day, but later the duke changed his orders to me. I was commanded to leave Moulins with the servants and the old nurse, and I was told only that Mademoiselle was being taken elsewhere."

De Marques pocked face shoved itself into his. With a shock Germain heard a rip and felt a sharp sting below his ribs: the man was pressing the tip of a small poignard into his side.

"Where!"

His father tried to intercede. "I swear to you, he has no idea. The duke does not take him into his confidence, he is only my son, an underling."

De Marques only pressed harder with the knife tip, gripping Germain by the arm. "Why would I believe that? Now tell us where that woman was taken or I'll carve my coat-of-arms on your guts!"

Germain, in fact, did not know exactly where Lyse-Magdalene was, although he'd been preparing to get her baggage and Gonzaga's gear quickly down to Clermont, where it was arranged that someone would be waiting to meet him. The only road to St. Piteu, which ended at the house, offered a thick stand of trees from where, Germain had discovered, the men who had trailed him remained to watch the manor. So during the nights Germain had bumped the baggage in carts right across the rough meadows and fields behind the house, hiding the clothes hampers and collapsed beds under the farm implements and sacks of millet destined as donations to the nearby Priory. The maid who wore Lyse's clothes, had been deliberately set to stroll about in the court near the wrought iron gates every day for a false impression.

From the Priory, which he believed wasn't watched, Germain was planning to soon ride out, integrating his laden pack animals into a travel group from the chapter who were departing to visit their motherhouse, the great Abbey at Souvigny.

De Marques pressed the dagger in harder. Germain clamped his lips against crying out and held his temper, even though he felt with alarm a warm trickle of blood sliding down his ribs. He was certain he could take on the solid, pock-faced Comte in a wrestle and still come out of it, but a knife under his heart was another matter.

He whined, "Monsieur, I am deeply devoted to Mademoiselle. Do you not think I am devastated to be thrown from her life in this manner, sent back to St. Piteu with her old nurse as of no value, and given no inkling at all as to what Monseigneur was doing with her?"

He allowed a tremble into his voice. "You may kill me, you may push that dagger so far into my side that I die, but as our dear Lord and the Blessed Virgin are my witness, I do not know where she is, nor does anyone here." And in fact, such was the truth.

The icy eyes bored through him, the sharp steel inched a bit deeper, and a dark blotch appeared on Germain's doublet. Then the knife was withdrawn. Deliberately de Marque wiped the dagger tip on Germain's sleeve, then let him go.

From behind them there was a small sigh from the *intendant*, who then volunteered, "Monsieur, if the lady is missing, she is most probably with her uncle, Monseigneur de Bourbon."

"Pah, she is not, he moves too swiftly, he eludes justice with the slickness of a weasel, impossible with a woman and her entourage in tow."

De Marques strode further into the Hall to look about, calling over his shoulder to his sergeant, "Dionne, see every cranny of this entire estate is searched for Bourbon-Tonnière, who has a fair face and hair like burnished copper. In fact, fetch here every woman from laundress to scullery maid for Monsieur de Lugny to inspect. Now you, younger Matz, bring me that nurse of hers you mentioned, I hope the woman will have better sense than to delay a royal inquiry. *Intendant*, bring food for us. See it is hot. And wine, your best. And something to dampen my throat right now."

He turned and unleashed a snarl at father and son. "If that woman is now discovered here, you'll be taken as prisoners to the cells at La Marse and after especially painful attention, left to rot there. And if I find her elsewhere and discover you lied in your teeth about knowing where she is, you will wish the hungry rats in a deep '*oubliette*' were your only fate."

As Matz hurried out with a guard, de Marques muttered to de Lugny, "If that young dolt truly has been used as a lure, they'd be stupid to tell him where they have spirited the wench. But putting fear into the lout's head doesn't hurt."

It took two soldiers to support the sodden nurse before de Marques, who, brandy goblet in hand, paced before a trestle table hastily set up to feed him and his party. The old woman, knees buckling, head shaking, was dragged up close to him so he could hear her mumbled reply to his demands. He drew back.

"Pfah, she stinks! And what's wrong with her?"

"Dead drunk, Monsieur. In the chamber where we found her she was screaming about great roaches crawling on her. There were none."

Germain was standing a few paces away.

"Matz! Is this one of the women who raised Bourbon-Tonnière? Lived with her all these years?" de Marques barked.

Germain nodded.

De Lugny put in, "But this old sot means little. The one of importance is her governess, de Dunois, who must be with her. That old gargoyle would never let the damsel out of her sight." He made a *moué* with his mouth, remembering his chagrin with the interference of his courting.

De Marques yanked up Nurse's lolling head by the crooked, white head-dress that was tied under her wrinkled chin. "Listen to me, woman, tell me where your mistress was taken, and by whom, and I will give you five big jugs of the finest tokay wine in France, eh? And a full stoup of ale, all your own. To last you the rest of your life! I swear it. Now, be good and tell me where is your mistress!"

Nurse's wrinkled eyes widened, finally focused and stared. "Five jugs!" she croaked in amazement, and hiccuped loudly. She opened her mouth as if to speak more, but instead, with a helpless retch, she bent forward and vomited over the *comte's* high boots.

Blood like evil fire rushed to suffuse the man's pocked face. With a violent curse, de Marques tore the sagging old crone from the men supporting her and slammed her several times into the stone edge of the chimney piece, as one would beat a dirty rug. There was a terrible crack of bone as her skull hit the stone and the bleeding old woman collapsed into a heap like a pile of dirty wash.

Suppressing a horrified groan, Germain immediately signaled the varlets who had brought in food to run with their towels and swab off the *comte's* boots. But the furious de Marques, stepping from the splat of vomit, grabbed a towel and threw it into Germain's face. "No, you do it, pig shit!"

Unemotionally Germain knelt at the man's feet and began wiping off the sour spew.

A soldier nudged Nurse's boney body with his toe as it lay, the head in a pool of gore and blood, the rumpled wimple soaked red. "She's dead, Monsieur."

De Marques, looking down at Germain's ministrations with an ugly smile, shrugged. "What matter? That broken-veined souse has drowned herself in an ale-pot for years, she wouldn't have remembered what she gummed for breakfast, no less where Bourbon's niece is. When my belly is full, whoreson, find us beds. Of good comfort, no fleas, no lice. We will leave at dawn."

He added coldly to Germain, "Listen, *crottin,* I don't believe you. But we are on His Majesty's business and I haven't time to waste squeezing answers out of you. We will find your mistress, soon. If we don't, rest assured I will be back to greet you kindly again, and your father. Now get your damned arse out of my sight."

As they wolfed down their food, de Marques growled to the *vicomte,* "The bitch is nowhere to be found in the Bourbonnais. So it had to be she left with those religious pilgrims that morning, then broke with them to travel the route where your man just 'happened' to break his neck. And I have a good idea in whose care she was placed—'tis a case of the similarly vanishing Italian, just when I had set my heart on bringing the whoreson coward down. Send a fast rider back to my brother, de Guise, and tell him he was right, the woman has probably gone south, and so will we. Bourbon has a fistful of fortified castles throughout the Auvergne that could have swallowed her up."

De Lugny nodded. But he wondered why Louis never mentioned that the youngest Lorraine brother had covertly arrived just after the King's celebration at Moulins and the very next day slipped away through the south barbican with only two companions. It was de Lugny's gossipy network of informants who had told him this, but he soon began to think the frustrated de Marques knew nothing at all about his brother's arrival and hasty departure.

Chapter 14

She was close to waking up.

She was well aware it was morning, but she had clung hard to sleep because it was so sweet. She cuddled closer to the smooth, naked chest of the sleeping man beside her, the strength of him drawing her, the heat of him arousing her lazy limbs, the leather and soap scent of his skin sending happiness flooding through her. In the thrall of love, she pressed worshipping lips to the side of his chest, but as lightly as she could, not to awaken him, who had ridden so gallantly long in the saddle to reach her yesterday—and had done the same last night in this bed. She wished him not to move his warmth one iota away from her languid, grateful body.

She had one arm flung across the rise of his chest and the two of them were breathing in unison, long, dreaming breaths that spoke, for the first time of no press of hours, no outer world in clamor. She had plenty of time before opening her eyes to savor and tell over like rosary beads the astounding heights of passion he had called up in her body and released. The very memory of her unblushing abandon with him, her wildness in seeking his deepest heart, made her quiver.

Quickened by her own lascivious thoughts, she kissed him lightly again on the rib she snuggled against, and wondered what blessing of God had brought this gift of love into her lonely life.

And then she felt his hand moving slowly on her back, lightly, as he came awake, moving lovingly down her spine and warmly onto her curled haunches. Somehow she knew his eyes were still closed, just like hers, and although she couldn't hear his heart for she was on the wrong side, she knew it was beating fast, ever faster, like hers. She passed her hand over the crisp, dark matting on his breast and up along the powerful tendons of his neck.

The arm around her could only reach to the side of her bosom, but the fingers partially slipped under the fold of her breast and moved, caressing her, making her nipples stiffen.

"You like that, sweet?" Came his confident, sleepy whisper. "So do I."

Still, she would not stir, or look up, for her hair was too tangled, her face surely blotchy, nor did she need to look at him, she could see his dark hair and engaging smile against the lids of her eyes. His visage, his essence were engraved on her heart for eternity. How long they had yearned for each other, how deep had been the silent concourse of their eyes at every meeting, until this chance arose.

Her hips moved against him in wordless need and as naturally he responded, carefully rolling his naked warmth over on her. She felt him hard against her belly, and her every nerve and muscle shot their hunger to her burning place below. Ah Jesu, how she loved him, she was shaking with desire

A huge explosion of noise!

The warmth against Lyse jumped up and was gone, the arms, the body, the pleasure quivering in her for release vanished into smoke! She surged up gasping, tangled in the sheet but fully awake now as the great dog that had been sleeping against her bounded barking to the window to attack a squirrel chattering on the ledge.

A terrible sense of loss dragged her down, who had been just moments before so close to joy. She suffered a pang of deep disappointment and unfocused anger.

At a dream? At a stupid dream caused by that tangled hound who had somehow sneaked into her chamber and leaped up to share the bed with her?

But had it been merely a dream?

No. It had been too vivid, too immediate, Lyse could feel the throbbing still between her thighs. It had been a 'seeing-back', a vivid memory, it was Mélline with her Templar, Bernard, happy and pleasured together, before whatever evil befell them had occurred! The fullness of love in Mélline's heart was still with her too.

Lyse glared at the wall, dumbly jealous of such love and such response by the ghosts in her head.

Finally she swung her feet over the edge of the bed, shoving away the dog, which had lost the squirrel and was trying now to lick her hand. She was intent on dispelling the pain of emotional frustration—for if the dog hadn't woken up howling, the next moment her dream might have given her something incredible, even if she wasn't sure just what. Nevertheless, she tried to separate that disappointment from the residue of Mélline's happiness still within her, a happier state to hold onto.

She succeeded in a way. When Marye came in with a sweet bread and barley tea, and in her strange Occitan language indignantly shooed the lolling-tongued animal out, Lyse was smiling. *Eh bien,* also because it was a lovely, cool morning, and the breeze had turned, bringing through her window the strong, heady scent of heliotrope from the graveyard garden.

And especially because Blackbeard had finally given in and was taking her today on the long ride to see Le Bézu from as close up as possible.

By the time she had donned her riding garb, with Marye's help, she felt normal, and even courageous enough to nail up a clear command in her head, 'Stay away, Mélline! For the sake of God, I do not wish to experience either your bitter grief or your adoring ecstasy, you are wearing me out with both. You have had your life. Now give me the secret to the Treasury and free me to live my own!'

She felt guilty though for the selfish wish. Perhaps her poor ancestress had in her life had suffered torture because she would not give up the knowledge forced upon her.

Informed that Don Ferrante was waiting impatiently in the Great Hall, she turned in her doorway for a moment to scan the room, and immediately knew it was here, at Rennes le Château, but definitely not in this chamber, where Mélline had entertained her knight. Her eyes widened as it swept into her mind that it was a much smaller room, a stuffy space with a low ceiling, like a nun's cell, and that the couch where love had so transported her ancestress was merely a wide, straw pallet upon which a thin mattress and velvet coverlet had been flung.

So where was it, that tiny chamber, where Mélline seemed not to fear intrusion, of discovery by her husband? It must have been a hidden room, still hidden now like the whereabouts of the Treasury, wrapped in secrecy and silence like so much else in the valley.

They had been at Rennes-le-Château over a month now, it was well into the summer. Madame de Dunois was still unconscious, in spite of the strong draughts poured down her throat, the smelly pastes rubbed into her spine, neck and temples, the burning of certain plants to make an aromatic but choking smoke. Two tables had been moved into the sickroom and were covered with the paraphernalia for making medicinal drugs: vials and jars and big wooden syringes, and they were worked at almost every day by one herbalist or another.

Lyse mostly languished about, much missing the company of the lady who raised her, poor de Dunois, as well she missed Germain and old Nurse. And not many flashes of ancient memories had come to her in this place, except the same ones, repeated.

Some days she strolled about the hilltop with Gonzaga, peering here and there amongst the houses, looking into Sainte-Magdalene, the château's own

ruined and unused chapel, parts of which were built in the remote ninth
century, and even following brush-obscured goat tracks partway down the
slope. They wandered in the graveyard among the flowers several times, stooping
to read the tilted headstones, and they always paused long before a humped,
earthen rise with steps going down to a tomb door, the iron portal marked
with unreadable runes and the name 'Blanchefort'.

But nothing seemed significant to Lyse, or brought a memory.

La Dame disliked leaving her hilltop except to aid the sick in nearby
towns, so Lyse also rode about the countryside with only two companions,
Gonzaga and the old *sieur*, who welcomed the distraction of playing guide.

Just past Couiza, the town at the foot of Rennes-le-Château's hill, a small
rise held the broken shell a castle called Coustaussa. The ruin was easily
explored, yet yielded nothing to Lyse but that same sense of stillness, the arrest
in time that, to her, pervaded the whole Razès. The Occitan-speaking peasants
in the area had no notion who had first built this château for the defense of
Couiza, they only knew it had been destroyed in the crusade against the
Cathars, and that it and some of the prosperous little towns of the region with
strange names that were relics of the Spanish-Catalan invasions, sat on land
belonging to the *marquis* de Joyeuse.

The *sieur* took his visitors every day upon a different path: into the
towns; into the hills to see the half-hidden, worked out and abandoned gold
mines, rediscovered every quarter century by avid, unsuccessful hunters of lost
treasures; and through the vineyards and across fallow fields to reach hills
honeycombed with grottoes. These high-roofed caverns of dripping stalactites
stretched away from their thresholds into stygian darkness, and as they peered
into them de Voisin repeated for them the legend that along the subterranean
rivers of the region lived a blind, troglodyte people who knew neither sun nor
stars, nor anything of the world above them.

But at the cave mouths the detritus of human exploration was everywhere, blackened fire circles, cracked jugs, gnawed fowl bones, a broken
leather strap, a split shoe, all remnants, Voisins cheerfully noted, of unsuccessful searchers for golden caches. He added that even the caverns that were
only reachable by dangerous scaling of the almost sheer rock had already
been combed over.

Discouraging news to Lyse. Expected news to the cynical Gonzaga.

Yet, vivid as these excursions were, they were fruitless as far as prompting
Lyse's memories to the surface. Nothing woke her mind, everything she
looked at or heard, from the hawk circling and whistling overhead to the noon

peals of a church bell from whatever village they were near, was her own, present experience.

Voisins took them to an isolated twelfth century construction which had once belonged to his family and had once been commandeered to imprison a number of captured Templars. Now it was simply a thick wall surrounding a heavy, square donjon, undamaged but deserted, the iron-bound portals of its gatehouse shut tight.

Looking at it, they remained sitting their horses in the wildflowers that had overgrown the track to the keep. Lyse stared hard at the top of the donjon tower, whose few shuttered windows were just below the roof, pitying Bernard if he had been imprisoned in that baleful pile. But no snap of memory happened to her.

She queried Voisins, "Did your family sell it?"

"Yes, some years ago. We have always been long on ancient lineage and short on money, and the place, as you can see, is solitary and has no producing land. The man my uncle sold it to years ago was a young count, Claude de Guise by name." Voisin's gaze swept over the silent stones with no regrets.

Lyse just happened to notice Ferrante's concerned look. The Mantuan remarked, "I did not know the Lorraines came any further south than Albi, and even Albi is merely one of the cardinal's farther-flung sees."

"Did you not know, Don Ferrante?" the *sieur* said mildly. "Why yes, they own some fine domains in the Corbière range, just north of here. The original Lorraines–their ancient name was Haurault, it is believed–were settled here in the time of the great Charlemagne, what, seven hundred years back? Now, of course, the family has big estates in the north, and moves with the royal court, and a Lorraine is rarely seen in the Razès. But this is an old, old area, and many families, Clerque, Baille, others, can trace their roots back a thousand years! My wife will tell you. She herself is a descendant of Bertrand de Blanchefort, who is buried in our graveyard."

Lyse's head snapped around. She had just read that name in her little book. "But Bertrand de Blanchefort was a celibate Templar."

Voisins winked cozily at her. "*Mais oui,* my dear, but many men joined the Order after marrying and siring children. In fact, Blanchefort was the fourth Grand Master of the Knights-Templar, and a most powerful lord, indeed. And suspected of being a Cathar, as were many of the Knights-Templar from this area, did you know that? Never proven, of course. In most cases."

He squinted up at the sun's position in the sky. "*Ciel,* my stomach growls. It is time to retrace our route, our dinner will be waiting for us," their host

declared with his usual chipper good humor, and beckoning for them to follow, turned his horses head.

Lyse stared at Voisins' retreating back, then demanded of the man riding
at her side. "Did you know this, about la Dame's family being Blanchefort?
And that the man buried in the tomb in the churchyard was that very Templar
Grand Master?" Ferrante only shrugged his answer, prompting her annoyance. "Then why you didn't tell me?"

"*Tiens,* why should I have? Isn't it more amusing to find out for yourself?"
he drawled. "Besides, Bertrand de Blanchefort was long dead when the Templars
were attacked, he had nothing to do with the lost Treasury."

This last slid past her because the word 'amusing' caught her. She was
envious over the Italian's ability to devise a pastime to amuse himself with.
He had purposely nurtured the friendship of the young architect who was
building in Couiza a good-size church in the style of Languedoc, of red brick
with polygonal towers. The young architect was impressed that the gentleman
from Italy, the very wellspring of architecture, also knew a good bit about
the art, so by invitation the Mantuan spent his afternoons at the site observing the work, conversing with his new friend and his master builder, and
squinting at the scaffolded construction and the plans covering the architect's
wooden table.

This left Lyse on her own most afternoons, for in the days' worst heat the
sieur napped and his wife closeted herself concocting her attars and perfumes,
with no invitation to her guest to look on. So, in a cool cotton bodice Marye
had quickly sewn up, Lyse spent the time lolling in a shaded chair on the
breezy gallery, legs straight out before her, reading, reading, from the château's
small collection of mildewed books, and often staring off toward the purple-
hazed mountains.

When Gonzaga finally rode up from the village he had taken the habit of
looking for her there on the gallery and they would share what they
learned—not that she understood the building techniques or devices he en-
thused over—or he would settle near her and she would read to him, smoothly
now, without even using her finger—from an exciting collection she'd found of
epic poems by the old troubadours of the area.

She knew her eyes lit with welcome as she watched him stride along the
gallery towards her in the cool of the waning day, but she couldn't help it.
She was glad to see him.

Yesterday though, having returned quite early and persistent in looking for her, he found her in the Sainte-Magdalene, the little church beyond the graveyard, kneeling in a shaft of sun coming through the broken roof and praying at the foot of a demolished alter for the safety of her uncle Charles. Twice a week Mass was held for the hilltop residents in the other, larger church, which Lyse attended with the rest of the Voisin household. But she much preferred to pray in the abandoned little sanctuary, and not just because it was named for the Magdalene, as she was.

It was an old structure of Romanesque arches, whose solitude and simple, whitewashed walls reminded her of St. Piteu's chapel. A feeling of peace washed over her every time she stepped through the arched portal onto the cracked flagstones. And God, of course, could hear you wherever you prayed.

So she spoke aloud to God, first begging for Madame de Dunois' recovery, and then asking fervently for Bourbon's health and safety, for his success, for the reversal of François' vendetta against him, her most dear uncle. She felt a certainty that especially from there, from that melancholy, empty chapel where birds nested and twittered in the rafters and honeybees buzzed in the flowering vines outside of the gaping windows, that the Lord would hear her. She finally bowed her head, finishing up her devotions with the *Pater Noster*.

A noise had made her look around and there he stood, Blackbeard, in fact he had been standing there a while, she suspected, silently watching her from the doorway. Ready to leave anyhow, she rose from her knees and walked toward him with a smile.

"I did not mean to intrude," he apologized. "I just wanted to make sure where you were." But his expression, lately so amenable, had shifted again and his green eyes regarded her with wary coolness.

She felt, in some strange manner, that she had to excuse her prayers. "I fear for my uncle," she said nervously.

"Your prayers were very loving. I'm sure they will help." he said. But there was little praise in his tone which one might expect to hear from a from Bourbon partisan.

She gave him a weak smile and then directed his attention around. "You know, this is a curious little building for an old church. There is no sculpture on these slim pillars, not a fresco on the ceiling, not even a painted saying or saint's portrait, or cross on the walls, or holy water font. And the altar is round and low, and see here, on the side of it, it is carved to look like tree bark. La Dame showed us this building so very briefly, remember, saying she didn't know when it fell out of use. But 'tis strange, that, since she seems to know everything else."

He took her arm firmly to lead her out over the cracked doorsill. "She didn't know perhaps because it is of no consequence. But you seem to have a thought on it."

"Could—could it have once been Cathar?" she asked boldly.

"There is a book in the library of this house I have been looking through. It has no title on its cover and its clasp was firmly locked, but age has eaten the leather strap and I opened it easily. It talks about the Cathar heresy. Their disbeliefs were strange: they abjured the saints, and even the Godhood of dear Jesus. But they admired simplicity. So, look at that old chapel..."

He didn't let her turn her head back, but continued to steer her out. "Lyse-Magdalene, that's enough of that. The Cathars are anathema, they brought Godlessness and terror to the Languedoc, they were proscribed by Holy Church and they still are. Even to read of them you are putting yourself in jeopardy if the priest at St. Pierre finds out. We are here for a purpose, keep your mind to that and do not discuss dangerous topics with anyone."

"Even with you? I thought you were more courageous."

"There was an execution in Paris when I was there this past winter, the stupid young son of a lawyer was condemned for following this new 'Lutheran' heresy from Germany, of speaking ill of Christ, of Our Lady and of the Saints in Paradise. His tongue was first cut out, then he was strangled and burned to cinders. The Holy Office is as vigilant now as ever. Perhaps in St. Piteu you hadn't heard of its severity."

"But you won't denounce me just for reading of the Cathars?"

"Of course not, but some might! I tell you, take your mind from those heretics. Let's hear of them no more."

Emerging from the old chapel, she had wondered at his vehemence, although she suspected that he, himself, was not at all afraid, only that he still believed her tongue would trip her up before others. Of course she had no sympathy for the vanished Cathars. But she was chagrined she could not talk to him about them, she was curious, they intrigued her.

He'd then broken the mood by dredging up a little congeniality. "Listen, walk back with me now, they've brought up fresh peaches and plums from Couiza and I crave a companion to enjoy them, along with a mouthful of cold wine. Eh, what do you say, my lady?" He was looking down at her, and anticipation of the luscious fruit had gotten his green eyes alight. So she put aside her resentment and nodded, giving him a mock curtsey and answering smile.

But there was more than just the Cathars swirling around in her head. By accident, she had noticed something in showing him the squat, round altar; a tiny parting between the carved grey base and the flagstones, the shadow of a depression showing beneath. A silent excitement had grabbed her at that sight. It might indicate a hole in which something was hidden!

Could that be it? Was the Treasury under the altar!

She didn't dare believe so, it would be too easy. But she wondered if she could possibly budge the heavy altar herself, for Gonzaga's dismissive attitude had disappointed her and she was loathe to ask his help in case she was wrong. Just imagine, if she found the Treasury with help from nothing but her own very clever observation!

All the rest of yesterday the possibility of moving the altar stone engaged her thoughts, and then, just before dark, Charles de Bourbon's exhausted messenger urged his horse up the spiral road to Rennes-le-Château and panted out to them that the duke was safe, delivered from France and on his way to Mantua. Lyse broke down with cries of relief, for her uncle's precarious welfare had hung like a shadow over everything.

The rider then handed a ciphered letter to Gonzaga, who took it to his chamber to translate it, insisting that Lyse come to watch, because he wanted her to know the method he used.

The code was keyed to a small history book he had brought with him, *Amadis de Gaul*. The letter was short and concise: after sending fond greetings to his cousin and to his niece, the duke got right to the point. He was in dire need of many more soldiers and so he was most anxious for gold. What was their progress in this respect? He would send a trusted courier every week so that they could keep in contact however fast he moved his base of operations.

"What progress in this mad venture, my lord wants to know?" Ferrante muttered, staring at the letter and irate once more to have been shunted from the main arena of action to this rural backwater. "*Cristos,* none. But were I with him right now I could call him up a thousand of the finest knights and men-at-arms in Lombardy, men who rode with me in a dozen campaigns—and just on my word that pay would be forthcoming and good booty to be had, they would fight at Bourbon's back forever. So I sit here on my arse amidst the damask roses, searching for a phantom. "

Embarrassed by her failure so far, aware that Gonzaga was barely stomaching wet nursing an ineffective woman he suspected of being half-mad, Lyse's shoulders sagged with her spirits. But stubbornly she caught herself up and rounded on him instead. "Monsieur, you don't at all believe in what we're doing, do you? You don't even think there *is* a Treasury to be found, here in these haunted mountains or anywhere else! 'O thou of little faith,' how then can we possibly succeed?" she demanded with unconscious pomp.

Was that a smile that brushed his lips?

But he declared flatly, "My faith doesn't matter, lady. I am here solely on behalf of Charles de Bourbon, who *does* believe you can find him a vast cache of money, so whatever I can do to aid you, I will."

This was no news, yet she felt jarred. Their agreeable weeks here had obscured the fact that in the end he was much the reluctant escort, the conscripted bridegroom. "Good, then if you want to help, I shall ask you once more to take me to Le Bézu. I just feel in my bones that I *must* go there."

"The devil's behind, it is a hard, overnight ride into those mountains. You had a narrow escape on just such a route as must be used, and I wish to spare you that."

"What needs to be done, must be done. My beloved uncle Charles is in dire trouble and I will not fail him. I'm not afraid to brave those ruins. Certainly, Signore, you couldn't be. Could you?" She knew the taunt was unworthy the minute she uttered it.

Stung, Ferrante paused. He studied the stubborn light hardening the girl's pale aquamarine eyes, and the determined line she made of her jaw, and marveled once more how a woman whose normal aspect looked so meltingly angelic could really be so wilful.

Bowing to the inevitable he said, "Lyse-Magdalene, I believe you are sore afraid of mountain heights, but I am convinced that for your uncle you'll go up there anyhow, with or without me. You are, Mademoiselle, either quite reckless or quite brave, but it doesn't matter, for I will take you to Le Bézu. Tomorrow. I'll arrange for a guide."

She deflated, the wind flown out of her sails by his sudden compliance. She chewed her lip, she *was* very leery of mountain heights since her fall. "Thank you," she muttered weakly.

But Ferrante's mind had turned away to the letter in his hand, drawn again into the distant preparations for real battle. "Tonight, after supper, I will write letters to two captains of elite mercenary troops making their headquarters near Mantua, and this courier can deliver them. I will ask they join the duke, on the written pledge of my castle and dependencies at Trina, until the Bourbon paymaster can recompense them."

She goggled. "But Signore, what a dangerous gamble you take, do you not? Trina is your home, it is where your wife lives."

"And an estate which adds welcome income to the 8,000 ducats yearly my father left me." But Ferrante shrugged his gesture away. "Charles would do the same for me," he informed her, then swiftly retreated from this sentimentality by raising one cynical eyebrow. "Besides, you *might* indeed find the Templar Treasury, eh, and then he will have to pay me back double." He shoved the letter inside his doublet and escorted her to the door.

"I know I will find it," Lyse declared staunchly, but with more certainty than she really felt. A hint of panic already tugged at her.

Chapter 15

On the early morning of their trip, as she descended the curved, open staircase wonderously cantilevered out from the wall of the Great Hall, Lyse decided not to mention the erotic 'seeing-back' she'd had of Mélline and Bernard de la Motte in her bed an hour before, in spite that it would show she had not lost her peculiar ability. Describing her ancestress's passion for her lover added nothing to their quest, and besides, it was too embarrassingly personal.

Even in a clear dawn the torchières in the big Hall were always burning. They dimly illuminated a pacing Don Ferrante, and a more patient-seeming group consisting of la Dame, Tournel, and a leathery-faced local guide, introduced as Joachim Bonpuy, who spoke Occitan and little French.

Blackbeard had exchanged his constricting doublet for a short, tan tunic and rustic leggings. A jaunty felt hat was tipped over his eyes, a mean, long dagger was stuck into his sword belt; his bulk, the knife, his knitted-brow, sun-bronzed face with its slash of undereye scar formed the very picture of a dangerous rogue.

Lyse thought he looked wonderful.

He was looking her over too, for by his order, and necessary to the rough hiking they might face, she was arrayed in faded boy's clothes similar to his except for a longer tunic, which la Dame had found for her. But except that leggings allowed her to ride astride which meant more control of the horse, she wasn't pleased with the male garb, for she thought it most unflattering; so, in revolt, she wore her hair straight down and loose below the soft tam she'd jammed on her head. Across her shoulder was the strap of a small leather purse, and in her belt she had shoved a little fly whisk of colored wool.

Reluctant admiration gleamed in the Mantuan's eyes. He drawled, "Very good, Mademoiselle, I see you've left off the court gown today. But we are fortunate in that you don't actually have to masquerade as a lad." For a moment she thought he meant her uncoiffed hair and was ready to argue with him, but his speculative gaze lingered on the bosom incongruously swelling her cotton tunic. She flushed.

"How many of us go?" she asked him, to change the subject. "The guards?"

"No. Only Tournel accompanies us, for Bonpuy here has discouraged a larger party."

Stifling a morning yawn, la Dame explained, "Le Bézu is thought a place of demons and ghosts, a haunt of the devil Asmodeus, who will send evil down on any perceived threat to his stronghold, like even a few men. So Bonpuy will take you only within close sight of the ruins. No other huntsman who knows the safe tracks up those mountains will even do that much, but your guide, here, admires the ring of silver coins more than he fears the wraiths of dead Templars."

Then their tall hostess, ever in grey, her smile and her perfumed aura of ripe womanhood always provocative, glided closer to Gonzaga to gaze into his eyes as she spoke. "You do well to go fully armed, Don Ferrante, even though Bonpuy carries a strong crossbow as well as a spear."

"Why? Do you believe a sword can stick a ghost to the heart, Madame?" His smile, his gaze was just as suggestive as hers.

"Of course not, but it will protect against the bears and wolves that roam that range." She looked over and saw Lyse's eyes widen. "Well, of course, *ma chère*. You demand to go into wilderness, which is full of dangerous beasts."

Patronizing and supercilious, la Dame ran her eyes over the enticing form outlined by the garb of Marye's fourteen year old son, and Lyse felt a secret shiver of triumph over the flare of jealousy in their silvery depths. Nevertheless, her hostess came and kissed her on both cheeks.

"Mademoiselle, I do not fully approve of any journey to Bézu, there are too many tales of strange disappearance in that back country, so I insist you keep always about you these guardians that I give you." Into Lyse's belt, next to the fly whisk, she slipped a small, needle-bladed poignard in a scabbard. Then she pulled from a pocket and clasped around Lyse's neck, a silver medal on a long, silk cord. "A talisman, to keep evil from you in that tragic place, niece of Monseigneur de Bourbon," la Dame intoned, then stepped back.

"We must leave. Lucco has our mounts waiting in the courtyard," Gonzaga murmured to Lyse, and gestured her ahead of him.

A few minutes later, la Dame watched the little party depart through the gate of Rennes-le-Château, her decrepit home. She fingered the silver-and-crystal earring hanging from one earlobe and pursed her full lips in a gesture of doubt.

They cantered south, and in an hour turned off the river road below Esperaza, and onto a path through the brush, a gently climbing track cut by flocks of sheep driven to pasture in the high meadows and easy to manage, even in the rapidly warming morning.

Riding behind with Gonzaga, Lyse pulled out the silk cord which la Dame had tucked down the neck of her tunic and examined the square talisman hanging from it. The medal was curiously embossed, showing two chain-mailed and helmeted knights riding double on one horse.

"Pray, what is the significance?" she asked Gonzaga.

He rode closer to examine it, rubbed his beard, and looked surprised. "The double-riding men was a badge of the Knights-Templar, it signifies either humility or fraternity, maybe both. Lora meant it as a guard against that Order's witchcraft for you. Such small objects can be found in many ruins, and I suppose that's where she got it."

But Lyse noticed how casually he had used la Dame's given name. She went on, trying to ignore the suspicion that leaped into her breast and burned there, that Gonzaga might be relieving his boredom with their hostess's company. "But why not a cross as talisman? I have a tiny gold one in my purse, of course, for Christ's symbol is the best protection against the Devil."

"I don't know. 'Tis a confused issue, for before their trials the Knights-Templar rode proudly beneath the splayed red cross. But I would trust Madame de Voisin, a native of this region, to know what would defend best against any of their unshriven spirits."

"Including the ghost of her own ancestor, the Grand Master, Blanchefort?"

"Probably *especially* him." He grinned at her concern. He took it as his duty to tease her when she looked so anxious.

Tucking the medallion back down her tunic, she said, "Anyhow, I still find it very hard to understand the terrible sins that destroyed that Order, or even believe in them. So does that make me a Doubting Thomas? Or worse, an apostate who questions the Church's wisdom? My religious instruction was not very deep, I'm afraid."

He squinted a look at her from beneath the beak of his tilted hat, then looked ahead. "No. That makes you intelligent," he growled.

For what information she had on the Knights-Templar Lyse was relying on the translated little book he had given her, written ten years before by an anti-French Milanese to examine one of the strangest events in Christian history.

The religious, celibate Order of the Knights-Templar, grown into perhaps the strongest military force of the thirteenth and fourteenth centuries, and certainly the richest brotherhood, was suddenly attacked by the church hierarchy and accused of heresy, of perpetrating the worst anti-Christ offenses, and even of worshipping the head of a Devil they called 'Baphomet!' All crimes punishable by death.

Even more mysterious, most of the French Templars, although protesting innocence, were taken from their fortified Preceptories and cast into the dungeons of the early Inquisition with hardly a struggle or murmur on their part! In the course of seven years of persecution, from 1307 to the execution of their Grand Master, Jacques de Molay in Paris, two hundred and fifty French Templars were brutally tortured for confessions, and over seventy who refused to admit any guilt were burned to death at the stake.

It was Philippe Le Bel of France who, out of jealousy and greed and not a little fear, in 1307 engineered the downfall of the stiff-necked Templar Order. The French monarch himself had quarreled fiercely with the medieval church, and had audaciously invaded Italy and actually kidnapped Pope Boniface, to charge him with demonic possession and moral disgrace!

After Boniface died, Philippe's agents in Italy then poisoned his legal successor, Benedict, because he had excommunicated everyone suspected in Boniface's death, including the French chief minister, Nogaret, a spiteful fount of hatred who lived in terror of magical attacks. So, for refusing to lift these interdictions, the new Pope Benedict was assassinated.

Strong enough now to put his own puppet on the Papal throne, Philippe tapped a French archbishop and anointed him Clément the Fifth, then the rampaging monarch invaded Italy, forcibly uprooted the papal officials themselves from Rome and installed the Holy See at Avignon in the south, where it became a mere appendage of the French crown for the next sixty-eight years.

With the Papacy under his control, but avid for more money to sustain his army, the French king decided to move against the Pope's special Order itself, the arrogant Templars, whose Treasury had always made him salivate, and who he suspected to be planning to take over Languedoc as their own principality.

The puppet Pope Clément was persuaded to abolish the Order of Knights-Templars worldwide. Then Nogaret, talented at compiling appalling charges, announced terrible accusations against the Order, gleaned from the shocking confessions of a so-called 'renegade' Templar. In a feat of incredible precision for that time, sealed arrest orders were issued to royal seneschals and bailiffs throughout France; these were opened simultaneously on the same date and were accomplished at once, with every power available.

Thus, by surprise raid, at dawn on Friday the thirteenth, October of 1307, almost all the Templars in France were seized and arrested. Their Preceptories were sequestered, goods confiscated, and their distinctive, round Templar churches closed.

But the great, alluring prize, the staggering Templar Treasury which Philippe coveted and thought was locked behind bars in the Paris Preceptory, eluded him. He raged, he searched, he tore down walls everywhere, but he never found the Order's wealth. Nor did anyone else.

The Italian historian who compiled Lyse's book in the more modern climate of their own century, believed the Templars had been pre-warned of the King's surprise attack. He surmised that the Grand Master, de Molay, had sent swift orders to all Preceptories ordering all records and paraphernalia of rites and rituals burned. Some Templars fled to remote fortresses, some discreetly escaped to safer countries, but the majority of those proud, French military monks stayed and were taken, submitting passively to martyrdom for whatever reason only God knew.

Not until seven years after Philippe's grand sweep were the small group of Templars associated with the Order's Treasury finally captured in Languedoc and executed. At the end, with the Grand Master de Molay's terrible, roasting death in Paris, the two-hundred year old international organization of white-garbed warriors for Christ was decreed dissolved by the Avignon Pope.

Not everywhere were Templars so vehemently persecuted. Edward the Second of England, doubting the charges, made half-hearted arrests, giving English Templars ample time to escape to Scotland or regrow their tonsures and melt into the population. In Lorraine, Germany, and Spain they were allowed to join other strong Orders. In Portugal they merely changed their name to Knights of Christ; and later, the caravels of Cristoforo Columbo sailed to the New World under the Templar's red, splayed cross, for the admiral was married to a descendant of a former Grand Master, a forebear from whom he inherited special nautical charts.

Lyse had lately started to read the descriptions of the hideous fates meted out to the French Templars, about the terrible tortures, the wild confessions to anything which were extracted from agonized flesh, the mass burnings at the stake attended by a populace in holiday clothes, even the tormented Templars' repudiating their confessions at death's door, but she quickly closed the book.

In the back of her head she had begun to hear her mother screaming, she had felt Mélline's horror and anguish starting to build inside her, she could not fall asleep the night she commenced that sordid section. So she fled that part, and went back to reread the Italian author's discussion of the accusations against the Order.

The Templars were accused of practicing infanticide during their highly secret rites; of teaching women how to abort; of giving obscene kisses at the induction of a postulant; and of homosexuality and sodomy.

Lyse was not sure what either of those two last words described, or obscene kisses either, but she was certain in her soul that Bernard de la Motte was not guilty of any of the accusations. She knew nothing about the long-perished knight, even what he looked like, but somehow her heart did, and never would the man have been capable of such vile things. And surely not of the most incredible charge of all–that these servants of Christ who had fought for Him on hundreds of bloody battlefields, in reality denied His Godhood, and trampled and spit on the Cross.

She couldn't have coaxed explanations of the charges she did not understand from Madame de Dunois, even were she better, for she suspected they were sexual in nature and her governess was strict about what unmarried females need not know. Although curiosity was driving her, she would not go to Lora Voisins about it either. She wondered if Germain even knew of such bad things, but he was far away anyhow, and so was the cook's daughter, who surely did. That left Blackbeard.

As they rode toward Le Bézu she glanced at the *condottiere's* strong profile, at the jagged scar below his left eye and at the confident bearing of birth no common man's tunic could disguise. Would he explain those strange charges to her–so she could know the Templars better and perhaps recognize what the 'seeing-back' showed her–and more, could she even ask him without turning crimson as a cardinal's hat? Would she dare?

In her deepest heart Lyse believed she was a timid person, that if she appeared bold it was because she strained to do so. Nevertheless, mischief crept into her expression as she considered asking him–sometime. It would shock him, such shameless curiosity from a lady. *Tiens*, what difference? He didn't think much of her anyway, except, as she'd discovered about other men, he liked her looks.

The path petered out into a faint trace. They toiled up a hill, crossed a saddleback ridge and faced even a higher hill. They kept ascending, at last through a wood of spreading oak and chestnut trees where the sun shone only fitfully through the leaves, and where riding was much cooler. But they were plagued with gnats that swarmed and buzzed and kept Lyse's ivory-handled fly whisk busy, and brought a steady stream of Italian curses from Gonzaga as he flailed at them.

At noon they stopped at a brook in a perfect little dell for a bite of the food they had brought, and here the Lord had been the gardener, providing flat boulders to sit on, gay wildflowers bobbing everywhere, birds twittering and flashing through the trees and frogs croaking in the cold mountain stream.

And the swarming gnats. So the four ate very quickly, with few words, and didn't linger. But before they remounted, Gonzaga noticed Lyse filling her eyes with the lovely hollow and on impulse he bent, plucked a pink blossom at his feet and solemnly pushed its stem under the band of her floppy hat. "That's for remembrance of this place," he murmured into her arrested stance, and immediately turned away to hold her horse steady while she mounted up. He regained his own horse but she was yet peering at him in surprise, so he smiled wryly and rumbled, "That pansy or whatever it is, very delicate and glowing–just like you."

He clucked up his horse and that was all, but the niceness of the gesture from such a man somehow lifted her heart, and were he looking at her he would have seen her pleased reaction.

The wood was a paradise for game hunters, they saw squirrels, pheasants, the white flash of rabbit tails, and startled deer crashing away from them, so many creatures that their guide slipped away from them during a rest and soon returned with a bloody brace of rabbits and two young guinea hens which he dropped into his grass-lined pouch for their supper later.

Soon the terrain grew steeper, the trees became evergreens and much denser, and their horses trod quietly over soft turf and thick layers of pine needles. To everyone's relief, a cool, sloughing wind blew away the biting midges and flies.

Their route was zig-zag, as they avoided parts choked with rockfall and brush, or trees with branches so low they couldn't pass. Among the thick pines now, they heard only the occasional call of a cuckoo and the sound of their own muffled passing as a horse's hoof snapped a twig or a saddle creaked.

That same, weird silence, the feeling that Lyse had that the whole Razès was holding its breath, had again descended upon them. They picked their way up the mountain through the trees, around, parallel and up again, always higher. Once they heard a menacing snuffling following them, an animal unseen in thickets of holly bushes, but they kept going, the men alert, the guide sliding his spear from its holder. But with a crackling of dry branches the soft snorting soon moved away and was gone.

"Bear. Young one. And uncertain of us, luckily," Gonzaga answered Lyse's unspoken, nervous question.

Finally the forest ended, but the steep, rocky grade became so tumbled it was wiser to dismount and leave the horses at that point, tied to trees. Lyse now understood the wisdom of her close-fitting male costume, her strong shoes and gloves, as they scrambled and stumbled their way up on foot over loose stones and between boulders and she willingly accepted Gonzaga's help to negotiate a leap.

The way was hard and she was panting and tired, but it was passable, and here there was no sheer drop. She wondered why they said Le Bèzu could not be reached, although looking up she could see nothing forward of them but more boulders.

At last, achieving the crest, they came around the flank of the mountain and onto a very broad, open ledge overlooking a gorge, and in the middle of the ledge stood a round brick tower with one side half demolished, so one could see inside where crude steps, white with bird droppings, spiralled to the top. Coming into the clearing, Lyse was hit by a gust of wind strong enough to make her stagger, like a hand shoving her back. "That is Bézu?" she panted, staring at the tower.

The guide heard the name, smirked and shook his head. He directed her gaze to the left and up, and there—above them and across the gorge, on a peak the shape of a ship's prow, were the bleached remains of Le Bézu, the lonely, distant fortress she had glimpsed from Rennes-le-Château.

"But we're nowhere near it," she protested.

Ferrante shaded his eyes with his hand, with the other securing his jaunty hat from the wind. "There is no way I see to get closer, unless to climb that cliff with ropes and Alpine axes. The road once carved from the mountain's edge was been pounded out of existence by deliberately-set rockfalls. Anyway, Bonpuy here won't take us any closer."

The guide grunted something and Tournel, who had picked up some Occitan, reported, "He says there are evil demons there who shriek all night. Even this far away he won't camp on this ledge, but wishes to go back, lower."

Bonpuy walked over to the tower, and beckoned to them to come. He pulled aside a bush and they saw a terra cotta plaque set into the wind-scoured brick. On it was a worn representation of two mailed men riding double on one horse.

"The Templar symbol," Lyse breathed, reaching to touch it with reverent fingers.

"Templar, Templar," Bonpuy nodded solemnly.

"This must have been one of their watchtowers," Gonzaga surmised.

Bonpuy made more unintelligible sounds, then seeing no one understood the guttural language, grimaced with his creased face and tried sign language.

"He means a lantern," Ferrante said, watching carefully. "So this was a signal tower. In fact, Voisins says they had a string of them on the high peaks, running all the way to Limoux. Using a code, they could send very simple messages by moving flaps on their lanterns."

The same thought then occurred to both Lyse and the Mantuan, but he voiced it. "Hah! And 'tis still done today. That is how the whole Aude valley knows in just minutes whoever travels that river road. They signal from peak to peak, with the advantage of high mountains where a light can be seen for leagues. No magic there," he declared, pleased to strip la Dame of one of her mysteries.

Lyse turned her attention back to Le Bézu, walking to the parapet at the other edge of the clearing and staring up at the wrecked fortress intently, the wind furling her back her hair like a red-gold flag. Sensing she needed room, Ferrante let her stand there by herself.

As she concentrated on the scene, puffy, wind-blown clouds were racing over the sun, making the sun seem to blink on and off

to match the flash of mirror, up there in the window of a tower, the main keep of the fortress rearing over the strong, crenellated walls, and on its battlements white banners whipped in the wind, each carrying a fat, splayed, crimson cross bright as fresh blood.

—flash, flash—flash—

A familiar voice explained in her ear, "Brother de Troncval signals that they will send twenty men down from Bèzu tomorrow night, in small groups through the well passage, since the road is so spied upon. That should make short work of our task."

"But so many to know the location?" She was worried. "And if they are caught and put to the strappado?"

"These are men who would give up their eyes, their limbs and their cods for the Order, they would scream to die but no word of betrayal would pass their lips. Nor mine either, in their place," the low-keyed voice vowed, and she knew it for the truth.

A horrible shudder ran through her at the thought that this man might also be captured; she was terribly afraid. She wanted to chain him to her and they would both run away, across the mountains, to Spain, to Africa, anywhere. A foolish dream, for never would he leave his duty until it was done. The chill touch of premonition wracked her again

Lyse's hair whipped back into her face and made her blink. Rough hands grasped her arms.

"Lyse-Magdalene? What's wrong?" Gonzaga's deep growl demanded, and he instinctively swung her away from the view of the Preceptory. His bronzed, bearded face swam into Lyse's consciousness.

"N-nothing, I'm all right, "she quavered. "Just–a voice this time. But Don Ferrante, I have remembered something! It was de la Motte telling me–Mélline– of a message from Le Bèzu. Their road was not safe, so he had come here–to this clearing–to read the flashing of that mirror."

"What mirror?"

"Why, that one," she began, disoriented, and turning, realized that the bleached, square tower showed black, empty windows and was naked of flags, and the walls surrounding it were broken and almost leveled in places. She gulped, and muttered, "That is, I thought I saw a mirror flashing in the sun-light, I could swear I did."

She felt his grip on her arms slacken a bit, as if he suddenly wanted to remove his hands.

"Well, no matter. What do you remember the Templar saying?" Now he did let her go, but walked her back from the stone parapet which edged the clearing.

She glanced over where the other two men were watching them at a distance out of earshot, where Gonzaga must have ordered them to stay. "He told me–no, told Mélline–that twenty men were being sent from Bèzu to help him in some work, and that they were worthy to carry a secret. And she was very afraid."

"Of him?"

"Certainly not," she retorted scornfully. "Afraid for him, for them both, because she loved him so dearly. And she did know what he was going to do. And–perhaps–where."

"Aha! And that was–?" The green eyes gleamed.

Miserably she shook her head. "And nothing. That was all. All that came to my mind, that snippet of talk about Le Bèzu. I had no definite sense of what they were discussing." She sighed. "I truly thought viewing this Templar redoubt would help me remember something of significance. Not just about twenty men going somewhere unknown to do something unspecified."

"Which is at least a signpost, lady." He tried to cheer her up in her deep disappointment, in spite that he shared it. "'Tis no disaster, take the view that you have put another piece on the playing board and it will fetch others to it. See, you were right to come here. It did bring some recall."

"I already felt they didn't bring the Treasury here. But there seems this forceful tie between Le Bèzu and Mélline? I just have the deep feeling there is something–something dreadful–more than de la Motte's danger."

Wondering why she thought that last, she turned again to stare at Le Bèzu, distractedly grabbing the Mantuan's arm to keep the wind gusts from staggering her. The sky was solid clouds now and the ruins looked bleaker than ever, empty, dead. She stared fixedly at the old stones, jagged against the sky, trying to will that sudden shift in her mind, like an eye opening wider, as the long-dead Mélline's memories swept in to capture her consciousness. But nothing happened. She was only aware that the wind had set up a low, eerie moaning and even in summer was carrying a chill to her bones from the higher, snow-capped mountains in the distance.

She stared harder, then cried out, "Don Ferrante, there is something over there, see, on the forward round tower, fabric or canvas, flapping, like a sail. Or a signal!"

He squinted at where she was pointing. "Aha, yes, I see it! 'Tis hard to tell what." He called to Bonpuy, jabbing a finger at the forward tower on the ship's prow, and making a questioning gesture with his hands.

But the huntsman had noticed the movement on the tower too, and his eyes seemed to have sunk into their sockets. He fired off a burst of words and backed away, gesturing strongly for them to follow him away from the clearing. They looked at Tournel.

"I think he says that the waving cloth is the signal for a gathering of witches tonight," Tournel reported. "My mother once told me that witches love windy nights, the easier to fly to their covens on the backs of goats and pigs. Bonpuy wants to leave here immediately, for he will not stay this close. Monsieur, I do not think we should either." The sergeant, ordinarily stalwart, looked nervous and crossed himself. "Even though there is yet some light, this is an oppressed land. And there are things in this world best left unseen."

Gonzaga looked at Lyse, an eyebrow raised in question.

They all could see that bit of forlorn cloth flapping about from the roof of that tower, it was no possessed memory of hers. Lyse stared another moment at Le Bèzu, then nodded, for the ruin unnerved her too. Bonpuy, with his talk of witches and demons had made her skin creep, for even if they themselves hid safely, she would dread witnessing the Devil's disgusting disciples swarming through the air on scaly wings, crawling over the rocks on clawed legs, rising from the ground shedding cobwebs.

She could try again to access her memories in the spirit-dissolving light of morning.

Seeing his employer's head towards the point where they had come into this clearing, the guide's face relaxed. There were stories of foolish hunters who had disappeared without a trace when making their camp on this ledge. A few scoffers said the unfortunates, many lost in the spring, were taken by ravenous bears, but Bonpuy knew better. That ancient, blighted stronghold up there had been cursed and abandoned by God.

They camped where they'd left the horses, just inside the tree line, where their guide deemed it safe from Le Bézu's spirits and the wind was greatly cut. The men built a fire while Bonpuy skinned and plucked his afternoon catch and soon wonderful, sizzling smells of roast meat rose up to the rustling branches and the low-hanging clouds which were making twilight darker. The food was delicious, and they were hungry, and they drank freely from the skin of wine they had carried along.

In a while, Bonpuy, who had a decent voice, sang them his traditional Occitan songs, to which Gonzaga reciprocated in Italian with folktunes from the Piedmont—so it fell to Lyse and Tournel to uphold the honor of France with the sprightly old songs at least three of them knew, while Bonpuy glee-fully rapped a stick on a log for a drum.

Lyse sat upwind of the woodsmoke with a blanket around her shoulders, well-fed and rested, and enjoying herself. The men's faces, relaxed by the wine, were cheery, in fact she was fascinated by how the leaping flames chiseled to hardness the planes of Blackbeard's features yet reflected warmly in his green gaze. To her the night was pleasantly cool, but he thought it was warm and had unlaced the neck of his tunic for comfort, revealing strong collarbones and a tuft of dark hair, and for once—absent his arrogant demeanor—it was easy to see an attractive man.

She began to think she was laughing too much, but the quantity of wine one imbibed was hard to measure when one drank it in mouthfuls from a skin, and besides, her companions were telling funny stories and recounting amusing exploits that sometimes befell fighting men. Even Bonpuy, suddenly taking on a personality, made them call out translations and roar until they wiped their eyes, with a detailed pantomime of a simpering, frightened noble-man whose company he once suffered on an unsuccessful boar hunt.

It grew late, the wine was gone. They threw more chunks of wood amidst the embers and prepared for sleep, choosing the foot of trees where the piled brown needles were springy and soft. Gonzaga, giving Lyse an expansive smile, patted a good spot on the opposite side of his tree. "Lie down here, Mademoiselle, here there is warmth but not smoke from the fire."

She accepted graciously, as if he were offering her a throne.

But Lyse had never been delighted with wading into bushes to answer nature, one could get stabbed with thorns, or worse, step on a snake in the dark. Now, forced to it, she found there wasn't much cover in the evergreen forest so that she had to go a little distance from the fire, and even in her light-headed condition this was dark and scary, and the God-forsaken points that laced up her boys tights—for the front flap did her no good—were hard to undo and re-do. She answered when Gonzaga called to her, but took so long re-lacing the tights with clumsy fingers, that she stumbled back to their campsite, gig-gling, just as Gonzaga was preparing to get her.

The little group settled down to sleep, with Bonpuy slightly removed to save the lady his snoring. He assured them that even so he slept so lightly, alert to the least sound or smell of trouble, that they needn't post guard.

Gonzaga had spread Lyse's blanket on the ground; she wrapped herself in it light-heartedly, yawning and suddenly drowsy. The fire crackled brightly, companionably, the pine-scented night air seduced the nostrils and lulled her, an owl hooted to his mate in the distance. She closed her eyes for just a moment, she meant to think about Le Bézu and Mélline and Bernard now that there was quiet.

And awoke, her eyes opening wide, her body stiffening as she went up on her elbows, straining to listen, for something was out there and lurking in the dark shadows beyond the light of their much-reduced fire. She must have fallen asleep, and now some threat had awakened her. Did she hear snuffling? Was there a stealthy treading on the pine needles in the blackness all about them where the fire's weak light did not reach? Cautiously sitting up, she glanced at the humped mounds of the sleeping Tournel and Bonpuy on the other side of the embers. They did not stir.

A wild screech in the forest and then a crazy hooting loudly descending the scale turned her blood cold. She clutched her blanket to her racing heart, but she could see nothing in the dimensionless black beyond the nearby trees standing like flat, cut-out images, barely illumined by their small circle of light.

The wine had worn off, and it descended upon her that they were deep in a wilderness, distant on every side from anything human—but not from the tragic and haunted Bézu, and the damned souls Bonpuy so feared. Her ears strained to separate sounds away from the background of soughing trees and the rasping of insects.

There, there it was, it was breathing she thought she heard, something heavy, breathing out there in the dark to her left.

But the men slept, none of the mounds moved, not even Blackbeard's, about two arm-lengths from her. *Mon Dieu,* that terrible screech could have woken the dead. But Bonpuy? He said he could hear the least sound of danger.

Eyes staring, she decided there was a lighter patch coalescing in the black at the edge of their camp, and wasn't it pulsating, or writhing, like a tormented spirit? Again there came the awful screech and demonic hoots, and she felt her hair lifting from her scalp. Gasping, she looked around wildly but not one of the men had stirred.

Dead, that was the reason. They were dead! A demon with a curled, forked tail and red eyes had killed them in this forest and now it was coming for her, not to kill her but to carry her as slave and sacrifice in its Satanic rites, to place her cringing, naked body on its stone altar and do evil things to her.

Whimpering with fright and not taking her eyes off the lighter patch wavering outside their circle, she pulled the Templar medal out of her tunic to clutch it tightly, for la Dame had promised it would save her. Still wrapped in the blanket, she began wriggling along the ground toward Ferrante, the choice being whether to suffer the heart-stopping swoop of the demon by herself, or at least have the Mantuan's dead body to cling to. The scoundrel! He was supposed to safeguard her, he had sworn this to her uncle Bourbon, and now he was dead and she was doomed.

She thought the lighter patch had started floating toward her and in a panic she quickly crawled on all fours the rest of the way to where Gonzaga lay on his side, half in shadows, with his head resting on one arm, and that arm atop his sword. She peered desperately at him to see if he were breathing. Then with a start she realized his eyes were open, he was watching her.

"Oh!"

"What is it now?" he whispered.

"You're not dead!" Relief flooded her voice.

"Not this year, foolish woman. Why are you not asleep?"

"There's–there is something out there, I'm sure I hear it. A wild animal, or an evil spirit, look, over there, something greyer than the night–I'm frightened."

He sat up and frowned around, then cocked his head to listen. "There is nothing, besides your imagination. And Bonpuys would hear any animal before you did." But he got up and built the fire up again with the store of branches they'd chopped. "*Voilà*, beasts don't like flames, it's good protection," he murmured as he returned to ease himself down next to her. Seeing she was still jittery, he added, "Look over there, our peacefully snoring hunter has his crossbow at his hand, ratcheted taut and ready to fire, if need be."

"You can't shoot a bodiless ghost screaming for revenge," Lyse shivered, although with the brighter fire the patch had been swallowed up into the featureless dark that pressed into their camp. Just then the wild screech pierced the air again, followed by the loud, crazy hoots and she jumped, trembling with the shrill assault, then hunched herself together in a frightened ball.

"Aha, that?" He pried out one of her hands, grown cold with fear, and heartily rubbed it. "Don't be afraid, lady, it's a night bird, a small one, strangely, for such a fierce cry. 'Tis called hereabouts a *Sortilège Bleu*. It is restless and will soon move on. I suggest you go back to sleep; I'm sure there is still a few hours before daylight."

She swallowed. He didn't understand that the bird's very name, 'blue sorcerer,' added fuel to her enflamed imagination, which she couldn't turn off. "*Ma foi,* that dreadful cry fills my mind with fearful images. Please, could I—could I sleep here by you?" She knew she was sounding like a tiny child who begs to hide from a nightmare in her nurse's bed, but her nerves were still jumping, and she wasn't convinced that the ominous grey patch wasn't still hovering just out of their vision.

"As you wish. If it makes you feel better."

And with nothing more welcoming than that, the Mantuan stretched out on his spread blanket, flipped a bit of it over himself and turned his back on her, moving his big shoulders to get comfortable and go back to sleep.

Lyse stared at his long form. Well, what had she expected from the boor, a scrolled parchment invitation?

She settled herself too, on the other edge of his blanket. She did feel more secure, she had to admit, close to his strength and sword. But the man was often unreadable. One moment he was chaffing her hand to warm it, the next minute he acts as if she were the Gorgon's snaky head asking to rest near him, and barely offering her a churlish 'yes'.

She didn't know what to make of him, nor of her own unmistakable attraction to him, which even so vacillated between fascination and distaste.

She comforted herself by contemplating again the future she was planning for herself, the unique unfettering of her life, from him, from her uncle, from any necessity of sad refuge in a nunnery, freedom purchased by the keen barter she would make for any key knowledge she finally remembered.

Ferrante couldn't return to sleep. He was very aware of the woman next to him and that he wanted her, in spite of the handicap of weirdness that so disturbed him, for that serious flaw, unfortunately, did nothing to mar the exquisite beauty of her face or the succulence of her rounded form. The attraction, doubtless, was also due to his long period without a nubile damsel, and because he had no intention of involving himself with the equally peculiar Lora de Voisin, whom he suspected could be as formidable an enemy as a mistress.

He rolled over and to his surprise almost on top of the Bourbon 'peculiar' to whom he was secretly betrothed, unaware that she had chosen to sleep so close. Clearly, in spite of her brave front, she was timid, afraid of the dark forest, afraid of her visions, probably afraid of many things, including himself.

She was sleeping on her back, one cheek pillowed on her copper-silk hair, and in the ruddy firelight her expression, minus its voluptuous pout, was peaceful and sweet. He stared at the outlawed Templar medal on the chain around her neck, stared at her a moment, then ventured a finger to snake back a strand of hair caught in a crease of her neck. She didn't move, so he slipped the medal back under the top of her tunic, for it shouldn't be flaunted before the hag-ridden Bonpuys. Not that Ferrante himself would relish any encounter with a sorcerer's jag-toothed minion. He just did not believe they dwelt in every shadow and lonely outpost.

Sighing for everything, he lowered himself on his side beside her and slid a protective arm lightly over her ribs, fighting an urge to draw her closer against him. Even the piney scent of the dark forest did not obscure from him the delicious perfume of her hair and skin. But whenever he suspected he could some day fall under the spell of Lyse-Magdalene's porcelain beauty and occasional radiant smile, he remembered his hard existence with his present, abnormal wife, and knew he would definitely resist the lure of this damaged woman.

As they slept, the wind changed; smoke from the pine-wood embers of the fire wisped towards them.

Ferrante bolted upright at Lyse's scream, in his hand a naked dagger from under the blanket, but he saw nothing around them in the grey dawn. His charge, however, was kneeling, arms hugging herself, eyes blank and wide and staring at nothing. Tears ran down her face. She coughed, and blinked. And grief flooded her face.

"Lyse-Magdalene! "

"His flesh is blackening in the fire, and it is me, I did it, I gave him up, O God help me, O Perfect God help me," she wailed, and threw herself blindly into Ferrante's arms.

He held her tight, shaking his head. Seeing their alert but puzzled companions on their feet, weapons in hand, he shook his head more positively and waved them back. "Shh, shh," he tried to calm her, patting her back, and in a few moments her trembling stopped.

Still, she leaned against him and muttered into his chest, "I saw him,

Bernard chained amidst the burning faggots again, and the hot flames claimed him, even as the rain began. Oh, oh, such horror struck me!"

"You must bear it better, Mademoiselle. The man was already dead, you know that, mercifully garrotted."

"No, you don't understand! It was Mélline, she did it, she gave him up, it is her hatred for herself that tears out my insides."

"But the woman loved him. She would never betray him."

"But she did," Lyse panted. "I–I don't know why. And she had to be restrained from running to the flames to die with him. Oh, "

"Shhh, lady. It is just the seeing-back, you yourself are all right, and look, the sun is almost up. I will bring you a sip of water."

He was murmuring in her ear.

She realized now that that she was in his embrace and so pulled back in confusion, in spite of being distraught. "I beg your pardon, Don Ferrante. For those few moments that the memories control me, I cannot separate that woman's life from my own. It is unnerving, frightening."

Looking into her panicked blue eyes, seeing her lips tremble, Ferrante felt sudden compassion for the girl, and even an anger that she must be so tortured by an inherited fault. At that moment, if he could tear that peculiar 'seeing-back' from her, that twist in her mind which might doom her to eventual madness, he would. Feeling helpless, lacking something to say, he frowned at her.

He would have even hugged her once more, wordlessly trying to give her some of his strength to fight off any evil, but she pulled away and staggered to her feet. "Please, may we go back up to view Le Bézu again?" she asked.

He rose too, cocking his head at her to try and fathom her. "You really want to go back there? It will distress you."

"Oh, but I must, I must! It is what we are here for."

After a moment he nodded his consent, grudgingly because he remembered his assessment of her timidity. Now he understood that the lady was determined to help Charles de Bourbon, no matter at what cost to herself. That was most sacrificing, for a niece. Beyond duty, perhaps. But then again maybe not beyond duty, if one considered what relationship they might once have had.

He explained brusquely to the concerned sergeant and their guide, "It is nothing, Mademoiselle has merely suffered a *cauchemar,* a nightmare." Then he grabbed up a wooden cup and strode off, stone-faced, to a nearby stream to get the damsel some water, his softened attitude towards her toughened once more by aversion for her hallucinations and the unworthy, dirty little suspicion that dogged him.

Chapter 16

Later, they rode back to Rennes-le-Château mostly in silence.

Lyse was glum, for there had been no further stimulation to her memory from a second viewing of Le Bézu, although as she had stared up at it her mind seemed to strain uselessly towards a revelation, like pushing against a door that wouldn't open.

Ferrante, when she glanced at him, was wrapped in his thoughts, and she could wager they were ill humored ones connected with his involuntary tie to her, a futile seer, wasting the days. She was glad she hadn't mentioned Mélline's rendezvous with Bernard. The Italian was put off enough by the emotional distress the 'seeing-back' brought upon her; *mon Dieu,* what would he think if she told him the shamefully sensuous turmoil that erotic 'dream' the night before had caused in her body?

His mild encouragement when she was disappointed on the mountain didn't fool her, or even his support when she woke in the night so terrified, for even without faith in their mission he wouldn't discourage her while they were where she'd demanded to be.

But her dejection lifted immediately as they rode through the gates of Rennes-le-Château and she spied a party of pack animals being unloaded by a couple of muleteers and the two brothers Collini.

"*Une miracle!* My clothes," Lyse cried out in delight.

"Finally, my armor," exulted the deep voice behind her.

And just then Germain Matz came through the château doorway. Lyse slipped from her horse before the groom had caught its halter, and ran with glad squeals to fling her arms about her friend. "Oh, heaven be thanked, oh Germain, how I have missed you," she burbled as they hugged each other. "But don't even look at me, I have been wearing the same few pieces of clothes for weeks," she exaggerated, forgetting that the Couiza seamstress had sewed her two new summer bodices. In her excitement she even forgot that at the moment she was sporting a boy's tunic and leggings, and that her straight hair swung loose down her back.

Mastering his eyes with an effort so as not to stare at her lissome form and shapely legs, Germain's plain face mirrored her delight. He shook his head. "You look beautiful to me, *ma princesse*. I am so grateful to see you again."

"Oh, me too, me too, Germain, oh, I have thought of you every day. "Ignoring that Gonzaga was rolling his eyes at her gushing, she tugged the young man along by the arm. "Let the others bring in the baggage. Come inside, we'll demand something cool to drink, and talk and talk and talk, I have so much to tell you!"

Ferrante's brows knit as he watched them disappear into the dark maw of the entry. He didn't care much for Mademoiselle de Bourbon-Tonnière's too familiar attachment to that fellow.

"So? How did it go?" he growled to Lucco.

"*Multo bene,* Signore," his sly-eyed squire assured him. "I didn't wait no longer than five days at Claremont and there came the lady's man with all your belongings, bragging he fooled those who had wanted to detain or follow him—a story I leave to him to tell you. At that collapsed bridge we took a chance on the downstream ferry, and although the fording 'twas rough, and the rope holding the boat from being swept off was near unraveling with the strain, the animals did not panic, we did not overturn or drown. Beyond Rodez we came upon a merchant's caravan that had just been stripped by *banditti,* the guards killed; 'twas but the mercy of God we had not come along earlier to fall into the thieves dirty hands. *E verro,* that Matz is not bad on the road, he is not much smart or crafty, but he does not rattle easily."

"As usual, well done, Lucco." Ferrante flipped up a gold coin which the squire caught in mid-air and pocketed with grin. "Let us get out of the sun. I'm anxious to hear why Matz thought he might have been followed."

"Eh, he had a good reason," Lucco declared, hustling to keep up with his master's long stride toward the château entry.

Lyse was so overjoyed at Germain's presence she didn't notice how flat his tone was when he assured her that her old nurse was well. But even though the tale he told, of the *comte* de Marques' aggressive search—not for Bourbon but for insignificant her—was confounding, she heard it more with surprise than with fear. She had Ferrante di Gonzaga, Tournel, Germain and the Bourbon guards surrounding her. The men on the watchtowers would report any strangers approaching. Here she was safe.

When she parted from the men, she literally ran up the stairs to her chamber, where Marye was already shaking out the crumpled skirts and bodices drawn from the traveling chests and hanging them on the crude pegs available.

Lyse, in her boy's clothes, danced among them as if they were golden treasures, and coming upon the traveling dress she'd presently been wearing to death, tossed it at the maidservant. "Here, take this away somewhere. I don't want to see it again for the next year. And thank you for lending your son's garb, you may have it back as soon as I remove it." She started to pick off the pine needles still clinging to the rough cloth.

The woman shook her head. "Monsieur de Gonzaga paid me for them, they are yours now, Mademoiselle. I'll brush them off and fold them away, maybe you'll use them again," she said, with no interest about where they had been.

"Then bring soap, I want to sponge all the dirt off me, and then I'd be happy if you'll help me dress and brush my hair thoroughly to rid it of dust and pine needles; wearing it loose was not so fine an idea after all. And look, there's my dressing mirror in that pack, oh finally, quick let us prop it up on the chests until it can be hung."

Lyse's tone grew giddy as they adjusted the little framed square of mirror. "I wish to look splendid tonight. I'll wear that marigold damask gown, the creases should come out if you keep shaking it. That, and the white satin kirtle showing, with three petticoats under, and my round-arched hat with the black fall behind, because I've never liked those gabled hoods. The scarlet stockings and the Spanish leather slippers, oh, what's become of them?"

She tore off the boy's clothes as she chattered away, and when Marye brought a round, wooden tub of water Lyse stood naked in it and squeezed the water onto herself from a soapy sponge, humming a tune as she washed, the warm, pleasant breeze from the window caressing her glistening skin and bringing occasional faint whiffs of heliotrope.

Encircled by men, she was determined to look just beautiful at supper: in honor of Germain's arrival; because Tournel had never seen her in anything but a monk's robe or her simple travel garb; and because it was fun to titillate the *sieur* and especially to make his wife jealous. These were her reasons for the care she took in dressing and in knotting up her coppery hair and frizzing the hanging tendrils, for at last the crimping iron was available to be heated over a charcoal brazier. She also pinched at her lips to bring up color in them.

The insolent green gaze that had studied with speculative interest her form in the clinging boy's garb had nothing to do with her powdering and primping and hours-long toilette.

Apparently the big Mantuan had been happy to see his wardrobe again too, for he'd spent the weeks tromping about the church site or hunting with de Voisin in his plain, traveling doublet and sturdy boots.

That night he also turned up in the Great Hall in his fine clothes: broad, padded sleeves, codpiece, square-toed shoes, fancy-hilted sword and all, once more the breast-plated *condottiere* and jaunty frequenter of fashionable courts. He met Lyse at the bottom of the stair, offered his arm and brought her to the table.

"Hola," teased the cheerful *sieur* at the sight of both of them, "what transformation! Could these be our two guests from the Bourbonnais? Mademoiselle, Signore, you have surely brought a whiff of the Court to these dreary old walls. Mademoiselle Lyse-Magdalene, I did not think you could gladden these dulled eyes any further, but so you do this night. You are marvelous lovely," he chirped in homage and fervently kissed Lyse's hand. She smiled charmingly, but flicked an arch, female glance toward his wife.

Gonzaga dutifully followed the old gentleman's lead and made Lyse a polite compliment, and Tournel bowed low, his dark eyes gleaming. Germain, too, invited at Lyse's request and his hair genteelly slicked down, made a deferential bow. One need only glance at his face to see his worshipful admiration of her.

La Dame, with a dry smile, said nothing, but when Lyse looked for a moment into the silvery eyes she was taken aback: they seemed to attenuate, elongate, and she had the disorienting impression of an empty, whirling vortex behind them. Then, in a moment, the grey stare resumed substance again, and it was just veiled female jealousy stabbing out at her over the heavy-lipped smile.

During supper they picked over Germain's account of de Marques appearance at St. Piteu, and of course, in front of him and Tournel, Ferrante handled the Lorraine's demand for the whereabouts of Mademoiselle de Bourbon-Tonnière as simple harassment of the fugitive duke's relatives.

"Ah, I believe this conversation both frightens and saddens you, Lyse-Magdalene," la Dame remarked in her husky voice, noticing a glisten in her guest's light blue eyes.

"Ah, *oui*, Madame, for St. Piteu is a small domain where I was raised and lived until early last spring, it was my home. And–" Lyse hesitated, since it didn't seem right to say it had been Bourbon's gift to her upon her betrothal to a man still married, "–and it has special meaning for me, and for Germain Matz too, whose father is *intendant* there. It pains me to hear it is gone."

"Your sadness is understandable then, for the place where I was a child is no longer available to me either. But you needn't fear that the King's henchmen will find you here, for they won't, and it is time I showed you why, after we have finished our meal. Both of you." Her pouf of silver-grey hair shimmered in the light of the torchières as her eyes engaged Gonzaga's and although the subject was serious, nevertheless the little, seductive smile played on her lips. Finally her gaze shifted. "You too, Tournel, for you will have to defend the lady, should it ever come to that. And–?" Her questioning look went from Germain to the Mantuan.

But Lyse indignantly forestalled Blackbeard's answer. "Of course Germain Matz is to be included! He is a trusted and loyal friend, who barely escaped with his life from that man, de Marques."

"As you wish, my dear," their hostess agreed smoothly. "In fact, I will cheer you. I have seen your symbol as I laid out my Tarot cards today, and I have seen that good news for you will be arriving here soon "

Lyse grabbed at this. "News from my uncle Charles?"

Her hostess shrugged her big shoulders. "You'll have to wait and see." She cut off any more questions by turning to Ferrante to chat.

When they pushed back from the remains of their simple meal, la Dame, true to her word, took the triple candelbranch from the table and led them beyond the shadowy Great Hall and across another large chamber smelling strongly of age, a vaulted, columned space so ancient it was attributed to the Visigoths. At its far end there was a round tower which formed a corner with the wall which had been built to seal off the residence from the ruins. The rooms of this tower were empty, she told them, its conical roof collapsed and wooden floors too rotted by rain to withstand exploring.

But la Dame sailed not towards the door that opened to the tower's crumbly steps, but to where the structure's curve joined with the straight wall. She stooped to examine, just off floor level, the wide border of decorative pink bricks which ran around the walls of the room in a geometric design.

"Look here," she said, and counted three bricks from the curve of the tower and one brick down. She pushed hard on a corner of that brick. It swung in on a pivot, scraping against something, they heard a ping, then the grind of machinery and weights pulling on chains, and in several moments, to their surprise, part of the curved side of the tower moved ponderously aside and gaped open, forming a narrow doorway.

"'Tis a hidden passage, built into the width of the thick tower wall. This ring on the inside of the door will pull it closed, and a mechanism engages to push the key brick back into place. I'm not versed in machinery, I have no idea how it works, but it does." La Dame stepped into the opening and lifted her candlebranch to reveal to their eyes a small landing, with narrow steps leading down into a well of darkness.

"Where does it go?" Ferrante grunted.

"All the way down, dug through the mount itself. It once led to Coustaussa, that château beyond the town, but the outlet there was blocked centuries ago when Coustaussa was battered apart by siege machines for shielding Cathars. From Coustaussa there was a further passage leading to Montségur, the most important of Cathar strongholds on the heights, but that was lost as well."

Ferrante stepped into the entry, filling it up, staring down the steps. "So we may hide here momentarily, but without any egress at the other end. If an enemy takes this place and remains, we are trapped."

The silvery eyes blinked. "No, of course not. There is another exit at the base of our mount, under a flat stone hidden by overgrowth, which can be pushed up and slid aside. I'll show you where it emerges outside tomorrow. Inside, you keep following the steps and the tunnels down, and the stone is marked with a sign you will not miss.

"Le *sieur* is fascinated with the mechanism of this door," she continued. "It gives us a sense of security as well, so he keeps it working by once a year applying grease to these chains and gears. And in this basket," she indicated a covered container on the landing, "are candles, a flint and striker, other necessities." She gave her throaty chuckle. "Just pray you never need to come up this stair. That many steps can kill all but the most hardy."

But Lyse had seen that the very narrow steps cut within the width of the tower wall went up, too, and she wondered out loud what they lead to.

"To a small chamber, hidden between a false floor and ceiling, once used as a temporary refuge for fleeing Cathar *parfaits*. It was not uncomfortable, and it had air from a concealed window. But 'tis too dangerous to examine it at present, the floor is weak."

The thought came so strongly Lyse bit her lip not to cry it aloud: that had to be it! That forgotten room was where Mélline met with her knight, in safety and in secret.

The truth was, she felt glad that the chamber of those lovers was inaccessible, viewing it would be too invasive of passions that should be private. Even as she thought of it, the memory of Mélline's ecstasy with Bernard produced a sensual picture of twining, naked bodies to flit through her mind and she brushed at her forehead as if that would wipe her sudden yearning away. A quick, guilty glance showed her that Blackbeard was watching her as he always seemed to be watching her lately, his expression neutral.

"Should the necessity come to use this escape, you will have time to prepare," la Dame assured them as Tournel pushed closed the heavy door, its fit so perfect when closed that one could not see any trace of it in the tower's brickwork. "Warning of any interlopers in the valley would be signaled to us early."

Now there was a sardonic gleam in Gonzaga's green eyes as he asked, "But what say your Tarot cards about such interlopers, Madame? Shall we expect them?"

"I have not yet inquired of the Tarot," she answered with haughty solemnity. "One must not peer too far into the future by that method. But, Mademoiselle, your good news comes soon."

After the Voisins retired, the remaining little group gambled at the cleared table until late, delighted to have in Germain a fourth bettor for a game of flux–a fast, mindless game where each drew three cards, discarded one for a fourth and whomever had all the same color first, or bluffed it, won the stakes, which could build into a tidy sum. They played for low stakes fed after every deal to accommodate both Germain, who nevertheless garnered a raised eyebrow from Ferrante for having the luck to stay even, and Lyse, who consistently lost, all the while sweetly suggesting that everyone was cheating.

"But you pass good cards from your hand without remembering what was given up, Mademoiselle," Ferrante finally lectured her, indicating the discard pile. "With such silliness an unscrupulous player could trounce you in a quarter hour of everything you own."

She bridled at the insult to her intelligence. "Well, you cheat. I saw you marking the trefoils with your ring's edge."

Ferrante sat back in disgust. "I did no such thing. You do not lose well, lady," he rumbled. A man he would have sliced in half for such a slur. With her he consoled himself with his view of the white breasts half-revealed by her yellow brocade bodice. She had been so enticing in her finery and elated mood he'd had difficulty taking his eyes from her all evening.

But, annoyed with her losing streak, she announced precipitously, "*Tiens*, if I am so stupid, I no longer wish to play," and she jumped up and slapped her cards down. "It is late, so I bid you all good night." Turning to Germain she vented more pique at Ferrante.

"*Écoutes*, Germain, the Signore and I take a short ride to exercise our horses every morning before breakfast. Please do you join us tomorrow."

Not the least bit shamed by her childish display, she nodded all around and swept away to her bed, skirts rustling, nose high in the air.

With a twist of a smile on his face, Ferrante watched her glide from the hall. It was damn strange how her rashness amused him when from another woman the same would have irritated him. Maybe he enjoyed the pouty curve of her mouth, or seeing the incongruous glare of disdain from such soft and artless eyes.

What he certainly didn't like was having to share their daily, high-spirited morning canter on the river road, and their companionable singing on the way back, with that glum, spike-haired varlet of hers. Tomorrow, maybe, he would allow it, but that was all.

The good news arrived a week later and from not very far, in the pouch of Madame de Joyeuse's liveried courier: invitations for all to come to the Château de Puivert for a fortnight's celebration of her fiftieth birthday! There would be banqueting, picnics, entertainment, and even a gala tournament, with gentlemen from as far as Gascony taking part.

Ferrante, although himself dubious over whether they should attend and draw attention to their presence in the area, thought Mademoiselle de Bourbon-Tonnière's ecstatic smile at the invitation would light up the whole Razès.

But in a private conversation la Dame advised him to go, nor was her reason frivolous. Puivert in centuries past had been famous for its stylish court, bruited for its celebrations and troubadours and poets and philosophers, a veritable magnet for the well-born all through Languedoc and from northern Spain as well. Old records told that some of the Templar leadership had sojourned at Puivert, and in all probability the Mélline of Lyse's memory had visited too. The short trip might be fruitful, la Dame argued, a trigger for other flashes of recall in Lyse's mind.

The problem was keeping this Bourbon presence in the area unremarked by anyone likely to inform the Lorraines. La Dame suggested that the young woman could go merely as Mademoiselle de Tonnière, an obscure person from unimportant St. Piteu, visiting her relatives, the Voisins.

"But it is you, *mon brave,* who can hardly be missed," la Dame purred to Ferrante, her gaze as sensuous as a caress as he paced the floor of her disordered chamber. "Some of the guests, the *comte* de Foix certainly, should he attend, will know you are Bourbon's man and might have charge of his missing niece."

"You forget, Lora, that thus far it is not actually the king who so actively searches for Lyse-Magdalene, but only the Lorraines. Would those villains enlist Gaston de Foix in their greedy quest by making much of the obscure Lyse-Magdalene?"

"You have a point."

"No, they would not, they wouldn't allow anyone else to share in what they hope to gain from her."

"Still, what would you, a *splendido* of the battlefield, be doing in the Razès when it is known that your close cousin Bourbon is in Italy building up an army? What, I ask? Recruiting the mountain goats? You are conspicuous."

Ferrante leaned a forearm against the high mantle while he scowled into the cold hearth, rubbed his beard, twiddled with his earring– He suddenly snapped his fingers. "Passing through. I am merely passing through the area on my way to the shrine of Santiago de Campostela to send up desperate prayers for my sick wife. And you have asked me to escort your guest to the Puivert festivities. *Voilà!* Simple."

"Not yet, my *bravo*. Would anyone who has met you before believe you are so devout as to make a pilgrimage for your wife?"

Or that I even care that much about my wife, the cruel thought echoed in Ferrante's head. But still he was not deterred. "Bah, then let them guess what I'm doing here," he said impatiently, "They couldn't imagine my mission in a million years."

"If he were informed of your presence, Claude de Guise could. De Marques could."

"I'll take the chance."

"And what if anyone else is present at Puivert who saw Lyse-Magdalene at Moulins and knows her for a Bourbon?"

"She only spent a few months at Charles' court. Jean de Joyeuse felt those gentlemen there from this area, at least any who were aware of her, would be in his military compliment, far away." He gnawed at his lip, then gave a decisive nod. "In any case, since it could trigger her visions, as you remind me, we are forced to take the chance. We'll have to handle what arises when it comes."

"You want to take her because she wants to go."

For a moment Ferrante hated the silver-haired woman. "I want to take her because it is expedient, as you mentioned."

Lora de Voisin's smile remained enigmatic. She stretched like a cat, fluttering her grey veils. "Tell me, have you no thought of telling her that her old Nurse is dead?"

"No, for what purpose? It would make her grieve, and the brutality of the death would frighten her. It's best to keep her mind uncluttered. That minion of hers, Matz, did well not to mention the murder in her presence."

Lora shrugged, she had just been curious. She toyed with her earring. "Le *sieur* and I will not go to Puivert, we rarely leave here, you know, but I will send with you a jar of my exquisite rose balm to the Marquise. However, Ferrante, I should like to keep by my side that fellow, Matz. It turns out he has familiarity with the medicinal blending of herbs and roots, and so he is helping to me to find a potion strong enough to revive Madame de Dunois. The woman is fast losing what small strength she has left."

In fact, Ferrante had several times noted la Dame with Matz as they entered de Dunois' chamber with trays of various boxes and bottles, the spiky-haired fellow's expression grave, his doublet usually streaked with some sort of powder or fluid.

"In that case I doubt Lyse-Magdalene will refuse you his company, and for my part, I make you a present of him."

"You don't like him, do you? Why not? He seems innocuous enough, he knows his place and keeps it."

"Yes, but it is the lady who doesn't know his place. She literally fawns all over him."

Immediately Ferrante was sorry he said it, for with irritation he could easily read la Dame's sly smile. It said 'jealous'.

Chapter 17

So their wardrobes, all washed, brushed and cleaned, were packed up again, and the steel of Ferrante's sixty-pound suit of armor, with its jut-visored helmet, was burnished by Marco into a mirror-like gloss. They departed Rennes-le-Château with Tournel and Ferrante's two menservants, and Marye's daughter to attend Lyse.

It took Lyse a while on the road to repair her spirits, for she had spent a most melancholy quarter hour at the bedside of the shrunken and immobile Madame de Dunois, holding her fragile hand in farewell, and she had murmured to her whether the unconscious woman could hear or not, begging the governess to return to the world. The tears that leaked from Lyse's eyes at that bedside were for her governess, indeed, but also for her uncle, her mother, her vanished world, herself...

But oh, at this moment it was a glorious, blue-skied day, and the crops were high and lush in the fields, and the fruit trees were heavy with their delicious burdens. The shadows lifted from her as they shared the rutted road west from Quillan with villagers, farm wagons, herders, or in contrast, other finely-dressed travelers on horseback or in litters, who were surely headed for Puivert.

Not in any rush, they stood aside to let a large, jingling equipage pass them, the front riders, under orange and blue pennants, whooping and hollering to clear the road. These were followed by a resplendent, supercilious noble couple who cantered by on silk-draped horses without sparing a glance for them, and who were followed in like manner by a procession of elegant ladies and gentlemen and a stiff-backed troop of guards.

"Did you recognize who that was?" Lyse asked Ferrante, wide-eyed and impressed as the little court disappeared in its own dust.

"The *comte* and *comtesse* de Foix, I think, from the device on their banners. He holds great power in the region just west of here, and he is sometimes directly at the King's back in his Italian campaigns. Fortunately he does not know me, although he may have heard of me as one of the duke's intimates. I shall do my best to avoid him."

She sniffed. "I am certain now that we should have taken along the rest of the Bourbon guards, so as not to appear insignificant."

"Insignificant will suit us admirably," he growled, and they continued on.

As they rode Lyse amused herself by discreetly studying the parties of gentles they passed, or who passed them, and with whom they exchanged courteous nods. Already two separate gentlemen had glanced very warmly at her in her green velvet cloak, and she thought each of them attractive too. If the reproving scowl Blackbeard tried to hide from her was for her flirting, she didn't care.

The road curved into a descent, and then there opened before them a wide valley of such beauty it brought a delighted gasp from Lyse. The vast sky was reflected below in an azure lake, inlaid like a huge and sparkling gem amidst the surrounding low, green hills, their undulating slopes striped with the pale gold of blowing grain and the smudgy, indigo blue of the pastel fields.

The spreading lake, as they saw its long length on coming down into the valley, was pristine and untenanted along its reedy banks, and only flights of wild ducks flapping above it marred the mirror of its tranquil, blue waters.

In the distance, on a low hill commanding the lake, loomed Puivert, an old castle built of orange-gold stone, and, were the day not fair to begin with, Lyse thought it would surely seem sunny just looking at the glowing aspect of the château, its old ramparts gaily draped with flower garlands to welcome the arriving guests.

This Languedoc seat of the *marquis* de Joyeuse was not especially large, but where Moulins had been overwhelming, and Rennes-le-Château depressing, Puivert exuded joyousness, even at a distance, even before one crossed over its irregular moat. In a froth of excited anticipation, Lyse thought the panorama of golden Puivert and its lovely, peaceful lake and valley the most beautiful sight she'd ever seen.

Her companion, squinting at it, agreed with her. "I'd forgotten its charm. In fact, it's one of the few castles in the Razès intact, you see it just as it was built in the twelfth century. Somehow Puivert escaped the violence this countryside suffered in the church's hunt for Cathars, and even in the raids a century later, when some of the Knights-Templar discovered here surrendered without a fight." He saw her staring up at the château, whose moderate rise they were approaching. "Well, have you any sense at all that Mélline was here?"

Reminded of why they had come, other than for enjoyable distraction, Lyse took the moment to concentrate, her gaze drawing inward and her pale brows knitting. "No, nothing," she admitted, finally. "At least, not yet," she defended herself.

"Well, don't fret, we've hardly arrived."

Stop pushing me and I won't fret, Lyse thought petulantly.

But just before they rode across the drawbridge, where stood a quartet of parti-colored musicians fluttering with ribbons, capering and playing cheerfully on lute, horns and drum to welcome the guests arriving that day, Ferrante noticed how the young woman's eyes shone and felt bound to recall her attention to their purpose.

From the side of his mouth he muttered, "Tell me, Lyse-Magdalene, do you love your uncle? Do you understand his dire need and what we are trying to do, as swiftly as possible?"

"Of course. Why do you always ask me that?"

"Then mind carefully what you say. Except with me, and only partially with Madame de Joyeuse, do not stray from the tales we have prepared, and answer any questions obliquely, if at all."

"I know that," she gritted. "*Ciel!* You are worse than Madame de Dunois. How can you think I am so frivolous that I cannot understand my position?" She kicked her horse and rode onto the drawbridge ahead of him, her white chiffon scarf flowing back.

"Because, *ma donna,* that is easy to believe of you," was his caustic thought, even as he admired the proud grace of her carriage in the side-saddle.

He was definitely not going to allow her to stray far from his sight during the revelries. To see she did not stumble in their deception, of course.

It was long past midnight at Puivert when Lyse returned to her chamber after a wonderful evening. As soon as her sleepy maid helped her undress and then retired to a small pallet in the corner, Lyse flung herself at the open window in a delirium of happiness, propping her elbows up on the slanted sill and smiling out into the moonlit night, as the merry, reedy music for the dance still went round and round in her head.

The breeze cooled her and played with her flowing hair and the soft chemise she wore for a nightdress. She drank in, like a heady draught, the shadowed sight of the hill-girt lake and the fields about, lying tranquil in the creamy light of a half moon.

The air was like silk, wafting the scent of late-blooming flowers and charming Lyse as she mulled about how practiced a dancer Blackbeard had turned out to be, how even the intricate steps and turned-out toes of the *branle* had not fazed him, and how, to the irked disappointment of several gentlemen who had noted her, he often claimed her at the first sound of the flute and drum. But strangely, the way he tried to monopolize her, pleased her. She liked dancing with him and she blessed Madame de Dunois for ordering the dancemaster who had come all the way from Bourges to St. Piteu last summer to teach her all the intricate patterns.

She loved it that the supercilious Mantuan was visibly intrigued that the little country mouse could handle herself so well in the demanding court dances. She loved it that the court finery she'd acquired at Moulins, seductively displaying shoulders, bosom and little waist, kept drawing that volatile green gaze to her, and she believed the elegance of her dress surely reminded him that she ranked, after all, somewhat higher than he.

There'd been a marvelous supper, with entertainment and dancing for the hundred guests already arrived, all splendidly garbed in satin, brocade and jewels, and in high spirits. These southern barons seemed friendlier than the aristocracy at Moulins, for even as ordinary Mademoiselle de Tonnière she was received cordially—except by the aloof Gaston de Foix and his wife, the ranking nobility of the entire area.

Lyse's stay at Puivert had already begun auspiciously, for Madame la Marquise, honoring that she was in reality Bourbon's niece, had assigned her this fine chamber facing the lake. She was to share it with a Joyeuse daughter, a nun, but the woman hadn't arrived yet and so she had it all to herself to loll dreamily at the window in the dead of night instead of going to sleep.

Even in this short a time, she adored Puivert. The château, all crenellated walls and square towers alternating with round ones, was built around a great, rectangular interior court. The ceiling of its Great Hall displayed the vivid banners of families in liege to the *marquis*, and in most rooms the walls were warmed by expansive tapestries depicting the coy romances of Roman deities.

Wherever she found herself in the animated castle, Lyse had the impression that its golden-orange stones had never known any sound but laughter and conversation and music. She had no impression that catastrophe had ever overtaken Puivert, and indeed, that melancholy, underlying stillness she felt elsewhere in the Razès was absent here, and thus did not mute the beauty of the Joyeuse's castle and its smooth mirror of a lake.

Francine, Marquise de Joyeuse, the wife of her uncle's chief advisor, was warm-natured, deep-chested and perspiring, with grey strands peppering her dark hair. The lady was everywhere at once seeing that her guests were cosseted and entertained, but she had asked Lyse and Don Ferrante to attend her privately, for they had been last to see her husband before he fled the country with Bourbon. She was under the impression, of course, that Lyse was here with truncated name in this far reach of France in order to dodge Francois' royal spite.

The messenger from Bourbon they'd received at Rennes-le-Château had also carried to the *marquise* a letter, but Jean de Joyeuse was no writer; his epistle was loving but short. So at the lady's request, her guests attended her in her cozy dressing room and imparted whatever more they knew of the duke's whereabouts and actions, which would include Joyeuse.

"Ah, child," the *marquise* finally murmured to Lyse, shaking her head, "when a woman marries a man of the sword, she leads a widow's life long before his death. I try to be cheerful, but in spite that my young son, and my daughters and grandchildren surround me, 'tis not the same as a dear husband by my side. Especially on this occasion." She sighed wistfully and patted tiny drops of perspiration from her upper lip. "*Ciel,* fifty! One wonders how such an antique age came about so soon."

"Were your appearance to describe the age of fifty, Madame, the whole world would consider it but a very tiny step from youth." Ferrante paid her the graceful compliment easily.

"Fie, you lie, Signore," the matron demurred with a pleased blush, "but oh, so charmingly." Her warm eyes studied them with wise perception, and although she did not say so, it was easy to see she thought them a striking pair. But she said, "Tell me, Don Ferrante, will you remain long at Rennes-le-Château?"

"As long as monseigneur le *Duc* assigns me to guard the welfare of his niece, Madame."

"Then it is the most pleasant task of all your cousin has awarded you," the lady observed, meaning to be cordial.

But Lyse saw Ferrante stiffen. She could read his mind by now, she felt his mortification that the *marquise's* husband risked his life to remain at Charles de Bourbon's side, while he rotted in safety with her. And she had surprised herself by feeling a dollop of sympathy for him, the manacled gladiator.

Now, at the window, still smiling to herself, mellow but unwilling to seek her bed, Lyse let her gaze lazily follow the shadowed contours of the lake's reedy banks, for she could see a good part of the large body of water from her height. The moon cleaved a silver, shimmery path through the water–

but she leaned out further anyway to see the lights, ah there, somewhere on the farther bank, a few points of light moving, bobbing in the dark, small as fireflies at this distance but seeming not natural, lanterns perhaps, or torches. She strained to see what might be happening and deep anxiety struck at her, oh, they

were much too visible, they could be remarked, in spite of the ravages and desola-
tion around them. The lights moved jerkily

—and of course, they were surely fishermen, plying their trade in small boats. So Lyse entertained a giant yawn and decided it was finally time to sleep. After the morrow's hunt Don Ferrante had promised to tip one of the *marquise's* falconers to teach her the rudiments of flying a hawk. She closed the shutters against the night air, padded to her bed and after punching her feather pillow into shape settled down on her back.

But her eyes popped wide open. What? Desolation? In this fertile valley? Around that lovely lake? Why in heaven had she thought such a thing?

Turning on her side, she tried to distract herself by conjuring up the engaging gentlemen who had paid her court that day with all their compliments and witty chit-chat. But all she could raise against her closed eyelids was Don Ferrante's sardonic image and the way his smile crinkled the scar under his eye. His face refused to go away. So she courted sleep by jerking into a curled ball—and remembered the firm clasp of his hand when they danced, and how, although he conversed little, his proprietary gaze was often on her.

Well, she wasn't his yet, in fact she had gone out of her way to flirt and tease the local gallants, just to prove it.

After the gala evenings that followed Lyse made it a pleasant ritual to take the air by the window and calm down before sleeping, doing so quietly, for she shared the bed with the *marquise's* daughter Louise, a Sister of Charity, as thin and invisible as her mother was plump and convivial, and the nun retired early in order to wake before dawn to say her morning offices.

In spite of staring, only once more did Lyse spot the lights of the fishermen, far across the moonstreaked lake, although she couldn't make out their boats. She wondered what fish they caught in those deep waters that kept them out so late, and surely their harvest appeared on Puivert's bounteous board.

She idly asked the question at a gathering of certain female guests who had been invited to take the noon meal with the *marquise* and her ladies in a spacious tower room whose windows overlooked the valley. The chamber had small and exquisite sculptures of musicians, lutanist, rebec player, flutist and so forth carved at the base point of each Gothic arch which supported its high ceiling.

"I've twice seen their lights. I just wondered what the fisherfolk catch at night," she queried brightly as she sopped the last of her rich venison gravy from the plate, and looked forward to the milk-and-cinnamon pudding that had just been placed on the long, damask-covered table.

The *marquise* had been half-listening to a trio of high-voiced young men behind her, singing madrigals to a hurdy-gurdy and pipe accompaniment, but now she turned her attention fully on Lyse. In fact, most chattering and conversation near them stopped, at least among the ladies resident in the area, who stared askance.

"I must say, there are no fish in our lake, Mademoiselle, save a boney little pilcher only a cat could eat. No fish at all," the *marquise* responded calmly.

But one of the *marquise's* attendant ladies cried out, "Oh, *Sainte Vierge!* Madame, she's seen them, the cursed lights! Oh, never have I, although I've looked and looked. Oh, the very thought makes my heart stop!"

Another quavered, "Could this be an evil omen, Madame? For 'tis seldom people see those lights without some misery descending."

The *marquise* frowned and batted at the woman with her napkin. "Hush you, Madame Gaillarboys, that is not true and you will frighten my guests. Tell us, Mademoiselle, where did you see these lights? Or perhaps you were imagining?"

"Why, in the distance, somewhere on the other side of the lake, bobbing as if being carried forward, or in a boat on the water."

The *marquise* raised her thick eyebrows.

The remark she was forming was forestalled by the first lady, who insisted, "Aha, see, 'tis him, the Damned One, I tell you! That's who!" Round-eyed wonder warred with fright on her face.

"Rinaldo! Please to sing softer," the *marquise* ordered the trio over her shoulder, then pushed her pillowed seat back from the table to make a little more room for her stomach. She stared a Lyse a moment, who was obviously disconcerted with everyone's reaction, then smiled to reassure her. "Don't be alarmed, *mon enfant,* you are not mad, you do probably see lights where no lights are. Others have reported the same for centuries, although our pastor says it is all folly, imaginings generated by bad digestion of tough *pisse-en-lits.* But we have had no dandelion greens to our plates lately. So I see I am bound to relate to you the unhappy story of our lovely lake."

"Oh, a tale, do tell us a shivery tale," one of the visitors said eagerly, and there were expectant murmurs and rustles from the rest of the long table as the ladies made themselves more comfortable in their chairs. Francine de Joyeuse clasped her plump, ringed hands on the table, took a noisy breath through her nostrils, and began.

"In our Lord's year of twelve hundred seventy-nine, Puivert was owned by a baron named Bruyères, who enjoyed, as his longtime guest, a young and spoiled Aragonaise princess, a relative of his wife. The name of this lady, reported a fine beauty, has been lost, but because she always dressed in white, she was always called 'la Dame Blanche'. This damsel adored our beautiful château, which the troubadours of the time made famous far and wide as one of the châteaux of Love and Dreams. So when she first saw, in the middle of the lake, a jutting boulder which, by caprice of nature, looked somewhat like a chair with arms, she gleefully adopted it as her own.

"It is said that every late afternoon, surrounded by her friends, she had four huge Saracen slaves row them all out to lounge on the rock, where they would admire how the vibrant sunsets danced fiery sparkles along the surface of the placid water.

"Then, unhappily, for several years in a row, the valley suffered unusual storms of rain all year, and the level of the lake rose and rose until, this year we speak of, the comfortable rock in its center was almost engulfed, to say nothing of the villages and fields bordering it, and the river that feeds it, which is named the Hers. Only the fishermen were delighted."

The *marquise*, an animated story-teller, looked about in satisfaction at her rapt audience hanging on every word, even though a number of them already knew the old legend.

"The White Lady was desolate to lose her rock and like any silly child who had lost a toy, she pouted and moaned and whined her disappointment to the Baron Bruyeres. He, one presumes, was covetous of the favors of this temptress, for when the weather recovered, to please her he went out one dark night with a company of stout diggers from the gold mines and attacked the lake bank, thinking to enlarge the lake's outlet into the river Hers and drain away its excess water.

"And so, of course, the lake level did go down and in a few days the White Lady's favorite 'armchair' appeared once more and she was in a transport of delight. Perhaps she even rendered the besotted Baron his reward." Francine chuckled at the witticism and winked at one of her guests. "Nevertheless, *his* reward from our Blessed Guardian On High for tampering with nature was not long in coming."

Her tone turned ominous. "On the first day that the White Lady and her charmingly-dressed attendants and rowers again ensconced themselves on their mid-lake perch, reciting poetry, declaiming on the beauty of the scene and singing, there was a rumble under the earth and the lake's banks, weakened by rain and the channel the Baron had dug, shook like jelly and with a heart-stopping roar totally collapsed. The lake rushed out over the broken banks and chuted down into the valley, a sudden huge wall of water, and it swept along to their deaths the unfortunate princess and her screaming friends, along with trees, rocks and boats. It drowned the bustling town of Mirepoix and a number of other villages, and carried along on its murderous tide hundreds upon hundreds of bodies and animal corpses."

The ladies murmured uncomfortably, looking at each other, and several crossed themselves. The hostess picked up her round parchment fan and began wielding it energetically. Her silk gown had damp spots under the arms and at the front of her tight, straining bodice.

"It was a frightful catastrophe the imprudent Baron of Puivert had unloosed on his unsuspecting neighbors for all those leagues down the flooded river, and the result, beside death and destruction all around, was that the lake drained almost dry. For thirty-six years it remained a huge, stinking depression in the ground, filled with mud and weeds and the broken bones of the hamlets that had been on its banks, with only the narrow channel of the swift-running river flowing down the middle. And the infamous, chair-like boulder had disappeared! Or at least, so it is said.

"When finally the Baron's son Thomas inherited this Château, he built, as a surprise for his bride, a strong dam where the far banks had been, and cleared and widened the river's inlet into the lake's vast hole. And in two years there was again a deep lake at Puivert, it again became the lovely jewel we see now, set like a sapphire in the crown of our countryside." The *marquise* showed her crooked front tooth in a smile of triumph at so pretty an end to a tragic story. But the lady who had spoken before looked around with a haunted expression and declared to them all, "Mercy on us, Mesdames, but even so the lake is considered cursed. The poor town of Mirepoix was rebuilt further away, but never again did the other flooded hamlets and drowned villages arise. And most fish do not survive in it now. The rest of the story is that the ghost of the White Lady was condemned to roam the lake banks every summer, ever searching for her special rock, never to rest into eternity."

Enthralled with the tale, Lyse nevertheless had to remark on the injustice that retribution fell only on the princess. "It surely was not all *her* fault," she declared.

"You have a kind heart, Mademoiselle," the *marquise* nodded. "No, she was not held to account alone."

The intemperate lady next to her again raised her excited voice. "Those are the lights some people spy, as you have, for Jean de Bruyeres's spectre pays for his dreadful folly, condemned to dig away at that far bank forever. But wherever he has excavated in the night miraculously becomes whole again before morning. Of a summer night the White Lady walks and weeps in the reeds and the cursed Baron digs his channel with his ghostly helpers, and those who are passing by when they appear almost piss in their breeches at the sight of them."

The haughty *comtesse* de Foix, peering stiffly from the jewel-edged, white gable of her hood and arrayed in a black lace-covered bodice, chimed in from her hostess's right.

"My husband, Monsieur le *comte,* insists 'twas not for love that Bruyere caused that disaster but for greed, in order to gain more land for himself."

The *marquise* only smiled weakly, unwilling to dignify with a response so crass a cause for her romantic story.

She said to Lyse instead, "But how remarkable you have seen those lights, Mademoiselle de Tonnière, for as a stranger to this area you did not know this history. I myself know of only one old man who swears he has seen them, for few actually do, no matter how many years of summer nights people peer across the lake. Monsieur de Joyeuse, of course, believes the entire tale is false, merely the peasants' manner of explaining a natural disaster. At any rate, even if true, 'tis not a matter of demons or evil witches reaching out to plague us, but only miserable, restless souls doing penance."

"Ah yes?" said her persistent lady-in-waiting to Lyse, "then ask Madame why fish restocked into the lake to reproduce do not survive. It is a cursed water, I tell you, and nobody ever takes a boat out on it. Nobody living, that is."

"*Mon dieu,* hold your tongue, Marguerite! It might be the same odoriferous minerals we have at our bathing spring which now seeps to the bottom of the lake and kills the fish."

"'Tis the souls of all those doomed people drowned by its waters that curse the lake!" Marguerite insisted to Lyse with relish.

The *marquise* left off her fanning, sat up straight and signaled the servants at the buffet to serve the puddings and orange jellies that ended the meal. Firmly she changed the subject, announcing to her pleased guests that, speaking of mineral waters, there would be a party tomorrow for both sexes to the nearby spa of Rennes-les-Bains where they would enjoy a soak in the warm, mineral baths, gentle massages, good food and conversation, and, of course, gaming.

Under the torrent of chatter this unleashed, Lyse had time to wonder why she had seen those ghostly lights. Or had she? Perhaps it was her weary excitement that produced them that first night, or perhaps they were big fireflies after all. But she was sure that for once it wasn't her weird 'seeing-back' playing tricks on her.

She turned to talk with her neighbor, a sweet, pleasant damsel from Foix, attendant upon the *comtesse* and soon to be married to a local knight. Plunging into an easy chat over the merits of certain wools to fill the background of tapestried pillows, Lyse meanwhile crammed the intriguing tale of the White Lady to the back of her mind. She would amuse Ferrante with it later.

Ah, what dances, farces and mummeries the *marquise* presented to them in her Great Hall those two weeks, what swirling dancers from Valencia, what entrancing ballets to the music of viols, what tickling comedies and tearful tragedies staged by a troup of Florentine actors! Enough, and more to uphold Puivert's ancient reputation for the arts. But Lyse's favorite entertainment was the imitators of old Provençal troubadours who, singly or in pairs, sang to lute or pipes the courtly ballads of unrequited love which so pleased their dreamy audience late at night.

And then there was gambling and cards and chess, continuous all day and night in various chambers, and tennis, newly played with racquets instead of the gloved hand, and wrestling matches on a grassy side court for the energetic in body.

Ah, the banqueting and toasting to the *marquise's* health and long life! Rich food, the finest red wine from the Rhône, the most succulent fruits to peel and suggestively pop into one's neighbor's mouth if one felt so inclined, all to charming music from the Hall's balcony.

Several paunch-bellied high churchmen held their own with the other guests when it came to celebrating, and even Sister Louise amused her mother by taking a cup or two of wine and becoming giddy. Even the servants and grooms of the invitees, their duties done, got drunk late every night in their own quarters.

Lyse even had several sessions with the house falconer, who taught her to fly a beady-eyed, black saker hawk with silver bells on his leg, a beautiful, glaring bird with the grace to swoop back to her leather-gloved forearm whenever she waved a lure made of red cloth.

The exhilarating festivities left hardly time for sleep. Little notes were delivered early every morning to Lyse's chamber for her to hurry and wake, and join this or that swain for this or that activity, but unless there was one from Don Ferrante, brusquely written as usual, she fell back into her bed—empty, by now, of Sister Louise. Because she often crept into bed so late the nights before, she often slept happily and soundly until the noon bell pealed out from the village nestled below the rear of the Château. Madame de Dunois would never have approved of such sloth.

Neither did Ferrante di Gonzaga.

"You missed a fine hunt this morning, the dogs brought to bay two stags and a doe, and a careless beater was tossed to the treetops by a deer with an enormous rack. I suppose they'll display the trophy this evening," Gonzaga said as they strolled along one afternoon a week into their visit, viewing the countryside from the battlements. "Especially since it was de Foix who claimed it was his javelin that dispatched it."

Although fall was beginning it still remained quite warm. Blackbeard had left off the short surcoat that went over his striped satin doublet with its tiny ruffle at the high neck. And Lyse's tight, long sleeves with big puffs at the shoulders were of lightest-weight gauze.

He lectured, "I couldn't imagine sleeping as long as you do on these perfect mornings."

"But it's delicious. Don't you ever sleep past dawn?"

"*Chère* Mademoiselle, a soldier either forms the habit of waking by first light, or he might wake up dead." He chuckled. Then flat smile circles appeared at the corners of his mouth, although he continued squinting at the countryside. "However—I suppose I could be coaxed to remain a few hours under the quilt of a morning, in certain promising instances."

Pretending she didn't understand him or even feel the peculiar stumble of her heart over the innuendo, Lyse chatted on.

"I'll have you know I won twelve crowns at cards last night," she announced proudly, wanting him to know her playing judgement was getting better.

"So what will you do with that fortune?"

"I don't know, buy some lengths of the best gold satin, I suppose."

But she had already speculated on what she might do with it. There was a bookseller in Couiza who displayed on a wooden rack an expensive volume of architectural drawings. Against all her better judgement, she thought she might buy that book and make Gonzaga a surprise present of it when they returned to Rennes-le-Château.

Just because she wanted to.

As the days went on, Lyse grew more and more jealous over Gonzaga, and she was well aware of it now.

At Rennes-le-Château her excitement over going to Puivert included the thought that there would be attractive gentlemen to once more charm and flirt with. *Ciel,* in her boredom on the hilltop she had even begun to miss the young pikeman at St. Piteu whose inarticulate ardor had soothed the urgent currents that flowed through her, for which she had neither name or outlet.

Instead, at Puivert, she was often distracted by jealous feelings, losing the thread of what she was saying, or a bit of a play's dialogue, as her gaze followed Blackbeard, smug amidst his female conquests. It was true she sometimes turned and saw his stare on the gentleman she was conversing with at the moment, but he seemed to have cast her loose after the first night, satisfied she would not trip over her tongue. It made some sense, of course, for them not to monopolize each other: they were supposed to be strangers after all, and he merely escorting her to Puivert.

Still he needn't act like a fox let into a coop of hens, she thought sullenly, as she watched him strut by with a damsel on each arm as she waited her turn at croquet, a partner smiling by her side. Ferrante wouldn't play croquet, he said it was too mincing a game for him.

Instead he spent much time in practicing for the tournament with the other contenders, charging his auburn-maned Bucephelus down the lists set up in the grassy Cour d'Honneur and spearing a small ring hanging from a swing arm on a pole. One of her gallants remarked the Mantuan was considered a 'rude lance', meaning his eye was excellent, his arm iron, and he seldom missed the mark—to the impressed approval of the women watching the practice from a wooden gallery above.

To Lyse he merely looked huge and powerful in his full suit of jointed steel, even quite sinister when the sharply pointed visor of his helmet was down. But she realized that to the other women about her, married or otherwise, the dashing Italian with his bronzed good looks and piercing green gaze, was a gallant who fair made them swoon with admiration. Although she tried to ignore their giggling remarks, coy or slyly lascivious according to how fashionably daring each lady was, her positive view of Ferrante di Gonzaga was sharpened by their sensual lip-licking over him.

Chapter 18

Thirty knights were entered in the tourney in the great court, which began with a blare of trumpet fanfares. The contests, alternating between battles on foot with swords and battle-axes and the more popular and elegant mounted jousting, drew everyone in the château to the escutcheon-hung stands and the timber balconies along the inner walls. And most of the townspeople and farmers for leagues around stood massed on either end of the field, where the contenders with their squires waited their turn.

Since it had gotten around that Don Ferrante di Gonzaga had won the championship for France at the famous Field of the Cloth of Gold tourneys, where the knights vied only in the name of Francois Premier or Henry the Eighth of England, his turn was always anticipated with hushed reverence.

The jousters, plumes aquiver, steel-covered biceps adorned with their ladies' scarves, galloped full-tilt at each other from opposite sides of a wooden barrier, the object being to shatter one's lance against the opposition's chest, but stay on one's horse. As heavy as it was, the long jousting lance with its blunted iron tip was still a lighter weapon than the lance used in actual warfare, for it was intended to break or splinter without sorely hurting its target. Aim and brute force was paramount, but skill as well, since the stub of the splintered lance had to be cast up in time not to cause the opponent damage.

The shock of the lance barreling into a rider in a square hit was tremendous, and it sometimes swept one or both riders off their horses to land with jarring crashes and lose many points with the judges.

The reward for the knight who splintered the most lances and stayed mounted, a grueling feat, was gold bracelets to be enameled in the winner's colors, and a grand prize of a diamond worth fifty crowns. An unmarried winner sometimes presented his prize to whichever blushing lady he favored, and during the stir and applause which greeted Ferrante di Gonzaga's repeated victories, Lyse's jealous glance often darted to his latest conquest, a lush blonde blushing fervidly amidst her envious friends.

No matter, she too was hugely impressed with the Italian's prowess as he leaned forward and almost standing in the stirrups, squarely hit with great force the red felt marker on the left side of his opponent's armored chest, hard to do from the back of a thundering steed. Especially when Blackbeard was himself able to avoid the full power of the lance aimed at him. Although the other knights acquitted themselves with commendable valor, she thought that Don Ferrante's opponents, chosen by lot, seemed to shrink within their steel plates when the formidable figure on the huge warhorse appeared at the other end of the barrier.

This thrilled her, that he was extremely skilled in the martial arts and claimed the awe and respect of every person viewing him. She watched him caracole his horse to shouts and applause, holding up his shattered lance in triumph, and excitement quickened her blood. Excitement seduced her.

There was a betrothal agreement which no one knew of here; he would, some day, be her husband, no matter how much that straw-haired strumpet over there threw herself at him. It was peculiar that watching a man in mock but dangerous combat, slashing away with a ferocious sword to drive his opponent to the wall or galloping like a devil to upend him with a resounding crash, should have so alluring an effect on her, who quailed at almost everything violent—but it did.

She did not celebrate each victory of his so vocally as most of the audience, but she sat amongst the *marquise's* ladies with a smug little smile on her face and a surprising pride in her heart.

Lyse had to admit that besides that temper tantrum at Moulins directed at Germain, and his always patronizing attitude, the Manutan had been fairly decent to her. He had saved her very life, to begin with. He had given her literacy. He had attempted to dispel her disappointments. What was stuck in her craw, and the very thing he had shouted to her that fateful moment as she hung hysterically over a foaming river below, was that he dealt with her on her uncle's account, not hers. His loyalty was only to his admired cousin, on whose behalf it seemed he would do anything.

Wounded vanity goaded her. She thought she was as pretty as the local belles fluttering about him, that brunette one in particular, Isobel de Somuir, whose husband was in exile with Jean de Joyeuse. The woman was a saucy, dimpled, voluptuous beauty, her red lips always smiling as she coquetted with Ferrante di Gonzaga over her parchment fan. To Lyse's disgust, the message of that challenging flirtation had obviously hit fertile ground, for by the end of the first week Ferrante and Isabel de Somuir could be often seen conversing together, his dark head attentively inclined to her, and they spent time together at the hunt picnics, or murmured companionably in window seats, or strolled in the garden. But as the days passed and she sneaked glances at the couple, she believed the challenge in the woman's gaze had softened, had turned into a smitten and tender regard, what she imagined a beloved woman might project.

Perhaps others might be fooled to think those two carried on merely a circumspect friendship, but having seen her unwilling escort rub up even to la Dame, Lyse knew what was foremost in his mind when it came to females.

But he was, after all, betrothed to her, wasn't he, like it or not?

It hurt her pride that he chose to spend his time with other women. So, when they did come together, she reverted to the facade she'd once reserved for her uncle, the side of her that was particularly charming, soft and vulnerable. This wasn't hard to do, since Gonzaga was well amused at Puivert and his physical aggression gotten out on the tilt field; he too had exchanged his impatient scowl for his roguish, amused smile, and in their encounters they meshed together very pleasantly.

Was it true, she finally confronted herself, mooning out of her midnight window towards the end of their stay? Was she suddenly craving all of his attention? Well, why shouldn't she? They were, after all, together in this nether part of France locked in the intimacy of a pressing, secret pursuit. She had an honest and prior claim on him, did she not? *Mais oui,* she answered herself, she did.

But it was the night before the last evening of the *marquise's* birthday celebration, which was to be the most gala feasting of all, that Lyse found herself staring in startlement into the air over the hand of cards she was playing, unconcerned that her partner, a high-browed young courtier with a sensitive mouth and cleft chin, was also fondling her knee under the table. A certain thought had escaped her control and invaded her head.

What? Did she actually want the Mantuan to make love to her? She was for a second shocked by the extreme notion. Then she was more shocked by the pleasurable strike of lightning that lanced through her at the idea, a thrill that made her toes curl; a reaction her partner at cards had failed for two weeks to produce in her, despite his cleft chin and devoted courting.

The answer to that was '*mais oui,*' of course. She suddenly felt faint.

Toast after toast was proposed for the *marquise*, whose eyes flashed with delight at every paean to her beauty, her wisdom, her this and that, as well as her fifty years. She wore a tilted hat supporting a forest of crimson and white plumes, and the deep, red brocade bodice framing her generous bosom was paved with a double row of large pearls and gems. Up and down the great u-shaped table littered with remnants of the huge supper, the gentlemen stood to honor their hostess and the varlets darted in with their pitchers to fill and refill empty wine cups.

There had been already been dancing, entertainment, and even the fanfare-announced, wordy presentation of a diamond in its silk-lined pouch to the great-sleeved grand champion of the tournaments, Ferrante di Gonzaga, who rose from kneeling at the *marquise's* feet to look around the room a moment. The gathering thought he might give his prize to someone, and waited for such fodder for gossip, but he merely grinned, put the pouch in his pocket, and bowed away backwards.

After the toasts the chief steward banged his staff to gain the attention of the babbling, laughing guests, and called out "the Scarf Dance!" which set off even more excited chatter among the wine-loosened company. The infamous dance, which had spread from the royal court itself to high society throughout France, was deliberately held at the close of long celebrations, just before the guests scattered, to allow its naughty revelry no chance of repetition and to stave off serious repercussion afterwards.

The ladies brought scarves to the banqueting place and left them piled in a heap as the supper started. When the dance was announced, always late in the evening and after copious wine and hard cider had loosened reserves, the gentlemen, according to rank, plucked scarves from the pile, ostensibly at random, although many an arrangement had already been made. Since the drawing was considered haphazard, even married couples were free to publicly indulge, with whoever befell them, in the indecorous courtship that the dance mimicked.

The dance itself was arranged in three parts: a graceful Ronde to begin, a slower Pavanne, and a wild Sauterelle to finish. The gentlemen, brandishing their scarves, first stood in the center of the floor, while the ladies circled about them, trying to be solemn.

Lyse's had allowed her eager, cleft-chin swain to pry from her the orange color of her gauze scarf with an enamel pin in the shape of a lion attached, for she did prefer him to any others who might draw her from the pile.

She had worn her very best for this last evening of revels, attaching her biggest puffed and slashed sleeves to her off-the-shoulder purple silk bodice above a pale green skirt. The *marquise* had insisted on lending her a lovely, floaty headdress—a high purple toque sheathing most of her red-blonde hair, with a filmy lavender veil secured to it by a wreath of flowers and pearls.

Because she had no special ornament to adorn the tender expanse of white breasts rising above her low neckline, she had drawn from its velvet pouch— for the first time–her gold and emerald betrothal pendant. Hesitating, she had let it sparkle in her palm for a moment, this symbol of secret marriage contract presented to her by a man who, at the time, was both a stranger and repugnant to her.

Now he was neither. Now she thought of him in a different way, yet the situation hadn't really changed. He was still her uncle's man, performing a sworn duty without relish. Sadly she contemplated the beautiful piece in her hand, green and glittering as piercing eyes under dark, winged brows. Although none would even realize what it represented, it still remained an empty symbol to her and she should not wear it.

And yet–it melded lushly with her string of pearls and her purple gown, it was impressive and it was hers. How sinful to hide its verdant sparkle in the dark of a chest! And she had to remember, even though passing as a lady of little consequence for her safety's sake, that the realty was, she was a proud Bourbon.

In a moment Marye's daughter was fastening the doubled gold chain about Lyse's neck, so that in her glass she beheld the lovely emerald warming it-self just below the beating hollow of her throat and framed by the creamy glow of the pearls Charles de Bourbon had given her. Between headdress and jewel and cheeks pink with excitement, she had finally felt like the princess she really was.

Now, on the floor, with the viols and pipes playing cheerfully, she and the other ladies slowly circled the large group of gentlemen, old and young, who were holding up the scarves they had chosen and gamely suffering the women's giddy comments and openly risqué scrutiny. There were squeals of delight or cries of resignation as each lady found her scarf. And some of the men pursed lips in regret as Lyse passed up their proffered scarves.

She was looking for her dimpled cavalier, but she chanced first upon Ferrante di Gonzaga. And to her astonishment it was he who stood brandishing her scarf, hand on hip, and a sparkle of mischief in his eyes. He looked splen-did, the great sleeves of his surcoat puffed and padded. A white plume swept down from his rakish, tilted hat to his close-cropped beard as he knelt down to her and pressed warm lips to her hands.

"Will you honor me with this dance, kind and beautiful lady?" he rum-bled out the set formula.

"Certes, Signore," she responded, much bemused at the turn of events, for he had danced with her out of politeness just once during the whole, long evening. "But how did you–"

"Have I not seen your scarf and pin on various occasions? And since I outrank your pretty beau, naught is left to him but to grit his teeth that I circled 'round his flank'." The *condottiere* chuckled with wicked satisfaction. But still following the formula, he grabbed her by the shoulders and planted a lingering kiss on each of her cheeks, then bent to allow her some dazed, quick pecks back, a required bussing.

Now paired off by the scarf, he led her to the growing rank of laughing couples waiting for the dance to begin.

To cover the shaky burst of delight she felt that he had abandoned his blonde and other nymphs to share this particular dance with her, Lyse murmured, "I am not too well acquainted with these figures, I'm afraid. I hope I will not shame you." In truth, she'd only entered the Scarf Dance once before, at Moulins, with de Lugny. It took a very good memory to recall the precise steps of all the fashionable court dances.

"Worry not, I'll guide you if you falter."

"Well, I won't," she thought, her spirit stiffened at his smug grin. And of course, he would know the libertine dance intimately, wouldn't he?

The music started up and they moved off, beginning with a grip held high, her scarf laced through their intertwined fingers, their other hands on hips. All through these first brisk figures of crossing and turning steps, the gentleman deftly drew the scarf about his partner's waist, but allowed her to coquettishly slip away from it, the catch being that if she wasn't fleet enough he could steal a kiss on cheek or lips or tip of nose. There was much giggling and laughter and light slaps from the ladies, and even the gallants who had drawn older but sprightly ladies pluckily smacked the wrinkled cheeks.

With graceful twists, laughing into her partner's eyes, Lyse was able to sidestep Don Ferrante, except for once, when he deliberately held the end of the scarf too long, so that, for a moment, he was able to kiss her full on the lips. She almost stumbled at the sparks that shot along her veins and sent flames into her face.

He saw her blush. Then his gaze fell to her bosom as they danced and an eyebrow raised. He said in a neutral tone, "I am surprised, Mademoiselle. You wear my emerald."

It was hard to tell if he was pleased with this premature debut. "I thought there was no harm. It is m-most beautiful," she stammered. "'Twas too much a pity to let it languish unseen."

He reached out with his strong, blunt fingers to lift it lightly a moment from its satiny perch. He hardly touched her skin, but delicious prickles attacked her arms.

"I am happy you favor my gift. Yet what more beauty could so blooming a rose truly need, Lady?" he murmured smoothly, smiling as he passed her before him and she turned her shoulder and pointed a toe.

Pleasant complements were *de rigeur* during the dance and this surely was one, but amidst her blushes Lyse could not take him seriously, painfully aware of his penchant for flirting with any woman who crossed his path. So she merely smiled back winningly as she twirled safely from the scarf's embrace. She was absolutely determined to enjoy this last night at Puivert. It might be a long time before another such festivity came around, and wasn't this wonderful fete the reality of all her lonely dreams at St. Piteu?

One more time Ferrante roped her to him with the scarf so quickly, before she could glide away, that her mouth was half-open as he brushed her lips again with his.

The first dance set flowed smoothly into the second, taken up by tambours and Spanish guitars in a much slower, romantic Pavanne, and here the couples each held an end of the scarf as they performed the measured steps, hands on hips, staring soulfully into each other's eyes, parting to the length of the scarf, then for a few measures coming close, many so close a kiss was only natural, and gentlemen truly captured could use the scarf to secure their partner tight against them with unabashed intimacy as they danced the sedate steps.

The passionate dancers somehow managed to step lightly, even as they kissed, and the cheerful spectators still quaffing at the table whooped encouragement and snapped their fingers for those couples who hardly came up for air.

Lyse, at first wearing the ritual, arch expression, soon took her turn to coquette by looking into her partner's gaze and smiling provocatively up at him from under her lashes. She let her lips part, even wet them with the tip of her tongue as the cook's daughter had once demonstrated, and moved her bare shoulders with beckoning grace as she stepped about him. But twice he pulled her close by looping the scarf about her waist, and his kisses were longer now and she swayed to him.

They were staring into each other's eyes. Her heart began pounding, her stomach fluttering, she wasn't aware that her smile disappeared as she sank into his gaze, which had turned intense, dark as green malachite, with an imperative desire so unhidden all must see it.

Not that she cared if they did. A great, devouring monster stirred in her, finally fully awakened, and the next time he pulled her against him with the scarf in both hands, she turned up her mouth and kissed him back greedily, and then he wouldn't let her go, guiding her faltering steps with his body, for her eyes were closed.

Their lips clung, the kiss turned desperate, and as if through wool ear-stoppers she hardly heard the clamoring, whistling spectators. Suddenly the stately music stopped to the onlookers great mirth, only the drum continuing.

They broke off and Lyse stepped back, breathless, reddening, thinking the laughter was for them, until she saw that a damsel had fainted and her grinning partner, whose ardor had presumably overcome her, was carrying her from the floor. The other dancers were also laughing, and one gentleman made as if to faint too, receiving a blushing punch from his lady.

The rollicking, *laissez-faire* mood was infectious. It, the copious wine, the unleashed monster that was breathing the heat of desire through her body, stripped away caution. Disregarding the danger she giggled up at Gonzaga and he grinned back at her.

"That was a delicious set," he bent to murmur in her ear.

"But you are an expert dancer, Don Ferrante," she coquetted back, allowing him to think she might mean more than that.

"So are you, lady, for a country maiden of so innocent an air. How do you dance so well these naughty measures?" His gaze lingered a moment on her mouth and his grip tightened on her hand.

"'Tis innate talent, I suppose," she teased, "Or my dancing master's lessons."

"In this dance?"

She giggled, enchanted with his proprietary amazement. "In one something like it. Of course, much more restrained than during the gaiety of a *soirée*."

"Your governess was being remiss with you. That dancing master would have been in mortal danger from me."

"Ah, but I didn't even know you then!" she laughed. As the last set started up they both grasped the doubled scarf, their free arms in the air with elbows bent, but Lyse thought her feet must be a length off the floor. She felt giddy with delight.

With a skirl a bagpipe started off a rapid tune, then horns and viols pealed out merrily against an agitated drum beat, and the dancers ran and dipped and stepped and whirled so fast that when the music stopped precipitously everybody bumped into each other with peals of mirth. Now it was the lady's turn to rope her gentleman with the scarf and quickly kiss wherever she could reach, but without him stooping or bending his head. All the women were sparkly-eyed and panting, excluding a few who were queasy from too much drink, and many had to jump, with laughing shrieks, to catch a chin or jaw, and some tiny damsels gaily had to make do with a mouthful of embroidered doublet or gold chain unless her beau lifted her up.

With her hands on Gonzaga's shoulders for leverage and a little jump, Lyse could clear the jaw-line beard and land a quick peck on his lips, which were working desperately to contain a laugh. But it took her two unsuccessful tries to succeed, since the whirling had made her dizzy.

The lively, driving music commenced again and they fell into the steps, and now he whirled her about, now all the couples, yipping and yelling like peasants, joined hands and danced wildly in a ring, and the music stopped again. No holds barred now, the gentlemen had the right to kiss their ladies wherever they liked—except on the mouth—and they pressed heated lips to smooth shoulders, heaving bosoms, velvety napes, a breast scooped from its bodice, and some fevered swains knelt to kiss their damsel's skirts at the level of the crotch.

With the scarf about his neck, Gonzaga swooped Lyse up and swung her around until her head fell back, then planted a long kiss on her damp, arched throat, and she felt his hot tongue taste her, perspiration and all.

As he set her dizzily on her feet again, she caught a glimpse over his shoulder of his abandoned Isobel, flushed, laughing and wantonly allowing her partner to suck loudly on her nipple to the cries of the delighted audience, but staring hatred at Lyse as their eyes caught.

Mademoiselle de Bourbon-Tonnière experienced a zestful taste of power she had never enjoyed before. Exhilaration flung her into the closing figures, and she matched Blackbeard quick step for quick step, hop for hop, turn and twist, her feet as light as her heart, stamping and jumping. The final figure, ending with a the music's resounding major chord, drew a chorus of ribald yells and cheers and pounding on the tables, the guffawing *marquise* as excited as anyone. The exhausted dancers fell panting into each other's arms, pelted by a rain of flowers that had been supplied to the onlookers to hail their prowess.

Over the pounding of her heart, Lyse looked up at the desire-narrowed, glinting eyes of her keeper, Don Ferrante di Gonzaga and the noise floated away from her, the world floated away from her, she lifted her head as his hands spanned her waist and she let him embrace her, let him kiss her long and deep, and although her legs turned to jelly, the heat of his lips, the unaccustomed probing of his tongue to open her mouth poured fire through her lustful, trembling body, and she kissed him back with clinging ardor.

When at last they parted, amidst other couples ending the Scarf Dance in the same hot fashion, they managed to bow to the spectators with the others, smiling triumphantly.

Then he tugged her by the hand right out of the Great Hall, through a few chambers and out into the welcome, cooler night air of the garden, which was dimly lit on its paths by torches shoved into the ground.

With a kerchief drawn from his sleeve he solicitously patted her glowing face, then mopped his own as she fanned herself with her hand, the driving rhythm of the swirling country jig still ringing in her head. Their eyes met. They burst out laughing, still captured by the abandon of the dancing.

She allowed him to lead her to a stone bench in the shadows, away from others who had spilled out after them, where he sat down next to her, absently unclasping the high neck of his doublet to cool off. But his mood was turning. He sat staring straight ahead into the dense bulk of the clipped bushes as if some message might be written there.

Peering at his suddenly solemn profile, Lyse began to feel herself adrift, roughly cut off from the Lyse she'd been when the banquet began—her own person, silly perhaps, but at least confident, compared to how she felt now, unsure, a woman who had lost control of her emotions. The vivacious Scarf Dance was over, the wives returned to their husband, the damsels to propriety, the lovers to discretion, but the man it had left Lyse desiring was Signore Blackbeard, the gentleman of a thousand moods and as many willing damsels with whom to indulge them.

No. She would not believe it was merely a peccadillo, the way he had gazed at her. There was more, she knew there was more in that last intoxicated embrace than just a passing seduction. She had little to go on, but the belief was intuitive and deep, in spite that her head told her 'You want such to be true, so you say it is.'

She closed her eyes a moment with the memory of that last kiss, the few instants they were fused together, his mouth burning on hers, his breath on her face, her lips yielding and parting under his insistence, and the hard feel of his body as he pressed her to him. Weakness flooded her, and her back arched slightly to contain it.

She opened her eyes and saw he was looking at her very somberly.

Yet he was still clasping her hand tight. He turned it over to press a passionate kiss into her palm, and then drew her to him. "I am wild for you, Lysette," he whispered in her ear, but so miserably that it seemed like a cry from the doomed. "I have been for a long while, but I was loathe to admit it."

In spite of his lugubrious tone, the words made her heart pound in her throat, and set her soul quivering like the plucked strings of a viol.

"Oh Ferrante! But why did you not say? It must be obvious I do not reject you." She swayed toward him—but to her surprise, he pulled back.

Starlight behind him glimmered off the hard outline of his face. His expression, his eyes were shadowed. His voice had a rough cast as he said, "Perhaps I want more of you than you are willing to give. More than kisses."

"A woman will give much in exchange for love," Lyse whispered, telling the truth, for her soul and body yearned for him. "And we are already betrothed, promised to each other in the sight of God. There is no harm—"

But he put impatient fingers to her lips to silence her and his voice came sternly out of the dark. "Yes, there is harm, and it is why we shall do nothing. We have come here to perform a miracle which depends on your fragile ability to remember certain facts hidden in the past. This trait grievously harmed your mother. It unsettles and disturbs you. I will tell you what I fear; that additional strong emotion, however happy but added to your burden of psychic strain, could drain your powers. If Eros becomes our master, if we become avid lovers, it could distract you. We cannot, we will not gamble. We are here for a purpose."

Lovers. The thrill of such an idea! Yet this incomprehensible man invoked it in one moment and coolly dismissed it the next.

Imagine, to have a lover. In her months at Moulins, gossip had drifted all around her in *sotto voce* detail, revelations of various illicit liasons over which the court had smacked their lips, and she had been envious, even dreaming back to the heady excitement of her sneaked meetings with the lanky pikeman at St. Piteu and the pleasure of being fondled and kissed.

But only now, reacting so passionately to Ferrante di Gonzaga as she had to no other, did she understand the true meaning of 'lover'? It was not at all giving oneself, as to her pikeman, out of deep curiosity and witless appetite, as lightly as a giggle. It was with a fury of desire no other man could assuage, a hunger for the arms, the flesh, the love of that one person, and a driving need to do everything, anything that would give him joy.

A veil had been torn from her eyes, indeed.

But could Ferrante's sudden caution be correct? A vision of Bourbon's boyish face and affectionate smile rose before her, and a tumble of memory of all the duke's kindnesses. Would she abrogate her dear uncle's trust and gamble his vital need by jeopardizing this quest by a devouring love? For she was aware, even much more than Ferrante, how deeply the memories of Mélline's overwrought life spent her; how much of her emotional strength she already needed to combat the 'seeing-back's' drain on her.

Even so, she might have disagreed with Ferrante—she might have wildly flung herself into his arms and dismantled with her caressing hands and her kisses his determination to ignore their feelings—except for the seeing that the big Italian's overriding allegiance to Charles de Bourbon had almost immediately intervened between them.

This dismaying actuality sent wounded pride rushing to cool off nerve endings where a moment before only desire had crackled.

She straightened up and looked away from him, glad he could not see her flustered disappointment. "Then, what shall we do? Now the milk is spilt."

"Nothing. We will continue as we have been." He turned her chin toward him in spite of her resistance. "I will behave like an honorable gentleman and you will remain the virtuous lady entrusted to me. Nothing more."

"Betrothed to you," she reminded him, so he would at least think her reaction in the dance fell not too far from virtuous. She tried to smoothe some nonchalance over the hurt in her voice. "*Vraiment,* Monsieur, you sound quite satisfied with the arrangement you propose." She wished she could see his eyes, but was glad he could not see hers.

"Hardly. If you think that, you know me little."

She thought about his paramour at Moulins, who Germain had told her about, his flirtatious playing with la Dame, his immediate dalliance here with the brazen blonde, his ability to take love or leave it. She stood up precipitously. "Not at all, Don Ferrante. I think such a thing because I know you more than you imagine."

He rose too, looking strained. "Just what does that mean?"

She refused to answer. "I believe I will retire now, the night has been strenuous and wine makes me tired. We have a long afternoon of traveling tomorrow." She saw he meant to escort her, but she held up a hand to stop him. "Please, would you allow me to go in by myself? I would prefer it at this moment."

"Lyse—"

"Don Ferrante?"

But, after a second's silence, he nodded stiffly. "As you wish. Will you attend the ten o'clock Mass tomorrow?"

"I hope to."

"I will see you there, then. Good night, Lyse-Magdalene."

"Good night," she whispered against the lump in her throat, for this is the man she wanted and he stood there, rigid as a statue, when she wanted him to reach out for her and kiss her mouth as hungrily as he had scarce a half hour before. In fact, they both stood still a moment, staring through the dark at each other. And then she turned and swept down the brick path to the Château, from whence still issued the sounds of music and the high cheer of voices.

Ferrante watched with envy her determined retreat from the situation they had just created; it just wasn't that easy for him. He was still shaken by the burst of desire for that angel-faced young woman that had caught up with him, meshing him in a silken net; desire for the Circe who had so fervently given him her lips, and yet had just as swiftly remembered Bourbon, possibly once her lover, and unprotestingly returning to her duty when reminded of it.

What, was he not human, Ferrante wrangled with himself? The girl concealed her instability and probably faulty morals with a sweet form and a face of dazzling beauty; even with the purity of her glance that could grab the heart of any man, that had pierced his armor and heated his blood almost to overboiling.

What irony. He should be grateful about her physical charm, since he had put his name to a contract of marriage with her, and a sack over her head would not be needed.

But he deeply perceived that for him, in the case of Lyse-Magdalene de Bourbon-Tonnière hiding her ardor under virginal aspect and radiant smile, giving in to the urges of his body could finally enslave his heart, all reason set aside. It was this he fought against, it was his dread of loving a woman with mental incapacity, and the imperfect children she might produce, that riveted back into place his emotional buckler and enabled him to withstand his aching frustration.

Yet, he would one day be her husband. What would he do then when she called him to duty in her bed?

Ferrante trudged along the path, a languishing champion who felt one hundred years old.

But suddenly he could not stop a mirthless chuckle at his terrible tangle of desires. "To be terrified of loving one's future wife because of hating one's present wife? How do you explain that, *condottiere*? Except that your brain is rotting, rotting and too distant from the creak of scaling ladders and the mélee, the beloved clangor of battle that overstrides all cares."

He grabbed a solution from the air: the answer was to speed up Bourbon-Tonnière's remembering of the Treasury's location, if he could, to dig up what was to be found, ship it out and be quit of this woman and this duty so he could rejoin Bourbon in his armor and astride his great warhorse.

He resolved to go to la Dame for help in this, who had several times hinted she knew a drastic method to induce the 'seeing-back'.

Ferrante greeted several revelers as he passed through the portal into the château. He wrapped his fingers around the encased jewel in his pocket, reward for his martial prowess, and smiled grimly. *Nom de Dieu,* he was too keyed up to go to bed—unless with Isobel, the rounded wanton who had already proven to him the fire between her solid thighs. With the diamond as his apology for tonight, she might do so again, and he would please her by the rugged style of mastery which she so enjoyed. Hah, life had not changed, nor had he, just because the fruit he had forbidden himself seemed all the more tempting for it.

But mysteriously, in spite of himself, his steps led away from the Great Hall where Isobel might indeed be still found, and up to the stuffy chamber he shared with two other gentlemen, and where a yawning Marco, kicked awake, helped him to unbutton and unlace, and where he fell naked into his solitary bed, only to toss and groan and struggle to chase the aberrant Lyse-Magdalene from his drink-blurred mind.

Chapter 19

Germain had followed the insight that with Madame de Dunois hardly alive, it would unstring Lyse-Magdalene to be told of her old nurse's violent death. Now he saw he had been right. The girl had returned from Puivert less like herself than he had ever seen. One day she was silent and pouting and melancholy, the next day flouncingly cheerful and apt to dance around by herself to the inviting music of the hungry, itinerant musician la Dame had given shelter in exchange for brightening her gloomy abode for her guests.

Germain had made himself useful to Lora Voisins, whose extensive knowledge of plant preparations impressed him. Thanks to years watching the monk running the pharmacopoeia at St. Piteu's monastery, he was able to mix elixirs and pound powders to the prescription of la Dame and the physicians who were still trying to revive the governess. He ran errands and messages for her, he re-recorded her hundreds of scribbled perfume recipes in his more legible hand, he helped her gather the roots and plants and blossoms growing down the mountainside and on the river banks, and he prepared them for drying.

He did this because he liked the work, but also because the Junoesque, silver-eyed woman fascinated him. He loved to watch her large, capable hands sweep together measured heaps of pulverized leaves and shaved roots into the exact blends she wanted, and admire the shards of colored light dancing over her intent face as she held glass jars to the sun to examine the suspensions and sediment of her potions.

For her part, pleased with his ability to understand measures and directions, la Dame smiled at him with insinuating, curved lips, and moved so that her exotic perfume wafted to him from her scented gray scarves. Germain thought Lora Voisins the most riveting female he had ever seen, and when she stood very close behind him to decipher some crossed-out and illegible notation in her writings, her presence raised the hair on his arms in a not-unpleasant manner.

Evenings, la Dame coaxed Don Ferrante to read to all of them in his rolling baritone, sometimes from Dante, from the poetry of the troubadour Betran de Born, or about Petrarch's beautiful Laura, the belle of Provence. But during the day Germain often spied Don Ferrante standing at the architect's table under the scaffolding of the unfinished church in Couiza and studying the drawings along with the master builder and his aides. This technical interest in building seemed to Germain highly incongruous in a man whose business was warfare, a cavalier who had roundly trounced all comers in Puivert's lance-breakings, so Lyse-Magdalene had reported. Still, since the builder of the church acquiesced to Don Ferrante's presence, this probably testified to the Italian's competent opinion.

The Mantuan had discontinued riding out with them every morning, leaving Germain to accompany Lyse-Magdalene and Lucco to exercise the horses. But for Germain things were not the same as they used to be. The girl he had known in St. Piteu had chattered him blind, had enjoyed an energetic, sweaty horserace, and had strewn all around her radiant smile that lifted the heart. But this lady was discontent and glum, and there was pain behind her crystalline blue eyes.

He could see that she had difficulty looking Don Ferrante in the eye, even when talking to him, and her fingers in her lap twined about each other like snakes. The big man didn't seem to take notice of this, perhaps because he seldom looked directly at her, either.

It saddened him that Lyse-Magdalene no longer confided in him, for when he asked her what troubled her she insisted nothing was wrong, she felt fine.

He suspected such growing apart was for them a function of becoming adult and being unequal; he had expected it in his heart from the moment they left the simple world of St. Piteu. He was the son of a very minor employee of the Bourbon household. She was a Bourbon *princesse*.

No matter, she would always be part of his youthful memories, his *princesse*, and his devotion to Lyse-Magdalene de Bourbon-Tonnière would never change.

The girl was sometimes hollow-eyed when they rode out, and she blamed it on lack of sleep because of frightening dreams that awakened her, the same ones over and over, dreams, however, she couldn't seem to remember in order to describe them to him, so she said. Other times she sat listlessly by de Dunois' bedside, sewing or reading, or keeping vigil with the priest who visited daily to pray over the prostrate woman.

She only seemed distracted from her melancholy when she sat out on the gallery with the itinerant musician, a slim lutanist named Ferri, and harked to the ballades his nimble fingers strummed as the breeze tumbled the fallen leaves of autumn along the stone gallery. Germain couldn't be resentful at how much time she spent chatting and even laughing with the soft-spoken fellow, sometimes along with the *sieur* to make a third voice in the songs they were practicing, for he, Germain, spent just as much time with la Dame.

He was just happy something pulled Lyse-Magdalene now and then from her funk.

But he couldn't say the same for the Gonzaga, who was visibly dubious about having a stranger in the household, even so harmless a one as a poor minstrel who was grateful to have found food and a roof over his head. But it finally came to Germain that Don Ferrante had more driving him than just cautious inhospitality to strangers–for, thinking himself unobserved, the *condottiere*'s mouth attitude went grim at the easy camaraderie between his charge and the musician. Germain believed the man was jealous, and suspected the Mantuan might have confronted the two openly with the hot-blooded suspicion of his race, were it not for his dignity.

Then there came a day, as he and Lyse trotted their horses past the ruins of Coustaussa looming above the main road, when she glanced at the jagged shell of the château and asked him bitterly if he had ever felt the terrible sting of drastic failure.

Surprised, he answered, "Of course, what man has not failed at something? For me, it has always been figures, summing up the parts of numbers an *intendant* must know to keep his estate records in good order. My father despairs of my head in that regard, try as I will to figure correctly. But Madame Voisins has taught me a method to easily add an eight part and a twelfth part, and now, when we go home, I shall astonish *bonhomme* Matz, the elder."

She wasn't amused. Her pouty mouth drooped. But then her head came up and she turned in her saddle to face him. "Germain, pray, will you help me to do something silly? As a secret, between the two of us?"

Glad to skip to another subject, he pulled off his felt hat and ran a hand through his spiky hair. He grinned. "Aye to that, but only if it would be more silly than dangerous. *Ma princesse*, I know you."

"Oh, *bien sûr*, it is not dangerous at all. You would just have to pry up and move something heavy. Very heavy. And then push it back. It will take strength."

"You've not to worry about strength," he boasted. "And when could I ever say you 'nay,' no matter what?" He gave in to make her smile, ignoring all those tricks and pranks this angel's face had gotten him into at St. Piteu.

Later he thought with much regret that her offhand manner should have warned him.

Nevertheless, the following afternoon he found himself in the old chapel connected to the cemetery, on his hands and knees preparing to try to push the ancient stone altar away from a minute crevice in the crumbly flagstones. The gap was barely wide enough to insert a fingertip, much less the end of the sturdy pole which he'd fetched in for a lever, a fallen part of old scaffolding behind the church once used for some repairs.

La Dame had gone to bring a vial of medicine to a peasant who worked their bottom fields. The old *sieur* napped, Gonzaga was in Couiza. The bored guards on their one rampart and tower roof, or lazing by the gate, paid them no attention as Lyse had led him through the tumbledown burial ground, past the Blanchefort tomb, the D'Harcourt and Voisin graves, the crazily-tilted gravestones eroded by age and almost hidden by foliage. And before one could say '*Vive le Roi,*' they were standing in the cool and wavery light coming though the chapels' gaping windows.

In vain he gave her one last, pleading look to change her mind before he turned his attention to the strange, round altar under which she proposed was a forgotten crypt, perhaps with bones of a saint or other holy relics, or even a gold chalice and plate hidden from invaders. His *princesse*'s imagination had always been lively.

Seeing no hope for it, he spat on his hands and bunched his muscle to push. Five gigantic, straining shoves against the waist-high altar later and nothing had happened except a sore shoulder and abrasions to his hands from the rough stone. "'Tis the strangest altar did I ever see," he muttered, and rubbed his hands on his tunic. "Carved to look like the broad stump of a tree, and as solid rooted. Mademoiselle, this can't be moved, unless with steel wedge and hoist."

She pleaded, "Oh please, Germain, try again. Somehow I know this church has a crypt, maybe we'll even find the lost relics of the holy Marys that came this way. The local legends here say that after Christ's death his mother Mary, Mary, Martha's sister, Mary Magdalene, and St. Joseph sailed from the Holy Land to a port near Marseilles, but that in time Mary Magdalene herself carried the Savior's words here, to the Razès. It's said from here she went to join God in heaven, although no one can say where she was buried."

Germain knew Lyse was using her limpid, light-blue, wide-eyed, gaze on him. It always worked.

"Pah, well, the sainted lady would never have been in this poor village church. There's naught under this base but foundation rubble, I'll wager, and that little gap is merely an age crack, like all the rest."

"Oh, please, Germain, try again. I'll help you."

His good-natured sneer discredited whatever strength she might add. He wiped his pimpled forehead with the back of his hand and glared at the truncated column of altar, and just then an idea came to him. "*Eh bien,* maybe you can help. I'm going to lie on my back." He stretched out on the gritty floor, placing his feet against the barrel of the altar, knees bent. "You kneel behind me, with your knees against my shoulders. Your task is to keep me, as best you can, from moving back."

Although the angle of pushing was much improved and his legs were strong, she made a frail buttress to counter his muscular thrust, so he had little hope anything would happen. But, with the second heave of his solid thigh and calf muscles against the stone, there was a sharp crack and a sound like small balls rolling. Startled, he stopped in mid-air, then gathered his strength again, rebent his legs and shot them out straight with all his might, causing another loud crack, the sound of rolling, a groan of wood and squeak of metal.

He heard Lyse's gasp behind him and raised his head to see the round altar had rumbled smoothly away a few inches from his stretched feet. He looked back to show her his own astonishment, then wiggled forward to gain another purchase against the stone, and pushed until he quivered and threatened to shoot backward himself, in spite of his accomplice's grunting pressure against his shoulders.

Then, with the protest of ancient wood hinges, the altar, riding on a flat metal base, swung ponderously away and came to a jerking halt.

"Jesu!"

Germain scrambled up and gaped at the round opening under where the altar had stood, forgetting to help his mistress up, who crowded forward anyway. But whatever Lyse Magdalene had hoped for, what they saw was a disappointment, especially since the altar had obviously been constructed to roll away. There was only a round, shallow pit cut in the floor under the flagstone, of the same circumference as the altar and only about the length of a hand deep. The depression was empty, it contained nothing at all.

But deeply chiseled into its dark granite bottom was an alarming symbol, one which Germain knew in his bones did not belong in a church.

"What is it?" he muttered. But when he looked at her, Lyse-Magdalene's face did not mirror disappointment. No, instead she looked appalled.

Then they both jumped to hear a sound behind them, and swung around to see they were not alone. The itinerant minstrel, Ferri, was practically staring over their shoulders, his soft boots having allowed him to approach undetected while they were preoccupied with their task.

So fascinated was the lute player that he was oblivious to their unwelcoming reaction and breathed, "Yes, what is it? Do you know, Mademoiselle?" He paid no attention to Germain's frown that he had sneaked up on them.

Germain had no love for the fair-haired Ferri. He couldn't say exactly why, except the lean, narrow-faced young man reminded him of a hungry whippet dog. The fellow played his lute handily enough, from what Germain's inexpert ear could tell, in fact he had a way of caressing it into fine tones, and he pleased the ladies, entertaining their meals and quiet evenings with a sentimental repertoire of ballades. He had even a refined air about him, the one-named Ferri, for he claimed to be the youngest son of a rich burgher family that had gone bankrupt at the death of the parents, setting him adrift and penniless to wander and play for his food.

But it was the fellow's eyes that put Germain off. When the minstrel was off guard, their sharp-edged attention somehow did not match his otherwise languid manner and loose-limbed stance.

But Lyse-Magdalene was too mesmerized by her discovery to care that Ferri had joined them.

"I can tell you what it is," she muttered, "'Tis a symbolic pentagon. A five-sided figure. Germain, can you brush away with your shoe the dirt obscuring its center?"

Gingerly Germain complied, grasping the altar for balance as he scraped away the dust of ages from the center of the pentagram. Suddenly, gleaming up at them was the gold-outlined shape of a pyramid, and etched into the middle and also outlined in gold was an unwinking, staring eye. The device glinted up at them untarnished, and both he and Ferri couldn't cross their chests quickly enough. Lyse copied them mechanically.

"*Le bon Dieu* save us." Germain whispered in horror. "Witchcraft signs! Do not look at it, Mademoiselle Lyse-Magdalene!"

But she said in fascination, "No Germain, they are *not* witch's symbols. They are symbols of an old Christian sect called the Cathar. I have an Italian book that says such a pentagram represented wisdom and knowledge to the Cathar, and that the staring eye meant truth. These are virtues they revered."

Ferri gulped. He had drawn back, shaken. "Knowledge, yes, but of the Devil! The Cathari were evil heretics. They were eradicated by Holy Mother Church to save us. A man dare not even read of them or he will become contaminated. They consorted with demons and sorcerers. They ate their children," he said with dread, and signed another forceful cross on his chest.

Lyse still stared at the eerie, gold-outlined triangle and mystic eye glimmering up at them in the diffused light. To her, Ferri spoke out of ignorance. "What you say is not the truth. The Cathars hated the Devil. They called Satan evil," she insisted—and at that moment endured a tremor down her spine because something had stirred sharply in her brain. It was as if a small edge of her memory was lifted up a fraction and then dropped down again, too swift for her to capture anything but the impression that an important thought had been there.

She glanced up and saw the revulsion on both her companions' faces as they stared at the anti-Christ symbols. Yet, strangely, she felt neither fear nor revulsion. In fact, she felt oppressively sad.

"Germain, do you think there might be something under that inscription?" she prodded him.

Reluctantly Germain took up the pole he'd carried in and poked and probed at the dome of stone forming the bottom of the depression. "Nah, not so. 'Tis solid rock, *ma princesse*, the mountain itself poking through here, and left in place in the foundations when the church was first built."

"So—there are only these curious symbols under the altar, and nothing more?"

Germain scraped hard at the rock. "'Tis solid, nor could one cut into this rock without making marks plain to see, like that pentagram. There is nothing under this."

Ferri, still somewhat nervous, nevertheless wondered out loud what were they looking for.

Germain saw Lyse-Magdalene collect herself and casually shrug her shoulders. "But we didn't know. I saw a crack under the altar and thought it might mark a forgotten tomb. Or buried reliquaries and chalice cups, as priests once did to avoid pillaging. Maybe even a lost treasure," she said with a disparaging laugh. "Everyone speaks of a lost treasure hereabouts. At Puivert there was even a lost lake, once."

"Do you refer to the Cathar Treasure I've heard about as I wandered this area?" Ferri asked.

She answered lightly, "I suppose so. But, too bad, it's surely not here. Or anywhere. La Dame said the whole of Rennes-le-Château has been spaded up and combed through for hundreds of years."

Staring at her across the ancient symbols that repelled him, Ferri insisted, "This church must have been one where the heretics held their vile services and need to move the true altar away to worship their symbols. Do you think the *sieur* and la Dame know of this?"

Germain moved quickly to defend the Voisins. "Surely not, or they would certainly have defaced the thing. They are pious Christians! But this place has stood as a ruin for over two hundred years. Nobody comes here. It was sheer accident Mademoiselle spied the little crevice that made her suspect there was a space underneath this altar. So we will tell them now and they will chop it out."

Lyse clamped her hand on his arm. "No. No, we won't tell them. You know how sensitive the *sieur* is, why, the tears just roll down his cheeks when Ferri sings of sad events. Think how upset they will be to think their old chapel had once been desecrated by heretical rites. If we roll back the altar into place these symbols will be buried deep and made harmless again, for even this deconsecrated altar of true Christian worship must retain some power of God. I refuse to repay the kind hospitality of the Voisins by so distressing them. Promise me you'll say nothing, either of you, it will be a secret among us. Do give me your word."

They promised her, of course.

Germain, who vaguely thought that the altar had moved too easily for not having been rolled away in centuries, did not actually consider la Dame too wispy to receive news of an abomination to be rooted out. In fact, he could imagine her directing with special verve its mutilation by a farmer with a pickaxe. But if Lyse-Magdalene felt sensitive and uncomfortable about giving her hosts such news, he would go along with her.

Ferri, too, did not resist the blandishment of those entreating, azure eyes, for he nodded solemnly to keep the secret and asked no further questions. His recoil and shock at the sight of the unholy symbols seemed to be wearing off.

With the two men pushing, the altar rumbled back into place more easily than it had moved before, this time sliding over the depression completely, with no crack to show that the altar base on its strong iron plate was actually a sliver's width off the floor.

As they trudged from the ruin, Germain asked Ferri, "How came you to find us in this old church?"

The slim musician, whose long-fingered hands flapped by his sides, playing tunes in the air responded, "I was walking back from the east parapet of the mount, for I favor the panorama over the countryside from there, and I saw you both enter the building. I was curious. I did not mean to be rude, nor did think 'twas a private meeting. I beg pardon, Mademoiselle."

Lyse shook her head. "Ah, but you've done no harm, as long as you keep your promise to ignore and forget what we've seen." She gave his shoulder a little pat.

"Indeed, so I will," he assured her with a bland smile. "A wanderer sees much and says little, as the best way to keep his neck from the noose. Discretion, 'tis the first law of the rover."

Germain hoped the footloose lutanist would remember that rule. His *princesse* was already hiding from her connection with the discredited *duc* de Bourbon. She didn't need any further suspicion to fall upon her by even being in the vicinity of outlawed symbols of heresy.

As for reporting their find to the exotic mistress of Rennes-le-Château, he had no wish to delve too closely into the mind behind those limitless eyes. That morning, as the woman slipped by him to take a jar off a shelf, she had brushed his privates with her hand and he understood it wasn't accidental. In spite of her middle age, if she did it again, he suspected he wouldn't fight too long giving the randy woman what she obviously wanted.

Lyse stood on the breezy gallery which seemed to float off edge of the mount and stared past the autumnal landscape below, stubbly fields where the grain had already been harvested and at the base of the mountains trees making riotous stands of golds, reds and orange, their cool weather glory underlined with a shiver of yellow aspens. She stood gazing towards the mountains and the pale blur that was Bézu, straining to recapture what had flipped past her memory in the old chapel, and returned in muddled dreams since, shards she couldn't grasp or remember in the morning, except they held tears, frustration and a connection with Le Bézu. Sometimes she wanted to just reach into her head with a hand and grapple them out. It made her moan not to be able to grasp Mélline's legacy to her, and sometimes she even felt dread that the edges of her reason were crumbling.

Behind her on the gallery Ferri lounged cross-legged in an x-chair and picked softly on his lute, composing a new song. Her eyes locked on the Templar's old fortress, which sent her mood plummeting.

But today that vague ruin in the distance hardened up Lyse's resolve. La Dame had hinted she knew a way to dredge her memories to the surface, fast and clear. She was going to demand that Gonzaga elicit the woman's help. She was tired of suffering failure, of the guilt of having little news to send back to her uncle as each messenger arrived.

She was tired and she was cranky because she didn't sleep well, and because her heart hurt her, and because her disloyal body yearned for a man who avoiding her whenever he could.

She wanted to be finished with the tormenting 'seeing-back' and to leave the lugubrious domicile of Rennes-le-Château, and the Razès with its peculiar, oppressive feeling, and go anywhere, to Puivert if the *marquise* would take her in, or even to Italy. After all, she was not totally helpless, she still had the considerable money the duke had allowed her. And Germain.

Ferri's voice interrupted her glum reverie. "You are so pensive today, Mademoiselle, and it makes me sorry. But just to tell what one is thinking can calm the mind," he invited. "Here I sit, your gallant receptacle, ready to hear."

She wished she could tell him the strange coil she was caught in. It would be easy to unburden to him. He was sympathetic, he was a romantic, an imaginative artist who could suspend disbelief, whereas Germain was not. Little could the wandering lutanist imagine how restricted, how beleaguered she was by a weird, draining talent she never asked for. She opened her mouth, then closed it.

For there came the sound of boot heels striking the flagstones and the clink and slap of a sword, and Gonzaga approached them along the gallery, a cool smile on his face. "Hah, there you are. I am at your service, Mademoiselle. My valet Marco said you wished to see me?"

She nodded, her breath pinched off in her throat at the presence of the man she never stopped thinking about. Outwardly he hadn't changed, there was the same glinting green eyes under the winged brows, the same stubborn, black-fringed jaw. And yet, there had been a change, ever since Puivert—the wary distancing had returned to his glance, distancing that etched more depth into his mild scowl and tensely set shoulders. She felt he was angry with her and she couldn't imagine why, since she was doing what he had asked, maintaining what he preferred as the attitude between them.

She wondered if he slept badly and tossed and turned all night too, and vindictively she hoped so.

"You will excuse us, Ferri," she ordered the musician away, her gaze not straying from the big Italian.

Slowly the minstrel unfolded himself, glanced at each, made a short bow, and departed, cradling his big-bellied instrument against his chest like a precious baby.

Lyse returned her gaze to the stunning view, not trusting to look at him, which might tell him things he had declined to know. She was wondering how to begin the discussion, but he helped her, advising from behind, "Another of the duke's messengers has just arrived, this time from Barcelona. Charles is well and will winter there, in Catalonia. He is planning an early spring invasion of France, as always from the north, in company with England. Besides his own supporters he has commitments from mercenary captains for thirty thousand men, who, can he pay them, will form the spine of a rebel army soon strong enough to annihilate Francois.

"But the captains, hard men all, distrust an exile, even one as illustrious as Charles de Bourbon, afraid that in the long run there would be no money for their sweat and blood. Charles writes that he desperately juggles funds to keep just the core of them together through the winter."

She turned about swiftly, pinning him with feverish eyes. "That, Signore, is just what I wish to talk to you about. You were the one who said my uncle must strike back soon, while indignation in France over the King's high injustice still runs hot. He needs gold, he needs it now, and I need to find it for him."

"Lyse-Magdalene, 'tis a bootless chase he's sent you on, you cannot blame yourself. "

She could mark concern in his eyes, it was sincere, his attempt to exonerate her, but she broke in impatiently, "Nevertheless, we are here in the Razès where his hopes lie, and I must do more than I have." She reached a hand out to touch his arm and forestall a protest. "The pity is, my governess knew of certain circumstances that brought on the seeing-back, and would God she had told me what. Still, when we first arrived, la Dame mentioned that she too knew of ways to hasten the remembering, and that is my object now, speed. I know Madame Voisins would hesitate if I myself asked her to do with me whatever is necessary. But she would not refuse you."

He looked away from her into the distance, his profile set, mechanically slapping his thigh with his silver-handled riding crop. "Then, lady, I beg you remember the rest of what she said. She said the method she knew was dangerous."

"She said it might prove so. But I will take the risk. I must, if my task is to be accomplished in a meaningful time. My uncle Charles trusts me. You cannot refuse me."

He turned his dark head to glare at her. "How commendable a loyalty— if you were a vassal lord and not merely a woman. Are you so dutiful a niece you will risk grave harm to yourself, maybe even losing your life in Bourbon's cause?"

"*Condottiere?* Is that not what you risk every time you ride to war at his side?"

His scowl deepened, a little vein throbbed in his temple. "*Mama Diabolo,* woman, that is not the same—"

"Oh please, Don Ferrante, allow la Dame to help me. I am devastated by my failure, oh can't you see that?" she begged him. And couldn't he see what was also devastating her, that she wanted him to comfort her and hug her in his arms and understand her duty to an uncle who had given his orphaned niece kindness and a home? But he stood stiffly, with his hands at his sides. Her eyes searched his face.

He finally relaxed a little, although his stare remained chill. "Very well. You make it clear that helping him is your heart's desire. We will go to Madame and ask her to describe in detail this method she mentioned. If the chances of harm to you seem small, I'll consider approval."

She let out her breath with a tenuous smile. "La Dame is in her cabinet with Germain."

"But she always seems to be in her dispensary with Germain," he remarked gratuitously, his eyebrow raised, deliberately prodding her jealousy. "Don't you miss his company?"

She recognized the goading and merely flicked a glance at him. "Yes, of course I do. But men always have compelling interests before anything else, and la Dame's work with potions and drugs fascinates Germain. He is my friend, I could hardly begrudge him his pleasure. Besides," she reminded acidly, "I have Ferri the musician to amuse me, and we practice rondelays together every morning, and in the afternoons duets on our lutes. That gives me great pleasure."

His lips pursed in wordless denigration of her new interest, but then, then he sighed and said, "I'm bound to admit, that was truly a charming tune you both sang last night at supper."

Her enthusiasm rose. "Oh, it was just a simple one, you understand. Today we began studying a two-part madrigal of much more complexity. I know it will very much please everyone when we perform it."

"I'm sure it will, Lyse-Magdalene."

She couldn't tell how genuinely he meant that, for his tone had gone flat. He stared at her a moment longer and then, with a shake of his head which could have been for his own behavior, he caressed her soft cheek with the back of his hand a moment, surprising her so much that she never moved.

But he was always surprising her. She thought he would have been taken aback at her story several days before of the Cathar pentagram and eyed pyramid concealed under the altar of the ruined chapel, but instead he was only angry that she had not consulted him first, before the endeavor, and had included strangers like Germain and by accident, Ferri—which necessitated that she remind him that Germain was not a stranger.

In fact, he had just about shrugged over her actual discovery, saying it was merely another uneradicated relic of the heresy that had once found fertile ground in the Razès. But he too thought they should not mention it to the Voisins, for it would discomfort them. It had lain safely undiscovered all these centuries, then safely hidden it should remain.

Talking quietly with her he had said, "I don't wonder it shocked you. The breath of the anti-Christ is as frightening as the very howl of Satan."

Lyse turned to him a puzzled face. "But I knew what those symbols were, and that they weren't of the Devil, but of people who had actually struggled to evade him by living good lives. It was Germain and Ferri who paled with fear, not me. Of course, they didn't know the Cathars abhorred Satan and all his evil servants, and that they yearned for God and tried to lead aesthetic lives in order to find Him."

He cocked an eye at her. "So? Indeed. Where did you learn all that, Mademoiselle? "

"Why, in that little book you loaned to me, the one written by your compatriot. He writes of the Cathars as well as Templars."

"Well, I would not mention it to others, either the book or what you've read in it. Here in France the Holy Office is still greatly wrathful over the old heresy, even after three centuries. We of the Roman peninsula have more forgiving natures once wrongdoing is punished; we finally try to see things in intelligent perspective. Hence that little treatise."

As a Frenchwoman she felt insulted. "Perhaps forgiveness is easy because you had no Cathars in your midst to defy your church and abase His Holiness in Rome."

"Hah, you are wrong, for there were many strong Cathar groups in the north of Italy. They were sternly dealt with, of course."

"If this subject is not to be discussed, then why did you give me that book to read?"

"Because I thought it might stir you, stir up your 'seeing-back'. Listen, there was always strong belief that many of the French Templars themselves were secret Cathars. The rumors even included Blanchefort, the great knight from this region who became one of the Templar Grand Masters!"

Lyse eyes widened. "But Templars were pious warrior-monks, reverent members of a Catholic order overseen by the Pope himself. They could not have believed in that aberrant faith."

"Why not? That German monk, Luther of Wurtemburg, whose writings we've been arguing and discussing these nights, and whose rebellious ideas are already filtering strongly into Languedoc, as Madame Voisins reports, is also a churchman, is he not? Perhaps it takes a man immersed in the very fabric of the Holy Roman church to understand what it may be lacking."

"I can't fathom the Knights of the Rosy Cross did not believe the dear Christ was God's only begotten son."

"Well, that is not the worst of what they were said to believe, or disbelieve," he responded.

But abruptly then, with a dismissive grunt, he had glanced impatiently toward the stables, making it obvious the conversation was lacking the interest of riding down into Couiza and viewing the progress of the church a-building. Lyse, seeing his attention thinning out, had deliberately swallowed her many other questions. She had no wish to bore His High Illustriousness.

But her wonder at Gonzaga's mild reaction to the symbols under the old altar remained with her.

Now, as they stood on the gallery and she still felt surprise over the quick, warm caress of his hand on her cheek, he rumbled, "Come, Mademoiselle, let us go and see what la Dame has to say about granting your wish to speed your recall. But if she has deep reservations, I warn you, I will not allow the process to take place."

"I only know of this treatment from old parchments, I have not conducted it before," Lora Voisins was candid enough to admit. "But it is simple to administer, nothing more than inhaling the smoke of our dye plant, the *pastel,* and it might be that the danger of derangement is in proportion to the subject's previous distress. Mademoiselle de Bourbon-Tonnière seems to receive her insights with relative élan, compared to what I know of her mother's grief, and that of the other females reported in old Bourbon accounts.

"I would say she has a very good chance of emerging unimpaired." Her big hands were playing with a small crystal pestle on her table. She gave them a wise nod and her argent eyes seemed confident.

Lyse looked hopefully at Ferrante, literally willing him to approve.

After a moment he gave a grudging nod. "Very well, Madame. I must rely on your assessment. The fact is, Lyse-Magdalene and I are both anxious to succeed for the duke as quickly as possible. Location of a treasure here is reported to have happened once before, to a Bourbon, so I must believe there is reason that it can happen again." He sounded as if he were convincing himself.

La Dame turned to Lyse. "You are not afraid, *mon enfant?* Will you trust that I shall do my best for you?"

"I am not afraid, Madame," Lyse lied in a steady voice, but her hands grasped each other tightly in her lap.

"Then, quit me now, both, for I must prepare everything. Return here at sundown. Lyse-Magdalene, leave off your stiff bodice that constricts breathing, wear a loose robe to be more comfortable. In the meantime, rest easy. I am certain there is little to fear."

Lora smiled sagely at them, as if to ease the uncertainty in their faces, but Lyse, although she needed to trust this confidante of her uncle's, thought there was a certain curve to the smile that she just couldn't read as friendly.

The two guests at Rennes-le-Château descended from the Voisins' tower with little to say to each other. At the base Ferrante turned to his charge, reluctance still shadowing his face. "Lady, you do scrape up much courage when you need it."

Such uncharacteristic, if grudging praise from him broke her facade down in an instant. Her shoulders slumped in their big, poufed sleeves as she said, "But I'm not brave, actually, not at all. Will you—oh Don Ferrante, will you hold my hand when she does whatever she does?"

She could have sworn his hard green gaze melted to embrace her, although he did not move.

"Yes," he said briefly. "I will."

A rug-draped couch had been moved to the middle of la Dame's chamber and elevated to match the height of a bowl-shaped brazier resting on a three-legged tripod. A little fire flamed merrily in this brazier, kept fed with small chunks of charcoal by Robert Voisins, acting as assistant and dispensing kindly nods of encouragement to a pale Lyse, who rested on the couch, head and shoulders propped high on pillows.

La Dame offered her Mantuan guest a stool so he could sit by the side of the couch, just beside the brazier.

It helped that the night outside was chill, for all the shutters were closed and the charcoal smoke from the brazier already rose and hung just under the ceiling.

With both hands la Dame held an unpainted earthenware pot of red clay, its lid held down by an iron clamp. "In here I have the blue leaves of the *pastel* plant ground up to a very fine powder. I will throw handsful of it on the fire, and you must inhale the smoke, Mademoiselle, deeply. That is all you have to do." Her instructions were brisk; her dark-rimmed, gray eyes stared down at Lyse, who was lying so stiffly.

"Will I fall unconscious?" Lyse asked in a small voice.

"I don't know, it depends. But should you, you will wake when the smoke is cleared. Close your eyes, relax your body and breathe deeply. Then say whatever comes to your mind. I shall begin now." She nudged her husband, who moved aside so she could stand directly behind the brazier.

Lyse gave a weak smile to Ferrante, who looked uncomfortable perched on the small stool. His brows were drawn in his usual semi-scowl, his gold earring glinted in the lively flames from the brazier, and his expression seemed more skeptical than ever. Yet ironically, his presence, Blackbeard's strong and dominating presence once so inimical to her, was now her very strength.

He took her hand firmly in his and winked. "Don't worry. This grip will be your anchor. I will not let you go."

She allowed past her guard the pain and the pleasure of remembering his mouth on hers, the unleashed passion in the kisses they shared that last night at Puivert, and she half-closed her eyes over it. A handful of powder hit the dancing flames, causing a hissing and spitting, and a cloud of bluish smoke was directed towards her by the *sieur* wielding a large parchment fan.

Another handful, more hissing, more smoke wafted under her nose. The smell of the burning charcoal mixed with the spicy-sweet anise odor of the dried *pastel* plant, but not unpleasantly, nor chokingly. Eyes closed, Lyse could breathe as the fumes enveloped her, with only an occasional cough.

She heard a muffled cough here and there from the others too, but otherwise, as the minutes passed in the still room, nothing happened. There came the hissing twice more, and she tried hard to concentrate on Mélline, even on Le Bézu, but her mind perversely skipped and jumped all around, and her eyelids kept fluttering. Was she failing again, oh no, she couldn't–

"Breathe in, Lyse-Magdalene, breathe more deeply," came la Dame's hoarse command.

She did, coughing and inhaling the scent of the smoke, spicy anise and lemon and a faint tinge of the mold on wet walls, but there was nothing else occurring. She heard the others cough. Out of embarrassment, bleak humor struck her. She muttered thickly, taking refuge in self-ridicule, "Isn't there, mayhap, some miraculous incantation you should pronounce–Madame...?"

Incaantaatiion...!

–a shift, a silent snap–

Chapter 20

"—nor incantation. No spell known will waft it there, my lady. It remains for us to physically transport it, now we are ready," the burly, black-robed brother exclaimed, punching his thong-laced needle through cloth one more time to draw together the tarred canvas which covered a pillar-like object taller than a man and shaped like a curve-armed Y.

"But how?" Mélline asked, feeling ill from the suffocating smell of the pitch softening in a metal pot over a brazier.

"Through these tunnels, as far as we can, and then across the fields in the darkest part of the night. Sir Brother de la Motte thinks we have run out of time, so to take it all the way by cart would be slow and dangerous."

Mélline felt her back prickle as she stared in reverence at the monolithic bulk they discussed, for under the canvas wrapping was a relic of the ancient desecration of the Second Temple in Jerusalem: Solomon's fabled Menorah, pure gold, heavily encrusted with the most precious of gems. And here this priceless treasure stood, anonymous and humble in its waterproofed shroud in a dimly lit, underground chamber in the Razès, as the Templar sergeants busied themselves around it, preparing to depart.

It was the last of the Treasury to leave this refuge for a safer hiding place, and as Mélline thought this, the splash of water and the image of smoothed stones dripping in the dark also flashed into her mind. But she was happy to see the last of this incriminating Treasury, the gold bullion and priceless artifacts the Templars had acquired in two hundred years in the Holy Land, which they called Outremer. The horde would condemn them all to death were it found at Rennes-le-Château.

Actually she had viewed only the outer containers of the overwhelming Treasury Bernard and his men had smuggled down from Paris, staggering stacks of caskets, boxes, crates, chests, and blanket-swaddled objects of immense value, one of them an ebony coffer bound with iron holding a large piece of the True Cross!

Her hands were freezing in the cavern despite it was summer, she put them inside her long, drooping, velvet sleeves to warm them.

"Will Sir Brother de la Motte return this way?" she asked, and her heart

hammered for the answer she deeply wanted. She had not seen Bernard in over a fortnight, not since he rode away escorting the plupart of the Treasury into hiding. She felt crushed by a sense of approaching doom.

"Mayhap he will," her Knight's tonsured adjutant shrugged, tying off the strong stitches that sealed the canvas' doubled edges, then sawing the thong from the long needle with his knife. "But we will be gone from here within the half hour. There remains only placing the ropes for lowering this most sacred behemoth." He tossed the wooden needle to a brown-robed aide who was folding canvas into a pad upon the crude sledge these last five Templars and two mules would use to drag the lashed Menorah through the narrow tunnels.

He added, "Grammercy to you, Madame, for the welcome food and drink you carried us, although I fear you have a sore way back up those steps."

Mélline slipped her arm through the handle of her basket and turned toward the passage leading to the twisting stair that mounted into darkness. She turned back. "Do you see your Knight Bernard, good brother, tell him the lady of Rennes-le-Château and her sire wish him well, and pray the that the God of Heaven's all-seeing eye rest close upon him. Upon you all."

The stubble-faced Templar aide smiled, but his dark eyes were sunk deep into his head from lack of sleep and hard work. "The Lord's blessings upon you and your sire, Madame, for your friendship in this hour of need," he responded.

Mélline's hand holding a lighted lantern trembled. "Perhaps—perhaps, brother L'Astre, the emergency will yet be proven empty?"

"I do not think so, Madame. I am told the knowledge of impending disaster for us comes from an impeccable source. Yet it is hard to know why God brings us this punishment." Still sitting back on his heels at the foot of the shadowed, en-shrouded Menorah, the brother rounded his fleshy shoulders and wiped the sweat from his gritty chin. He looked at her sadly, from the depths of a confounded soul.

"I will convey your message to Brother Knight de la Motte, good lady."

—water again, surging into her mind, the swish and great splash of disturbed water, the crash of a large object into water—?

Lyse rolled her head, she ground her teeth and groaned, she fought to breathe, but still the smoke rolled into her nostrils—

Mélline coughed hard, but she didn't know why. The ugly black smoke still rising from the burning farmstead beyond the bend in the road below did not reach their tower's rampart, and the grimy plume of dust kicked up by a troop of riders approaching from the opposite direction along the river, billowed away from their eyrie.

Her stiff, veiled hennin, so heavy on her head, offered no shade that would help her headache. She reached up to loosen its transparent chiffon draping, and pulled it down to shield her eyes from the bright day, and she stood close to her husband as they peered over the area through a wide crenelation, for even the old man's presence blunted a little the fear that ate at her.

The two of them were ready for the invaders sending up dust in their fast progress toward them, for beacons had earlier signaled the numerous presence of troops in the Razès, and one need only spy the massed, rippling ensigns they flew to know that they were royal troops, soldiers of the monarch Philippe le Bel.

But of all of the residents in the peaceful valley who gaped in surprise at their ranks, perhaps only the forewarned baron and his wife knew the terrible intentions of this swoop of heavily armed soldiers here—and at the same moment throughout France.

The baron took Mélline's nervous hand as she stared down, the thunder of hooves finally rising to their ears. "They will not ride up here. We are only a little hilltop village," he reassured her. "This château could not stop a mosquito who wished to enter, so who would chose it for refuge? I am sure they will pass on, through Quillan and thence to Perpignan, where there is a large Templar preceptory and church. And there they will make their arrests."

"And Le Bézu?" she whispered through a cough.

The old man's facial muscles drew taut. "They would not dare defile Bézu!" he said.

Her jaw wanted to tremble. "De la Motte's superior was right, then, to send the Templar Treasury into hiding here months ago, for what they suspected then has happened. But I cannot believe it! On what grounds can the King be arresting monks of an order which is under the protection of the very Pope himself?"

Her husband squinted down at the flashes of sun upon steel as the long, bristling column of visored men arrowed out of their own dust, noting the trio of powerful bombards on carriages that kept bouncing pace behind, and, lumbering more slowly in the rear, a great siege engine for hurling boulders that could crack thick walls.

He didn't answer the upset young woman beside him because he didn't know the answer. The whole attack, if it followed what de la Motte's superior, the Templars' Master of the Treasury, had learned, was shocking. Unbelievable. Terrifying.

A servant hurried out on the rampart. "Householders at the château gate, Monsieur. They have seen the soldiers and are frightened and wish to shelter in the court."

"Yes, of course. But tell the people to be calm. There is no reason for any of us to fear. The troops will pass us by."

The servant hesitated. "But the Guimets, they were arrested at dawn and their place burned to the ground."

His master lowered his white eyebrows in a frown. "The Guimets were accused of witchcraft, simply that, just as were those two brothers in Limoux two months past. Eh Bien, we have no witches here, we are safe," he stated sternly. "Courage and silence, that is our watchword."

"Oui, Monsieur, I will tell them," the servant gulped, backing away.

"Yes, calm is what is needed, and our usual courage of the spirit. Say that I demand that."

The Baron stared at the man's retreating back, and sighed heavily to his wife. "I would wish that our leader were here. His pure and shining presence would be reassurance to us all."

Mélline was staring south at the column of black smoke from the burning farm still spiralling into their boundless, azure sky. She tried to lift up her own spirits. "At least, if Pope Clément's word still holds, all will still be safe at Le Bézu."

The old man's troubled eyes followed hers to the snaking, black scar against the sky. Clément the Fifth, who had been the archbishop of Bordeaux before the determined Philippe had tapped him to be Pope, had a nephew who was the Templar Preceptor of Le Bézu! And even more uncomfortable for the Holy Father in this debacle, his very own mother had been a Blanchefort, a descendant of the great Templar Grand Master.

"As long as Clément's dear nephew is the commander of the Knights-Templar at Le Bézu, the Pope will not allow the fortress to be touched, not by King Philippe and his man, or that demon Nogaret, or anyone else. So no one will dare bring evil on those pure spirits whom Templars shield."

"Even though the Pope knows there are one hundred and five Cathar Parfaits and Parfaites secretly sheltered at Bézu? I know de la Motte told us that, but how strange it seems that the pontiff does not move against them! Clément was put on his papal throne by King Philippe, after all."

"Mais oui, he knows. But it is just as true that his blood ties are strong enough—and Le Bézu remote enough—for him to persuade the King to stay his hand."

"And if this Pope dies, conveniently, like the others?"

"Alas, my dear. The cleansed souls who absolutely will not hide their truth have no where else to flee, and so they will be taken. What will happen, will happen. Which is why de la Motte would not hide the Treasury at Le Bézu, it is too risky."

Mélline's sigh came from the depth of her heart. She was not as sanguine as her devout husband. "But you do not worry about your son?"

"Ah, he is young, and a good man, and learned in the good ways. Think, at Le Bézu he will at least have the rite of the Consolamentum to raise him to

Heaven, should he need to die."

Mélline felt a scream rise in her, she ached to tear to shreds her husband's peace and calm faith with the reality of the danger that swirled about them. Or perhaps it was just her guilt over her sins against him rising to overwhelm her.

But a trio of horsemen, the Bishop of Albi's soldiers, had been dispatched up the precipitous mount to Rennes-le-Château. Now they clattered officiously into the courtyard where the priest of Rennes stood protectively before the nervous villagers in his black and white cassock, a round-brimmed hat over his white cap.

But the soldiers were looking only for the Assistant Treasurer of the French Templars, Bernard de la Motte. They made a quick search of the château and village, and not finding their man then made it clear that anyone giving the Templar refuge would be executed.

The little priest spoke up, his stentorian voice bigger than he was. "But the man is a Knight-Templar, a monk, a brave soldier of the Pope! Why do you seek to arrest him?"

"They are all being arrested, mon père, every member of that Order, from lay brother to Grand Master, right now and everywhere in France. By orders of his Holiness, the Pope, and his Majesty, King Philippe. They are accused of heresy, witchcraft, and blasphemy, for which they will surely all go to the stake. Any man who gives them refuge is a fool, for we will smoke out every last one and their accomplices will pay too. With their lives."

The brusque, helmeted soldier glowered all around to emphasize his words, then remounted his horse and rode out of the gate with his companions, threading down the mountain again to catch up with their troop

—Lyse moaned in her darkness, waggling her head to get away from the clinging smoke, it made her cough, made her cry bitter tears, it made her heart race so fast—

"The Guimets are accused of sorcery," the royal bailiff reported, placidly sitting his horse, along with the Baron and his wife who had come to meet him, and surveying the still-smouldering ruins of what had once been a prosperous farmstead. "Their neighbor swore to the tribunal that they had sickened his cows and goats and withered his field; what's more, he swore they had trampled a cross into the dirt, twice. They have been taken to Carcassonne for interrogation by the Holy Office." He shrugged. "I hear they were not faithful churchgoers."

The bells on the embroidered halter of Mélline's palfry jingled softly as the mare shifted. She covered a cough produced by the acrid smell of charred wood.

"That does not make them evil, Monsieur. The old ones were frail, they just could not easily get about."

But the bailiff, self-satisfied in his dark blue gown embroidered with the golden scales of justice, his porcine eyes almost obscured by fashionable bangs, grimaced and declared, "Then be not shocked, Madame, when I tell you, but they are Cathar, that is what they are! Damned heretics!"

Mélline appeared to be startled and she crossed herself.

"How could that be? The last two hundred of those people were destroyed at Montségur even before we were born, Monsieur. There are no more Cathar."

Her husband smiled thinly. "How naive you are, dear wife. All were not found, at least not here in the Razès. They scurried and hid, they scuttled into the new orders of humble friars that had commenced—such as the Franciscans, which suited their sense of sacrifice—or they moved away and sheltered elsewhere under a mantle of devout Christianity. But in their hearts they still abjured the Cross and the teachings of Jesus' Roman church, and this they have secretly taught their children and grandchildren."

The bailiff spat at the side of the road. "They like to kiss the arses of cats and dance with the devil, the wretched fools." He turned his pudgy face toward the lady to be his hostess for several days and his smile became treacly as he admired this most sheltered and delicate woman, her brow as virginal as new-fallen snow. "Well, no matter to concern yourself one bit, Madame, for they'll soon dance at the end of a rope or on a pile of faggots, Cathar or sorcerers or whatever they are. They will be blotted out."

Mélline was silent, although her stomach churned. But she wished she were a huge wildcat with fangs long as daggers; she would rip the stupid bailiff into a dead, bloody mess

—Lyse writhed, coughed, frantically tried to get away from the smoke, her eye seemed glued shut, something was holding her, she moaned and put up her hand to ward off the smoke—someone pushed her hand away—

eyes flying wide, ogled the little scroll of parchment he had pressed into her hand as if it were a snake ready to strike.

"Of course I will keep it, Bernard. But it is so heavy a burden to guard."

"It is a safeguard," he said, as she kept staring at the scroll in the tiny flicker of the candle's light. He was standing above her, looking down at the tender, white nape of her neck where her braids were coiled. "You know I would do nothing to put you at risk, sweet lady. Four couriers were sent on their way last week in four

different directions, each to make his way, direct or roundabout, across the Channel to the Scots Templars, each with the same ciphered message, the location where the Scots will find our Treasury. But I give this copy to you because I trust you with my life and because you are beyond suspicion, even if your husband is not. If, by the worst of luck, all four messengers fail, the Scots know to eventually, secretly seek you out."

Mélline dropped and flung herself forward to hug him hard about the knees. "I am so afraid for you, Bernard." she keened. "You should not have come, even through this dark night, and you must escape that old cave. They have thrown every Templar in France into prison, accused of the most incredible falsehoods, and they are combing the countryside for you, to torture you into revealing the Treasury. Go to Le Bézu, my heart, and never leave there."

"No, I will not jeopardize that last refuge by my presence. The cave is cleverly concealed, it is safe enough." But he raised her up to distract her, saying softly, "Ah, Mélline, are you not glad we are together a while longer? God help me, I have been burning for you."

"But I will not say adieu," she snuffled. "We will succeed. We will yet see that far, cold land of Scots where your brother Knights offer safety. I love you, I will not say farewell, Bernard."

"We will not say farewell," he murmured into her hair. Mélline felt the tremor of emotion that tensed his muscles. Then he picked her up and laid her on the little cot. She closed her eyes, despairing to sense his underlying resignation as he gently kissed her eyes, her lips, her throat, as he caressed away with worshipful hands the misery that bound her. Soon, as it always did when they could express their love and cling together, everything inside her ignited into one huge, obliterating flame of desire for him

—she could feel the chords in her neck standing out, she could not pry open her eyes, she whipped her head about to avoid a black orb hurtling to kill her, she couldn't breathe—

—crackling, burning, hissing, the terrible, choking smoke… and they held her shrieking to the ground, held her kneeling and gasping in the mud made by the rain that would never put out the fire, never, never, it was too late to quench the searing fire, too late to relieve her guilt, too late to save the consuming love for her Knight that had lit her life with its radiance. She raised her streaming face into the grey, racing sky as they held her by twisting her arms and the spit drooled from her mouth as she screamed, "You are the Devil, You, You there above, the Devil,

Satan, Evil! You have taken my Bernard, O my Bernard!" she screeched, agony in her contorted face. And the sky rumbled and flashed and roared back

—hurting her, gripping her by the shoulders, slapping her face, stop, stop it, but she couldn't, she screamed and screamed the horror of it, for what she had done was too great. She wanted to tear it from her mind, cleanse it away, not to think of it, to be empty, empty, no more anguish, think no more—

Her face was crushed against a shoulder. Hard arms were around her, rocking her back and forth, "Lyse! Lyse-Magdalene! Shh, shh, you are safe, you are here now, don't weep!" The deep voice went on whispering like that in her ear, the strong arms not allowing her struggle, the anxious but reassuring words chipping away at the tight mass she had made of the writhing worms in her mind, to keep out the truth and the pain.

A woman's voice urged, "Here, make her drink this. 'Twill calm her immediately."

"I think we've done enough to her—" came the protesting rumble.

"I insist. Listen to me. It will help."

Cool metal touched her lips and Lyse shuddered. Her breath was coming in animal gulps, her weeping eyes seemed to her open in horror although their lids were closed. She was being forced to drink, forced, and she didn't care, life held no meaning for her but horror, she would drink and thank them for the poison. Cool bitter liquid poured down her throat and she swallowed, then swallowed again, grateful to die in order to stop the pain of living.

She didn't know how long she was racked with convulsive shudders, but at some time they lessened and finally stopped. She could breathe. Because her head pounded with pain, she realized she was not dead. She realized that the arms had never let go of her, except to shift her to a more comfortable position, and that a callused hand was stroking her face. Her eyelids fluttered. The unknown horrors she had seen against them had at last slipped away, and now she knew that she could open her eyes, with effort. So she did.

They didn't focus for a moment, but then there was a face above her and she thought it smiled. Dreamily she smiled back, for he was her love.

"Bernard!" she whispered.

"No," came the relieved response. "Ferrante. I hope that does not disappoint you."

Her eyes uncrossed. Bernard? The brooding green stare and bearded jaw swam into clearer focus above her, the strong nose, the sensuous lips, and she knew him. He was Ferrante di Gonzaga. So she was Lyse-Magdalene de

Bourbon-Tonnière. Was she not? Lyse? Mélline? Everything was tumbling about in her aching head.

A silver-haired, grey-eyed woman came into her view, fixing her with a stare, forcing her to know who it was, Lora de Voisin. She also became aware of a miasma lingering in the air, and the odor of anise. She was back to her senses and she suddenly hated that smell.

"I'm all right," she muttered, trying to stir, and winced. "But my head rages with pain."

"You need to sleep, Mademoiselle," la Dame husked. "You have had a difficult time."

Lyse stared wide-eyed at Ferrante. "But—we've won! I remembered—some important things. Almost what we were seeking, almost, almost ..." She trailed off wretchedly, for 'almost' was not the success they needed.

La Dame insisted, "No, now you must sleep in order to heal your mind. You will not forget that which you recalled. Signore, do you think you can carry her to her chamber?"

Unable to summon up volition or strength, Lyse closed her eyes again and felt herself lifted off the couch, and, drifting, she thought that it was the velvet-covered pallet where her beloved Bernard had brought her such joy, and she murmured about it. Then she was deposited again on a soft bed and a sheet was drawn over her. She gave a long, shuddering sigh, and turned her face into the pillow.

Ferrante, badly shaken himself by Lyse' violent reaction to the *pastel,* surveyed the drugged senselessness of his charge. "Is she all right, Lora? *Sang de Dieu,* it took too long to bring her back. That hysteria, such cries and anguished weeping, it almost tore her apart. And she confused me with that Templar, Bernard de la Motte. What else can we do to help her return to herself?"

"Nothing. She is exhausted. But I looked deep into her eyes once she had quieted and I saw Lyse-Magdalene, I assure you. We are lucky that her sense of identity is strong. Just let her sleep for a few hours, Marye will stay with her. You come with me, *condottiere.* The *sieur* has in his chamber a flask of strong *eau de vie* from the Gascons."

"You have a knack, Madame, of divining a man's greatest need." The chuckle was ragged.

"I know. So perhaps you should allow me other ways to prove such a talent, Signore, *hein?*"

Her insinuating, throaty laugh bubbled up and then died away as the door closed softly behind them.

Incredibly, a twinge of jealousy invaded Lyse's blurred mind, even as she was sinking into deep sleep, since she had not seen Ferrante's negative expression.

It was a sleep of quiet, happy dreams which lapped over her like cool water; dreams of her handsome, smiling uncle Bourbon when she was a child as he presented her with a frisky colt; of Madame de Dunois patiently teaching her to embroider; and even of Germain, her constant playmate, showing her a bird's nest.

But once, for a few seconds, she was shot to the surface of her dreams by the loud creak of a door opening, and she was aware that Marye noisily got up from her seat and went to it.

There was an unmuted whispering. "No, I assure you, she is fine. 'Twas a faint or something, but she rests and her color is very good," Lyse heard the maidservant grunt, and heard her firmly shut the door. "Nosy minstrel," Marye muttered, returning to her post, "thinks everything hereabouts is his concern, has to know everything."

But Lyse was already lost again in the healing dreams and memories of her own life.

Chapter 21

Finally she woke, just like that. Her eyes snapped open and she lay still for a while, breathing quietly. Taking inventory, she realized she felt fine, perfectly normal. And she remembered everything; the 'seeing-back', the things that had happened to her—no, to Mélline!—lay crystal clear in her mind. But would it stay that way? And where was Don Ferrante? Or la Dame? A snort made her turn her head around, to see Marye snoring in the chamber's one chair, hair askew beneath a white cap, hands folded over her stomach.

Sitting up, wrapping the sheet about her because her clothes and even her shift had been removed, Lyse hung her legs over the edge of the bed. She reached to tweak the woman's skirt. "Marye! Wake up!"

"Eh? Eh?" the woman gargled. "What's wrong, Mademoiselle? You feel sick?"

"No, I'm really quite well. But I want to see Don Ferrante. Please fetch him for me."

The maidservant blinked around her and her face fell into disapproval. "But Mademoiselle, regard the window. There is no light coming around the edges of the shutters. 'Tis still full night. He will be asleep."

"Wake him, then. Do as I say. It is very important."

Marye balked. "Pray, Mademoiselle, I have no stomach to tangle with that man, he has a temper. Maybe he will not wish to be awakened from a good sleep in the middle of the night?"

"Yes, I know about his temper, but I swear to you he will come without reprimand. Go quickly, it is urgent!"

With a sour look, Marye levered herself up, found the straw slippers she had kicked off, and, yawning, shuffled out.

Lyse blessed the health that had snapped her back into reality unharmed. She secured the soft sheet more carefully under her arms and waited, and as she thought of Ferrante, in spite of herself his image blended with what she believed Bernard had looked like, and tendrils of Mélline's emotions still clung around her heart. A little smile appeared on her lips and she could feel the blood pulsing through her veins. She wondered what she looked like after the ordeal.

Oh, *le bon Ciel!*

The room was warm from several charcoal braziers. Dropping the sheet she ran naked to the mirror, only to see that her hair was streaming loose, and that her lips and face were white as a ghost. There were little lines of strain under her eyes, although at least the whites were clear. She poured cool water into a basin and vigorously patted her eyes and face with a cloth wrung out in it, bringing a tinge of color up in her cheeks. She rubbed the wet cloth over her neck and chest too and arms too, enjoying the fresher feeling.

She quickly touched some scented oil between her breasts, hooked the river of copper-silk hair behind her ears, then streaked back to sit on the edge of the bed, with the sheet wound around her again. In a moment she peered into the large goblet on her table, and seeing it held water, drank it all down.

Then there came a peremptory knock on the door. The Mantuan entered, cocked his head to see her sitting there, sheet-wrapped but seeming much herself, then ordered Marye to wait outside.

He'd come swiftly from where he'd fallen asleep in a chair, just as he was, still clothed in his shirt, undone at the neck, and his tight, striped breeches, but sans codpiece, and stockings. Running his fingers through his tousled hair, he walked forward to squint at her in the low light of the few candles burning, then demanded, unsmiling, "How are you?"

"I am quite fine, Signore," she murmured lightly. As proof, she looked him up and down, and raised her eyebrows. "Heavens, do you always sleep in your clothes?"

He growled, "I dozed in a chair, sitting up. In case you needed me. I wasn't sure la Dame's last potion would serve to calm you, you were in a convulsive state. Though now—you seem to be quite normal, I am relieved to note."

"I apologize for asking your presence in the middle of the night, but I need to tell you everything I remember, right now, before it might leave me."

"Ha. Quite right," he eagerly agreed. "You sometimes spoke out loud under the *pastel's* trance, but otherwise there were lengthy silences when we were not able to follow what you were experiencing."

He glanced over at the chair Marye had been using, but Lyse, in control for once, patted the high bedside next to her. "No, if you would sit here? It still—badly unnerves me—to recall Mélline's grief. The chair is too far away. In case I faint. Please?"

He hesitated, then did as she asked, gingerly folding his big frame on the bed edge next to her. His obvious reluctance to come that close annoyed her. Did he think she might bite him? Or that her strange gift was infectious?

With one hand she held fast the sheet, with the other she took a last sip from the goblet, and then, in a steady but low voice, so that he sometimes had to lean closer to catch her words, she recounted to him the glimpse of the Treasury she had gotten, the dread sight of the royal troops riding to arrest the Templars, and the burning farmstead, but next to most important, the astounding fact that the Templars of Le Bézu were sheltering Cathar *Parfaits*. She finished, finally, with the most important, Bernard's farewell visit to the hidden chamber to give the written key to the Treasury's location to Mélline.

Ferrante's semi-scowl had disappeared, he listened totally absorbed in her words. "But did you—did she look at it, this record he gave into her keeping? Had you any glimpse of what it said?"

"No, that time no," Lyse admitted unhappily. "But in fact Mélline didn't want the responsibility, she took the scroll unwillingly. Anyway, its message was in cipher, so Bernard said. She probably couldn't read it.

"Or just as probably, she could. She seems infinitely involved with de la Motte and his task, more than was her husband, certainly."

But Lyse was troubled and regarded him with haunted eyes. "Ferrante? It is my suspicion that Mélline was a Cathar herself. And her husband too. Perhaps some of the people who lived on this mount as well. Even so many years after the Holy Crusade to destroy that heresy, there were still Cathars!"

She thought he would be as shocked as she was, but he looked at her levelly. "So your Bourbon ancestress might have been a heretic, you believe? An apostate? Does that distress you so mightily?"

But why shouldn't it distress me, swept through Lyse's mind, there should be revulsion that the blood in my veins was tainted centuries past by a woman who thought herself Christian but repudiated the dear Christ, His Crucifixion, and the Annunciation, and who believed in two Gods at once. Lyse felt a chill run up her arms as Mélline's last, harsh, wild screams against God echoed in her head...

And yet, it was only great pity she felt for Mélline; and the idea wouldn't leave her that, after all, no matter their weird, dissenting tenets, the Cathars called themselves Christians and strove to reach Heaven in a state of grace. And their holiest people, the *Parfaits* and *Parfaites,* led humble lives of study and sacrifice reminiscent of her own day's most exemplary Christian Orders.

So she answered him simply and with courage, "They were mislead, indeed. But I don't believe they were evil."

He studied her a moment, then cleared his throat and gave her an unexpected half-smile. "Neither do I."

Startled, her eyes scanned his face but there was nothing more she might read on it. Her mood dipped again. "Still, none of this has brought me one whit closer to discovering exactly where the Templars hid their Treasury. There is more I must remember and I know I can. Don Ferrante, I must avail myself again of this magic smoke."

"No. It is too dangerous. Since you feel you are close to remembering what we want, you will do it as you always have, naturally, when it comes to you."

"Too slow, too slow," she agonized. "The answer is atop me, I can feel it. But you see, there is something–something more that is tearing poor Mélline to pieces, even more dreadful than Bernard's execution, something that makes her curse God! I must remember, I must."

He took her hand to rub, for she was upset. "*Doucement,* lady. We will talk about it in the morning, with la Dame. Now you should finish your sleep, rest some more." The green gaze smiled into her eyes, but he did not rise. She could see he wanted to ask her something. Finally he said uncomfortably, with a clearing of throat. "Tell me, did de la Motte take his lady love to bed in that secret chamber in the old tower you've mentioned?"

She glanced down sideways, biting the corner of her full bottom lip, embarrassed, feeling as if she had been peering through keyholes. "Yes," she finally murmured, "Their hearts were joined. They made love with each other."

"And, do you recall all of that? As intimately as it occurred?"

"Yes," she admitted, and felt heat flood into her face. "This time yes, and other times too." The confession just tumbled out. "Especially, I can see now, when the heliotrope was blooming outside my window. I prayed not to remember their meetings, I disliked it, but in no manner could I help it. Afterwards I would feel so lonely. I felt bereft–shorn of Mélline's delight with, and love for another, and of her joy to know her love was returned. Alas, I have no control over this unseemly peeping."

She thought he might laugh or make a suggestive joke, but he surprised her. "Ah–don't look so sad," he sympathized quietly. "Remember, 'tis not your life."

"But I am sad," she answered, lifting her face to his. "It is sad and terrible to feel the hopeless passion of ghosts."

Ferrante swallowed and felt the bump in his throat bob. He shook his head doggedly. "Ah, Lysette–" he began, thinking to once again explain their own situation in terms that wouldn't hurt her. But he stopped, once more drowning in the lash-fringed beauty of her crystalline, pale blue gaze. A rush of pity for her scattered his resolve; the urgent need to lend her his strength crumbled the self-protective wall he had built against her, and shredded his intention not to confuse her recall, not to exacerbate her overwhelmed emotions with the added excitement of the erotic pull between them.

Her lip quivered. All reason fled him. He opened his arms and she came into them, and he hugged her to him, the poor, bedeviled woman.

She cried against his shoulder, her fingers digging into his flesh. "I think I am Mélline sometimes and I want to hold on to her, to her world. It is like another person lives inside me. It frightens me because I was born Lyse-Magdalene, and I am alive here and now, and I don't want Mélline's life. But sometimes I just—am her. Ferrante, will I end like my poor mother? Will I be unable, finally, to come back to myself? Will I die of Mélline's grief?"

"No, no, you know you have a deal more mettle. It is that accursed blue powder la Dame burned, it is too potent a filtre for you. I swear we will not use it again." He paused for a moment, his grip tightening around her as he felt her shiver, and he searched for words to distract her, to distract himself, murmuring into her hair, "Ah well, take heart, Lysette, at least the season for heliotrope is over." It was a clumsy, stupid joke and he knew immediately she thought he was mocking her for she stiffened and tried to pull away.

But Ferrante held her right where she was. His avid will to avoid this peculiar female was totally deserting him, for her back was partially bare, and his hands, by chance, had encountered her warm, smooth skin there. *She* was not a ghost, she was a rounded young woman of appealing beauty, and resolve be damned, he could not take his hand from her, he could not stop from caressing the silken skin that thrilled his touch.

She leaned back in his arms to peer at him and the sheet she still held slipped to the curve of her breasts, displaying the enticing white flesh that often rose half-naked above her square bodices, a female fashion invented to make men crazy.

His eyes traveled over her face. He marveled in a whisper, "*Nom de Ciel.* How can it be? You have the immaculate face of a Virgin, yet the most voluptuous mouth I have ever coveted. The mouth of a beckoning Siren."

She made a little face. "Thank you, my sir. How gallant you are in your turn of phrase."

"Yes, you are like the enticing Sirens, whose celestial singing wreaked utter havoc with poor Ulysses in spite of his powers," he said accusingly.

"Indeed, and I can sing too," she added.

"And you will wreak havoc with me." There was almost a groan behind the words.

Her short laugh was bitter. "Say then, Signore, how better to amuse yourself hereabouts?"

This bold invitation made him angry; he continued the litany of her faults. "You are quality, born and raised up so. Yet see how you invite me like a tavern wench."

"Wrong, Signore. For 'tis not I who has my fingers within your clothes."

His hand started to jerk away from her back, but he stopped and instead gave a bark of laughter for the jab. But Lyse saw the gleam in his green eyes turn wicked, and knew she had teased and toyed with him too far.

"Very well, my demoiselle. I am only flesh and blood, and no less immune to temptation than the Greeks or Sampson or David. God is my witness that I have done my best to ignore you as a woman."

"Or even as a man," she quipped, even though knowing she was teetering on the edge of a precipice. "But surely, Don Ferrante, you didn't do that scandalous Scarf Dance with a man?" Her fingers crept to the nape of his neck and toyed with the dark curls there.

"No. With a lady. A most enchanting one." His breath caught, for he saw she was boldly watching his mouth. "I've forgotten her name but there is a way to identify her," he said, and shifted his grip to her bare arms and pulled her close.

His kiss, which was searching at first, as if he were still fighting with himself, in a moment turned hungry, and Lyse recklessly followed him along that path, her heart hammering, her head shutting out the worry that her shameful secret could soon be laid bare.

She opened her mouth to his insistent, probing tongue, she met him feverishly, tasting him, twining with him. Her heart was ready to burst with joy because he wanted her, there was no doubt of that—this great, dashing Mantuan who had barely cared to speak to her as they signed a marriage contract, who had suddenly turned her away at Puivert—he desired her now, fervently, and she desired to yield to him.

With a moan, but without releasing her lips, he pressed her back down on the bed, so that she was partially beneath him.

Panic struck her. No, she had only been playing with him, she should not give herself to him unwed. And when he discovers she was no longer *intacta...!* She dragged her mouth from his, gasping, and wriggled to free herself, the enticing movement only making things worse. Or better...

He strung fervent kisses along her throat, and as if they didn't belong to her, her arms clasped tighter around his neck, and the sheet slowly slipped away from her grasp.

It was different, making love with him, it was heart-stoppingly different from what she thought she knew—the kisses, burning her lips like hot embers, yet sweet and heady as strong wine, his lips upon her mouth, her throat, her breasts, her belly, and her shallow, panting breath barely sustaining her. She was not prepared for the waves of melting sensation he extracted from her, pleasure that made her quiver, pleasure she had never before experienced, never even imagined.

When he bent his dark head to nuzzle and kiss her nipples and then suck strongly on them, she thought she would faint from the intense excitement lancing through her, or fly off the bed, and her fingers dug into his shoulders. She could do nothing but give herself completely to his ardor; her head went back, and uncontrollable, soft little moans came from her throat.

Somewhere her mind realized that the simpleton man-at-arms had taken the maidenhead from her but he had not made love to her, not like this; he'd known none of the tender seduction that Ferrante was using to drive her body wild.

She ached in her groin, it was like a tight drum down there, pulsing, pulsing. Her back arched sharply as he trailed his moist tongue down her belly and with his fingers reached down to touch her private soul. A fire swiftly ignited there and even the slipperiness dampening her thighs did nothing to put it out. She was sweating, she was panting. Her knees came up, frantic.

With heavy, half-closed eyes she saw him quickly unbutton his bulging breeches. Then his gaze locked with hers, his green and relentless gaze, and it was blazing with desire—

O mercy of God, how it was different this time from that one misstep she'd made. He knew she was ready for him, yet he came into her slowly, slowly. The stretching, filling pressure inflamed her and she thought she would explode with yearning, she needed him more, more, for something urgent she couldn't quite pin down or express.

Then he almost stopped for a moment.

Above her she heard his low oath, she knew what he had realized, but she didn't care, she moved her hips under him, in a panic to urge him further.

He propped up her hips and rode with her, fast, faster, grunting softly, and his cod inside her seemed to expand to fill her whole body, her soul, her universe. Convulsively she pinched her muscles together down there and heard his gasp.

And then something was touched and her body tensed, coiled, and a great, exquisite flare washed over her, beat, beat, beat, and she thought she was breaking, she thought she was crying out, her wits were leaving her—in some vague dimension she was aware that his body too had stiffened as she shook, then he plunged once deeply, with a great shudder and a choked, "Ah, my God !"

She seemed to be whimpering loudly then.

She felt a hand clamped on her mouth and his warm breath on her face as he murmured, "Shh, shh, Lysette, you will wake the whole household." He withdrew from her, and ridiculously, she felt resentful, like he was taking some of her away.

She had to give her poor, surprised heart a moment to stop racing, her body a moment to draw back together, before she could form the words flooding her. "F-Ferrante, what was that? What happened?"

"What do you mean, what happened? Were you not here?"

"To–to me, I mean. Suddenly. Something took me, the strangest, wild sensation just shook me–I thought I was dying!"

He stared down at her intently, straining to read her expression. Then incredulousness spread over his face. "Why, you're not lying. You don't know, do you? Have you never before felt that special taste of Paradise?"

She shook her head, dumb, lips parted.

His disbelief turned into a smile, and he pushed the hair back from her eyes. "Well, you know now, my lady," he said softly, and there was a certain pride in his voice. "The word it is called, is *jouir*. It is an ultimate gift of pleasure that happens to both the man and woman when their lovemaking is fervid. Did you like it?"

Her eyes were huge. "I think so. I was surprised. A little frightened, too."

He stared at her bemused, but suddenly, as if a curtain had dropped across his gaze, his eyes went narrow, the undereye scar seemed to whiten. It was as if invisible hands were pushing them apart again. His tone was dark, frighteningly quiet. "The face of a Madonna, yes. But it appears you are not virginal where it matters, Lyse-Magdalene de Bourbon-Tonnière."

Shame and fear struck her. Now it had come, now she must pay for her curiosity, her stupid, thoughtless, waywardness at St. Piteu. She had ready a tale to tell, but would he believe her? Was she to lose his respect, and even worse, lose him?

She sat up and faced him, her lips trembling that she would lose him, that he would despise her, but she looked at him squarely as she spoke. "Ferrante, you may ask my old nurse when next you see her. It was a riding accident in my fourteenth year, I should not have been riding a-straddle, but I was. My mount bolted and jumped a high wall, and while I did not lose my seat I came down hard in the saddle and jounced with the horse's flight until another rider grabbed the bridle. There was bleeding and pain, Nurse told me I may have broken my maidenhead. That is what happened."

"You have not had a man?"

"No." The lanky, young man-at-arms was more a boy than a man, she rationalized to herself with the desperate lie. "I swear before God, on the life of my dear uncle Charles, what I've told you is true." And in fact it was, the most of it. Germain's father had beaten him black and blue for allowing her to ride such a nervous horse. And being deflowered by accident sounded better than wanton, careless coupling with a guard.

"Bourbon also made sure to tell me this little possibility before we signed the betrothal papers. It is not an uncommon accident."

"Then why do you look at me like that, Ferrante?"

"Hah! Because 'tis a hoary tale, that one, told by a thousand ruptured maidens to duped bridegrooms!"

"Because it happens. It does!"

He said nothing.

White-faced, she went on. "No matter how I swear my innocence, nothing will make you believe me virtuous unless you want to. Ah, Ferrante, I beg of you, will you punish me for a childhood accident?" She did not add, 'or a young girl's stupid curiosity?' Lyse's very heart stood in her eyes. A single tear trickled down her cheek.

He brooded down at her a moment longer, then let out his breath. "Charles de Bourbon is too dear to you, you would not swear falsely on his life. Thus, I believe you. I do."

Neither of them moved for a moment, Lyse paralyzed that he might not mean it. So he leaned forward and took her anxious face in his hands. He kissed her gently on the lips, twice. She could not tell if it was her heart or his beating so loud in the breathless silence. "I believe you, Lysette," he murmured, and the ugliness that had threatened to come between them was gone.

Then he dragged off his shirt, muttering it was hot, and lounged back on the pillows, the shirt fallen across his thighs.

Lyse peered at him insecurely, but although he had closed his eyes, the half-smile had reappeared on his lips. Reassured, she drew breath again, and since he wasn't looking, she could study him in the dim light. Her eyes grazed the damp locks on his forehead, and the dark lashes against the high, bronzed cheeks. They traced his sensual mouth, and the strong column of throat, which nevertheless, to her eyes, seemed touchingly vulnerable as he lay there. His expansive chest, sprinkled in the center with dark hair descended to a narrow waist and muscled stomach. Her eyes admired the breadth of his shoulders and the bulge of muscles in his long arms.

She thought he was beautiful, like the Roman sculptures she had seen at the Château de Moulins.

Timidly, she placed a hand on the warm skin over his ribs, then impulsively, because she had to, she pressed her lips hotly to his taut stomach where she felt the pulse beating. She heard a rustle below where the shirt was, something moved slightly. Now she smiled. She knew what that was, at least; 'reawakening the beast' as her guardsman had called it.

She was glad it had been only once her curiosity and her body had driven her into allowing that fellow to take her, in a quick rutting in which she lay mostly passive. It was so different with Gonzaga, her reluctant betrothed. She wanted with all her heart to touch him, to feel him, to kiss his face, his hands, every part–every part, she thought with astonishment–and her hand came up as if unattached to her and grasped the rock-hard shaft risen under the shirt.

He made a pleasured grunt.

She showered small kisses on his chest, his ribs, then felt his hands pulling her up on top of him.

The glittering green eyes were half open. "Let me take off my breeches," he whispered, and somehow he managed to do so without displacing her.

Naked together in her soft bed, and locked in embrace, they molded themselves to each other, and if she had died right at that moment Lyse could have asked no greater joy than the feel of him wrapped about her.

He whispered in her ear, "Do you want that sensation again, to *jouir*, eh? Is that what you crave?" he teased. His hand cupped her buttock, she could feel his cod long and hard against her stomach, and she nodded against his mouth.

"Hah. So do I, lady."

This time it took no longer than before, because his knowing fingers teased and drew and rubbed her, knowing just where to connect her with his purpose, her purpose, knowing just when to withdraw so that he could thrust himself inside her, just in time to join with the huge spasm that ripped her apart with joy. When it was finished she laughed softly. He drew back to look at her, and seeing the joyful wonder on her face, he chuckled too.

"But you're supposed to cry a little, Lyse-Magdalene, it is a very emotional experience."

"Sometimes when I'm very happy, I just laugh," she murmured. "Is that wrong to do now?"

He shook his head and kissed her forehead. "Nothing is wrong that happens in the bedchamber, my mistress. You only delight me," he husked.

"I always rise at first light," Ferrante said. "I'll leave you then. So sleep now," he ordered. He tucked up her against him, one arm wrapped around her to hold her breast. "Your hair smells of flowers," he murmured, drawing in a long, relaxed breath.

Lyse's limbs were heavy and languid. She closed her eyes. Everything was all different, the world had turned inside out and become very small, in fact it was all here, warm against her spine, all that she wanted. She recalled her first glimpse of him in the church at Moulins, Blackbeard she had named him, a gold-earringed swaggerer flirting with another girl. And remembered how he had bullied Germain and been rude to her.

Now, against her drowsing eyes she saw only Ferrante, a tender lover who had kissed her and said, 'I believe you'.

She remembered his bleeding hands from the rope on the cliff, his amused guffaw for having given her a lewd Boccaccio tale to read, the way he'd held her hand so tightly before the blue smoke overcame her the evening before. She remembered his piercing, cyncial glance, but also the several times those strong arms had held her in sympathy. She remembered everything that had happened between them.

But when, Lord, had she fallen so deeply in love with him?

Chapter 22

La Dame quickly squashed Ferrante's jubilant idea that the tarred canvas sewn around the ancient Menorah meant the Treasury had been hidden in water, possibly bricked in below the water line of a large well, or even drowned deep in the water of an unused one. Of course!

No, she dissuaded him, with a smug curl to her lip, such an idea was not new. All the wells in lower Languedoc wide and deep enough to accept large coffers and objects had been sounded, tapped, inspected through the centuries, with nothing more discovered than broken jugs, insignificant jewelry, animal skulls and an embarrassment of human skeletons. Locally the river edges had been scoured, as well as the banks of Puivert's lake.

"Hooks have even been dragged from boats in Puivert's lake, which is very deep in the center," Lora added. "Nothing submerged was ever found."

Crestfallen, Ferrante bounced his crossed leg, glaring at her without meaning to. "But, it is somewhere," he responded in frustration. "Lyse-Magdalene's memory tells us that now, without doubt. The Treasury was concealed in this area. Somewhere."

"Yes, she had quite a significant rush of recall under the influence of the *pastel*. So then, shall we try it again?" The smell of anise still clung amidst the clutter of la Dame's chamber, in spite of open windows; it was making Lyse faintly queasy as she sat listening to them.

But Ferrante launched himself from his chair. "Absolutely not. I will not allow it."

"Still, Signore, you read me the letter the courier brought this morning. Monsieur de Bourbon is in distressed circumstances. He urges our swiftest efforts."

"Madame, winter is almost upon us, no campaign of his can be mounted now. We have a while to rely on Lyse-Magdalene's natural memory, without exposing her again to that dangerous nostrum." His brows knit together like a threatening storm. "In view of the turbulent effect of the plant's smoke, I absolutely forbid you to use it."

La Dame pursed her full lips and shrugged. "But what does Mademoiselle wish?" The unusual eyes slid to impale her Bourbon guest, who had said little.

Lyse's stare went from one to the other, from the satirical challenge which glinted in la Dame's silvery gaze, to the stubborn whitening at the corners of Ferrante's mouth, for he was looking at her now with the possessive gaze of a lover.

The latest letter from Charles had upset her, made her feel useless and ungrateful, unworthy of the great Bourbon name. She had to do more. But her eyes locked with the apprehension in Gonzaga's green stare and her heart melted like butter. "I will obey Don Ferrante's wishes," she murmured.

"I see," la Dame said with a flare of nostrils, and it was obvious she did indeed, for her guests, with their constant glances and quiet smiles, could not hide that something between them had changed.

"Then we will continue as before. But I have one small bit of heartening news. With the help of Matz, I may have found a certain medicate which will revive Madame de Dunois's brain. An hour after we administered this potion to our mute and senseless patient the attendant who was sitting with her swears the lady moaned softly and moved her head and arm. I will strengthen the formula and try again this afternoon."

Lyse had jumped from her seat. "Oh, Madame—"

"One groan does not make a cure," la Dame cautioned.

As if the fates called, a rapid knock on the door came just then and, in response to Lora de Voisin's permission, Germain almost fell in, his spiky hair standing up like a sheaf of wheat. "Madame, come quick! She is uttering strange noises and her eyelids flutter, as if she tries to open them. And she moves her head!"

They all hurried back to the sick chamber with him, entering into the heavy atmosphere where the odor of garlic still couldn't overpower the acrid, gagging smell of other potions invading the air. But now the governess lay as still and waxen as ever upon her linen pillow. They stood over her bed a while.

"But she did move, and she was trying to speak," Germain insisted.

His mentor, la Dame, laid a comforting hand on his arm.

Rather familiarly, Lyse thought. Germain's attention was lately totally divided between la Dame and Madame de Dunois. Lyse felt he hardly remembered she was there, which would have hurt her if Ferrante wasn't filling her mind so totally.

"Be not upset, Matz, we will reach her again," Lora's lush voice assured her assistant. "But come now to my chamber. We must quickly work on augmenting the Xantheria in the formula. Or it was possibly the pinch of hog-weed that succeeded."

Leaving the unconscious woman to her nurse, the four went from the chamber, Lyse and her lover to enjoy the late fall day on the gallery, where the gnarled butler served them a second breakfast of crusty bread and jellies and cheese to hold them until dinner. Ferri came out on the far end and audaciously perched on the balustrade, strumming his way gently through a complicated piece and paying them no attention.

Midway through the little meal, punctuated by their teasing and laughter, Ferrante picked up Lyse's hand and nibbled on her fingers and then rubbed them against his soft fringe of beard. Neither of them ever stopped peering into the other's eyes, she with adoration, he with amused enchantment.

Lyse had never felt so utterly happy—nor so utterly helpless—never before having been enmeshed in love's binding toils.

At the beginning of December two separate messages from Italy arrived for Ferrante di Gonzaga from his brothers, the *Duca* di Mantova and the *Cardinale*, both relayed through Bourbon. The prelate stormed that Ferrante's wife was indeed dying, which for the family's honor absolutely demanded his immediate attendance at her bedside, and the *Duca* demanded his brother's presence and personal attention to the numerous legal adjustments Aliesa's death would necessitate.

Ferrante offered Lyse the letters, letting them slip through his fingers as if glad to be rid of them. Her heart gave a jolt as she read both strong pleas, for of course he must go. "When?" she asked, with assumed bravery.

But he was pacing the floor of her little chamber, where a cheerful fire was taking the evening chill off. He stopped to pound an impatient fist against the stone mantle, along which Lyse had strung dried yellow and orange flowers amidst deep green spruce boughs.

"*Merde!* I'm not going. She has been dying for years. It is another trick to get me back, and I cannot bear that mean woman."

"But she is your wife, your responsibility. And the appeal comes from both your brothers this time. Surely it must be the truth. You know that."

"Ah—*sang de diable,* you are probably right," he conceded unwillingly. "So, then, she is dying. But I cannot leave you here alone. I will ask my brother Federico to handle my affairs for me and beg my mother use her vast diplomacy to deal with Aliesa's family, the Sforza's. Those two will understand my deep obligation to my cousin, Bourbon."

"Dear one, your obligation to the woman you took before God as your spouse is greater. You cannot let her die alone. I know you now, you are not made of the same steel as your breastplate, your soul would suffer such a sin the rest of your life. You must find the first ship from the coast and hasten to her."

"And what of my oath to guard you and help you in your task? How lightly do I observe my cousin Charles' dire need?"

She moved close and leaned her head against his arm, hating every word she was saying. "I will be fine. I have Germain and the Bourbon guards and even Ferri. And no one comes here. If they did, the watchtowers would signal and I could hide forever in the tunnels. And you will be soon back–"

"Soon? The journey alone might take four weeks each way through Genoa, depending on sea transport, not to say how long the rest of my obligations would endure once I reached Mantua. Probably the entire winter and well into the spring."

She blanched slightly. "That long?"

"It is possible." He grumbled, "Besides, the Bourbon guards have gotten fat and lazy here, your fellow Matz is besotted with Lora, and that skinny vagabond musician couldn't swat a fly."

"Why, 'tisn't true about the guards, Tournel has not let one day go by without seeing his men in trim and alert," she said indignantly. "We've all heard him barking at them."

"No matter. I cannot go. My mind is made up."

Lyse was torn in half. All her soul wanted him no more than a finger's length from her in any direction, this broad-shouldered warrior whose knowing touch and heated kisses aroused her to ecstasy, and in whose strong shadow she felt safe. And yet her soul backed away suspiciously from a man so unfeeling he could leave a woman who once shared his bed to die alone in crippled anguish, no matter how despicable her character.

This was what she once thought he was, long ago at Moulins, a callous swaggerer, until she began to see him clearer, day by day, and learned the decency beneath that exterior. She could not allow him to be less than that now and become a man she could not love.

But she had some knowledge of Ferrante di Gonzaga. Pleading and whining at him would do no good, nor tears, which would more strongly convince him that she was weak and needed him. Only frontal attack would work.

She threw her arms around him, imprisoning his arms and waist in a wild grip, the side of her face pressed into the heavy silk brocade of his doublet. "Don Ferrante di Gonzaga, my dearest love, you must go home, you must," she cried fiercely. "For love of me, if not for that suffering soul. I cannot bear your heart to be so cold, you will always regret it bitterly. Go, go, I beg you.

All will be well here, certainly through the cold winter when nothing moves, nothing, neither armies, nor spies and evil-doers." She squeezed him with ferocious will.

"You are wrong, the King is not paralyzed by frost, nor are the Lorraines. They may move." She heard his voice rumble in his chest.

"They are not even aware of where I am!" she insisted, and looked up to plead into his stormy face, "Nor do they even care, so I believe, in spite of what you say. Oh consider, Ferrante, the lasting sin of turning away from your God-given duty as a husband, as against the small risk of a few uncertain months here."

His expression hardened into a scowl, he did not like her telling him his duty. He easily freed his arms and let them hang loose by his sides. "You seem anxious to get rid of me, lady. To clear the field for someone else, perhaps?"

"What?" She was taken aback. "Who?"

"That wolf eyed minstrel whose pluckings and warblings you so dote on and who constantly fawns at your feet!"

Her eyes opened wide. "Ferri? You think I want him?"

She balled her fist and hit him as hard as she could on the shoulder. "Oh, you villain," she cried, "what a terrible thing to say! Have you no pity for the dread loneliness of my life without you? No one can take your place in my arms, no one, not Ferri, not all the gentlemen of the Razès, not even the King of France himself...!" she finished, two tones higher, and smacked him again on the shoulder. "How dare you!"

He caught her fist, squinting, and for a moment she thought he was on the verge of adding someone else to her imaginary list of rejected suitors, but instead he flushed and shook his head. He put her hand to his heart. "Forgive me, please. That was ugly of me, nor did I even mean it. But it destroys me to have to break my word to my good cousin Charles and to leave you. "

"You must, can you not see that? And can you not see, over my words, my own despair that you must sail away?"

He led her by the hand a few steps to the window where a luminous moon was flooding in full, and with a bitter smile studied her in the lambent light. "Can I not see? I see a beautiful, copper-haired lady, a brave one, who could be in more danger than she knows, but who is, in this instance, damnably right. And who shows, on her incredible face, a very fine intelligence..."

Her titter was forced. "Oh, so I no longer have a virginal face?" she bedeviled him, switching moods.

"...and who is in danger from me, right now," he warned softly, his finger tracing her warm lips.

Her breasts felt as if they were swelling against her bodice. "But the *sieur* awaits you downstairs to play at cards."

Nevertheless, she sealed her fate by lifting her mouth, half-open, to his.

"Let him wait," he growled a minute later, and scooped her up. He carried her to the bed, where he deftly removed her bodice and busied himself licking a stiffened nipple while his hands rid her body of skirt, underskirts and chemise. By that time she was quivering.

He opened his breeches before they might burst, and she slid down to do something with her mouth and tongue she never dreamed in this world she would like, but oh, she did, and his hard cod grew even harder while he shucked doublet and breeches. He pulled her up into his arms. The touch of skin upon skin was shocking, his kiss was probing, his fingers below played where her entire being was gathered, and in a few moaning moments he pushed into her and together they moved deliriously toward the joy he had shown her lived in her body and his.

The release was so great this time he cried out, and so did she. The thick walls probably kept them from being heard, but they heard each other, and gasping, clutching each other as if swirling in a maelstrom, they felt wonder at the perfection and the marvel of their union.

He buried his face in her neck and she could hear him breathing in the scent of her skin. Limp against him, she wondered, now would he say it? Now would he say finally say, 'Lyse-Magdalene, I adore you. I love you and no other. For all eternity.' Now would he tell her that of all his other women only she held his heart in sweet bonds? She ached to say the truth to him, that she loved him desperately, but she couldn't. Not first. She was afraid to. He was a lusty man, cooped up with her here, and perhaps he was only taking what had been consigned to him eventually, anyhow? Overwhelmed, she waited for her lover's words to caress her heart.

Instead his hand moved over her hip and then her rump. She felt his lips hot on her throat.

"I cannot have enough of you," he groaned softly, his hand cupping and squeezing her breast. "See, look what you do to me—like a callow boy, too eager to know when to stop."

Something long and hard rubbed against her thigh. It pleased her enough to shut off, for the moment, her constant yearning for his declaration of eternal love. She happily closed her hand firmly around him.

Don Ferrante di Gonzaga, with his two servants and horses, left Rennes-le-Château for the busy Mediterranean port of Narbonne, where there was a good chance of finding a ship bound for a northern Italian harbor. Lyse rode down to Couiza with him, but so did the Voisins, and so they said their public goodbyes circumspectly, Lyse even kept the tears from welling in her eyes, or the terror from her heart that he might never return. Dear God, how she would miss him the next months.

She watched his shoulders square as he cantered away from them with his servants, free of 'sitting on his damned arse,' as he once put it, and wondered painfully if even now he was forgetting her and determining not to return.

Don Ferrante di Gonzaga, her protecting escort and secret betrothed who had been enjoying her body so well, had never once said the word 'love' to her.

Chapter 23

The scraping noise woke Lyse up; the sound was not loud but she sat up groggily in her bed to see if it would come again. It did, from outside, a muffled clank and scrape, metal on metal. She grabbed the extra blanket on her bed to wrap around her, pushed the curtain aside and slid to the floor, her curiosity flaring, although without much cause. It could have been the flap of an owl, or the horses being restive in the stable, or even a hard sneeze from the guard on the tower roof.

She always left the window shutter slightly ajar, so she could tell whether or not it was morning, but at this hour no light came through the slit to compete with her dim little oil lamp. She opened the shutter quietly, peering out into a clear night with a wintry half moon riding the wind and vaguely illuminating the garden and the burial ground below, all blanketed with the usual, biding silence she always felt like a dampening layer just above the tree-tops. But nothing seemed amiss in the dark vista before her, nothing stirred.

And then, from the corner of her eye she caught a moving shadow amongst shadows, lighter than the rest, and she fastened her attention on the low portal of the Blanchefort tomb. The soft, scrapping noise came again; the lighter shadow seemed to stoop and bob, but finally turned so that the shielded light of a small lantern appeared, to barely reveal the outline of a cloaked and hooded figure, with what seemed a sack over its shoulder. Lyse swallowed, releasing her clenched throat, for it was definitely not one of the fearful wyverns or loping basilisks that sometimes lurked in cemeteries after midnight.

The lantern flickered on the greenish metal of the door to the sepulcher and then the door must have opened, for a greater blackness swallowed up the figure and in a moment Lyse heard the same low scrape again. Then she heard only the blood pounding in her ears, and only the wind stirred the cold night and rattled the dried flower stalks between the ancient graves.

She blinked hard and stared about her room to make sure she was not in a memory, but there was her own bed and chests and clothes hanging on pegs. So in truth she had most certainly seen a person entering one of the old tombs below in the dead of night!

Her feet were freezing, she padded quickly to pull on her woolen stockings, then blew out the little night lamp and hastened back to the window, for the stealthy prowler might emerge before first light. She couldn't imagine why one of the guards didn't hear the noise that had awakened her and come down to investigate, unless they were all snoring up there. She should, of course, alert Tournel, and let him drag the ghoul out. But in spite of her brave heartbeat and resolve, her feet were stuck to the floor and her eyes glued to a slit she left between the wooden shutter and the stone window edge.

Suddenly, like a celebratory burst of the fireworks she had seen at Moulins, her head had the answer! There it was! There was the Treasury, of course, resting along with the dust and bones of the Templar's greatest Grand-Master, de Blanchefort! How stupid they had been.

She thought fast. The creeping graverobber, whoever he was, had come prepared with a small sack, but he could not steal much that way, and since she had no wish to alert the guards to what the sepulcher contained, it was best to let the thief go for now. He could be apprehended the next time he came to mine the lode he had somehow discovered. The thing was to see his face when he slunk past below her window.

Jubilation was flowing over her like a purling stream spreading over dried-mud banks, for at last she had earned her uncle's faith and would recover the vast monies which would enable him to invade France and retrieve the Bourbon heritage. She could even have back St. Piteu again, and much more indeed, she would see to that. Now she could come to her marriage with Ferrante as a woman of substance and wealth.

Happy, she felt neither the chill or the fatigue of standing as she waited patiently at the window, peering down from just behind the shutter. She reveled in the release at last from the weight of shame and depression that had almost broken her as full winter claimed the Razès and the 'seeing-back' had given her nothing more than she already knew.

The months since Don Ferrante di Gonzaga had ridden away had been endless and cruel ones.

Elinor de Dunois had died just after Christmas, having regained consciousness of a sudden to croak a loud and rusty, "The smoke, the smoke!" her sunken eyes gone wide and wild, darting about and then rolling up in her head. There was a terrible gurgle from her throat and a gasp, and the poor lady just stopped breathing.

Two women came from Couiza to wash and wrap the bony body first in a cotton sheet and then in one of de Dunois' own heirlooms, her finely woven bedcurtains. The village priest sprinkled holy water and intoned his prayers, the saddened *marquise* de Joyeuse arrived two days later with a daughter and a few ladies to pay homage to her dead sister-in-law, and for the bereft Lyse's sake the governess was buried near the old chapel, along with the provision that when Mademoiselle de Bourbon left Rennes-le-Château, the body would be reinterred in the family ground at Puivert.

A deadly winter ague struck at the valley and la Dame and Germain exhausted themselves trying to cure the victims of their high fevers and enflamed lungs, and neither had time to be with Lyse. She wanted to help them in order to dull her grief, she could pound dried leaves for medicine, or even nurse the sick, but la Dame forbade it. Her silver eyes weary, la Dame had responded to Lyse's petition, "I must follow what commands I have been given, Mademoiselle, and that was to allow you few distractions from your main objective. It is our coldest, dampest winter in thirty years. I believe this dreadful malady of the lungs comes from the bad air down in the valley, smoke and dust and putrid, evil vapors held down by the constant mists. I will not expose you to that."

"But nothing enters my mind other than flashes I've already experienced, no new recall, no progress upon what we already know. It is so lonely here." Lyse had pleaded. "The *sieur* sits close to the fire because of the aches in his bones and falls asleep on the chessboard. I have read every book in the château. I must do something."

"Why do you whine as if this was my fault? Germain will ride to Esperanza and purchase what new volumes are available, if you give him money. And what of our musician, engaged for your sake? He has gotten you quite proficient on the lute. Practice the instrument—it is a favorable ability for an unmarried female to offer."

Lyse bridled at the derisive tone of the 'unmarried'. She wished she could fling in the woman's glib, large face the fact that she was to someday marry the man la Dame had failed to seduce, and that in fact Don Ferrante was already her lover. "If it weren't for Ferri I would go mad in this moldering place," she ground out.

"Yes, he is amusing, I suppose."

La Dame had murmured this with such condescension that Lyse had twitched her skirts around her and walked away from the coldly-smiling woman, who stood with back straight, unyielding.

In Lyse's pocket where she could finger it often crackled a second letter from Ferrante, three weeks old, a short one full of news. His wife, extremely weak and so paralyzed she could barely breathe, still clung to life in spite of all predictions. He had gotten his own affairs in better order, and had also pulled together some Swiss and Italian mercenary companies and committed them to Bourbon. He suffered to have left her alone in that poor shell of a house. He thought of her constantly.

That was all. No voluminous writer or believer in flowery phrases was Don Ferrante, no mention at all of love or a longing heart, and neither had there been in the first letter she'd received in January. That had come via a traveler to the area, and offered her no way to respond. But the one in her pocket had been brought by a hired courier a week past who was returning, and she was able to respond quickly, to tell him she was well, nothing more had come to her memory, the weather was cold and damp, she missed him very, very much.

She could have said more, she could have said that she had fallen so obsessively in love with him that day and night she yearned for his presence, that she remembered the way laughter sparkling in his eyes erased his mild scowl, and longed to see the gentled green glow of them when he gazed at her. She missed his striding footsteps on the flagstones, the comfort of his voice, the feel of his breath suggestive on her ear, the tickle of his cropped beard and the passion of their lovemaking.

She could have said how astonishing it was that his faults, his quick temper, his abandonment of his wife, his ill-concealed dislike of her 'seeing-back' affliction, no longer were significant to her, dismissable under the glory of everything about him that she admired and adored.

She could have written all this, but depression over her failure to remember the treasure stilled her. She did not know yet what to make of a man who had signed a marriage contract for her and taken her heart and body, but never professed love. Even her ignorant man-at-arms had stammered out the word as they lay in the grass!

Love was not necessary to betrothal, everyone knew that, or to marriage or childbearing. But when it happened, so achingly fierce and tender at once, was it not tragedy for it to be one-sided? Or for her to be unable to erase the suspicion that his loyalty arose only from his duty to her uncle?

She longed for the man, her dark-bearded, commanding *condottiere*, she missed him dreadfully, and the days of leaden skies and bone-chilling cold only eroded her spirits further, already limp with boredom. Even the *marquise's* several invitations to Puivert had to be refused, in respect for de Dunois' death, and also because Gonzaga had extracted from her a solemn promise that she would travel no further from Rennes-le-Château than Couiza, at the foot of the mount.

His letters from Mantua spoke of little to warm up her heart, except that he thought of her often. But what thoughts? That she was a useless 'peculiar'? That she was failing in her mission?

The messengers from her uncle in Barcelona came by ship to Perpignan and thence overland. Charles de Bourbon had been greatly buoyed by news of Lyse's strong and important memories under the blue powder, for they confirmed his hopes. But while he stopped short of demanding the use of the dangerous smoke again, he kept prodding and exhorting Lyse to greater effort, whereas she was at her wits end to know what more to do, except to use the *pastel*. Even Madame de Dunois had croaked out as her dying advice, "The smoke, the smoke!"

Nothing further came to Lyse no matter how she tried to invoke new memories, nothing happened, except her mind felt wrung out. The recall, when it happened, was always unexpected; a momentary sight, a random action, an evocative odor jumped her into Mélline's life. Often she wasn't sure what was the cause, but the memories brought up were the same, the red Templar cross on Bernard's cloak, the sightless churchman at whose feet Mélline wept, the shining Menorah being enclosed in its shroud, her ancestress' tortured grief.

At least she had learned how to emerge instantly from any recall that repelled her, to chop off the horror of Mélline's collapse and curses to God, to shred away into nothing the vivid visions on her closed lids of Mélline and Bernard lying in each other's arms, two passionate ghosts–although as winter wore on and then waned, the intimate intrusions, at least, had stopped. Only her own erotic memories of loving Ferrante remained to warm her loneliness.

Each impatient missive that came from Charles de Bourbon deepened her sense of failure. And then one day Germain picked up the news in Couiza that all of the land and properties of the former Constable of France were now under royal control and their ex-owner, having escaped Francois' justice, was ordered captured or killed on sight by any citizen sighting him, along with a dozen co-conspirators named enemies of France.

Only two names on that list of conspirators held meaning for Lyse: The *marquise* de Joyeuse, brother of her ill-fated governess and husband to the warm-hearted Francine, and Don Ferrante di Gonzaga, the man who had become her very reason for breathing.

Under such an edict Ferrante could not, must not return to France!

Lyse's sense of urgency to complete her mission grew agonizing, yet all she could think to do was to return to Le Bézu, in the hope she could trigger remembrances which included the location of the Treasury—or else persuade la Dame to break her word and use the blue *pastel* plant again. Despair over the arrest warrant for Ferrante and a growing feeling that doom was approaching overrode her fear for danger and she inveigled Germain into smuggling her a spoonful of the blue powder on the frivolous pretext of using it in melted yellow sealing wax to make a pretty green.

But no matter what method she tried to ignite it in an earthenware dish, she could not get it to burn.

The soft, scraping noise came again and roused Lyse from her reverie like a musketshot in her ears, and with a gasp she crawled up from the floor where she had wearily subsided and glued her gaze again onto the tomb. In a moment she triumphantly made out the moving, dark figure weakly illumined by the moon against the static black of the background, the shielded lantern throwing a tiny gleam of yellow on the earth.

The man moved away from the tomb and towards the château, and suddenly Lyse thought he looked up directly at her window, but as she was in darkness herself, peering only through a small gap between the shutter and the window edge, she was sure she could not be seen.

The figure, tall, hooded, approached closer, his feet knowing where to step not to crackle dry weeds or shrubs. Just before reaching the low gate that separated the old château from its garden-cemetery, the shrouded one lifted the lantern a bit to close its shield entirely. The head that bent forward from the hood sparkled argent a moment, the hand that slid the little panel was large and wore a familiar, huge silver ring on the index finger.

It was la Dame, Lora Voisins.

And even in the somber shadows of night Lyse imagined she could see eyes like silver-bright whorls deep within the hood.

As the figure passed from her line of sight and entered the château, Lyse fell back, hand to her mouth at the calumny of the woman, the lying deceit that had put them all through months of torment trying to find a treasure already found. She knew, she had felt all along, that there was something hostile about the eccentric Lora Voisins.

But what could she do now, accuse the greedy woman to her face and be laughed at? She couldn't even order Tournel to arrest la Dame, not in the woman's own home, not without revealing the why of it.

She had to see for herself what was there in the tomb.

Calm overtook her now that her exhausting quest was over, and she thought carefully. Her best move was to send a victorious letter to her uncle and allow him to arrange the removal of the Treasury. And until he could find a safe way to do so, it was wiser to keep the Voisins—for surely the *sieur* was in on the deception—unaware of her knowledge.

But—would she, could she enter that shuddery repository of the dead all by herself in order to verify her discovery, by herself brave the bones, spiders, worms and disturbed spirits she would certainly meet? Sweat broke out on her forehead, in spite of the cold seeping through the shutters.

She ran back to her bed, but sat up staring into the darkness, trying to make a plan. It occurred to her to wonder why she had been awakened by the scraping noise and the Bourbon guards had not, and as she concentrated on the question two parts of the problem connected.

La Dame had a curious ritual every Sunday night without fail: as a salute to the close of the Sabbath, everyone in her household, to the servants and the guards, had to partake of a drink of wine and herbs poured from a flask blessed by the priest. It was a custom, she said, handed down to her by her grandparents. The small libation was taken by everyone at the close of the evening meal, with the old butler dispatched to bring glasses on a tray to the four men-at-arms on duty, three patrolling the walls, one at the gate.

Offering his glass to the continuing glory of the Lord, everyone got a few swallows of a delicious, sweet liqueur tasting of raspberries which rolled easily down the throat, a pleasant way to see in a new week. Lyse loved the flavor of the tipple, (Ferrante had not, it was too sweet, but pleased his watchful hostess by tossing it down anyway) but depression had made her increasingly tired and so this particular night she had begged to be excused early, before the *sieur* began his Sunday night reading from the Old Testament books.

In carrying her little glass of liqueur across the Hall to drink it before bed, one of the slobbery dogs dashed after a scrap the servant dropped from a plate and jostled her so that almost all the liquid spilled onto the floor. Swearing at the great beast, she turned to go refill her glass, but the table seemed so far away for her weary limbs that she decided to forgo the treat for the first time since she had arrived at Rennes-le-Château. God would forgive her.

And later she had woken up to the slight sound of the door to the Blanchefort sepulcher scraping.

One could presume it was not the first time la Dame had gone with her small sack to plunder the Treasury and opened that ill-fitting old door. Could it be possible the tasty liqueur was drugged, to insure everyone slept heavily on Sunday nights? And this once, having spilled hers, the very person whose chamber squarely faced the cemetery, did not? Lyse gave an excited snort.

What worked for the Voisins could work for her as well: by planning carefully, and if she could manage to wait, to bite her tongue and clench her fists and damp her excitement until the Sunday next, she could get into the tomb without waking the guards or anyone else.

Nervous beyond measure that week, she kept fumbling the fingering in a piece of music she knew well, to Ferri's curious interest, and twice had to cut out poor stitches from the tapestry pillow she was making. She ate little and constantly wove her fingers together. She saw Germain glancing at her when they took their meals, and by Friday, joining her for an early morning ride along the windswept road to Esperaza, he voiced his worry that she was not well.

With her gentlest smile to this loyal friend who she could not include in her greatest adventure, she insisted her health was fine, she was merely unhappy with the chilly weather and disgusted with isolation just as bad as it had been at St. Piteu.

"It is not fair that I am made to suffer as much of an exile as my uncle," she pouted, picking what might explain her jitters, even if it sounded childish. "'Twas not me, after all, that the King's mother sued. Why must His Majesty take his grudge out on all the Bourbons?"

Germain shook his head at such a snit. "Because that is the way of monarchs and a lady of your high birth should know how to endure. Patience, *ma princesse*, his fury will cool."

"And I will grow old and die here," she flounced, and not all of her ire was simulated.

She studied him a moment and was surprised to see how much older his stolid, honest face seemed, serious, crease-browed; in less than a year he had matured, taken on a little weight, even his pimples had disappeared. Where had her friend's youth gone while she was so occupied with Ferrante and her secret duty? And was her face so changed too, her mien more decorous now that her heart knew a mature love? Wistfully she said, "I miss you, Germain, *mon ami*, we spend so little time together, laughing and talking like we used to, riding hard across the fields, telling stories."

He gave a little laugh. "We didn't know when we were well off at St. Piteu. But you must forgive my neglect, please, this terrible phthisis is spreading up and down the valley, children and old folk are dying, and Madame Voisins and the *medicins* are overwhelmed. I make up plasters and draughts and administer them, I mix solutions and drops and salves for a Christian must help the sick where he can, must give his attention, and it takes long hours. But I wanted this little time with you to make sure you were not suffering illness. I would not let you be sick, *ma princesse*."

Touched by his anxious solicitude, Lyse assured him again she was well. She straightened in the saddle and told him she would try to be more patient, but in her triumphant mind she was thinking, "Ah, my dear friend, just wait until you see how well we shall live very soon, my uncle will make all of France ours, the finest château in Europe, the finest attire, you will be astonished..."

She had thought to say she was sick on Sunday night and not descend at all to take dinner in the Hall, but Germain was too uneasy about her and might insist on giving her some nostrum or other that would make her sleepy. And so, along with the Voisins, Tournel, Germain and Ferri, she picked at the juicy roast joint and capons provided by the duke's money via Gonzaga, the turnip pudding and onion pie, until the Lord's libation was served and dutifully ingested by everyone.

Lyse saw the silvery eyes staring hard at her and took a deep breath. "I will go to my chamber now, such a delicious feast makes me weary. A good sleep will help."

"But drink your Sunday offering," came Lora's deep voice pouring out like dark honey.

"I will take it with me, as last time," Lyse smiled, "and down it after I say my prayers, if you please."

"The custom is to drink it when served to you."

"Ah, I could not get another morsel or drop down right now, so good was the meal." Lyse smiled, pushing her chair back and the men stood, respectfully.

"Mademoiselle, I insist." The honey had drained from the voice. "You have already breached this old ritual once. Do not bring bad fortune upon us."

Le *sieur* put a restraining hand on his wife's arm and piped, "Let the lady go, my dear, she will offer to the lord when she blows out her candle, will you not, Mademoiselle? It is all the same to God."

But la Dame was frowning with great displeasure; the strange eyes seemed depthless, ire sparked in their silver infinity.

Lyse saw she must do as ordered, or else the woman might decide not to steal into the tomb that night. But she had expected as much. With her most wide-eyed, innocent expression she demurred, "Ah, Madame, I did not mean to upset you," She raised the small goblet on high, then drained it in three swallows. La Dame smiled at her, the grey eyes turned opaque again.

Nodding goodnight to all, Lyse walked quickly from the Hall, although Germain insisted on accompanying her to her chamber door. On reaching it, to calm him she whispered it was merely her monthly female complaints that wearied her and swiftly slipped inside.

Feverishly she searched in Madame de Dunois' small coffer and found the vial of white liquid the governess had always used to induce vomiting when a bad fish assaulted the belly. Standing over her basin, she choked the chalky stuff down, panted anxiously a few minutes, then her stomach clenched, roiled, heaved up into her throat and exploded into the basin, smelling of the sweet liqueur. She must have taken too much of the emetic for she retched and retched and her whole dinner came up through her mouth and nose.

Finally sweating and miserable, she swabbed off her face and forehead with a wet cloth, covered the noisome basin with a towel, and gulped down some water. But she was sure she had flushed the sleep-inducing draught from her system.

The fresh air at the window revived her. In for a long wait, she wrestled her twist-legged table up to the window, placed her low hassock covered with Turkey carpet atop it, and scrambled up so she could sit instead of stand, eye just on line with the little opening between shutter and stone, the room dark.

She must have dozed; with a start, she found herself with her arms and head cradled on the cold, sloping sill. Something had awakened her. She stared down into the burial ground and in a moment, thanking her good luck, her eye found the moving shadow in its tiny gleam of light, somewhat bent under the weight of a back-slung sack. Aha. Her lips curved in a silent smile. The shadow flitted across graves and empty flower beds, halted at the recessed entrance to the Blanchefort sepulcher and stooped, concentrating on something.

The moon was only a quarter now, and low in the sky. Lyse strained to see, prayed to see, la Dame must surely be unlocking the door, but how? There was a large iron ring on the door, and a keyhole, but she and Germain had noticed months before that a key had been broken off in the lock and rusted tight, completely stopping up the hole. Maybe the door was not locked at all, for who in this forsaken spot would bother to breach the portal of an old crypt?

Suddenly the lighter lump of the shadow passed before the greenish copper plates of the door and disappeared, like water swirling down a drain. La Dame had entered the tomb. Silently. No small scrape or clank now!

Lyse waited, alert, for without the tell-tale scrape she could only use her eyes. The question of what la Dame could be carrying into the tomb in the sack flitted across her mind but she dismissed it; it was what the woman was taking out that counted.

She passed the time, perhaps an hour, constructing letters in her mind, announcing to her uncle, to Ferrante, her discovery of the treasure, although not saying where it was. And figuring how to put her demand for a tiny part of the gold so that it seemed more a request, for as she had heard in the gabble of the ladies at Moulins, a woman with money under her own control was not beholden to the men who directed her world.

The stillness of the Razès wrapped the sleeping château in its arms, the faint moonlight touched the treetops with luminescence, bats flickered across the sky. An owl hooted softly. Lyse crossed her arms and rubbed them, shrugging the mantle she wore closer about her neck.

There! The black-cloaked Madame Voisins had emerged once more from the tomb.

Lyse ducked closer to the sill and watched the tall figure make its way to the gate, but not as bent under the weight of the sack as before. The head raised. Lyse held her breath as la Dame's eyes, deep in the hood, must have raked her window and seen nothing but the closed shutter. The figure lowered its head and, shuttering the lantern, returned to the château. Fortunately for Lyse, the Voisins' quarters in the tower did not face the cemetery.

Waiting another half hour for the woman to go to sleep was not very hard, it took that time for Lyse to plump up her courage, to tell herself that if Lora de Voisin could enter that tomb time and again and emerge unharmed, so could she. With flint and striker she lit the candle in the lantern filched from the kitchens, which she would have to shield with her cloak. Finally she tiptoed from her room, putting up the hood of her cloak. In her deep pocket she had slipped the small dagger la Dame had given her before the trip to Bézu. Just in case there were...snakes?

Flitting from the château was easy; the guard outside the main portal was hunched on the step, nodding heavily. He did not hear her light tread.

Chapter 24

The weathered old tomb was at the edge of the burial ground where it slanted off down the slope. Half-underground, it had a stepped entry well of low brick walls, a metal door, and a stone roof arched in a barrel vault. It wasn't very tall, unless one went down the few steps to stand level with the door, over which, in old lettering, was carved large the name 'Blanchefort'.

Lyse pushed at the door with all her strength and turned the iron ring right and left with no success; holding up her lantern she squinted into the large keyhole and saw it was still blocked and rusted. Then how did la Dame get in? She had stooped to do something, but what? The brick stepwell was featureless, the strip of earth before it hardpacked and pristine. She pressed a few of the round boltheads studding the metal door, but that was silly, too obvious.

And suddenly the mechanism that opened the door to the escape stair in the tower popped into her head. Here, the low brick wall to the left was where la Dame had seemed to stoop.

Placing her lantern close, she counted up three courses of brick, and then to the third brick from the tomb wall. And pushed. And gasped in panic as the rough brick yielded and moved in.

With neither scrape nor clank now, the heavy portal opened when she shoved at it, and stygian darkness yawned before her with a cold, dank breath. Staring into it with cowering heart, Lyse wanted to run back to her bed and hide under the covers. She wanted Ferrante's strong arm beside her, she wanted Germain with his sturdy club, anyone to move forward with her and hold her hand.

Inside, she urged herself! Inside is the incredible horde of gold and treasure that you are here to find, the answer to everything. Enter, she ordered herself, and didn't even know she shook her head, terrified.

The owl hooted again, further away, a soft, mocking sound, reminding her that the cloaking night didn't last forever, the dawn would come. Her feet moved a pace forward. She took a shuddering breath and entered the crypt, leaving the door open.

It was dark, cold, and damp, and the air smelled of dust and age. Holding her lantern high, she walked down an aisle between stone sarcophagi, four on either side, each massive lid bearing the full-length, lifelike effigy of a knight in tunic and chain mail. Their old-fashioned, raised-visored helmets framed somber, carved faces with closed eyes, their hands were clasped as if in prayer about the hilts of broadswords whose points reached to their feet. The dust of centuries lay thick on the stone, and mortar, fallen from the ceiling, lay like snow on the still forms.

Scarcely daring to breathe lest she wake the dead, Lyse raised her light higher. The stone blocks of the walls and ceiling were unadorned, the floor of black and white mosaic was cracked, and tree roots, poking through crevices in the half-buried walls, reached out like the gnarled arms of a withered crone.

Ahead of her, in an alcove which seemed to end the tomb, two sarcophagi rested on pedestals which had been draped with white fabric, now hanging in wisps. And cut into the curved wall behind them was a Templar cross.

Within her little circle of light she approached the larger of the two sarcophagi, resolutely looking straight at it, for to look back into the dark aisle of death she'd just crept through would have made her knees buckle. On the thick lid the sculpted, moustachioed knight clutching his sword lay prone, his head on a carved pillow, his stone feet resting on a stone hound. On his chest was a round medallion depicting two men riding on a horse, and above them was carved a hand, fingers together, thumb up.

The smaller bier held a woman, her sleeping effigy prim in a simple robe and headdress. Lyse was sure this pair must be the fabled Grand Master Blanchfort and his wife of the years before he joined the Order. The dust of centuries lay undisturbed upon their remains.

But there was nothing else in the crowded tomb, just the silent, hulking sarcophagi. Where was the great Treasury? Lyse stood rooted, only moving her eyes and the lantern across the walls and the coffins, the light wavering as her hand shook.

Then she looked down at the gritty floor on which she stood, and thought she made out blurred footprints which went behind Bertrand de Blanchefort's resting place. Following the faint marks into the rear of the alcove, she saw that the lower part of the stone wall there was of brick.

Heart hammering, she swiftly knelt at the edge of the curved wall, counted the bricks and pushed on one. Nothing happened. Frantically she pushed on several, with the same result. Chewing her lip, she rose, carried the lantern to the opposite edge of the alcove's wall, on the lady's side, and trembling with nerves, performed the same operation.

Immediately, with scarcely a grind, a part of the curved wall swung back, and Lyse's eyes went wide as she peered through the door, for she expected to see the gleam of gold. But the only gleam she saw was flickering yellow candlelight. She was looking into a low-roofed chamber from whence a warm, fetid stench hit her like a blow. She raised her lantern and at the far end of the space, on a cot, sat a human figure which moved, a patriarchal figure out of the biblical paintings hanging at Moulins: white-haired, full-bearded, ragged.

"You have forgotten something, my daughter?" the figure croaked, voice tattered as the coarse brown robe and heavy shawl enclosing his thin frame.

The shock of finding a living being in a half-buried tomb drove the Treasury from Lyse's mind. Involuntarily she moved forward over a cleanly-swept dirt floor, breathing shallowly against the stink of unwashed body and charcoal smoke which permeated the stale air. The chamber seemed to have been cut into the rock of the hillside itself. Darkness spread away behind the cot, but to the side was a wooden table, at either end of which a tall, fat candle on a pewter dish made a yellow radiance. And close by a large, smoldering brazier kept the damp and cold at bay.

Something moved; in the old man's lap there was a big cat which he was stroking, a velvety grey cat with luminescent silver orbs; and two more grey cats were curled on the fur coverlet of the cot. Their slitted eyes shone like jewels in the light of her lantern as she approached.

The old man coughed feebly. "But I detect it is a lighter tread. Say, is it you, Lora?"

Lyse was close enough to see his eyes were white disks; the old man was blind. And as she stared at the heavily lined face there was that silent snap in her head—

Mélline, pleading at the feet of a purple-robed churchman, looking up into his opaque and sightless eyes for some pity, for mercy, but there was nothing in that stern visage but remorseless command

Blinking wildly, Lyse battled her way back to the present. It was a strain for her voice to come from her throat. "No, it is not Lora de Voisin. But I will not harm you, old sir. Do not be afraid."

There was a puzzled silence. Then the hermit said, "But I know that voice. Come to me, my child. Let my fingers see you, for my poor blind eyes cannot."

Lyse should have been fearful, the old creature could be half-insane, might grab her and strangle her. But she approached him and bent, as if very familiar with the act, to let the bony fingers pass spidery over her features.

The fingers hesitated, as if in surprise. The skin on the sunken cheeks crinkled, somewhere under the bushy beard the aged creature was smiling. "Ah, 'tis Mélline! It has been a long, long time, Madame," came the soft croak.

Lyse jerked back as if he had branded her. "Heaven help you, old man, I am Lyse-Magdalene, not Mélline! But how did you know of that name?"

The rusty voice, speaking slowly, seemed to echo off the walls. "I have known you all your life, *ma fille*. Did I not witness your birth in your father's house? And marry you to the baron? Did we not pass together through the valley of dark despair? But sit down, sit down and talk to me. Lora has never allowed a visitor, although her father did, once."

Lyse felt as if she had been turned to stone. "Who are you?" she whispered.

"Is this visage so changed then in its solitude? I am Guillaume, Archbishop of Quillan, and in this safe and secret place I sit to avoid execution. Here I live with my furry friends who discourage rodents and with the faithful Madame de Voisin to sustain me until such time as God shall deem me pure and release me from the Devil's grip."

The poor creature was harmless, Lyse could see, but mad. Any churchman of Quillan who knew Mélline would have been dead over two hundred years! Nevertheless, she had to ask, "But why would an Archbishop be sentenced to death? Why need you to exist in a tomb?"

"Why? But you know this. Soon after the King's men murdered all the Knights-Templars, they came for me. People scream things out under torture, and several had given away my Cathar leanings. But Giles de Blanchefort rescued me and brought me here so I might continue my quest towards humility and perfection and ready myself to enter into God's kingdom. Many centuries this cell has been used for refuge for our people. Look behind me, and you will see. "

Lyse raised her lantern and drew in her breath sharply. A crude door cut into the wall sprang into being, and above its flat lintel, carved deeply into the rock, was a triangle in a pentagram, and in the triangle an unblinking eye.

The man was a Cathar? Two hundred years old? She looked around and saw a bench with a sprung straw seat. She sank down on it.

Why would la Dame be hiding this madman? Who was he really? Her pulse pounded as she stared at the Cathar symbol dug into the wall, the exact same one as under the altar.

The ancient sat with his blind eyes turned towards her, stroking the cat on his lap, an expectant look on his face. "Why have you come here, my child? Lora tells me the King has gone on persecuting what Cathari remain in the evil world. I thought you too would have been swept away, but my heart is happy you are safe. We have too many martyrs. "

The demented, driven from their wits by devils, wandered the streets of towns and villages all over France, dirty lice-ridden, competing with dogs for offal to eat. They often raved but were usually harmless if left to their delusions. So, collecting herself, Lyse knew better than to strip this oldster of his.

It had to be the grey-clad chatelaine of Rennes-le-Château who had told the old one everything he knew of Mélline and the Archbishop of Quillan. Maybe he knew more about the Treasury and its location than she did. She had to try to be clever. Shivering now in the fetid air, she pulled her woolen cloak around her and played along with him.

"Ah, Your Grace, do you, by any chance, remember a knight in the service of God named Bernard de la Motte? "

"By chance remember?" the old man husked. "And how to forget when I watched the Templar's dear soul depart his body on that dreadful pyre of flames in Albi? And clutched to my heart not the abominate gold cross I wore, but the interior solace that, in spite I had not yet reached *Parfait*, I had managed to deliver the *Consolamentum* to him that opened the gates of Heaven. And later I attended you, poor daughter, as you lay prostrate with grief on the hard ground."

Lyse stared at him. La Dame had told this unknown hermit all that? Still she went on, constructing a story to fool him as she spoke.

"The knight de la Motte was the assistant treasurer of the Order, and told Mélli—me—that he had conveyed their Treasury here to the Razès, and hidden it securely against the day when Scots Templars could spirit it out of France. But the location of it has been lost and now—now the Scotsmen have made their way here. I must tell them where it is, will you help me, please, Your Grace?" She held her breath.

A bewildered expression came over the wrinkled face. "But I do not know that! Even after the Grand Master Molay was put to death in Paris and there was not a Templar left in France, the search for that accursed horde of wealth was frantic in this valley. Many suspects were racked, or branded with hot irons, and screamed whatever came to their heads. Even I was taken from my cell—" The hermit drew up his robe a little and Lyse stared horrified at terribly deformed and twisted feet wrapped in heavy bandages—"but I could not tell them what I did not know. I still do not. I am but an old, old man, waiting mournfully for death."

Lyse believed him. It meant that la Dame did not know or did not tell him the Treasury's location. Crestfallen, she focused at the dark wall behind him and the crude portal. "What is in the space back there?"

He shrugged under his rags. "A natural chamber in the mount, in which a little, underground stream flows swiftly against one wall. It furnishes water to me and my little children here, and we take care of our bodily needs. The good Lora brings food to eat, char to burn and candles for my pets to see by, for I have no need for light. Air comes from somewhere unknown to me, the smoke from the brazier is dissipated by it. God and my prayers keep me company."

Mired in disappointment, she jumped up abruptly and picked up the lantern. "I must look into the other chamber, old man."

He shrugged again. "As you wish. I shall pray God to give you strength in His Cause, Mèlline, my daughter, for the world outside is harsh."

Opening the door, she had to pinch her nose against the stench of odure, but the ancient had told the truth. The long chamber was quite empty, with only the purling stream flowing through via small openings in solid rock walls, with no other entrance. There was no Treasury in this place.

She backed out and stood again before the pitiful blind sack of bones, noticing there was a bulge of padding under the robe at his knees, so he could creep on them. She had one more question on her mind perhaps he could answer. "Tell me—Your Grace—for anguish has caused me to suffer bad loss in my memory, what was my husband's name?"

"Dear child! Can you not remember anything, *ma pauvre?* And the man not so long dead? D'Harcourt, of course. A great friend to you Bourbons."

So! There was information! It was Mélline D'Harcourt she remembered, who might have been a Cathar when the family was yet small and provincial. How much the devious la Dame had told the hermit but hidden from her, it was scandalous!

She blurted out, "And Madame Voisins told you all this?"

Bewilderment again flooded the ravaged, sightless face. "Told *me?* But we all know these relevant things. The Blancheforts were my rescuers from the dungeons in Carcassonne, and their kin Lora has inherited my care. She is a good woman, Mélline, and she has great healing powers, she keeps me alive until I am ready. I teach her the Truth of our Cathar beliefs and she takes it to the others in the Razès."

"The others?" Lyse echoed weakly.

"Those who remain of us, in secret, of course." Now the sparse brows over the milky eyes frowned. "When I gave Bernard the peace, he confessed to me his love for you, a married woman, and confessed the sin of adultery that joined you together in the hidden tower room of the very château above us. I gave him the *Consolamentum* in his last hour of life, but you, my child, have you worked to erase such stain from your immortal soul?"

Her heart jumped. "Y...yes, I have," she stammered, almost struck dumb, for she had told these circumstances to no one, except Ferrante.

Her head whirled. She stared at the noisome, disheveled hermit sitting on his cot, grotesque, his ruined feet stretched before him, very old–but over two hundred years old? And believing himself to be a prelate long turned to dust? Yet he knew so much, and obscure people dead centuries were sharp in his memory. She was lost as to what to think.

"How long have you hidden here, old sir? How many years?"

He gave a faint cackle. "'Tis hard to reckon time in this silent place, but if I count from de la Motte's martyrdom, perhaps ten, fifteen years."

Bernard de La Motte was executed in the year 1314, it was now 1525. Of course, the man was deranged.

But one more question nagged at her, one that ravages her when certain fragmented memories of Mélline's flashed into her head.

In her mind's eye she saw a blind Bishop in his purple robes staring sightlessly, relentlessly down at the grief-stricken head of her ancestress. "Your Grace, again I tell you that horror has erased some of my memories. Why did I appeal to you once in great agony to relieve me of some obligation? What was it I had to do?"

The hermit listened, then sighed deeply and did not answer.

"Monseigneur?"

The sightless eyes lowered to stare stubbornly at the ground. "So God has granted peace to you by removing your memory of that bitter event? You are blessed, daughter. For your terrible sacrifice you are blessed, where I am not, for I must remember. I will not destroy the Lord's mercy on you."

"But–"

"Do not ask me, dear child, I cannot. Your lapse is a gift from God. 'Tis bad enough those strange visitations you sometimes have in your mind, of a woman long dead who lived in the court of the Merovingian Kings and suffered beating and rapine during the sack of Rennes-le-Château. But others fear your unwonted moans and screams; I have protected you behind my purple robes from being named witch and possessed by the Devil. The misery of those visions, the affliction itself, evaporated when your baby came, never happened more, the Lord be thanked for His mercy. So now how shall I give you more to suffer...? No, no."

He sighed again, deeply. "Go now, Mélline, the Dame of Rennes-le-Château never remains here so long lest morning overtake her. Go, and I beg you not to return, ever, it is very dangerous for you."

Lyse backed away slowly. The grey cat raised an imperious head to watch her.

The creaking voice followed her. "Be silent, my daughter, as to my whereabouts. The Holy Office searches diligently for me and their sinister piles of faggots wait. I fear not death, but my prayers and enlightenment are not yet finished."

"I will not tell. Nor will you tell Madame Voisins that I have been to visit you, for she did not give permission."

He was silent, then he answered, "I see. *Eh bien,* you have my word. Heavenly angels lead you, Mélline D'Harcourt."

"Farewell," Lyse muttered, but as she felt the curve of the open wall behind her, she stopped a moment, uncertain, taking one last look at the blind ancient, whose head was drooping.

The madman's voice came to her, whispering back from the rock walls. "There is no Treasury here, child. Only the treasure of learning God's mind."

She fled, pushed the brick that rumbled closed the wall to his dungeon, hurried down the aisle of sarcophagi, and shielded the lantern with her cloak as she came to the greyish square of night that meant the open tomb door. Outside in the waning dark she feverishly operated the mechanism that closed the door, and blew out the lantern before she faced the château.

The cold, fresh air cleansed her lungs, washing out the choking breath of the grave and sending life to her limbs again. She flitted swiftly and quietly, barely able to see her way and avoid dry foliage that could snap. She reached her room without encountering anyone, not even the dogs, who slept in la Dame's tower.

Ripping off her cloak, she flung herself face down on her bed, overwhelmed by the clamor of voices and thoughts in her head. Only to the absent Ferrante could she repeat this weird encounter and weep her suspicion on his shoulder, that la Dame, and perhaps everyone in this valley of curious stillness behind its living pulse was the inheritor of a despised heresy.

Or—she raised her head—was that the reality of two hundred years ago, and the mad old man thought it was now?

He was perhaps Lora Voisins' father or grandfather and la Dame kept him alive but hidden because she feared his addled stories would be believed, putting her at great risk with the zealous Holy Office. Who was he? Where was the Treasury? How could she free herself and get away from this brooding mount, with its mad hermit buried alive?

The weight on her shoulders, the suspicion she was surrounded by heretics, was too heavy to bear alone. But with whom could she share it who was not a thousand leagues away?

Germain. She must lay her heart bare to him, even though it meant breaking her word to her uncle, for Germain must smuggle her to Le Bézu, immediately, in spite of snow on the high peaks, take her at least to the clearing facing the unreachable ruins. Something inside her drew her there, nagged and nagged that important new memories would fill her mind if she once again set her eyes on that haunted fortress.

That was it. Her good Germain would help her stumbling feet toward her goal.

But, emotionally exhausted, she slept so late the next morning, that when she woke la Dame and Germain had left already to go down to Couiza.

Morose, Lyse wrapped herself in her wool cloak after a few bites to eat, and wandered the mount's tiny village, sparing a smile now and then for the respectful, red-cheeked neighbors she encountered. It was the wind that made the day cold, the constant wind soughing through the trees, bending the branches and whipping them about, rattling the curled, stiff cylinders of the rhododendron leaves in spite of the hint of buds ending each twig.

When she spied a little procession coming back up to the château unusually early, she hastened to meet it where the road entered into the village, a peculiar foreboding striking her.

Lora Voisins was in the lead on her horse, and some villagers followed behind leading two donkeys with a canvas sling between them supporting a man wrapped in a blanket. Approaching, Lyse saw it was Germain in the sling. La Dame called out that he had been felled by the sudden high fever of the winter plague, in spite of wearing the garlic-soaked gauze about his nose and mouth, a device la Dame had hoped would counteract the putrid air.

Distressed, Lyse ran along beside the sling, peering into eyes inhumanly bright that hardly knew her. He had complained the day before of an aching head and back, and had been obviously in need of rest; that imperious woman was working him too hard.

She was on foot, the mounted group forged ahead of her and took the litter in the residence. But when she reached Germain's chamber Tournel was stationed at the door. He repeated politely but adamantly that he had been ordered not to let her in. In fact he agreed with the order. For her own well-being she should not go near the sick man. From outside the door she could hear her friend's violent coughing and loud wheezing, as if he could not breathe, and when la Dame emerged, she shook her silvery head and admitted that Germain was ill indeed.

For Lyse the dreadful news was the last straw, and especially since Ferri that morning had mentioned he would be leaving them, come somewhat warmer weather.

She hated gloomy Rennes-le-Château, and the wind-swept, disturbing Razès. She disliked la Dame and distrusted her, especially now for placing Germain in jeopardy. It was already March, a few days from April; her uncle wrote, hiding neither his disappointment nor despondency, that it was almost too late for him to mount an attack against Francois Premier this summer. He said he did not blame her for lack of success, he knew she did what she could. It probably took more time.

But Lyse's heart had lurched as she realized that he might keep her shut into Rennes-le-Château for years, with Ferrante on arrest order and unable to join her or perhaps finding more amusing climes. If she ever wanted her life back, she had to make a move, now, however she could.

She went to find Ferri.

She tried hard to tell him only what he needed to know, that she had recurrent nightime dreams about finding some sort of treasure secreted in the Aude valley, only she couldn't tell where she had found it in the dreams. But that the very night previous she had dreamed that the answer would come to her if she went as close to Le Bézu as she could get, and prayed there very hard for its location.

They were sitting in the château's somber Hall. Ferri lounged by the side of the hearth, one foot up on a stool as he cradled his lute and enjoyed the bright, crackling fire. The minstrel's almond-shaped blue eyes peered at her in startlement, then he gave a little chuckle, as if she were being ridiculous.

"*Tiens*, Mademoiselle, I dream every night I have found the Sultan's ruby, but that does not mean the next day I will fling myself on a leaky ship to go after it. Dreams are not always what they seem."

"But mine are!" She jumped up from her chair and sank down next to him on the hearth steps. "My dreams are vivid and they often come true. *Dis-moi*, Ferri, would you not like to share in a great fortune?" Her voice came breathlessly. "For you would, you know, if you took me to Le Bézu. So much money would be yours you could toss it up into the air and dance under it for an hour ere it finished raining."

"A treasure in this valley, dear Mademoiselle? Ah, you are listening to that stupid Marye's stories, about those Cathars of yore and the dirty gold collected by their sect, which they spirited away."

"Yes, yes, that's it, a great treasure, and I think I can find it."

"No one else has been able to. 'Tis a fool's venture."

It was her turn to be surprised. Ferri was so imaginative, she thought he'd be less stolid than Ferrante or Germain, and relish the chance to chase even a chimera. "But no one else has had my dreams, and I just know they are sent by my namesake, the blessed Magdalene, who wants me to find it." She gave him the full force of her light blue, crystal gaze. "Yet I cannot go to Bézu alone, I need help. And I must go now, or it will be too late!"

The vagabond musician didn't seem interested; the solitude of the winter had been making him edgy. He plucked a string and slid his other hand up the neck of the lute to make a singing, climbing sound. He kept his fair head bent over the instrument an Instant, then looked up to drawl, "Dear Mademoiselle, it is barely past winter, the high trails are still icy and full of snow, even if down here the hawthorne bush fruits. Anyhow, the tale-spinners at the wine tavern I sometimes frequent in Couiza tell of climbers who have died at Le Bézu, and others who struggled and found nothing at all. Go back and conjure somewhere else beside that haunted ruin to amuse your sleep."

For once, Ferri was exasperating her. Her Germain would have given in quickly. She plucked his slim, callused fingers off the taut strings to get his full attention, anxious to convince him she was not just being silly, ignoring that for all his geniality he never liked to be touched. It was urgent for him to take her seriously.

"Listen to me, Ferri, this has happened before, you see, and la Dame found a way to clarify my dreams, to make what I dream greatly specific. Once, when that special method was attempted, it turned out my dreams were true. So must this dream of Le Bézu and treasure be too." Her hands felt damp; it was hard to force someone in a direction and keep them ignorant of the whole of it at the same time.

But his ears seemed to have perked. "Sweet lady, everyone knows dreams are strange, twisted things, even a necromancer cannot explain them sensibly. And you have found a way to do it? To give clear explanation of those garbled visions? Your pardon, my lady, but 'tis hard to believe."

"Yes, yes, and in my dream, I knew that Le Bézu would provide answers to where there is a treasure—"

"Too far. Too cold. We will be floundering in snow. Too many have failed there."

"Look, it is not Le Bézu where I see the treasure in my dreams, but somewhere else. But in my sleep the past nights I think I am close to that old fortress, gazing at it, and suddenly, into my head comes the exact location of the treasure. Only–in the morning I do not remember. I will if I actually go to Bézu."

"Are you saying that the treasure could be anywhere? Even far away from Bézu, or from here?"

She shrugged. "Y-y-e-es," she admitted, feeling she was losing control of the veil she was trying to keep over the situation, "but it is in the Razès, I know it. But I need to make it more explicit, my dream of finding treasure, and at Le Bézu this will happen, as the Magdalene tells me."

Ferris's foot was tapping now and he twiddled with a strand of his fine blonde hair. He still looked dubious. "But what was the other way to interpret dreams that you said la Dame tried? It has to be easier than toiling up a wild mountain in the cold?"

"Yes, but that method of clarification of dreams is very, very dangerous, it could kill me. So I will not do it again."

"Ah, Mademoiselle de Tonnière," he teased, and struck a chord on the lute like a quivering laugh, "It could kill you? How vivid is your imagination!"

"No, 'tis true, Ferri, I swear, 'tis the blue powder–"

He sat up now, and drawled, "What blue powder? Such invention. Do you also fly without wings amongst the birds, my pretty damsel?"

Lyse bit the inside of her lip, for too much had already slipped out, even though he thought she was only babbling. But she had to convince him she had real knowledge. "You know the blue *pastel* plant from which they make dye here? It has potent smoke, it makes you dream, but very precisely, as clear as reality, and you speak out while you are dreaming, although waking, one remembers it all."

Now she fibbed desperately, to convince him, "In that one attempt with it I was able to lead Don Ferrante to the exact spot on the riverbank where I dreamed a gold ring had been lost–and there it was! But I almost died from the powder's effects, and although it works I cannot use it again, for fear of my life. Isn't that a stupid irony that I dream not of a silly ring now, but of coffers full of gold waiting to be found? But suddenly Le Bézu has come into my dreams as an alternative, a glimpse of which will give me the location of the hiding place no one has ever discovered!

"Ferri, please, you must accompany me there, I beg you. We shall be rich. You could buy ten Moorish lutes from Cordoba, inlaid with mother-of-pearl; you could buy a castle of your own! And I will not have to live in this dreary ruin of a château the rest of my life or finally creep off to a convent."

She looked away from him, her gaze sweeping over the somber reaches of the Great Hall outside their little circle of firelight and true unhappiness pulled the corners of her mouth down.

"What will Madame Voisins say?"

"We cannot tell her, there are reasons—oh, you must believe me. I can turn to no one but you, dear Ferri, for with Germain so sick, I am quite alone."

His almond-shaped eyes stared at her quite attentively now, although she couldn't tell whether with sympathy or rejection. But she continued, "I fear to wait too long. In my dream I am always running, running toward the place of treasure, because I know I must hurry or it will be gone—"

She was so entangled in her semi-fable now, that she truly believed she'd had such a dream. "I know the way to the vantage point for Le Bézu, I was once there," she hurried on, for at least the slim minstrel wasn't shaking his head and turning away. "It needs but a day to reach there and back if we start very early. Just a day."

Ferri put up the lute and began to wrap it in its velvet cover. "Mademoiselle, you jest. Sergeant Tournel has been appointed your keeper. He would never let you from his sight, or allow such a journey—"

She had already thought this out. "See, I know a way to leave Rennes-le-Château on foot without being seen! But how to find the horses we will need after that is a problem."

Ferri drew in the cheeks of his narrow face. He pursed his lips, thoughtfully weighing the peculiar journey, fingers drumming on the cushion of his stool. Then his normal, nonchalant expression returned. "I can get horses, if you have the money to pay. My friend the peddler, whom I often see at the wine tavern, can buy them for us and have them waiting below."

"Yes, yes, I have the money," she said thankfully. "*Écoutes,* this house was built with a secret stair down the mountain, with an egress close to the main road, by the big rock below the Coustaussa ruins. If your friend will bring the mounts there, we can ride off unseen."

"Ah, is that right? But your guards will chase you as soon as they learn you are gone. La Dame is clever, she'll puzzle out where you've gone and they'll race after us."

"It will be no matter, for we can steal away at night, and be so far ahead of them by dawn our business will be concluded before they reach us. And what will they do to me, after all? I am no prisoner, merely a female overly protected."

"The question is, what will they do to me?" Ferri asked wryly, but now caught up in the adventure still seemed concerned over it. "Are you not scared to ride in the dark? We could be followed by brigands and our throats cut."

"Ah, you must know thieves don't like cold nights," she replied airily, hoping bravado would convince him. "I lately don't rise before the sun is well up; it will be eight in the morning before I am missed. If we climb up the mountain near Bézu at daybreak, there will be plenty of time to reach the viewing ledge before we are collected. And then it won't matter."

She could see he was intrigued.

He murmured, "How much would I get, do we finally find this treasure the saints whisper about in your ears?"

"A money coffer full of gold écus!"

"You promise before God? You wouldn't forget the poor, as so many gentility are wont to do?"

"How could you even think that?"

Smiling, he stood up, cheeks drawn in tight." Well, I have done even sillier things before, and the heavy winter has worn on me this year. But I must have time to make arrangements for the horses with Pierre Loup, the peddler. I won't mention your part in the journey, and he's not the curious sort anyhow, caring only for his pots and pans and pocketbook."

"How much time do you need?" she asked anxiously, wanting to go that very moment.

"A day or two. 'Tis just as well, for we must wait for a dark night but a fair one, no rain or mist. I'll borrow the stableboy's donkey and ride down right now and find him."

"You won't change you mind? I promise I will protect you from the Voisins' anger, I'll say—I'll say I threatened to lie that you raped me if you didn't do just what I ordered."

A twist of a smile enlivened the itinerant musician's whippet face and he raised almost invisible flaxen eyebrows. "You see? I can't imagine why I attach the truth to the tales of a lady so inventive. Yet, I have always been fond of adventure," he confessed.

"Oh Ferri, thank you," Lyse trilled, and grabbed his hand in both of hers.

"But for this you must practice your interval chords with much more attention," he demanded with mock ferocity, and casually withdrew his hand.

Chapter 25

Their descent of the hidden stair la Dame had shown Lyse was dizzying and hard in places, the ceilings so low at times that Lyse and Ferri barely walked upright.

Initially the stair spiralled around as in a well, but the passage soon turned into a combination of sloped tunnels interspersed with rough steps, and sometimes a path that threaded through natural caves with elevated roofs and steep inclines. Moisture glistening from some of the walls had dripped mineral cones from the overhead rock and made the way slippery underfoot.

Ferri went first with a flaring torch, turning to help Lyse, in her boy's tunic and carrying a lantern, negotiate high, crumbling steps.

Except close about them, the dark was stygian. The weight of the rock above them seemed to press on their heads, and although there was still, heavy air to breathe, Lyse desperately fought the feeling of suffocation. Through the caves the echo of their footsteps bounced into a silence broken only by the gurgle of an underground stream, possibly the same one, Lyse thought, that kept the daft old hermit alive.

In places the path was so precipitous they might have slid down but for the rusty, iron chain strung as handhold. Remembering Mélline's glimpse of the golden Menorah being prepared for transport in a cave below her home, Lyse marveled that the woman must have come down here with food for the brothers and then had to struggle her way up again. Clearly, her ancestress had been no fainting flower.

Winding, but always angling downward, the descent from Rennes-le-Château seemed interminable, the menacing, surrounding dark fighting to overwhelm the torch's flare, and she stayed close on Ferri's heels. Again they heard water coursing, but now there were steps once more and they soon arrived into the less dusty air of a small cavern. Ferri raised his torch high—

so bright! There were so many torches in iron holders illuminated the work area, and brown-robed men busily moving about, nailing carry-handles to chests or sewing up canvases. The brother in service to Bernard took the letter from her hand and shoved it securely under the studded-leather belt about his waist, "I will see he receives this, my lady, never fear." Mélline's long braids hung down, she'd had no time to pin them up. She trembled, wringing her hands. "Brother, brother, I think I will never see him again," came tumbling out of her mouth, "something in my heart warns me."

"You will see him again, Madame, my heart tells me God in His Mercy will grant that."

Lyse squeezed her lids together and blinked hard, and the fearful dark rushed back to surround their two pools of light. Yes, she knew this place.

"Ferri! I think there should be a tunnel opposite to us, wider and higher," she whispered.

They walked forward and he raised the torch. "There it is," he said, not questioning how she knew, and preceded her into the passage she knew had conducted the brothers and the last of the Treasury outside to a secret resting place. "We must be close to the base of the mount," he added after a while, voice sounding like a whisper between the muffling walls.

"We are. This tunnel once went on to Coustauzza, but the egress is totally blocked there. We should soon come to a closer one—oof!" She had bumped into him, for Ferri had stopped at the foot of a dirt and rock fall which obstructed any further progress. Dismayed, Lyse raised her lantern to shine its dancing flame above, at the top of the ramp. "*Mon Dieu*, there it is," she cried, "the egress stone." She swallowed in relief, for always there had been the nagging doubt of la Dame's credibility.

"Agh, and just as in the chapel, that same pyramid with its all-seeing eye!" Ferri muttered, and quickly crossed himself. "This forsaken region is truly devil-ridden."

"Disdain nothing if it leads us out from inside the earth," she urged him. "The stone must be pushed up."

The square block had been so skillfully cut it almost seemed one piece with the roof. "It is old. It will not give," he worried, reluctant to touch the heretic carving.

"No, it has recently been attended to, you will see."

Scrambling up the slope, Ferri hunched his back under the all-seeing pyramid and shoved. The block creaked, but it budged. Realizing it was on a pivot, he moved to the right, pushed again, and the carving disappeared as the heavy stone swung up to reveal another patch of blackness, but admitting at the same time a cascade of dirt and dried leaves and a welcome whoosh of wind that extinguished the torch. Ferri threw away the dead torch and pulled himself out of the hole, struggling through a tangle of dead cane and briars, and finally reached his hand back to Lyse to pull her through into the dark night.

The cold air that hit her was welcome, clearing her brain, and she stumbled up, scratched and dirty, to see they had emerged in a chest-high thicket at the base of the mount, close to a huge boulder whose silhouette rose about one hundred paces north of the road up to Rennes-le-Château.

They fought their way clear of the thicket and onto the packed earth of the main road, keeping the boulder south of them. Now, suddenly awakened from the dreams she had fabricated, Lyse grew starkly aware that she was standing in boy's tunic and hosen under her cloak on a forsaken road in the dead of the night. She swallowed and husked, "Where is the man with the horses? I think we've lost much time."

Ferri's whistle was loud but short, very like the pipe of a nightjar, and the same sort of signal was returned. In a moment a man slunk out from behind the boulder and signaled them. "Hsst! Over here. All is ready."

The figure had on a round-domed hat, like the old one worn by Ferri's pudding-faced peddlar, from whom she'd even bought knitting wool and a thimble once. Lyse's heart started beating again in relief. Now they had mounts, they would be on their way to Le Bézu in a moment. But she'd purposely brought a scrap of white fabric, and now she stopped to tie it unobtrusively to a bush a few paces from the pivot stone, which, pushed closed, could not be easily distinguished from other's forming the rocky ground. They need not return the way they left, but, just in case.

"Come, Mademoiselle, the mounts are hidden behind the boulder, and we've two hours less now to give us a wide lead," Ferri urged, stepping back to allow her to precede him.

Lyse nodded to the peddlar, who also stepped back, eyes glinting darkly in the small light of her lantern, and she hurried forward towards their horses. Quick as a snake's strike the lantern was snatched from her hand, she was grasped and spun around, and before her astonished cry could be more than a squeak, it was cut off by the cruel smash of a fist against her jaw.

The dark world spun crazily around her, lights popped out all over, and then they vanished.

Gagging, Lyse came to her senses and raised her drooping head muzzily, feeling the roll and lurch of a conveyance under her.

She gagged again, because a wad of cloth had been stuffed in her mouth and tied there. She did not think she was blindfolded, but if not, she was staring into unrelieved dark. She tried to move and found she was bound by her shoulders and waist, sitting up against a flat, hard object, her wrists tied behind her, her feet secured too, with something soft but heavy weighing them down.

Fright flooded through her. She could hardly breathe and the left side of her face throbbed with pain. She shook her head; dizziness buzzed at her. Blind, immobile, battling to breathe the fusty air through just her nose, she grabbed at her panicked thoughts.

What was happening? Was she Lyse—or was this Mélline? Lyse led only a dull existence, so she must be the woman she suspected had been a Cathar, who had led a life full of tribulation? Staring into the dark she blinked hard, using the control she'd practiced to will the upsetting memory away and let her own life back in again. But the effort only brought her around more fully, and she trembled to realize that the jaw that was hurting was her jaw. And she was being transported somewhere bound like a trussed animal and almost suffocated by an attempt to keep her from crying for help.

Her own memories came flowing back, and the bland, jowly face of Ferri's peddler friend lanced into her thoughts. That man had knocked her unconscious and was taking her someplace! But where? And how long had she been unconscious? Was it still night?

It was easier to breathe if she leaned her head back, but the warm air she drew in was burdened with a confusing mixture of scents, leather, spice and lamp oil. She tried to slow the heart pounding rapidly in her ears, a state which called up her terrible tumble down the cliff on the trip to the Razès, and how Ferrante had calmed her hysteria as she clung to that brittle bush so she could help save herself. In her head, afraid and shocked, she cried out to him now—

and suddenly his commanding voice called out over the crowd, "Courage, my dearest heart, try to think clearly, have faith—" There were tears on his cheeks but she imagined that the unflinching green eyes stared directly, steadily, hungrily into hers as the hooded executioner behind the post stepped close to him, ostensibly to check the ropes holding the condemned, yet when the dreadful one stepped away moments later the dark head of his victim hung grotesquely sideways, a sight immediately obscured by obscene puffs of black smoke

Lyse-Mélline's aghast scream came out as a bare murmur behind the gag, she blinked hard and shoved down nausea and by a twist of will fled from the horrible memory. But it was Bernard, and not the green-eyed Ferrante who had been throttled! "Go away, Mélline!" she shrieked in her head, "go away!"

She concentrated hard on herself, Lyse-Magdalene de Bourbon-Tonnière, and on the dreadful situation she'd gotten Ferri and herself into. The loathsome peddler had abducted them and this was certainly his merchandise wagon. He thought to hold them for ransom, no doubt, having laid his nefarious plans the minute Ferri had asked him for help and mentioned they would have no escort. Dearest Lord, what had the villain done with Ferri? Was that the weight she felt on her legs, Ferri tied and gagged as she was? Or dead? She quailed, for the scoundrel might have killed the poor minstrel both for defending her and because Ferri was a rootless roamer no one would pay a sol for.

Her straining ears could hear nothing over the racket of traveling. It was hard to breathe and stifling warm, even in the cold night, so she thought a canvas must be hiding the two of them, tossed above them over some of the merchandise the itinerant carried—iron pots, bolts of fabric, chests of sundries, pottery, boot spurs. She was familiar with the wagon for the peddler came to Couiza often and invited her to inspect his goods as she strolled past with Ferrante or Germain. He was an innocuous-looking sort with eyes like raisins and a thatch of reddish hair under his hat.

His wagon had deep sides which he would let down to display his wares, and a roof of woven-straw arched over hoops. On either end the openings were shielded by patched curtains. Right now, from the awful bumps and thumps shaking her, the man's two mules were galloping full speed. They must be heading north on the main route, toward Carcassonne, for the road southward climbed towards the Pyréneés and was steep; a heavy conveyance could not keep up such a pace. So it must still be dark and the road deserted, for in daylight such breakneck speed of a merchant's vehicle would be noticed and reported to any pursuing guards. If it was still night, they might not have come very far. Tournel would surely catch up to them come morning.

But in a short while the clash and clang of the ungainly, iron-clad wheels and jouncing merchandise diminished as their speed slowed, and she could hear a voice hauling the draught animals back, "Gar, gar, pull it up, you whoresons, gar," and gradually the wagon slowed, made a bumpy, deep turn to the right, and stopped.

A heavy silence engulfed Lyse, as profound as the darkness she stared into. Then the peddler's voice came again, close and clear in the sudden quiet, and she realized she must have been stowed forward in the conveyance, just below the driver's perch.

"Ah the Saints! What a course. Only the Lord has kept us from striking a hole and turning over. You have a charmed–or should one say charming–life, Monsieur. The road we face now, climbing up, is harder. The poor beasts need a rest, half an hour at least, and by then it will be dawn. This path must be negotiated in some light anyway."

There was no answering voice. Was the brute talking to himself? But no, to an accomplice, of course. He would not have attempted such an attack alone, for Ferri, poor Ferri, might have been armed. Grief squeezed her, for the fate of the gentle musician she had led to his doom, and for her own unknown fate. She was chilled with fear. And alone. Her head drooped.

Then another voice said, "I suppose we've enough of a lead to stop, methinks we'll easily reach Château Valmigère before the hue and cry is raised, even with the signal towers these people use. Did you send off your man as I ordered?"

Lyse's head snapped up, her eyes widened. The light, melodious voice she heard was Ferri's!

"This morning, *mon cher*. He's a fast rider, he should reach Albi in three days. Give some time for turn-around, and three days more back to us and we'll ride out of this valley with an escort none of the petty knights in this region would dare confront." The peddler's staccato laugh tittered out, satisfied with himself.

"Pierre, 'tis the meanwhile I worry about. The Razès swarms with Bourbon supporters, although I was told Valmigère is an easily-defended redoubt even by the mere three score men we've kept there."

"And the *comte* de Marques is already there. So as not to attract attention, he had ridden south with only two men when I met with him. *Diable,* but that man chafed at the delay in this whole proceeding."

"Well, for that delay I've learned something so valuable to us it should swiftly calm him down."

"Anyway, I would trust your brother to safeguard us, dear creature, he's very good at these soldierly manoeuvres. If he wants to keep this bitch for himself, he'll have to step quickly."

"I told you, 'tis not the woman he wants, but what she knows."

"*Bien sûr,* and you said you would tell me all the rest of it too, I'm just burning to find out."

"I said sometime."

"*Cochon!* It was dreadful playing this peddler role for months, sleeping with the lice on dirty straw, dealing with the louts and peasants stinking of garlic, driving back and forth along the Aude until I knew every hovel and ditch along the way, every lumpish goodwife from Carcassonne to Couiza. I did what you paid me for, so far that is, *cheri*, and you promised an explanation."

"I promised a further heavy bag of gold when the job is done, Pierre, don't forget that." The minstrel's voice went syrupy. "And something more, in case your fickle heart has forgotten. Has it, *mon beau?*"

The false peddler laughed softly. "Ah, no, that delight to come is what dragged me from bed of mornings and accompanied my tired sleep at night. But give me another little sample, sweet princling, a little kiss—?"

Silence, then the squeak of the wooden driver's seat, then a little slap. "Greedy!" Ferri's laugh was light, almost a giggle. "I will admit I've been excruciatingly lonely, dancing about with two bitches, a sniveling old man and some flea-bitten hounds. I'm farting happy 'tis over."

"O, you liar. Lonely, with that Mantuan stallion strutting about in all his muscular glory? What, are you losing your eyes, or your touch?"

Another soft slap and a laugh. "The warrior had eyes only for my Bourbon lady, and the damned strumpet gave him everything he wanted. He was even jealous that she spent so much time with me, imagine!" Another giggle. "He hated me, oh, I knew it. The next time I see that *bravo* I'll put my dagger right between his eyes—or legs. If Louis doesn't do it first."

"Ah, demon, you!" There was another short scuffle. "But look down there and make sure your guest is comfortable, Monsieur. You tied that gag to nearly strangle her."

"No, *mon beau*, I need her very much alive. I was very careful."

Lyse, scarcely breathing, the hands tied behind her clenched into fists, heard the canvas a handspan over her head being twitched aside and cool air rushed down at her with lifegiving force. A tap on the top of her head made her jerk it up.

"She's alive, she's fine, and glaring, could I see her great big eyes," Ferri reported from behind and above her. "I'll wager she'd been eavesdropping on us, haven't you Lyse-Magdalene, not that 'twill do you any good. Can you hear me, Mademoiselle de Bourbon-Tonnière? I've known who you are since before I arrived here, our man managed to find your trail from Moulins in spite of his partner's broken neck. You are my prisoner. Probably for the rest of your life, which could be pleasant once you have answered our questions satisfactorily. Just relax there and think of your minor scales, would-be lutanist, our journey will be over in a few hours. Then we'll try to give you more comfort."

There was a snicker, a parting tap on Lyse's head and the canvas was drawn back over whatever object kept it off of her.

Lyse was really fighting now, struggling to keep down the vomit that could not be spewed out and would choke her. Tears of shock and fury ran down her face and began to stuff up her nose, her only means of breathing. Threatened with suffocation, she instinctively threw back her head and inhaled as deep as she could, once, twice, the air filling her lungs pressing down the nausea, her frantic will stopping her tears.

Pierre's discontented voice rolled over her. "I still don't understand why we don't go north to Carcassonne right now and pick up an escort there for Albi."

"Because the locals signal each other from the high peaks. By morning Rennes-le-Château will realize she is missing and flash out the word. We'd be stopped and searched even before we got to Limoux. This way we disappear off the road and into the mountains, and it might be days before they remember our deserted château and come to search it. That gives the cardinal's men time to get here from Albi and remove us safely."

"Suppose that witch-woman, Voisins, smells it out quickly? Château Valmigère, I mean?"

"Pah, what has she got, some Bourbon guards and mayhap a small rabble to attack a fortress? The day Gonzaga left, I knew we had a chance at the peculiar. I had to wait as long as I did because I wanted to discover whatever method they had to unlock her lips. I have it now."

"Ah—"

Against the lids of eyes screwed closed in anger, Lyse pictured Ferri's narrow face. The thin smile she once thought shy now was sly, the almond eyes once ashine with the pleasure of an artist now gleamed with deceit. The vagabond musician who had wandered up their mountain needing a roof over his head was a spy, one who had gained her trust in order to abduct her. She thought she knew who he was now, a Lorraine, for the *comte* de Marques the two mentioned as his brother must be the Louis de Marques who Ferrante had spoken of.

And what else could they want from her but the location of the Templar Treasury?

The miserable, lying villain. Did he think she would tell him, even if she knew where it was? Even if they tortured her, she quailed in her heart. He was stupid, he should have taken her to Le Bézu, she might have truly found some answers. And then, with a stab of horror, she remembered. She had told Ferri about the *pastel,* the blue powder. And that it fostered her 'dreams'.

The pseudo-peddlar was smacking his lips over something he was eating. "What could that baggage, a Bourbon female hardly anyone at Court is aware of, know that would interest you, much less our august *duc* de Guise? Eh? My nose is quivering on the scent of this mystery."

"Stop it, Pierre, *cheri*, your nose is too long and could bring you the grief of being chopped off. You know I find you so—especially attractive, but my brothers dislike you. And I am so prone to being swayed by them, don't you know?" Ferri's tone was coquettish, even in serious warning.

"*Bien sûr*, you're fickle."

"Ah, let's not battle, just when the whole ordeal is almost over. Keep your silence, dear one, and you'll like the reward, I promise. All of it."

Lyse recognized Pierre's mollified grunt as unwillingness to displease the powerful men employing him. She heard his "Hyup, hyup!" to the mules as his whip cracked, and the wagon jolted slowly on its way again, slanting upward. And again the noise of travel erased what her captors might be saying.

But it did not erase her towering disgust with herself, to have given Ferri the weapon of control he needed, when her uncle and Ferrante had begged silence from her. And now they were both too distant to save her from a disaster of her own making.

Dread took her over. No one knew where she was, or could even help her once they reached the Lorraine stronghold. Disobedience and pride had brought her to this grief, and would surely cause her death at the hand of these rabid enemies of the exiled Charles de Bourbon. Once the Lorraines sucked from her what they wanted, they would do away with her like an empty marrow bone.

Suffering every jolt and jounce through the creaking floorboards under her, she used all her strength to keep back the despair that would surely choke her. Regret was useless. Nothing was left but to find somewhere the means and the courage to kill herself before she gave the Treasury to the Lorraines and totally betrayed her beloved uncle, Charles.

Ferrante's out-of-the-blue arrival at Rennes-le-Château, with his two men and baggage mules laden with gifts, did not fetch the happy greeting he expected. Instead, a grim, mortified Tournel said a few words at the gate and quickly escorted him right to the Voisins in their tower.

With Tournel's bad news sharp in his ear, he strode scowling into la Dame's chamber, sword slapping against his thigh, and barely greeting them rapped out, "What does this mean, Lyse-Magdalene is gone? Gone where? When? How?"

But la Dame, angry-eyed herself, was in no mood for bullying. "Two days ago. We believe she must have been abducted. Sit down, then, so we may discuss this. You have no idea how the surprise of your presence relieves us."

"Surprise? I sent a letter some weeks ago to say my business in Mantua was over and I was soon leaving for Genoa to take ship."

"Bad storms, many along our coast this season," the *sieur* piped, for once wrinkle-browed and anxious. "Your courier was probably lost at sea."

Ferrante took a deep breath, visibly controlling himself. He looked about, dropped his frame into a chair and leaned forward. "Quickly. What has happened here?"

His hostess answered without wavering, "Mademoiselle has either run off with that scurvy lute-player, Ferri, or somehow been abducted by him. The Razès has suffered a contagious disease of retching and high fever this winter, it has caused many deaths, and she was unnerved when Germain collapsed with it last week, which still grips him. She has been restless and discontent all winter, and her fear for Germain's life must have pushed her into some action. Two mornings ago she could not be found, neither the minstrel. But the château's portal was seen still barred on the inside, and the guards swear the two never passed from our entry gate."

Ferrante's hard gaze stared into her silvery one. "So. The hidden tower stair?"

"That was the only answer, and we found their footsteps in the dust there. So Tournel galloped south with some men, for I was certain that if she were not kidnapped, she had gone to Le Bézu, which seems to draw her as if by an invisible cord. He did not find her, but other guards rode north and made inquiries, and they came across a goatherd with a curious story:

"He had drunk too much wine from his leather flask and fallen asleep in the brush at the roadside, kept alive in the cold night by the warmth of his few goats. The rumble of a vehicle awakened him. He could see only the outline of a tall wagon halted on the road, and two blurs of figures, but he could hear their voices clearly. He sneered to our guards that they were men-lovers, and best not to believe their evil mouths, still, they spoke to someone inside the wagon, so there was another person."

Impatient for the point, Ferrante sat with the foot of his crossed leg twitching. The Voisins had just finished a meal at their small table. La Dame poured some wine into her glass from a glazed pitcher and handed it to him. It went down his travel-parched throat in an instant.

"The peasant could not remember all of the conversation he heard, but certain things he muttered prompted the guards to shake more out of him. It seems the pair he eavesdropped on were driving the wagon to the Château Valmigère, to wait for a large escort coming from Albi. They mentioned Rennes-le-Château, they spoke of Bourbon and a Mantuan. And they mentioned a de Marques, who was brother to one of them."

She put out a hand to contain Ferrante in his seat.

"Ferri had been friendly with a peddler who had a tall wagon, and who brought him from Carcassonne strings for his lute, and rosin powder, sometimes a crumpled sheet of music. What's more, the Château Valmigère, outside the Razès and abandoned for decades, is the property of the *duc* de Guise. It becomes apparent it was Ferri and his peddler the goatherd saw on their way to Valmigère, and they were taking Lyse-Magdalene there, to await reinforcements to escort them from the valley."

Ferrante swore under his breath. "Where is this château?"

"Just north of the Razès, in a mountainous area. We have learned that the castle was regarrisoned last spring, not a great force, perhaps fifty men. But, with more soldiers coming from Albi—"

Beating one fist into the other, Ferrante jumped up to pace what open space there was to relieve the pain of his guilt. "I knew it. I knew de Guise would somehow trace her. How could I have so carelessly set you two to keep watch on her!"

"Mademoiselle went nowhere beyond this hilltop without an escort. But I could not chain her to her bed, Signore!" Indignation pitched la Dame's stern voice even lower than usual.

The *sieur* broke in, "Ah, softly, you two, I beg you, recriminations will not help the poor girl who is now, evidently, an unwilling guest of the Lorraines. And that clan has always been unpleasant hosts. Don Ferrante, we have sat here desperate to think of a way to retrieve her, but our little force is a useless number against such a mountain stronghold. We are stymied. We would have sent word to Monseigneur de Bourbon immediately but his last message said he was just departing for Italy. And we had no idea when to expect you."

"Bourbon has been forced to promise the Holy Roman Emperor to mount a campaign against Padua this summer. There is not enough gold in his coffers anyhow to pay for the great force he needs to invade France. His hope now is the Templar Treasury, and that is the reason why we were sent here on so chancy a mission—and the reason why the minions of the *duc* de Guise followed and seized a woman they knew could 'see back'."

Ferrante's anger went boiling over, even though he knew it was unfair. "And it was you, Madame, who brought that skink-eyed Lorraine informant right into the midst of us!"

La Dame rose up, seeming to grow in height. "Do you dare suggest—are you daring to impugn my loyalty to Monseigneur de Bourbon? I wanted only to bring a bit of life to these old stones, for your entertainment. And as the vagrant fooled me, so he fooled you too."

Regretting his impulsive accusation, which was prompted by worry for the young woman whose beauty and dazzling smile in his memory had given him heart through a bleak winter, Ferrante hastily retreated. "Alas, Madame, forgive me, I had no intention of accusing you of deliberate wrong. I most humbly apologize."

The *sieur* patted his wife's arm and tugged at her to reseat herself. "Madame forgives you, of course, don't you, my dear? You are understandably upset, Don Ferrante, as we are too. But the milk is spilt. Now we must struggle to get it back in the pitcher."

La Dame shook off his hand, but the taut muscles in her neck went down. "Very well, *condottiere*, what do we do?"

They stared at each other. Ferrante sat down again and glared at the flagstone floor to concentrate. "Whatever we do, it must be quickly. The Episcopal Palace in Albi is built like a fortress, with a large complement of soldiers. The kidnappers will certainly transport Lyse-Magdalene there, once they have enough guards to withstand any attack on the way. The Château Valmigère is surely smaller, and certainly more isolated than Albi, our only chance to extract her must be from there. I presume you can get the landowners around here to supply us with at least twenty more men to reinforce our Bourbon guards?"

"Quickly. I have always told you extra men-at-arms would be no problem."

"But how can I breach stout walls with less than forty men-at-arms?" Ferrante growled, and chewed at a corner of his thumb, the scar under his eye puckering white.

A spin of light seemed to rise behind the woman's opaque, silvered stare, "I can handily get you in. Breaching the walls of the château is not the problem. It is getting her out that will be hard."

Ferrante seized on this. "Explain."

"You forget, Signore, how these mountain redoubts were connected by secret tunnels. I have old parchments in my possession, so old they almost crumble at a touch, that indicates there is an escape passage connecting Valmigère with its half-destroyed neighbor on a lower ridge, which once belonged to a Cathar family. That tunnel may still be open, or it may have collapsed, as at Coustaussa. If it is passable, it will conduct you directly inside the

Lorraines' lair. The place has been abandoned for so many decades, I'll wager no one there at this moment remembers the location of the old escape passage, or even knows that there was one."

With a slow wolf-grin appearing, Ferrante gave this piece of news his approval. He strode to the door, flung it open to bark at Lucco, waiting outside, "Get Sergeant Tournel, as fast as you can!" When he turned back to the Voisins, there was relief on his face. "*Grazie*, you have been more than helpful, Madame."

Her big mouth twitched. "*Écoutes*, the tunnel could be impassable now, at one end or both, or even in the middle. Send scouts first."

"There is no time. We will take charges of gunpowder to clear the way in the tunnel. Will you allow me to copy your charts?"

"Of course. And what will you do once inside Château Valmigère, with so few men?"

"Strategy, Madame, create a diversion to draw all attention. A fast rider to the *marquise* de Joyeuse ought to fetch me eight or ten more men-at-arms from Puivert, evening the numbers more. But we must get in and out of Valmigère before the escort from Albi arrives."

"Count by presuming the worst, that a messenger left for Albi the day Ferri absconded with her, which was two days ago, that rider will have arrived today at Albi. Then a day for them to prepare, and three or four more for the journey south."

"Say you have two days to take her from there, not to cut too closely."

"One. Assuming my reinforcements ride like the wind from Puivert." The wolf-grin had never left Ferrante's face. This is what he knew, what he understood, a contest, fast motion, the clever manoeuvring of plans and forces to destroy an adversary wishing you in hell. "Do you know, Madame, if Valmigère is laid out as usual, a keep, a main house, four towers? Is it moated? From our angle as moles we will have to divine where Lyse-Magdalene is being kept, in a chamber, or the keep, or a dungeon."

La Dame leaned back in her chair and picked a shelled nut from a bowl. "They want to take something very delicate from the girl, her ancient memories, so I reason that they would not stupidly tamper with her health by throwing her into a cold cell. My guess is, she is held in an ordinary chamber that can be warmed, even given a few comforts." She nodded, satisfied with the deduction. "Not all of the Cathar records were lost or burned as people believe." Now her huntress smile matched his. "Beside the tunnel chart, will it make you happy to know I also have the plan of the Château Valmigère, and of most of the fortress-dwellings in the Aude valley?"

"Madame, I salute you," Ferrante murmured with admiration, and made the strange sign of quick fingers to lips and heart. His hosts followed suit.

The *sieur* piped up nervously, "We must pray that Ferri realizes Mademoiselle has given us nothing to act on, even in all these months, so that they will not quickly lose patience and try to torture the Treasury's location from her."

Seeing the thunderous expression return to Ferrante's face at the thought, la Dame interjected, "Pah, the Lorraines are not fools, they will give her a little time to recover the 'seeing-back'. Thanks to God, they can know nothing of the *pastel,* at least they cannot menace her life with it."

A knock on the door, and Lucco's voice, in Italian, announced Sergeant Tournel.

"Come in, Tournel," Ferrante growled at the still crestfallen officer, "We have a diversion to figure out, and an underground march to perform as fast and smooth as if it were on the king's royal highway."

"Don Ferrante, I apologize abjectly–"

"Not now, man. Now is for rapidly repairing the error made, not bemoaning it. But first name me a man who can carry a message to Puivert as quick as shouting it over."

"Grenet," the sergeant said without hesitation. La Dame brought paper and ink, and Lucco was dispatched with the message to find the guard Grenet and send him on a flat-out gallop to Puivert.

Chapter 26

In the chamber just beyond the door of the room that was her prison, the argument between Lyse's captors over waiting or not grew louder and angrier; she hardly cared, for help was so remote it didn't matter whether they carried out their plan to tear her memories from her right now or later.

For two days she had languished in the barren, gritty room, her bonds and gag removed, but her heart leaden. It was not the cold dungeon cell she had expected, but it was little better, a straw litter and quilt on the floor for a bed, some old, rude furniture, and a slop-pot. A small amount of light came from an unshuttered, high window. The guards brought her food and drink, not that she could eat it, and built her a fire every morning in the shallow chimney place. She was even given a woolen stole to keep her warm, in addition to her cloak.

Ferri had obtained the wrap from somewhere and tossed it in her lap that first morning as she huddled miserably by her fire, rubbing her bruised wrists and sore jaw. He seemed to have no shame at all over his duplicity, his only apology being that the old castle had been long abandoned and so he could not offer more comfort. She stared at the fine, narrow features of her erstwhile teacher with the familiar, indolent expression so common to male lutanists, and wondered how she could have ever told he was a fraud.

He offered, "Be patient, you will be better accommodated when we reach Albi, Mademoiselle de Bourbon-Tonnière. The Episcopal Palace in which dwells my brother, the cardinal of Lorraine, is very luxurious." Hands behind his slim back, he rocked lithely on the balls of his feet as he gazed down at her. His voice had descended a few tones from the one she'd heard him use with his lover.

"Dear God, Ferri, I cannot believe this of you," Lyse whispered.

"Why? Did you imagine that because a man can bring angelic sounds from a varnished box with strings, he himself must be an angel?"

"I thought there could be no harm in a person we showed both kindness and respect."

"But of course, no harm, Mademoiselle, we mean you no harm. And for seven months my music and singing and my deprived existence surely repaid your charity to a wanderer."

Lyse did not answer this, her stony look condemning his charade.

His smile had turned closer to a sneer. "We might have gone to Le Bézu first, you and I, but when you said the *pastel* smoke could unlock your–dreams–even better, Bézu was naught but a waste of time. You yourself sealed your fate."

Still she said nothing, so he hooked the rush-seated chair to him with his foot and sat down on it close to her, teetering casually.

"*Écoutes,* Lyse-Magdalene, your situation is exactly like the scale of C major, simple, with no distractions. My family has always known some Bourbon females had strange abilities to remember the past, in fact as did your mother–and that your traitor uncle has probably sent you here to recover a lost fortune, either the Cathar's evil horde, as my brother Claude strongly believes, or the Templar's Treasury, also lost in the Razès according to tale-tellers. You haven't yet dredged up the location of either, or Gonzaga would not have departed for Italy. But since he was serious about returning, it means that Bourbon still hopes more from you–in which case, so do we.

"Once you told me of the efficacy of the *pastel*, there was no reason for me to bide my time longer. 'Tis a pity the strapping Italian let your female wiles stand in the way of his goal, for it occurs to me that the time you were so stricken, it was surely from their experimenting with the *pastel* fumes, and I think he wouldn't allow you to undergo them again. Happily, we are not so easily deflected. You are young, healthy, you might survive however many sessions with the blue powder it will take to release your powers of sorcery."

Numb with despair, Lyse spit at him, and the wet dollop hit his sleeve. "You nauseating, unnatural flit!"

He was still wearing the worn doublet and hose of a poor musician, but he grimaced fastidiously and brushed the spittle away.

"That was not very clever, lady, I am your only friend here. You met my brother, Louis, he of the ugly pocked face and uglier disposition, he is totally without patience. My brother Jean, the cardinal, one of the country's highest prelates, is greedy and ruthless. He would stretch you on the Inquisition's rack for a witch. So, until our most powerful family member, the newly-anointed *duc* de Guise, arrives from Albi to oversee our peering into your head, I am your only bulwark against mistreatment. I advise you, do not insult me."

"Vermin!" she muttered through her teeth. "One cannot insult a louse."

The chair scraped on the dirty flags as Ferri abruptly stood up. "The faster you tell us where the horde of gold is, the faster we will let you go. And the Lorraines are not uncivilized; we may even give you for yourself a portion of what we find. Eh? To make you independent of the criminal Charles de Bourbon? You are a good subject of our good King Francois, why should you suffer for your uncle's sins? My brother Claude, the *duc* de Guise, can help you. You see? Life is not so bad."

Lyse had turned her head from him. "Leave me in peace."

Ferri had sighed, narrow blue eyes filled with sympathetic spite. "For the moment, lady," he had agreed.

And now, outside, in the only other partially-furnished chamber in the château, there was a great row going on between Ferri and the *comte* de Marques, who had been waiting here for the spy to make some move. Their voices were loud, the argument came right through the old door.

"...waited long enough. I want to know now, now while we are here, butting arses with the Razès and its secrets. How do we know Bourbon hasn't already learned where to look and is merely waiting for the king to take his troops out of the country to the Piedmont before sending a force to recover the monies. I say let us squeeze the woman now, I say that every moment counts, and waiting for Claude may bring disaster—we will find an empty cachement for all our effort. I am sending a man down with silver enough to buy some of the *pastel* from the dyers in Limoux."

Ferri's melodious voice dripped scorn. "And without an alchemist and his equipment, how do you powder the plant so it will burn? She explicitly said blue powder."

"Fah! The stalk were harvested in September and would be dried by now. No matter, they will burn, powder or not."

"I say no. Claude will be furious."

"God rot his fury. My dear brother needs me now more than I need him." Compared to de Marques hoarse, rough tone, his younger brother's voice rose with soft disdain. "And he will need you in greater measure when you've your claws into the lost gold, eh Louis? You will make the stiff-necked *duc* de Guise bow to you then, just as you've always dreamed, eh? Well, I say no! This ancient revelation can wait a short while for Claude to arrive in Albi, so no one has an advantage. "

"Wait for Claude, wait for Jean," de Marques mimicked him, "you ignorant fluff. Don't you know that once we get to Albi our dear Cardinal will have the advantage and grab the prize from us in some way or other, even if he has to slam cell doors on us? You are too trusting."

"And do you think you can defy both our senior brothers at once, one insatiable for gold, the other avid for the French crown no less? You'll end up a corpse. I say leave the Bourbon bitch alone until our business with her can be done right and all share in the results."

"Shut up! You make me sick, you cowardly little arse-fucker."

There was a cry of rage, then a thump and a jolting bang, as if a body was slammed against a wall, and Lyse quailed and drew further into her stole like a turtle. De Marques' jarring, grating voice was more than audible.

"You think that little pig-sticker can intimidate me, brother? Drop it! Now, before I twist your scurvy head off." Steel clinked on the flagstone floor. "Next time you threaten me, Ferri, I'll happily forget what your name is, I promise you that. I applaud your sneaking role with that bitch, you performed it successfully, but now 'tis my turn, that is what I've been sitting here in this pile of stones for. Go along with me or I'll throw you and that sodomite lover you fuck in the dungeons. Take your choice, either I'm in charge, or you are in irons."

A small scuffle and then came Ferri's sullen surrender. "Ah, let me go, I have no power. So you are in charge. But you'll be the one to answer to Claude if the woman dies and we know no more than before."

Lyse heard footsteps coming closer to her door.

"Life is a gamble, baby brother. We could also be controlling a very valuable secret by the time the duke reaches Albi from Paris."

"We? You have the intention to let me hold the strings too?" Ferri sounded sarcastic.

"Surely. You have earned it. Now collect that knife and leave me to concentrate while I make a list of what we must have to send our weird *princesse* into her trance. It doesn't seem a difficult trick if we make an excess of the *pastel*." Lighter footsteps receeded now, and a door closed.

Lyse could hear de Marques' whistling through his teeth. A key grated in the lock and her door was flung open, making the flames that were warming her jump in the grate. The de Marques stood in the opening, hands on hips, legs wide, his hugely-padded sleeves filling the doorway. "You heard all that, eh, Mademoiselle?" he rasped.

Not waiting for an answer, he came towards where she stood. His lips smiled, but his small blue eyes, a darker, colder blue than Ferri's, held no humor. "I hope it is clear that I will not dance a sarabande around you, even though you told my brother that the *pastel's* smoke which summons your 'dreams' as you put it, can seriously harm you. I will use it, never fear. That is, unless you can tell us of your own volition where the Cathar treasure is hidden. Eh? 'Tis a good way to protect your health, *ma chère*. I am not a mean man, it is not my wish for you to undergo an unnecessary ordeal."

Lyse backed up against the edge of the high chimney piece, he was coming too close to her. Her mind scrabbled. What if, in a bid for time, she told them anything at all, sent them on a wild goose chase, praying meanwhile for a miracle? No, it wouldn't work. "Monsieur de Marques, you are despicable, but I don't fool myself that you are stupid. Even if I had any idea where any treasure has been secreted, you wouldn't believe what I said, not on my word alone."

The mirthless smile flattened out. "Not without corroboration from those fumes whose results you cannot control. Very good, my lady. But in the long run you will be smarter to first cooperate with me."

Lyse pressed her lips shut. The situation was hopeless, it would be a waste of breath to beg for pity from this ruthless individual, a waste of energy even to hope for rescue. Still, her one tiny hope was time, time for Sergeant Tournel to somehow find her and with a handful of men somehow extract her from the lofty old citadel that otherwise might be her grave. Minuscule as it was, she still had to cling to the possibility of rescue.

De Marques was physically crowding her now, grinning, enjoying her discomfiture. She edged away from the hearth and along the wall, but soon found herself boxed into a corner. She breathed, "Monsieur le Comte, from time to time my memory does advance towards remembering the location of a treasure, but without using the dangerous blue powder. My uncle had patience with this, in concern for me." She licked dry lips. "If you consider this approach, I swear before God I will repeat to you whatever recall comes to me regarding any treasure. Lately it has seemed as if my efforts to remember were getting close."

He shoved his pocked visage into hers. "Listen, *ma belle,* what are you, nineteen? Twenty? Am I to wait then until you are grey and toothless, just because you'd prefer to chance death with the blue powder old than young? You are Bourbon's blood, he was easy on you. And your Mantuan watchdog preferred to fondle your white body rather than bury it, so Ferri tells me. Not that I blame him, the *odure,* for Bourbon or not, you are a luscious piece." He chuckled and ran a rough finger along her jaw, and she jerked her head away.

Both his hands shot out to slide over her tunic and grab her buttocks, pulling her up against him. "So delicate and innocent, my little bird, yet with the smell and feel of a juicy woman," the hoarse voice murmured and his fists kneaded the firm roundness with growing excitement.

In spite of his fine doublet, De Marques smelled from sweat and garlic. His eyes gleamed meanly. One hand came around and yanked away Lyse's stole. She saw his nostrils flare, and with a frantic squeal she tore away from him, ducking under his arm. She ran across the room but he caught her as she vainly tried to keep the table between them and, snarling, slammed her against the heavy wood edge and crowded her up against it. She could feel his hard thighs through the flimsy boy's tunic she wore, and another pressure as well, which was no codpiece.

His gravel voice was smarmy. "Be nice to me, *ma douce,* show me how nice you can be. It could save your life. It could make you happy, eh? Mmmm, but you have charming lips, ripe for biting–"

Gripping one of her wrists he was pressing her hard enough against him to immobilize her. Her back arched, she jerked her head away from him, but behind her panic her free hand began to grope on the table for the pewter spoon left from the supper she didn't eat, for someone had filed its cylindrical handle sharp to act as a one-prong fork.

Turning her head frantically from his insistent kisses, she felt the spoon under her fingers. No, no, exploded in her brain, no, the scum will kill you, don't, don't, but her arm, propelled by dread of his snorting ardor, came up and over, aiming for his throat. He caught the movement and dodged; the sharp point plowed through the padded velvet of his sleeve. He yelled and flung her hard to the floor.

"You scurvy whore–!"

He aimed a kick at her side, but reflexively she rolled away doubled up and gasping in fright.

"You want to play, eh vixen?" de Marques snarled in rage, unbuttoning the triangular flap of his tight knee breeches and standing over her in a straddle.

The half-open door slammed back and Ferri scurried in.

"Louis, stop! Don't be a fool," he cried. "She's not a peasant wench to skewer and toss away. If you rape her or hurt her we may never get out of her mind what we seek. Leave her be for now. Later you can use her any way you wish." Grunting, he managed to wrench the fuming de Marques away from his victim. "Louis! Use your head."

Curled cowering on the floor, Lyse dared a quick look at the heavy features above her, contorted with frustration. A small, dark stain where the sharpened spoon had nicked de Marques shoulder was spreading on the blue

velvet of his voluminous sleeve. The man touched it, then looked at his reddened fingers. His hand grabbed the hilt of the sword by his side, he shook
off his brother's grip and stepped toward her, but Ferri cried out sharply,
"Claude will give you to the headsman. Will you risk her great worth to us for
a moment's revenge? Later, It will be all the sweeter later."

The anger slowly flowed out of de Marques' pocked face, replaced by granite
iciness. He rebuttoned his breeches, never taking his eyes off his victim. He
promised hoarsely, "He is right. Not now, lady. Later, if there is a later for you.
Be patient."

He whirled and stalked out through the open door. Lyse heard him yell,
"Brisolet! Bring a bandage, damn you, I'm bleeding. And catch me the donkey's
behind who left that woman in there with a sharp implement!"

Ferri offered Lyse a hand up, but she hitched away in disgust

He shrugged, went to pick up the blood-tipped spoon where de Marques
had kicked it, and then leaned casually against the table. "Sit there, then. I just
saved you from the ignominy of rape, Mademoiselle, to say nothing of the
pain. My brother Louis has no finesse, but you shouldn't have stabbed him.
He'll never forget that. Louis likes his women docile."

Lyse staggered to her feet. "Ferri—" she croaked desperately. "Please listen,
there is no guarantee in this world that the dreams, the memories coming to
me, no matter how they are induced, will ever indicate the exact location of
any treasure. I appeal to you, leave me alone and ask a ransom for me. My
uncle Charles, Don Ferrante di Gonzaga, either one will obtain whatever gold
you ask for my deliverance. Help me, I beg, Ferri, speak to your brother to
accept a large ransom."

"Brothers, Mademoiselle," the erstwhile troubadour drawled, "and the
answer is no. The house of Lorraine has no interest in a paltry three or thirty
sacks of gold Bourbon might scrape up for you—or might not. Have you no
idea of the extent of the lost riches for which this region has been torn up
through the centuries? But I've done what I can for you anyway—Louis will
not molest you, well, not before tomorrow, at least, when he plans to see what
your blue powder will draw out of you."

He slipped the spoon into his doublet and prepared to leave. The sly
smile continued to light his whippet face. "In fact, it had better bring as much
as Louis gambles it will, or the *duc* de Guise will strip the skin from his bones
for not awaiting him." One hand on the door latch, he snapped the fingers on
the other with evil delight. "Ah, how could I forget? An unforeseen benefit
from all this is a little secret I still hold all to myself: that I have discovered

dwelling at Rennes-le-Château a nest of disguised Cathari, and once in Albi I will report this personally to the Grand Inquisitor of the Holy Office. No, it is not just the Voisins and the ancient church I saw defiled by that heretic symbol, but I believe all the inhabitants of that hilltop village are so tainted."

"Mercy of God, that isn't so! "

"That very week we moved the altar I went to mass in the 'new' church that is used, but now with open eyes; in the apse there were depictions of Jesus and of the Marys and Joseph. There were sculptured angels, even the Old Testament prophets in the windows, but nowhere a holy Cross on which our Saviour died, nor a Saint's statue, and the baptismal font is thick with dust."

"Ferri, it is a poor church, they cannot afford many works of art, nor even support a priest full time. And there are few children on the hilltop, none under five. You are imagining dreadful things."

He shrugged. "Let the Holy Office decide that. To root out such evil infection they will examine everyone in Rennes-le-Château, maybe even the whole Razès. No heretic's sins stay unconfessed under the persuasion of the thumb-screw." His eyes alight were with sadistic fervor. He peered at her with false solicitude. "But you must sleep, now, Mademoiselle, rest and strength could help you survive what you say will be an ordeal."

And he went out, locking the door.

Left alone, Lyse slowly glanced around the bare stone walls of the room as if one place in it might be better than another to nurse her despair, then chose the stool by the hearth to slump on. Her thoughts swung miserably from her own dire predicament to the doom which was hanging over the heads of the people of the valley. If only she could send a warning to them, to the Voisins, if only... She shivered, contemplating again how alone she was. How could anyone even find out where she'd been taken?

It was insane to feel anger that Ferrante was so far away, it was she who had sent him away against his will, and ignored his warnings. She forced away everything in her mind but her picture of him, her dashing Mantuan; she remembered the revelation of their passion in the Scarf Dance, and of eyes the shade of summer leaves glistening when he was amused with her. She clung to the memory of the grace and patience behind his strength as he guided her in love. Her fingers tingled, as if she were smoothing her hand over the bulk of his naked shoulders, the hard muscles of his arms; she could feel the warmth of his throat as she pressed her lips there.

She closed her eyes in yearning, as she had done for months at Rennes, and rocking back and forth, pictured how they had lain intertwined together, for that moment becoming less than two and more than one, unable to let each other go. She hammered back the invading thoughts of Germain's grave illness, her poor governess' death, her uncle Charles branded traitor and bereft of his title and lands, and of Ferri's opinion that Rennes-le-Château harbored Cathars. She clung only to Ferrante in her mind because she drew strength from thinking of him.

He was probably at this moment a penitent widower, free now. Tears began to leak from the corners of her eyes, for her heart told her she would not survive to see her bright star again, her dearest love. She sat rocking on the stool and crying quietly in her captivity.

In a while she dragged herself over to the rude bed and pulled the wool blanket over herself, for she was shivering in spite of her cloak and stole. Her lips moved in a prayer that she would give the Lorraines nothing for their pains, that she might find enough control over her babbling of Mélline's knowledge to omit the Treasury's location, did Mélline even know it. She knew the best that awaited her afterwards was being flung into an *oubliette* and left to expire there. So she prayed God would let the *pastel* close down her mind and cause her to die.

And finally she prayed that Ferrante had at least loved her a little and would remember her with pity and regret when she was dead, and not as a 'peculiar' who was finally of no value. She prayed he had not seduced her only to counteract the weary months of inaction at Rennes-le-Château.

The superstitious De Marques had brought a priest to Valmigère as safeguard; not knowing what manner of sorcery might have to be dealt with. The cleric was a Dominican, wrinkle-browed, with bony shoulder under his white cassock and a gold filigree pectoral cross. In the morning this Father Plautus, who had spoken to Lyse before briefly, visibly half-curious and half-repelled by her, was again let into her chamber. She was sitting listlessly by the little fire once more, the bread and milk breakfast on a table barely touched.

He approached her cautiously, hands in his sleeve. "Will you pray with me, daughter?"

"Father—do they mean to murder me?"

Although the dark eyebrows went up in negation, the gaze underneath was non-committal. "Surely not. Because I am confessor to the *comte* de Marques, I can honestly confirm to you that he is a devout, God-fearing man. He merely wishes to help you to remember certain things."

But Lyse rose and stepped closer to him, hands clasped to her chest, for he was a man of God, after all, vowed to pray the Lord's mercy. She pleaded, "Father, the method they use to 'help me' will grievously harm me. Please, I beg you to dissuade them, I beg you—"

A jolt—the short cleric seemed to elongate—

"Stop, my daughter, do not ask what we cannot give," the sightless bishop thundered down at her bent head. *"There are two hundred Cathari refuging in safety at Le Bézu, along with numerous <u>parfaits</u>. We may not trade all those precious lives for that of only one man. His Holiness, Clément, has heretofore turned a blind eye to his Templar nephew in that remote eyrie, and to the nephew's guests as well, but now he will do so only if de la Motte is handed over to the Inquisition. As shepherd over the whole Aude valley, I must make demand of my flock to produce him. I make it now, to the only person who knows where de la Motte is. You must obey me, Mélline!"*

She raised tear-ravaged eyes to the milky orbs of the churchman whose secret sympathy with the beliefs of the remnant Cathars had for years sheltered their pitiful number from Catholic zealots who suspected their existence. Sad lines drew the man's mouth down into his fleshy jowls, but his jaw was set, adamant.

She grasped his hand to her breast. "I beg you, your Grace, I beg your mercy, oh, take this cup from my lips!"

With his other hand he stroked down her flowing hair, for she had had no time to array herself before his surprise, midnight visit. "Only you know where Bernard de la Motte is hiding, my daughter, only you can give him up. In your hands rests many hundreds of lives! In your hands rests the fate of your own soul at your death. God and the Devil battle for you now."

"But Monseigneur, Bernard will never give this murderous king the Templar Treasury, not if the Dominicans torture him to death. And so they will try, Monseigneur, most horribly," she moaned.

His sigh was deep and resigned. "I can, perhaps, mitigate the worst of that. There are favors to call in, and I promise I will ease him, trust me. But give the man up, you must."

She shrieked, "I will fling myself on the pyre first."

"Will that help the poor souls sheltered in Bézu? You alone will fling them on the pyre too!" the prelate thundered, grasping her shoulders with hard hands. "My Archbishop will not be deflected from his desire to please both Pope and king by delivering them the Templar gold; he hopes a cardinal's hat awaits him in Avignon. Since he has finally received the Holy Father's permission to invade Le Bézu, he demands de la Motte or else rivers of blood will spill at Le Bézu. Where

is your strength, woman?" the old man pounded at her, "where is your moral fiber to know where your duty lies? How will you cleanse your immortal soul of such heinous sin as the slaughter of so many of the Perfect God's innocents?"

Mélline collapsed at his feet, burying her hysterical sobs in her hands. "Ah, Dieu me sauve, I cannot—"

"You must, and you will, my poor child."

Lyse started, blinking, and discovered that tears were rolling down her cheeks. Father Pontius had backed away a little and was looking at her with trepidation. "You need not shed tears, daughter, no harm will come to you. Only relate to Monsieur de Marques what he wishes to know and, *voilà*, you will be freed." The priest's tonsured head nodded in a gesture of reassurance.

But Lyse dashed away the tears and felt herself filling with rage. "Get out!" she screamed, helplessly combining the terrible grief she had just remembered with her own present terror, "get out, you liar!"

He recoiled. "Mademoiselle!"

She pressed her hands to her ears. "No, I will not listen to your lies. I have nothing to tell these men and yet they will hurt me, and you, sworn to uphold the love of God, know it and will allow it. Get out!"

The priest frowned, then shrugged in assent, for he was not loathe to remove himself from the presence of this woman his patron said had witch-like powers. Turning at the door, he jabbed an accusing finger at her and cried, "None of us know when it is our time to die. Fall on your knees, lady, and pray God, if it is your time, to forgive your sins and cleanse you soul!"

His voice rebounded from the bare wall of the room, it mingled with the remnant of a blind bishop's voice demanding a dreadful sacrifice and Lyse blockaded her ears. She stumbled about the room in a tumult of emotional pain greater than her fear. Had Mélline really sent her own beloved to his death, the Knight Templar who had Ferrante's eyes?

"No, no, " she whispered brokenly, "dear Jesus, no!" and suspected at that moment that if the blue powder did not affect her reason permanently, the terrible, unrelenting burden of Mélline's agony would.

A few hours later they wrapped her in her cloak and blanket, wrists again tied behind her, and guards took her up on the battlements, for Ferri feared she was too weak and pale to withstand the coming session, having eaten very little in a couple of days; he decided she needed some air to revive her. Two of her captors stood very close, in case she thought to escape by launching herself into space.

The fresh breeze striking her face and blowing her tangled, coppery hair did call her back to life, enough even to note that the wide sky over the ranks of peaks before her was a brilliant, clear blue. She filled her lungs with the pine-scented air and she could smell it was spring. She lifted her face into the bright sunshine, letting its golden warmth soothe the ache of her spirit.

They allowed her only a short time up there and then prodded her below once more, and into the chamber where the Lorraines had quarreled the night before. De Marques was there, also the priest, but he was ordered to wait outside, so only the two Lorraines would hear what the *pastel* dragged out of her. A small table had been brought in, there was a brazier on it with charcoal aglow, and a chair before it. The guards made her sit on the chair, bound her to it, and when they left Ferri stationed himself by her side.

De Marques, behind the hot brazier, was smiling with pale lips. "Do not look so frightened, Mademoiselle de Bourbon-Tonnière, I am not the Grand Inquisitor, there are no branding irons heating." He opened the collar of his doublet. "You merely have to breathe in some of the smoke I shall make with this," he took a handful of dried and curled blue leaves from a sack, "and you will remember what we must know, for that is what you related to Ferri would happen with this treatment. 'Tis simple. And then we will release you."

"And what if I remember nothing," she asked faintly. "Will you release me then?"

"Remember nothing? But, lady, you will cooperate better than that or we shall just go on trying, you see, we have plenty of *pastel*. This might prove too much for you, as you have warned, that the plant may be deadly to your mind. So you will gather your forces quickly under its influence and make one great effort to 'see-back' and unlock the treasure's whereabouts. Eh, don't you agree?"

As he spoke, de Marques crumbled some leaves between his palms and scattered them onto the hot coals. For a few minute nothing occurred, and Lyse dared hope that the *pastel* wouldn't burn at all in this coarse form. But then there was a crackle, a pop, and a wisp of blue smoke erupted upward from the coals, followed by a larger plume. The two onlookers murmured, and de Marques made a sardonic bow to his prisoner.

Lyse stared at the rising smoke, traumatized, for it came not in the fine, mistlike cloud la Dame had evoked, but in dense puffs. De Marques had a fan made of a sheet of parchment in his hand; with his other hand he crumbled a great fistful of leaves and dropped them into the brazier as if scattering pearls. The red-orange glow of the coals cast a demonic light onto his bad skin and reflected in his shadowed eyes; if her wrists were not bound behind her Lyse would have crossed herself.

"Monsieur de Marques, for the sake of God," she croaked.

"Who is your God, woman, is it Beelzebub?" He gestured and Ferri kneed her chair closer to the brazier, then with cruel hands shoved her head forward and held it rigid into the smoke, so close to the heat her face felt as if it were baking in an oven—

withering heat, as screaming she darted toward the leaping flames to burn with him, for she had murdered him, that strong, vital life so dear to her, so committed to die for his brother Knights

Lyse coughed spasmodically, choking. The pressure on the back of her head lessened, she jerked back, searching for air. Her captors did not seem affected by the *pastel,* or in standing they were above the worst of it. Implacably, de Marques wielded the fan, sending a bluish cloud to envelope her—

dragging her by the waist away and back, pinning her arms, laughing roughly, "Stand back, woman, we've no order for roast hen today!"

Another hand grasped her, held her, she saw her husband's ring on one finger, she heard her husband's aged voice saying calmly, "Public spectacles always excite my poor wife. I will look after her, soldier."

"Good, Monsieur," the fellow agreed, his attention shifting to the animated crowd shouting their approval of the executions: eight malefactors crisping in the flames, four murderers, two witches and two Knights-Templars, the latter wretches probably the last they would see in these parts of these evil practitioners pretending to honor Christ.

She fell to her knees, baying her pain, and then a hard drop of rain hit her brow

Lyse blinked wildly, gagged, panted for breath, the fanning stopped and she was allowed to lean back, away from the heat of the glowing brazier that swam into her focus, away from the thickest part of the smoke. Her eyes teared, she felt exhausted, as if she'd been racing to catch hold of Lyse who was being obscured, crumpled up and torn away, and thrown so far she was dwindling from the earth.

"What does all that babbling of hers signify?" Ferri asked.

De Marques answered roughly, "She seems to believe she is at an execution.

But regard her. She uttered scarce twenty words and she is already looking sick and faint."

Ferri's attitude was scornful. "Not at all what we seek, is it. How do you intend to arrive at real information?"

"How should I know?" de Marques snarled. "But now I'll ask her questions, to the point. We'll just keep her at it, as long as we have to. We've a few days."

Ferri shuddered delicately. "The cords stand out on her neck, she shivers and cries out, she stares unseeing, like a demented one. We may kill her too soon and gain nothing. Louis, discontinue, I say, and let us get the sure advice of an alchemist who is learned in these things."

"*Merde*, what things? Who would have experience with such ability as this 'peculiar' claims besides a true warlock, who might ensorcel us all and take the gold for himself. You are too dainty, you flit. We will continue now!" he barked, to make Ferri move.

And to his fainting prisoner he barked, "The Cathar treasure, woman, the treasure, where was it hidden?"

Lyse felt Ferri press her head forward again, holding it steady by gripping her hair.

Her ears heard a hiss and crackle as more crumbled leaves hit the coals, and then a fresh, thick wave of choking smoke closed around her, closed over her head as if it were water; she thought it was water and that it was beautiful, and her suffocating, shrinking consciousness understood that she should not fight it, that this time she should drown forever in its blue, blue grip–

Chapter 27

One of Tournel's men yelled out and ducked as a skeleton tumbled down on him from a ledge where it had been stuffed; his cry reverberated from every corner of the vast cave through which the troop was passing, the sound impaling itself on mineral stalactites high above, sparkling like crystal from the light of their torches.

Ferrante gestured for his spread-out men to follow him, for he had found, in the wilderness of boulders and pinnacles covering the cavern's floor, the continuation of the upward path connecting the natural grottoes honey-combing the mountains.

There was a dull pounding behind his brow, not, he thought, from the restriction of the rough-hewn passages, with ceilings that often made him stoop, but from the tension that they would penetrate the Château Valmigère too late, that the young woman he had sworn to safeguard might have been already mishandled, perhaps even destroyed by the Lorraines' animosity toward Charles de Bourbon. With Louis de Marques he couldn't credit the shepherd's report that the abductors would wait to reach Albi before questioning Lyse-Magdalene.

It was not only his failed duty to Bourbon that caused him pain, far from it, for the angel-faced 'peculiar' Charles had bound him to had wormed her way under his skin. He had hoped once he re-entered the bustling world again that she would fade from his mind until he returned to Rennes-le-Château. Instead he had thought of her constantly through all the dire days of Aliesa's death and funeral rites; through days of recriminations heaped on his head by Aliesa's father, as if he had killed the deathly ill woman with his own hands, and by his brother the duke of Mantua's sour looks through the endless pro-cession of advocates and notaries to his cabinet—for his crippled wife had been an heiress twice, through aunt and grandfather.

During all of it, including his own gnawing remorse, the memory of having caused Lyse-Magdalene de Bourbon-Tonnière's lovely smile to often appear in their days together, redeemed him to himself a little.

It was not just that the copper-haired beauty hid an explosive passion behind her wide-eyed innocence; he'd taken to bed some females as seductive as that and yet escaped their clutches eventually. Nor even that Bourbon-Tonnière possessed bravery and a quick, bright mind. It was something else besides, maybe pity for her suffering under the weird ability which left scars on her mind, or pity for her solitary past. Or, on the other hand maybe it was even her fluting laugh, which touched a chord in him and set up a resonance linking him to this woman far beyond the duty of the betrothal documents.

It seemed Charles de Bourbon, during his short stay in Mantua, had confided the existence of this betrothal to the duke Federico, a liaison which any other time would have erased the ruler of Mantua's irritation with his younger brother, but whose impressiveness was reduced by Bourbon's disgraced and exiled status.

So it was not political importance either which made her different to him, this young woman so eager to taste the pleasures of life, yet so uneven, yea, suspect in her experience. But once the doomed Aliesa finally found her peace, he had strained like a dog on a leash against the affairs requiring his presence in order to return to the simple life of Rennes-le-Château and the 'peculiar' in his charge. To risk his life, in fact, against a royal warrant in order to bring her safely out of France. Again pity, perhaps? Or was he wound around her finger by her beauty and lush delight in sexual matters?

Or—a thought that upset him—was he in love with her? Was his attachment to her the bonds of a heart filled with love?

Swiftly repudiating the idea, he was almost certain what he felt was not love. Viewed against his previous performance with his wife, or with other charmers he'd encountered, he truly suspected he was incapable of the sacrificing spirit necessary to deeply love a woman: he was too selfish a man.

And yet, now his head ached in his panic for her safety, he who feared little else beyond the horror of being carted from a battlefield hopelessly blind or with missing limbs.

Lowering his torch he plunged headlong into the dark maw of an upward-slanting tunnel; and so acutely did he feel urgency that he preceded the guide la Dame had provided and loped along almost at a run. Behind him came the panting breath of armed and breast-plated men, Tournel's best soldiers.

Except for their own soft clinkings and footfalls oppressive silence reigned in the cold, constricted tunnels, the sort that Lyse always said she felt in the Razès, as Ferrante himself had sensed on both journeys to this mountain-girt arena of ancient slaughter and persecution. But he considered the tunnels less overwhelming than the five huge and echoing caverns they'd traversed in their small haloes of light, like flies creeping across black velvet voids.

The passage widened and a slap of air hit Ferrante's face, a draft from somewhere that guttered his torch backward. The guide behind him raised his own flaring torch as they came around a turn. "Look, Monsieur, we are at the end—" the man began, but inhaled the rest of his words.

A stair was carved up one wall, leading into darkness beyond the stone ceiling. But at the foot of the stair and in a swathe around it lay the skeletal remains of men fallen where they were killed, eye sockets black in grinning skulls, bones chalky in the light of the torches and overlaid by double-edge broadswords, rusty iron pike points, and crude metal casques. Any wood or leather had rotted away, but tattered remnants of chain mail gleamed dully amidst the carnage, and steel blades glinted in the dead embrace of white rib cages.

Ferrante's second in command, a wiry, experienced soldier from Reims, emerged behind him. "Wah! These poor souls must have been companion to the one that tumbled down on Coultoir's head back there."

Ferrante's nudged a corroded iron helmet with his toe. "'Twas quite a battle from the looks of it."

Another man emerged and crossed himself, goggling. "Who were these men, Monsieur?"

"Ancient attackers as we are, trying to breech the castle above and failing, it seems, long gone to heaven or hell. Sweep these remains from the stair, we have no time to commune with them. There's a draft coming down that stair, which means we've reached our goal."

Laying about with pike and sword, several men cleared the steps, the bones crumbling to dust as they struck the floor.

The treads were steep and entered a narrow shaft. Ferrante mounted first, ducking to avoid overhanging rock. Uneasy, he wondered why there was a breeze filtering down to them. La Dame's parchment showed the hidden entrance to the château via a door concealed in the chimney piece of a chamber used as a kitchen. At least, when the plan was drawn...

It had not been easy to access the secret pathway into Valmigère. The guide had brought them into a broken lower fortress via a precipitous goat path behind it, so de Marque's sentinels on the higher ridge would not spot them. But a huge boulder had come to rest on the cracked flags of a courtyard there, right atop the trapdoor that concealed a long, iron ladder down into the bowels of the mountain. It took the last failing hours of daylight to fell saplings to jam underneath the great rock as levers, and three straining men to work each pole before the obstruction groaned away.

And now they had no idea whether the outlet they sought at Valmigère would be bricked up, or baking behind a roaring kitchen fire, or ringed with guards eating their supper.

Their trudging, sliding, laborious descent-ascent within the belly of a mountain had been so disorienting Ferrante could only guess at the time. "What hour do you judge it?" he launched a loud whisper down the steps to one of Tournel's men who was celebrated for having an hourglass in his head.

"We have been negotiating the passage from the ruined château almost seven hours, Monsieur. Above, 'tis still night, perhaps an hour from dawn."

"Excellent. Just as we planned." At that hour if there were a kitchen fire it would be banked, they could easily scatter it.

Ferrante's plan, conceived in much haste, was dangerously simple. He had two advantages: the Lorraines would not be expecting any rescue attempt, thinking to have covered their tracks and location; and attack from within their own walls would not even be considered. Surprise, therefore, would work for him. Against him and his small party was the castle's larger force and his uncertainty as to Lyse-Magdalene's location. La Dame had ruled out a dungeon or *oubliette*, guessing that they'd keep her close to the main tower of the residence, where her captors probably slept.

Once he'd found her, getting her out was the trick, heavily dependent on going back through the tunnels, if they were not discovered, or, if that way was blocked, through a rear postern gate and down the forested mountain to where horses would be waiting.

Stealth, silence and luck would be their allies, along with correctly timing their foray with the dawn arrival at the gates of Tournel, with a force of Bourbon and Puivert men-at-arms and thirty village volunteers along with a siege cannon loaned by the mayor of Couiza, grateful to la Dame for having doctored his wife.

The plan was full of risk, relying on the careless vigilance of an enemy smug in the belief that no one challenged them, but Ferrante had no choice. Once the Lorraines' heavy reinforcements from Albi arrived, no force in the valley would be strong enough to wrest away their Bourbon prisoner. And once in Albi, in the bowels of the Episcopal Palace, Lyse-Magdalene would be unreachable.

The stair ended at a brick wall. Ferrante ran his fingers over this, finding a hairline, vertical crack running to the floor, then took a heavy knife from one of the men and, working quietly, carefully dug away at the crumbly mortar until hidden hinges were exposed. The men passed up a small vessel with a long, plugged spout. Ferrante wiped his brow on a forearm and poured olive oil liberally from the spout onto what was exposed of the hinges, top and bottom.

They waited for the oil to seep around the contact points of the rusty iron. Then the men in front put out their torches, and some crossed themselves.

Ferrante knelt, fumbled for the right brick, and scowling, pushed at it. Nothing. Drawing in his breath, he pushed again, harder. Nothing. The rustle and breathing behind him seemed abnormally loud.

They could blow up the door with gunpowder, but that would be heard. Ferrante's hand fumbled across the wall again, three up, three along—ah, he had been too high, he discovered, had miscounted— Heart backing up his throat, he spread strong fingers against the proper brick and with a silent Paternoster, shoved.

Several soft clicks as a spring let go, a faint sound of balls rolling, a dragging sound, and with only a tiny protest from the heavily oiled hinges, which nevertheless sounded to them like a cannon shot, the hidden door to Château Valmigère opened a crack, showing a faint glow.

With a soft snort of relief, Ferrante motioned to Lucco to hunker down with him, and they peered out into the kitchen, already wanly illuminated by the false light of pre-dawn from the clerestory windows.

Fortune was with them. There was only slight heat on their faces from cooling embers in a small grate on the hearth between them and two shadowy mounds snoring on the kitchen's great stone table, where it was a bit warmer than sleeping on the drafty floor.

"The cooks," Ferrante whispered. "Maybe one or two other men to either side, where we can't see. *Eh bien, mon homme,* give them leave to join their maker."

Lucco nodded with relish. He traveled as lightly as he trod, with only two wicked knives in his belt and a strangling cord. Feral concentration claimed his swarthy face, reddened as a devil's goblin by the embers' glow, as with stealthy care he pushed the door further open and stooped through.

One side of the wide hearth was blocked by a massive kettle hook and cauldron. Lucco tiptoed around the other side of the fire grate, then crept around a stack of firewood and out of sight to the left. Half a minute later there was a tiny squeal, hardly heard over the vigorous snoring of the blanket-wrapped men on the table. Ferrante smiled. So there had been a third man sleeping in the faded warmth of the kitchen fire.

Lucco reappeared, an indigo shade gliding silently toward his remaining victims. His arm lifted and fell, there was a slight convulsion of the mound he had chosen, and the snoring sounds were halved. He stepped around and in another moment all sound had fled the chamber as Lucco withdrew his twisted-blade dagger from the pierced throat of the last man, and wiped it off on the corpse's shoulder. He signaled to Ferrante to come ahead.

As his companions quickly stooped through the door in the back wall of the huge fireplace, Ferrante glanced anxiously up at the windows, where the light was somewhat rosier than when they'd arrived. They had made their goal just in time for Tournel to accomplish his part of the plan.

"We must wait, now. Throw those bodies in a cupboard," he ordered, "the watch might send someone for bread and cider. Stand to each side of the door. Lucco there, behind the table."

Ferrante helped drag the dead soldiers out of sight, and then ducked behind a stone cooking oil jar almost his height. Each moment that the dawn light brightened at the windows reminded him that this kitchen was where luck might leave them. His ears strained for the boisterous voices of men approaching, hungry for breakfast. His pulse was beating in an ominous rhythm, like the boom of a galley-master's drum.

Then they heard it, even through the thick, old walls, the shrieking blasts of the lookout's horn above, and a minute after another pitch of horn below the walls, again and again, like blessed Gabriel trying to wake the dead. Ferrante smiled to himself in relief. "Stand open the door," he hissed to his second, "let them look in and presume the three who were on duty here have hastened to the ramparts."

There was a confusion of shouts in the castle now, the pounding of running feet in the corridor, the clank of metal amidst loud curses, all heading away from them and toward the main gate, where Tournel had emerged from the forest-girt road with a bristling company of pikemen and cock-bowed archers, deployed so one could not tell how many were behind them. They were never enough to threaten a garrisoned castle, but enough to engage the attention, and the ridicule of the Lorraines' men.

Tournel's job was to hold the château's attention by whatever means, offering various ransoms, threatening a siege, even firing the cannon, anything to draw the defenders to the battlements and out of Ferrante's path.

Through their windows they heard his voice shouting at the battlements, but the words were indistinct. Then some soldiers clattered toward them, who, in the next moment glanced in the open kitchen door quickly as if hoping to grab some bread for their empty stomachs, thought better of it and hastened on their way. After this their vicinity was quiet, only the shouts from outside, angry from below, insulting and jeering from the walls, came to the raiders' ears.

Ferrante led his men out, swords drawn, and they loped through several empty chambers to a spiral stair housed in one of the towers, whose roof above surely held some of de Marque's archers. Quickly and silently they padded up one floor and then flitted through a series of rooms undiscovered, to Ferrante's relief.

Their object was the largest tower. La Dame had concentrated her strange eyes on the ancient plan and decided it was there the Lorraines would make their headquarters and guard their captive. Ferrante agreed; the staircases in the château towers made them quick of access and their windows gave inhabitants unobstructed, three-sided views of the territory.

They had better be right, Ferrante thought grimly as they pressed through a narrow corridor, for although Tournel would try to aim his siege piece away from the main tower, he had no experienced gunner, the stone balls shot wildly could kill them as well as their opponents.

Voices and footsteps in a hurry were approaching, but from behind them. His men slipped through the next doorway and Ferrante motioned them flat against the wall on either side of it. Two helmeted, half-armored guards hastened through and made it a few paces into the room before sensing it was inhabited.

One whirled with a grunt, his razor-edge pike blade horizontal, but too late to deflect Ferrante's sideways sword slice to the neck, delivered with such power it removed the man's head in a spout of blood; the gruesome, severed object, strapped into its peaked helmet, bounded on the floor and rolled away loudly. The other soldier fell right along with his companion, run through the guts by a Bourbon guard. Ignoring the fountaining blood, they managed to catch both bodies and avoid the loud crash of their metal breastplates meeting the ground.

"*Andale!*" Ferrante waved his soldiers on with his bloody sword. "Hurry." If the noise of the bouncing head had alerted someone's curiosity, their only ally was speed.

Two chambers further and in spite of their hurried stealth, they almost emerged within sight of a single guard standing before a closed door; they drew back just in time. Deciding they had found their goal in the mostly uninhabited castle, Ferrante nodded at Lucco, who adjusted his hat, drew the leather thong from his pocket, balled it in his fist, and sauntered from his doorway towards the guard.

They could hear the soldier, startled by this new face, demand to know who he was, and Lucco's accented, cheerful fabrication, just a local who had brought barley and fish to the cooks and wanted to wander the old castle. The puzzled guard lowered his halberd and turned to watch as the stranger ambled to the left of him towards another door, then he remembered that the kitchen was two floors below and called out to the interloper. He did not hear four of Ferrante's men creeping forward, but a sixth sense made him whirl, croaking a challenge, then defend himself with his halberd against the intruders' swords.

Lucco, forgotten, jumped on his back and staggered him, there was a flash of hand movement and the guard, eyes bulging, dropped his weapon to clamp hands to the cord strangling him, and then crumpled. He had been given no time to yell for aid.

The closed door was unlocked; they shut it again behind them. The chamber was empty but it had been inhabited and hastily left: a fire burned on the hearth, there were two cots, half-eaten food on the table, a chest with its lid open, and a belt purse of embroidered velvet. Ferrante sprinted another door at the far end and found it firmly locked. "Open it!" he barked to his men, and three of his raiders battered at the moldered wood which soon splintered and gave, and they stepped through.

There was little inside but a pallet near the embers of a fire where a still form lay, wrapped in a blanket, one pale, slim hand trailing lifelessly.

"*Sfaccimo!*" Ferrante swore, heart tightening, and dashed forward; only a dead person would not have heard their entrance. He dropped to his knees, grief beginning to grip him, and pressed the cold wrist for a pulse. It was shallow, but it was there.

They had not failed yet. Lyse-Magdalene was alive but more a wraith than a living person, still and pale as ice, lips colorless, crystalline blue eyes open but unseeing, staring at the ceiling. Dribble leaked from the corner of her mouth, her chest barely rose and fell. He lifted the blanket and saw she was dressed in her boy's clothes, and physically unharmed outwardly. Ferrante called her name and rubbed her cold hands in his palms, but her eyes never moved, no expression crossed her face.

"Lyse, it is Ferrante, I am taking you out of here. Please, *cara,* hear me, hold fast," he begged, dread overtaking him that the 'seeing-back' had claimed another mind.

"Signore, time passes," came Lucco's urgent reminder.

"Listen, we cannot take her through the tunnels, the way is too hard, she would never survive it," Ferrante snapped. "We'll have to chance the postern gate." He wrapped the limp woman more securely, rose and scooped her up. His men, nervous but alert, waited for orders. "Move. Back the way we came, and then into the kitchen court," he rapped.

Just then a great roar and a crash penetrated the room, and dust cascaded down from the ceiling, shaken by a close hit from Tournel's cannon. Another shout came through the window, coming from the battlements above, "Archers! Fire!" A whirr and then cries of dismay from below.

Ferrante ducked with his burden through the splintered door of Lyse-Magdalene's cell and into the larger room, just as Louis de Marques opened and stepped through the opposite portal, several soldiers at his back. Ferrante's scowl grew deeper. Their luck had run out.

"What! You?" the Lorraine goggled.

Ferrante allowed a cold smile to join his hostile expression

"I might wish you good morning, de Marques, except it will not be such a one for you."

Recovering fast, Louis returned him a poisonous sneer. "So, you somehow managed to get into my stronghold, you dung, but how did you think to exit with your useless prize? One of my men has already run to summon others here to me; what, I have triple your followers! You will never see the sky again."

Ferrante passed the staring woman that he carried to Le Caus, who quickly deposited her in a corner, out of the way of the coming struggle. The men at Ferrante's back had known from the beginning that no matter the odds, the scowling *condottiere* would never surrender.

"What did you do to her," Ferrante snarled.

"Why, not a thing, only just what she suggested to us most willingly. We treated her with every respect due a noble lady, of course, but this blue powder she told us about seemed to have adverse effect on her." Louis gave a casual shrug, although his eyes did not lose their wariness. "Of course she told us much before she finally fell silent, in spite of our efforts to revive her. The rest remains for the more expert questioners in Albi to extract."

"You have no remorse that you may have cruelly exposed this high-born young woman to insanity, or to death?" Ferrante's voice was hoarse with rage. He glared hatred at the same blackguard whose deliberate and vicious blow years ago had almost cost him his eye, and he wanted their game over with. Only one of them would ride away from this old hulk of a fortress.

Louis shrugged again, an oily smirk of confidence still on his face. "A Bourbon? After all, what are they worth now? "

More of the Lorraine men crowded in behind de Marques, swords and pikes ready for the outnumbered intruders at bay in the center of the room. Ferri pushed to the front of them, not a lute but a sword gripped in his slender hand now, and he sent Ferrante an arch, mimed kiss.

Another boom and heavy concussion shook the room; a wooden shutter on one hinge fell from a high window to crack on the floor. They heard a distant, distressed shout, "There's a ball through the drawbridge portal! Archers to the barbican rampart!"

The drawbridge was immobile, the guide had said, could not be pulled up. Ferrante wondered if Tournel could actually cross it and battle his way to them.

De Marques laughed, reading his thoughts. "You think that small rabble outside will help you? My archers have already gotten most of them."

Ferrante grated, "De Marques, let it be just you and me to fight for the prize. Whoever wins leaves here freely, along with the lady and his detachment of men, and who loses, dies. Let us gamble for it, Monsieur, unless you are afraid."

Louis square mouth grimaced. "Why should I fight you, Italian? I already have the prize, damaged as she is, and you, besides. My soldiers will finish off that riff-raff you are thinking can rescue you. There are strong *oubliettes* below, where the rats need company. Someone will find your skeletons a hundred years from now and kick your bones into dust." He slammed his sword back into its scabbard in deliberate insult and turned about. "Take their weapons from them," he ordered the guards behind him who wore the heraldic maroon tabards of the house of Lorraine. "I'm going to see that mob and its siege piece demolished."

He began to push through the path they opened.

"Do you tremble, you poltroon, you puling coward, do you walk away that your arm is not equal to mine? Nor has it ever been!" The fact was that de Marques was considered one of the most practiced and cunning swordsmen at Francois' volatile court. The Lorraine halted and whipped around, spine rigid.

Legs spread, sword held low, Ferrante sneered at de Marques. "Hah, Monsieur le Comte, so you expose to these men how you fear my sword? Fear it even more that the lance that sat you on your arse in the dust at the Cloth of Gold, and made you the laughing stock of all England and France, even to this day! Do you run away now, you sniveling, suck-arse coward? You owe me more revenge than just making you scared and ridiculous again."

All eyes stared at Louis de Marques, the brother of the powerful *duc* de Guise and feared for his brutality.

But Ferri warned, "Pay him no mind, Louis, he plays for time. You owe him nothing, let the great pig rot in a cell." The fine tip of his thin nose seemed to quiver with delight.

Ferrante chuckled darkly and pressed on with his taunting. "You piss in your breeches with fear of my arm, don't you Louis, hiding behind your guards. You know your men will have to kill me before they take me to a dungeon. But you they will surely recount to all of France a cowering chicken."

With a snick De Marque's gleaming sword seemed to jump to his hand, and in his other fist was a long dagger. He tore his short cape from its fastening at his neck and stepped forward, flexing thick shoulders. The pocked face was wiped of emotion. He spat, "You dare challenge me? If you still live when I've done with you, *éspece de cochon,* you will eat those very words because I promise to cut out your tongue and cram it down your throat!"

He advanced, and Ferrante backed up, and the Bourbon men behind him scattered to give them room. The woman whose secret memory each pursued slumped in a corner, forgotten under the tidal bore of male aggression.

Ferrante's desperate goal was to disarm de Marques, grab him, and use him as a shield to get them and Lyse out of the castle and behind Tournel's small force. But the bristling, enraged swordsman opposite him, filled with hate, would fall on his own weapon in defeat rather than suffer another humiliation at his hands. Ferrante did not fool himself. The Lorraine was a formidable dueler and had a superior force. Escape, even if he won, was unlikely.

As they circled before an opening attack, Ferrante, with the passion of the challenge pumping energy through every vein, made a swift gesture with the hand gripping his knife, flicking the thumb to his temple, lips and then to his heart. He heard Ferri's indrawn hiss and saw him, behind de Marques back, staring in comprehension. With an inward curse, he realized both his slip and the special knowledge behind the despicable 'dolly's' reaction. Now he needed to eliminate both Lorraines to clean the slate, and how many more were there in the room who guessed at the centuries-old covenant to which he belonged?

Chapter 28

A milky veil lay across Mélline's eyes through which she peeped but she could hear nothing, except for what sounded like the slap of the little waves she had once watched strike against the *quai* at Narbonne, and which now lapped at her temples.

She seemed to see warriors before her, both of them in shining steel breastplates, warily stepping about each other in a murder dance, swords and daggers ready to strike. How peculiar was their clothing, what of it she could discern through the blurring veil across her eyes. And she felt so sleepy.

And one of them was her love, Bernard.

She wanted to go to sleep now. In sleep there was peace. Forever.

When the stockier man finally attempted a purposeful strike it was as if he were floating through a blur; and the other man so languidly parried the heavy blow and so languidly danced back. She could make out that man's broad shoulders and the dark hair that had overgown his tonsure now, but not clearly his face. Even so, it was her beloved knight, her heart knew that. Then she thought dully, but how could that be? God has already received him.

And she, for her sins, had been cast into paralysis, all movement and hearing and speech gone, her very sight damped and wooly, a just punishment for all her horrid sins, nor not even enough. She would sleep soon. She had drunk down the blue death.

But the baby, this tiny daughter of Bernard's, whose life in her belly had stayed her sinner's hand, and whose birth had saddened, had drained her? Oh, calamity! And all *pour rien,* nothing, for nothing at all...

The duelers, with faces all blurred, sometimes floated about each other like dancers in a fairy glade, sometimes crouched like the hungry beasts of dreams. They clawed each other but she could not hear the clangor of deadly steel upon steel as they struck, or their grunts and heaving breaths, although she could imagine it. Oft had she watched Bernard and his brother knights, on their visits, practice swordsmanship on the grassy court.

Perhaps time passed. Perhaps it didn't. But the protagonists swimming in and out of her fixed and bleary vision did not tire of hacking at each other. Bernard was the more graceful, as always, his sword had always been swift as a serpent's tongue, but his dogged opponent was skillful at escaping being cloven in two, in order to aim slow and powerful blows and slashes of his own. Ah—and so again did he, the man's sword tip ripped the Templar knight in the thigh, and instantly followed with a crossbody strike. The sword with the rosy cross in its hilt flew up in an arc into the sky—slowly, so slowly, and then tumbled downward.

What could she do? She was dying.

The fighters, her knight with only a dagger, circled; the shorter aimed a sword blow, the other with bleeding leg vaulted away, over a table, then kept the table between them.

Mélline heard nothing but felt the floor shake beneath her. And the peculiarly armored men who watched the duel looked uneasy. But it was the monarch Philippe le Bel's forces, of course, his sappers mining the castle, invading to arrest the Knights-Templar, all the brave Cathars, and the poor female sinner who had taken her own life. She would sleep. Soon her eyes would close.

A swarthy fellow darted and scooped up the fallen, too slim sword, pursed his lips in a whistle she couldn't hear, and slung the weapon hilt-first, so that it flew slowly—very slowly, right into the taller man's hand. O, she knew him, her Bernard, now she could almost see his beautiful, assured smile.

Once more the blurry and silent dance of death commenced, one of the two antagonists must be killed, their swords were thin but very sharp. She remembered how the big broadswords whistled as they clove the air, wielded so powerfully they could sever arm or leg in one blow, even pierce chain mail.

Bernard's thigh was bright red.

But—her sweet knight had not died by the sword, he died as a martyr!

She wanted to blot out the grisly sight of the dreamily hacking, murderous pair, but she could only blink now and then. So she drew up her mind like one would close a drawstring purse and diminished it into darkness.

And opened it later, with someone's shout echoing away in her brain, in time to see the stocky one's blade slip off Bernard's steel cuirass, in time to see her Templar knock the offending sword away and lunge forward with his long, gleaming dagger, and rip upward from the crotch. She saw the other man in profile, mouth open and gushing out blood, weapons slowly dropping from lifeless fingers, a body slowly crumpling to the floor.

The tall champion, sweat glistening his face, his whole left leg crimson, stood over his victim. But when had he grown a beard to his face? She struggled to discern his expression, and made out it was righteous and stern, as befit a religious warrior; yet curiously bereft as he stared down at his dead enemy. Ah, Bernard, beloved, so tender was your heart—

The watchers seemed to surge toward each other with weapons seeking blood, and one group was larger than the other. With lethargic curiosity she saw some of them turn around toward a door as if at an intrusion, and then the others of their surprised group turned, they began hacking back through the door, and thus some were cut down by the men they had turned their backs on. She let her heavy lids close for just a moment, but when they crept open again all the combatants had disappeared.

The minion who had thrown the sword was binding one of his own white stockings tight about Bernard's wounded thigh. A soldier entered with a chest salute for Bernard, and Mélline, through her misty, slow sight, imagined she saw her knight's appreciative nod. And then with his determined scowl, as he gave an order.

But Bernard?

Bernard de la Motte had already sacrificed his life. Bernard was with God.

She was too dazed, too weary to care more. She longed for peace, for sleep, to join her lover in Heaven. But no. She was a fornicator, an adulteress, and a heinous betrayer. The torments of Hell would always be hers, they already were and by her own hand, the just price for her sins. She would not let the Holy Office's torturers abase her, no! She would sleep the blue death, eyes open, drift away, away, to embrace her eternal fate—drift away—

She felt a stinging blow to her face, painful stinging. Bernard's deep voice came breaking over her, "—come back! Devil take it, you will not leave this world—" Then there was a long time of motion, choppy, like that of a horse, the movement reverberating in her breastbone, although she seemed to be held like a child in God's arms. It faded finally, the rocking. But not completely. Drift away...

More stinging hurt on her face, both sides, shattering her peace. She resisted pathetically, she did not wish to remain in this world, leave me be, leave me...

She was choking again, a flame seemed to run up her nose.

Lora Voisins rubbed the fingers that had slapped the Bourbon girl's face so hard. "Her pupils have dilated," she announced victoriously to Ferrante. "See, there is some comprehension in her eyes, she is coming back to her senses.

Ferrante watched the woman's fingers press hard against the soft, white temples as Lora once more concentrated her otherworldly stare into the patient's open, unblinking eyes. Then she picked up the ammonia-soaked swab again and held it once more under Lyse's nose, in spite of the girl's coughing and weak head thrashing.

When la Dame relinquished her place beside the bed, Ferrante stepped in to take his mistress' cold hand in his. He noted that some color had come back into her lips, although her cheeks were still alabaster. "Lysette," he called to her, "please hear me. You are safe, we are in Rennes-le-Château. Wake up, Mademoiselle."

Her reddish lashes blinked, a faint frown creased the skin between her brows, and she struggled to focus her eyes.

Premature relief flooded Ferrante when he saw a small movement of her lips, as if she would speak. "Speak to me, lady, say how you are," he urged softly.

She was looking at him. Her eyes began wandering his face and his heart leaped as he saw them brighten.

"Bernard!" she whispered.

Impulsively he planted a kiss on her hand in gratitude. "Ah, *Deus gratias!* No, I am Ferrante. And you are Lyse-Magdalene."

"Bernard." Sadness touched her voice. She drew her hand away from him. "You must not touch me," she whispered, "your dear blood is on my hands. Do not hate me."

Cautious, non-plussed, he tried again, emphasizing her full name, and the year, and his name, and where they were, and reminding her of her uncle Charles.

But the young woman on the bed stared at him blankly, as unreceptive as if she did not understand the language. She seemed to be reading his lips. "I pray you, do not despise me, sir. Do not curse me in my purgatory."

"Lyse-Magdalene, I am *not* Bernard de la Motte. This is the fifteen hundredth and twenty-fifth year of our Lord, and I am Ferrante di Gonzaga of Mantua. Listen to me, look at me! Open your mind again."

There was hazy awareness in her eyes as she obediently watched his face, but it was evident she was seeing a different world than his. He shook her gently by the arm and reiterated who she was, recalling to her St. Piteu, Madame de Dunois, the dancing at Puivert— But she gave no sign of recognition, nor even of much interest, merely repeating, "*Mon* Bernard, forgive me," in an uninflected voice and an empty tilt of head.

He rose and asked harshly of la Dame, who observed with a smoking potion in her hand, "What shall we do? She is totally lost in her own mind.

How do we bring her back?" He did not care that his anguish showed in his tone.

La Dame leaned over her patient. "But, you know, she may be irretrievable," the husky voice opined coolly, little pity in the tone. She glanced up at Ferrante's scowl. "We must always face that, *condottiere*. I will need some time to consult my old Greek tomes for other strong specifics to clear the brain. Galen had many such medicines."

"We have only a few hours to restore her at least to traveling health. When the soldiers coming from Albi discover what has transpired at Valmigère they will send back to the Cardinal for instructions, and he will certainly dispatch them to this mountain at all speed. Worse, if one of the Lorraines is in command of that escort, they will ride here directly. I dare count on only twenty-four hours to get her to safety, and even that lead is doubtful."

"Where will you take her?"

"Out of France. To Collioure where the ship that brought me is probably still taking on cargo, or failing that, to Perpignan for a sailing to anywhere out of Francois' long grasp. Some of de Marques' men escaped the additional Puivert force the *marquise* had dispatched, who had come through the tunnel and attacked the Lorraines strongly from the rear. They will give the arriving troops a good description of me, the raider who stole their prisoner and killed Louis de Marques. De Guise will proclaim his brother's death as murderous Bourbon vengeance, which will enlist the king's regiments in capturing Lyse-Magdalene and myself."

"But the Treasury you came after?"

Ferrante shook his head at the present enormity of completing their task, but he answered, "If I could only find out how much she recalled under that murderous dose of *pastel*, and how many of de Marques people heard her."

La Dame blew out her lips with a denigrating puff. "You may be certain it was only Ferri and de Marques, and perhaps their priest. Would you want any more people privy to so precious as secret as the location of the Treasury? But would they have had time to send off their findings to the cardinal at Albi?"

"That is my deep concern. When Lyse-Magdalene recovers–" Ferrante refused to believe she might not "–and if she has recalled the Treasury's location, I will find a way back into Languedoc with enough men to transport the horde out. But if the cardinal or de Guise already know the location, we are lost, and so will be the cause of Charles de Bourbon."

"I wish good fortune for you. And for him." A mean smile spread on the generous mouth. "Don Ferrante, if you have need of strong persuasion for that lying maggot we hold down below, I have a tincture that scorches the insides like the fires of Hell, but does not kill for a long while and until many doses." But Ferrante did not want any help. "Madame, turn your attention to Mademoiselle and the meagerness of our time. I will be concerned with the Lorraine."

La Dame made a frustrated *moué*, then shrugged.

She turned to administer the foaming draught in her hand to the patient, who was limply propped against pillows, and who had followed their conversation with uncomprehending eyes from which tears leaked unheeded, and from whose mouth now issued weak, mewling noises of grief as Ferrante stalked from the chamber.

Below the tower where the Voisins resided was a dank cell barred from arched ceiling to floor, ordinarily the domain of rats, now a cage for Ferri, hands manacled, sitting head on bent knees on a heap of dirty straw, a single candle outside the bars lighting the musty dark. As Ferrante came down the stone steps with Tournel and LeCaus, torches flaring, the prisoner lifted his head a moment, then dropped it, as if he had no interest in them.

Ferrante left his companions on the landing, out of earshot, and descending further, took out a key for the heavy padlock la Dame had furnished. He scooped up a battered chair leaning against a wall, and pulling open the chain that had secured the door, entered. He deposited his armless chair and sat backwards on it, contemplating the top of his prisoner's fair head with cold eyes.

"I promise you, Monsieur, it will behoove you to speak with me," he said evenly.

After a moment, Ferri raised his head, revealing a spiteful expression. "Truly, *condottiere*? I cannot imagine why. No matter what I do, you will eventually murder me." The oblong eyes glared balefully into his jailer's glittering gaze. "Just as your men ran through my friend, without mercy."

Ferrante shrugged. "Once a man picks up a sword, he has already made his wager with death. But you are wrong about my intentions towards you, you treacherous viper, although I would be happy to string your lute with your own guts. What will keep the breath in your lungs is your value to me as a hostage, in exchange for safe-passage from France if your brother de Guise and his men apprehend us. Nevertheless, I must have your frank confession as to what you learned from Mademoiselle de Bourbon-Tonnière."

Ferri snickered and stretched out his straw-flecked legs. "I could tell you anything at all. Why would you believe me?"

"Because you won't tell me anything at all. You'll tell me the truth. I will know it when I hear it," Ferrante said in a pleasant tone.

Ferri laughed insolently and shut his mouth. Languidly he picked straw from his shoulders, and acted as if Ferrante had disappeared. Ferrante had to give the unnatural bugger credit for courage.

The chair shot away with a clatter as he lunged and yanked the slight man almost into the air by the front of his doublet. "I suggest you take me seriously, Ferri, I have no compunction about crushing your fingers so thoroughly you will never use them again to strum your ballades or deceive women into harboring a snake. Tell me, what did Mademoiselle say once you began suffocating her with the blue smoke? "

"Nothing. She coughed," Ferri got out in a strangled but defiant voice.

Ferrante let loose a smashing, flat-hand blow to his captive's face; blood erupted from the musician's split lip. "That is with an open hand, Monsieur. The next one will scatter your teeth. I only promised to try and keep you alive. I didn't say in what condition." He yanked Ferri's red-blotched face back by his hair. "You have five seconds to speak or my men will bring down a vise which will oil your tongue. Both thumbs crushed first."

He had hit the right threat; making music and raising sleek hounds were Ferri's only real love.

"Yes, yes, *arretez*, I'll tell you! Why not, since I've already sent the information to Albi in time for the imminent arrival of my brother, de Guise." He wiped the blood from his cut lip on his raised shoulder.

Ferrante's heart sank. This was a death knell to Bourbon's hopes. But he growled, "How do I know this is true? Why would you send a message off to Albi if the troop you were expecting would soon convey you there in person?"

"Because it was at my miserable brother Louis' insistence that we questioned Bourbon-Tonnière ourselves, to gain a more favorable share of the prize. I was against crossing de Guise."

The collar of his doublet was cutting into his throat in Ferrante's grip, he choked and Ferrante opened his fist, letting the slim man collapse onto the straw. But panting, Ferri got up on his knees.

"*Écoutez*, Gonzaga, when I saw my former lady of the lute with bloodless lips and shallow breath, my courage left me for my elder brother's wrath," Ferri muttered, Adam's apple bobbing. "Claude de Guise is remorseless, he has made even blood relatives disappear off the face of the earth for less than the killing of a woman who might have put untold new wealth into his coffers. I sent off a messenger in secret, to deny any hand of mine in the business and curry favor by providing what Louis planned to withhold."

There was no mistaking Ferrante's disgust. "That treachery seems consistent with your nature. But who else was privy to that session with the *pastel*?"

"No one else at Valmigère, just Louis and me. The priest you've taken prisoner waited without the door, in case she fared badly and needed absolution. We would not have let her die unshaven, without the Lord's words." He made the sign of the cross on his chest and staggered up to his feet. "In any case, Father Plautus can confirm I sent off the messenger that night, to Albi. It was easy, Louis was in a drunken stupor, the imbecile."

Ferrante raised an eyebrow. "You seem not to have liked your departed brother."

Ferri stared down at his dusty boots, then turned up eyes full of malice. "Because he liked me all too well when I was a child, seven or eight. He took my virginity as easily as he took my sister's, but me he beat unmercifully where it would not show, so that I would not tell anyone. I have always hated him, the whoreson." He suddenly flicked Ferrante an arch look and added in a higher voice, "Some men are so brutal."

Ferrante tossed the chair over to him. "Sit on that. We are wasting time. Tell me swiftly and clearly everything that Mademoiselle de Bourbon-Tonnière said under the influence of the *pastel*."

But Ferri had withdrawn into himself, as if fighting reminder of his nasty childhood. His eyes stared at the straw and his mouth pouted. He didn't answer.

Ferrante lost patience and grabbed one of his wrists. He snarled, "I swear to you, we may not have such sophisticated equipment to wring you out as the Grand Inquisitor, but you will not at all enjoy our attentions, Monsieur." He seized the musician's long forefinger and middle finger and squeezed them hard in his fist, there was an ugly crack and Ferri screamed.

"Talk!"

Tears of shock leaked down the lutanist's cheeks as he cradled his throbbing hand against his chest. "Mantuan dog! My brother de Guise values me, he will kill you for this," he gasped.

"Those broken fingers will heal. The crushing work of the vise will not, and in the end the ruined hand must be amputated, if not the whole arm." After a moment of silence, with the Lorraine only glaring at him with swimming eyes, Ferrante stepped to the bars and summoned Tournel to bring in the vise.

Hastily Ferri cried, "Very well, I will tell you, for whatever good it will do you, now that de Guise will soon know the same." Ferri's narrow face had greyed, his arm trembled. "The woman moaned about fire and her sins and the death of a man named Bernard. We made out, finally, that he was one of the heretical Knights-Templar condemned by the Holy Church. Much that she mumbled made no sense, and at times she said nothing, merely moaned. Then, finally she talked about a parchment this Bernard had given her, and then she seemed to be reading aloud from it."

Suspense made Ferrante's heart pound. "What did she read out from that parchment?"

"For God's sake, just numbers," the Lorraine moaned in pain. "A list of numbers in no special order, twenty-one, fifty-six, one hundred thirty, ninety, in that manner. A code, of course, corresponding to words in some book, and I wrote down as much as she muttered. But that was all, I swear by all the good Saints. We were sore disappointed, but it was interesting to discover that it was the vast Templar Treasury you were after, not the old Cathar coffers."

Ferrante scowled down at him. So far Ferri had given de Guise only what his own camp already knew, except for those numbers. But what and where was the code book? "What more?" he prodded. "Surely she must have pinpointed the location of the Treasury to make your almost murdering her worthwhile?"

Ferri could not hold back a taunting smirk. "Ah, but I see neither do you know it."

But at Ferrante's step forward he held up his good hand, and it was shaking. "No, no, leave me be, I'll continue. She seemed to speak to somebody then, in agitation, crying that it was the work of the Devil and shriveled her poor soul; that she was going to throw it, something, into the fire. She sobbed and said only one clear phrase more, then began to pant shallowly and drool, and her pupils grew to the size of her eyes.

"We brought her into the air, but we could not rouse her, she seemed reduced to paralysis. Louis decided to leave her be until Albi, where the physicians could revive her."

A tangle of sensations raged within Ferrante, fury that these men had callously endangered Lyse-Magdalene's life, and relief mixed with chagrin that the Treasury's location seemed as elusive as ever.

"And what was that, the last phrase she said?" he growled, and as a cooperation reminder pulled one by one on his own fingers so that the knuckles cracked loudly.

The slight lutanist huddled abjectly on the low chair moaning over his broken digits, shuddered at the sounds. "She said a few words only making no sense. She cried out, as if bad tempered, "It has drowned!" Several moments later she grabbed at her belly and screamed. Then she uttered no more, just stared as if her senses had left her." The tilted eyes slyly slid up to the bearded Italian looming over him. "Did it ever occur to you, Gonzaga, that your lady might be mad altogether? I hear her mother died foam-mouthed in a raving fit."

It had once occurred to Ferrante, and the Lorraine's words sped like arrows to bury themselves painfully in his brain. He struggled to contain his need to crush the malicious young nobleman like a bug.

"You *odure!* Did you think she was insane when you instructed her for hours on the lute and sang pretty songs with her?"

"No, she was pleasant and handled the music decently. But women–! Who can know about such crafty creatures, eh?" Ferri had turned arch again.

"And so you wrote all of this to the *duc* de Guise?"

"Just as I've told you. To dig out the rest of her knowledge would have to await Albi where she would be shifted to the cardinal's tender mercies." Ferri made a careless gesture with his good hand, as if it no longer mattered to him.

Ferrante rubbed his beard to think. He believed Ferri, mostly, that the ab-ductors had learned little to help them. He intended to question the frightened priest they were holding upstairs for what corroboration he could supply, and then he intended to question Ferri again, for if the treacherous bugger was lying and Lyse had actually supplied them the name of the tome on which the code numbers were written, Charles de Bourbon's invasion hopes were over.

Well, they were over in regard to Lyse-Magdalene anyway, for Ferrante knew he could not allow the poor girl to suffer another assault on her life just to coerce her memory. He had to hide her under his own brother's powerful, protecting wing. But to do this he had to remove her from France, and to do this he had been candid; the youngest Lorraine would be their living shield until they reached Italy.

With an icy stare he contemplated Ferri. "Someone around here may be merciful enough to splint your fingers for you. Meanwhile, think again, musician, of what else you might have learned from poisoning Mademoiselle and remember the terrible sound of fingers breaking. Mayhap your hands, too, in our next session."

He refastened the padlock on the chain, stared hard at the intimidated, softly moaning but sullen musician huddled on the chair, and then bounded up the steps to where his men waited.

The trembling cleric was happy to blurt out whatever he knew that might save his life; but it turned out he thought the Bourbon woman had only been abducted and put to the question so the Lorraines could learn Charles de Bourbon's whereabouts. Still, he corroborated that Ferri had surreptitiously sent a messenger off to Albi as soon as Monsieur *le Comte* de Marques was too drunk to know.

This confirmed Ferrante's sense of urgency, no matter the good distance between Rennes-le-Château and Albi, a city almost as large as Toulouse. The duke de Guise would come after them relentlessly for his brother's death, coveting all the more Lyse-Magdalene de Bourbon-Tonnière and the last piece of the special knowledge that could be wrung from her–if Ferri were to be believed that the 'key' code was still unknown.

Ferrante could not protect her here as he could in Italy. And anyhow, he believed that the Razès and Rennes-le-Château had already worked any magic they had, beneficial and destructive. What remained of the Bourbon princess' 'seeing-back' might be forever locked up in her damaged mind.

He knocked, then let himself into Lyse's chamber, and Marye got up from her stool and retired across the room as he approached. He uttered a quiet greeting to la Dame, who stood by the bed, a small glass rod in her fingers.

He felt his tense features relax and a relieved smile come up, for the young woman he had held in his arms months back, and taken several times to bed, was sitting up and smiling too. She looked fragile and still tired, but her sweet, guileless face was alight with recognition. Her flowing, silky hair was held back by a white cloth, and smoking leaves in a little dish released the happy smell of mint into the air.

He walked up to her and murmured with pleasure, "Lysette!" not even wondering any longer that the very sight of this damaged and haunted 'peculiar' could set his heart jumping in his chest.

"O, Bernard, dearest one! How come we to rest in God's lap together?"

Ferrante stopped dead, his smile freezing over, but she went on eagerly, radiant, although she seemed not to look quite squarely at him, "O, my dear love, how much I have suffered, but the Lord of Heaven has forgiven me and brought me to you."

It was like a physical blow to the stomach. She was still wandering in her mind! He could see now that her guileless face as she looked up at him was empty, void of the complex shadings of personality that made her Lyse-Magdalene. Distressed, Ferrante glanced at la Dame, standing tall and straight and studying her patient. The lady shook her head.

"I have given her first an antimony purge and then an infusion to cool the brain, of cucumber seeds, violets, aloes and camomile, also a plaster to her feet of pigeon dung and gentian, and as you can see she is very much brighter–the same effect as if I would have allowed that barbarous bleeding, but with no drain on the strength. Just now I put seven slippery elm and quinine drops into each ear to drain through and lubricate her brain, for in a moment

I will administer a strong sneezing powder, of hellebore root, to rock her loose from her ancient memories."

She saw his dashed disappointment. "Speak with her, if you will, but only for a moment, the ear drops need to be followed up quickly."

Ferrante sat down next to the slim form; her light blue eyes with the baby-like crease under them followed him, blank as the turquoise and pearl orbs of a doll. For the time la Dame allowed him, he patiently repeated to Lyse who she was, who he was, the date, he even recounted her near-fatal fall in the gorge, hoping the frightening memory would bring her to herself. Dutifully she listened, but said nothing.

At last she patted his face, and with a hopeful smile, whispered, "See, my well-beloved, I divulged them nothing."

La Dame turned about from the beaker she stirred, and Ferrante held his breath. Was she breaking through at last?

The wide eyes blinked. "The letter you left with me, to the Scots Templars, you were right not to invest me with what it said, for the churchmen threatened me with the question and I had no fear to betray you again, no matter the worst they could do. But since the letter was delivered to the Scots, and my duty done, naught moved me but that I should join you in the world of the consoled, Bernard, and I wept for God to forgive my tortured soul its sins.

"And so he has, for regard -" Her gaze wobbled about the room, "-we have escaped the wheel of the evil world and climbed, both, to Heaven. How happy I am!"

She did not notice Ferrante's miserable sigh.

La Dame muttered, "In her body she will be able to withstand a journey by tomorrow, she eagerly swallows the nutritious stew we put in her mouth. And she may ride too, if you go slowly and watch her."

"And her mind, by tomorrow?"

"Who can say? I shall spare no effort in the short time we have. But the mind of a young woman is delicate and the *pastel* is shattering in too high a dose. The slippage of her memory may be irreversible."

"Do you mean she is mad?"

The silvery eyes the Junoesque woman swung to him again were like whirling vortices. "You must face the possibility, Don Ferrante. I have read in my old tomes that women with this strange 'seeing-back' affliction seldom escape that. But return here at midnight, when the moon sets and Jupiter is in the south. I am brewing the most powerful brain stimulant I know. It did not reach Madame de Dunois in her coma, but she was physically hurt and unconscious. But for Mademoiselle, I have another idea on how to administer it."

La Dame's full lips clamped into a stern line. Madame de Dunois' death had upset her, challenging her herbal medicine and then invalidating it. She would not welcome another failure.

Her patient having fallen into an exhausted sleep after sneezing painfully hard forty times, la Dame returned to her own quarters in the tower, where the *sieur* awaited her.

Robert de Voisin followed her around as she extracted with a metal pincers a small bezoar stone from a jar, two pearls the size of a baby's fingernail off a thin strand, some theriac, some shredded viper's flesh, and a selection of spices, and began to pound them together in a marble mortar.

"Do you not think we should also quit the Razès for a while, Madame?" he asked, somewhat nervously. "We could sojourn a few week with my brother in Montpelier."

"And leave my cabinet here to invading soldiers who will destroy it, for we have no time to pack it up properly? And what about Monseigneur in the tomb? The old man will starve to death."

"Might we take him along? "

She brought the full weight of her stare to bear on her husband and he wilted, hangdog. "Your concern clouds your judgement, dear man. His heart and old body would not survive the shock of the world beyond his hermitage. No, we remain here. We will claim ignorance of everything, leave it to me."

"They will not believe you. Everyone knows the *duc* de Bourbon is admired in the Razès, and that we have sheltered distinctive and distinguished guests lately."

"Ah, guests? We merely offered a roof to an obscure young girl and a foreigner. But if we run we admit complicity in any crime for which the authorities seek redress." She continued pounding in the mortar, grunting, her wide, folded back sleeves shaking with the effort. "I have not had to do this heavy grinding of late, I miss young Germain's strong and willing arm, but, thanks be, he will soon don his apron again. Still, I believe he will be too weak to leave with his *princesse*." She smiled down with satisfaction into her the mixture she was pulverizing, which she would then combine with ass's milk, a few drops of ammonia and a drop of urine.

But the normally cheerful little *sieur* could not tolerate her calm; with uncharacteristic assertion he grabbed her pounding arm and cried, "For the Lord's sake, cease, Lora, how can you ignore the terrible danger this fraudulent musician below represents to us all? Did not Germain relate to you how the three of them tinkered with the round altar in the old church and found our

Cathar emblem of wisdom? The Bourbon Mademoiselle, she has learned to keep certain damning things silent, and Germain you can control, but the prisoner down there is a Lorraine, a fervent Catholic of Rome, and he has witnessed the Single Eye of God here in Rennes-le-Château. He will confess it to those who know what it signifies, perhaps he has already confided in the priest they captured with him. Do you wish the harsh attentions of the Holy Office? If they come to focus upon this area again we are all lost. We must do something!"

"Yes, *mon ami,* I know," his wife answered, gently removing his grip and reaching for a wooden spatula.

But still he confronted her. "Don Ferrante is taking the Lorraine along to use as hostage, in exchange for their safety. I understand that they need such protection from de Guise's power, but we, you and me and all our brethren, cannot afford any breath of exposure. If the Mantuan gives the man up afterward, back to de Guise, it may be disaster for us."

"*Mais oui,* I know that," la Dame said calmly. "After all these year, do you tell me my duty, husband? I intend to take care of the problem."

"Perhaps Gonzaga will not let you? I trust him, certainly, but he is obviously smitten with the young woman and intends to protect her by any means, and the heart will bend any circumstance in favor of the beloved. Do I not know this?" he said, looking at her with puppy eyes.

"Then trust me, I beg you. The Mantuan will have nothing to say over it." She stopped her mixing and stared into the distance, as if considering something. She absently began twisting the large ring on her finger.

Late that night, la Dame, carrying a double candlebranch through the dark rooms, first visited the priest, Father Plautus. She was given access by the sleepy guard before his door, who, when she left, a quarter hour later, looked in to see the tonsured cleric from the back as he sat hunched at his table, reading in a little book. The guard nodded and closed the door.

Then the chatelaine of Rennes-le-Château returned to her tower for some straight, sturdy sticks and binding, and descended to the dungeon, where she greeted the Bourbon guard by name and showed him the splints. He nodded and obliged her request by strolling out of earshot as soon as he had unfastened the cell's chain. The rattling had awakened Ferri. He came alert quickly, like a nervous dog.

With her large smile la Dame showed him the sticks to set his fingers and his lips trembled. He eyed her suspiciously and relaxed only very little, but he held out his hand, with the two fingers grossly swollen and muttered, "I thank you."

Chapter 29

At dawn the next morning Ferrante stormed into Lora de Voisin's tower chamber before she was quite finished with her toilette, so, dismissing Marye, she faced him with her thick silver hair flowing about her olive face. He wore a scowl so furious it would have cowed any lesser woman.

"What has happened to our prisoners?"

She chuckled low, without mirth. "Life, I suppose."

"No, Madame, death, and well you know it! At my touch the priest fell out of his chair, blue and cold. No marks upon him that one could see."

"Ah well, the Lord join him to his spirit, his heart must have stopped. He was not young."

Ferrante strode over and grabbed her arm in his fury, but she barely blinked. He bit off, "No, but Ferri was young! *Was,* Lora, for he too lies dead and cold in his locked cell, with no mark upon him, and the guards say they only admitted you. What in damnation have you done!"

She jerked her arm away, imperiously. "Yes, 'twas me, no point in denying it. A little poison on a needle in my ring, a quick jab they barely felt, and in minutes it reached the heart and they expired, no foam on the mouth, no convulsions, did they not look peaceful? 'Tis an old Arab preparation much beloved of the Bey of Egypt. Very convenient and neat."

"Beelzebub take it, woman, why? You know I intended to use the Lorraine as a shield. He was important to me. You had no right..."

She rounded on him. "I had every right, for you are forgetting what is most important in your zeal to rescue that girl. Ferri had gotten a glimpse of the All-Seeing Eye, which Germain innocently mentioned to me. But our little troubadour was a Lorraine, a deadly enemy. Any hint of Cathar leanings whispered to the Holy Office by so illustrious a family and the Catholic torture chambers would ring with our shrieks. He had to be silenced, amidst prayers that he'd had no time to inform anyone else in his wish to keep the glory of uncovering us only for himself. Remember who you are. What are a few lives, yours, hers, the *sieur*'s or mine, against the safety of so many? Think! Recover yourself!"

Her harsh words washed over Ferrante like the shock of a cold wave, dampening his anger. He deflated, letting his breath out slowly as he glared at her, but he subsided. His next utterance was less heated. "And the priest? Did you think Ferri confessed to him his suspicions?"

The fleshy shoulder shrugged. "One doubts it. I reason, why would he share the glory of such discovery with a non-entity when he could personally take it to the Chief Inquisitor and alone reap the laurels? Still, care had to be taken."

"I had every intention of doing away with the Lorraine flit once Lyse-Magdalene reached safety. You should have trusted me."

"And if he escaped first? Or you were forced to trade his life for hers?" la Dame's wide mouth turned up sardonically. "Oh, I knew in the long run you would remember where lies your greatest duty, but I only thought to spare you such pain, *condottiere*."

He responded coldly, "I did not need your help, Madame. You should have consulted me."

"This is my home, Signore, I need not consult anyone about what goes on in it," she rapped, just as coldly. "The deed is done, and chance of misfortune for us lessened."

Scowling into her eyes, Ferrante again felt as if he were falling into them as the silver stare seemed to whirl and deepen and lose its bottom.

He shook his head with a flip to clear it, but his irritation still smoldered. "You are right, the deed is done," he growled. "Now my need is doubly great to remove Bourbon-Tonnière from France."

"Good," she agreed, and her voice changed to a purr. "So let us go to your charge and see her condition; she was calmly sleeping when Marye came to me. If she is addled still when she wakes, I have another formula to try."

"One way or the other, we both depart by noon."

"Both? Only two?"

"The least number draws the least attention. I have already sent one of the Collinis ahead to Collioure, where the ship I arrived in may still be loading cargo for the return trip. Lucco will book us accommodations, and contact the friend there that you mentioned."

He took stock of her steady look, which was reminding him he'd forgotten something, then grudgingly inquired, "How does her minion, Germain Matz?"

"He will survive, but he is very weak, he could not support the ride yet."

"You will keep him here, then," Ferrante agreed, knowing that was what she wished, and that was the end of the subject. Impatiently he gestured for her to precede him through the door.

They found Lyse still slumbering. Marye's daughter showed them the small remains of the bread and meat soup the patient had devoured for breakfast and then gone back to sleep. The girl reported in bewilderment, "Mademoiselle was smiling, and well able to walk about the room, and she gazed from the window wondering why the stables seemed so dilapidated and old. But she did not know my name, and she speaks of a person called 'Bernard'."

They stood at the bedside looking down. Lyse-Magdalene slept on her back, her face turned from them, but they could see healthy pink in the cheek on which lay the fringe of coppery lashes.

"Physically, at least, I believe I have given her back her health," la Dame murmured.

Ferrante's lips compressed as he watched the girl's easy breathing. "I want her mind back," he whispered harshly.

The silver-grey eyes slid towards him cynically. "Yes, I am sure you do. I will do what more is possible. She is strong and she has come a long way from the somnambulist you fetched here yesterday."

"But I want her as herself," Ferrante demanded. He saw a shadow of female jealousy enter la Dame's expression and was quick to add, "We can't forget she is still quite necessary to Monseigneur de Bourbon."

He nodded and turned on his heel to finish travel preparations.

Handkerchief to nose, Claude de Guise stalked away from the sprawled, bloated bodies in the room, one of which was his own brother who had been ripped from groin to stomach, and twitched his head at his guard captain. "Bury them," he commanded tonelessly. "Wrap Monsieur de Marques in a shroud, knock together a coffin and send the corpse back to the cardinal in Albi. When you order this done, return to me."

He continued walking, heading up to the battlements, accompanied by several gentlemen in his retinue who knew better than to breech his silence. De Lugny was among them.

On the crenellated battlements of the derelict castle he breathed deep of the chill wind that tugged at his feathered beret, and some of the deathstink blew away from his pinched nostrils. De Guise hated these ranges of low mountains, in fact the whole Aude valley region, for it remained steeped in that eerie, breathless quiet he had sensed on his few prior visits, as if the very place mourned catastrophe. It was a feeling that made him very uneasy.

Sometime back in antiquity, his ancestors had lived in this region before striking north to where the political power was coalescing–lived here and, he'd always suspected, some had been infected with the spiritual blight only generations of piousness and returning to Christ had cured. And now Louis lay dead on those hoary tiles which were still part of the Lorraine inheritance here, slain by Charles de Bourbon's kinsman.

And young Ferri was missing, along with the Bourbon woman who was their purpose here, and even de Marques' confessor as well. There had been an unexpected, large force of attackers, so the few retreating men who met them near Carcassonne had reported, led by a strapping, bearded Italian *condottiere*—as they'd heard de Marques call him—who de Guise knew could only be Ferrante di Gonzaga.

According to the messages forwarded to him from Ferri, those at Rennes-le-Château were not expecting Gonzaga's return from Italy so soon, so the *comte* de Marques must have been taken off guard. The violent feud between the Mantuan and his brother was long-standing, always due to end in the death of one of them. Louis was an accomplished swordsman, but too erratic and ridden by temper. Claude had always feared his brother's blinding wrath pitted with a cooler opponent would some day sweep him away.

He would miss Louis, but he was not surprised by his end.

It was Ferri's fate that worried him, for Gonzaga would not be gentle with a man of such treachery; but it was the loss of the Bourbon who could 'see-back' that especially tasted to him like wormwood, for clearly she still had special value to the rebel Bourbon.

In his pouch were several copies of a warrant he had at last obtained from the king to detain the woman for special questioning; and another warrant re-issued for the Gonzaga, Bourbon's long-time henchman.

They couldn't have gotten far in three days, and if he were the Mantuan, he would keep Ferri alive to use as a hostage. The man would not tarry at Rennes-le-Château now they were discovered; it was best for him to hustle his charge out of the country. West would take him into the well-patrolled domains of Gaston de Foix, a Bourbon enemy. South, through the still snow-covered mountains was difficult and slow. A ship from one of several ports on the Bay of Biscayne was most likely, and if there were none leaving port immediately there was a good chance the fleeing party could be intercepted. De Marques' remaining guards reported the Bourbon woman was very sick; Gonzaga might not dare travel too fast with her.

He had kept his composure at the sight of his skewered brother, for hatred at a distance was energy wasted. But he turned to one of the gentlemen who was doing his glowering for him and clipped out, "Take enough men down the valley to Rennes-le-Château at all speed. You know Ferrante di Gonzaga, if you find him there arrest him and the young Bourbon woman he accompanies in the king's name, and transport them back to the Episcopal Palace. The lord of that moldering hilltop is named Voisins. Question him and his wife however you will, if you cannot discover the ones I seek there."

He addressed another, "You will take men and hasten to Narbonne to make a thorough search of departing ships for Don Ferrante di Gonzaga and the woman, and he is probably holding Monsieur Ferri as hostage. I will furnish you with a letter to the city governor, and copies of my warrants. I myself will ride to Collioure."

De Lugny wondered, "But my lord, do you not wish to capture your brother's murderer yourself? Perpignan is much closer, there are more ships..."

The duke's degrading stare pinned the courtier as if he were a dead bird dragged in by a cat. "That is why I go to Collioure, *imbécile,* the man is no fool. You come with me, for you know what the girl looks like. A reward of five thousand livres above the king's promised royal purse for the man who brings these fugitives to me!"

La Dame's friend, a shipper of wine, oils and fats, lived in Collioure in a tall, half-timbered house with stained-glass bay windows. Polite but taciturn, he welcomed the arriving fugitives to the house for a few days, settled them into rooms on the third floor, presented his servant for their use, and left them.

Ferrante led Lyse, smiling and docile, to her bed to rest after her jouncing journey, partially on horseback, partially in a litter slung between two donkeys. She immediately fell asleep.

Lucco returned from an errand and informed him there were only two ships fit for passengers and soon to sail, one departing immediately, a carrick for Tunis in Africa, laden to the gunwales with milling sheep, and the other the large galleon Ferrante had come in, loading assorted cargo, including dyed woolens, leaving on the morrow direct for Livorno on the Ligurian coast. Ferrante thought they could chance waiting a day for the bigger ship whose destination was fortuitous, and went with Lucco to book passage.

He noted there were town guards strolling the piled-high wharf to deter pilferage, but they gave him only cursory glances. "Good, so far." he grunted to Lucco, "De Guise has not yet informed the port towns against us. Only one more day, Domine, give us one more day."

His thoughts dwelled again on the ravaged mind of his charge. Although she steadfastly believed him Bernard de la Motte, other things were muddled to her. Sometimes she thought they were fleeing to Scotland together, and sometimes that they were together in heaven, forgiven of sins, and a pitiful happiness shone in her eyes. But then she looked around in puzzlement, and Ferrante could see her fourteenth century memories struggle to make sense of their modern sixteenth century dress and inventions.

But she was childlike, wondering but not at all questioning, and her innocent smile could break one's heart.

But when he looked into the light blue eyes whose beauty still entranced him, they were empty, uninhabited.

He should have felt pity and he did, but also aching disappointment. And for the first time, wrath gripped him against Charles de Bourbon for risking this innocent in such a foolhardy quest, for exacting from himself that he wed this spirit-possessed female, and for other sins Bourbon might have committed in the past, perhaps.

On their way to this port they had slept one night in an abandoned shepherd's hut already dwelt in by a small family, but there had been room in a far corner. Lucco had contrived her a pallet of a blanket over a heap of dead leaves and pine needles, and Ferrante had stretched out along side by her. She thrashed in her sleep and sighed deeply. He stroked her shoulder and, watching her mouth in the light of the dying fire on the crude hearth, leaned to kiss it softly. His heart had moved in his chest then, but he quickly steeled it, and rolled away. What he felt he had to believe was only lust for her physical beauty.

Images of his dead wife Aliesa flipped through his mind, sitting for years with her face contorted with hatred, demanding all about her pay for her affliction, her limbs twisted and hurting under her lavish gown; and then on her deathbed, small, shriveled, made old by terrible pain. He may have shuddered at how terrible her poor life had been. But he had never, ever felt desire or love for Aliesa.

But with this pretty female, Lyse-Magdalene, his secret betrothed, it had been different: after his repugnance for her eerie ability receded, at first she had intrigued him, then amused him, then drawn him in, and finally, in giving herself to him in passion she of the virginal aspect but sensuous soul had become the very sun in his days.

Nevertheless, did he not at last deserve the chance to sire legitimate children on a woman who was without illness or blemish or demented? On the other hand, not an hour ago, as he bid Lyse stay and rest, and that he would return in a while, she nodded lamb-like, radiant with the desire to please him, and he was hit for a long minute with deep sorrow for the lively, headstrong girl who had been so unjustly wrenched from her body.

It was possible that she might someday heal and return to her own senses. But he quashed his spark of hope in this, for then what? Would she weep and rave and suffer every time some trigger loosed the memory of de la Motte's execution? Or would she be in his arms, but remembering and responding to the love-making of a dead Knight-Templar?

It was too much.

He let his horse pick its way along the street edging the curved harbor. He peered carefully at an old fortress on a headland across the bay. He watched the small waves beat up against the stone retaining wall of the *quai*, he studied the sturdy lines of the hulking, square-rigged galleon soon to carry them away from France, now with cargo hoists and striped-shirted seamen working hard.

He was wretched.

That night he tried again to reach her as she sat passively in the cushioned window seat, hands in lap, staring out into the dusk coming down on the town. He folded himself alongside of her, with one finger turning her face to his. "Lyse? Listen to me. Do you not remember your dear uncle, Charles de Bourbon, the Grand Constable of France?"

Lyse' brow wrinkled a bit. "*Mon cher* Bernard, but I have no uncle Charles." She saw his face fall, so she added hopefully, "But I have an uncle Raimond on my mother's side, he was in his youth a Crusader in the Holy Land with King Louis."

"Ah, Lyse-Magdalene, try! Surely you cannot forget your own governess, Madame de Dunois, who suffered such untimely death? Elinor de Dunois, the lady who reared you–?"

"But why do you call me that name? That is not my name, Bernard, I don't understand."

He pounded savagely on the wooden sill, frightening her, then sighed and gave up, impatiently throwing up his hands. But the look she gave him because he was not pleased was so woeful that he relented, as one would with a child, and drew her close to kiss her on the forehead. She emerged from this chaste embrace smiling once more, and so warmly appealing that his resolve just let go. His mouth descended on hers and he kissed her with a burst of desire so fiercely fanned by her passionate response, it almost overcame his despair for her condition. For a minute he reveled in her, in the sweet, yielding feel of her in his arms, in the remembered ardor of her lips that had set his heart on fire. But then, abruptly, he tore away his mouth and put her away from him with none too gentle hands.

She watched him, the 'peculiar' did, with eyes as gently startled as a gazelle. But he got up and stalked away, for she had, he was sure, been making love to Bernard.

In the next hours the smiling Lyse-Magdalene seemed not to notice his preoccupation, even when he pointedly, thought gently, unclasped the arms she sometimes slid about his neck. Both Collini brothers hung about the harbor, hearing plenty of gossip but nothing of any fugitives sought by the authorities. Ferrante was tense about the passing hours, knowing they were cutting it fine, but finally, when they inquired the next morning the master of the galleon had posted notice that the ship would leave on the afternoon tide, earlier than expected.

A few hours before anchor was to be hoisted, Ferrante rode through the market day throng to deliver in advance their small amount of baggage into their quarters below the high poop. In advance for no reason except that perhaps the angels were whispering in his ear.

With little interest Mélline-Lyse peered from her window at the townsfolk passing below, but suddenly there was Bernard, and he was riding away leading a baggage mule. Her lower lip pushed out and she pouted. She remembered one other time when he had ridden away from her to accompany a large and laden wagon—to Bézu? Or was it to that fortress? A wave of profound grief squeezed her heart and she whimpered. No, he was going to find sanctuary with the Hibernians. And she too? Didn't he say that? Ah, they would finally be happy!

But uncertainty nagged at her, she didn't feel sure. If he were not taking her along, why then, he must be going to Le Bézu. She gasped. Oh no, she must warn him, his life would be forfeit there, bartered for others, that dear and precious life that had given meaning to her own. What did he tell her? Did he tell her before he departed to take her rest? But she was all rested. She felt fine. Never, never would they lay hand on Bernard de la Motte again, the king's cruel men, she must run after him and warn him away from the eagle's eyrie of Le Bézu. Run, run...

Wide-eyed, with a shiver of anxiety, she whirled to descend to the street but there in the room was that disheveled-haired servant with the foreign accent set to watch her, probably, by her old husband. She had to be careful, she realized, and she smiled at him calmly. He smiled back in a shy manner.

She thought she would tell him she was very hungry, she would order him to fetch her some soup. She did so.

And when he was gone she flung her cloak about her shoulders, but the door was locked when she wiggled the latch. A crafty look appeared in her eyes. She pulled a chair over to an odd side window which she knew, from previous curiosity, only opened onto an enclosed, spiral stair. Standing on the chair she managed to hoist herself onto the window ledge, and peer over. But the window was too high on the other side, she would have to manage to hang full length and then drop. There was a good chance she would tumble down the step to the bottom, breaking numerous bones.

As she stared, irresolute, something wavered in her head, her vision shifted,

and she saw leaping flames of lurid orange and billowing smoke, and she was screaming, screaming as her dead lover's hair caught on fire

With blinking eyes and a frightened squeal she clambered up and over and managed to lower herself by her fingers, stretching with desperate toes for the step below her, and knew she was not quite tall enough. She inhaled a breath, and dropped the hands-width distance. Her feet hit squarely, but left her teetering, off-balance. She made a successful grab at the looped rope strung as a handhold and saved herself from a nasty tumble down the hard steps. As it was, she immediately discovered she had given her ankle a turn.

She limped down the stairs quickly, emerging into the arched alley cut through the house to give access to the stable behind. There, like a gift from God, a saddled horse stood quietly, reins in a loose hitch around a post. She had meant to run after Bernard and his companion, but now her ankle was turned and here was a splendid opportunity.

She used the mounting stone by the doorway to get up on the horse and smiled with great happiness, but then a puzzle slightly wrinkled her high, smooth forehead. Who was Charles de Bourbon? Who was St. Piteu? She closed her eyes a moment and waves seemed to lap in her mind, and there against her eyelids was a bearded knight who kissed her on the forehead with lips that burned. But then she remembered, she had to follow after Bernard, to save him.

She urged the horse out into the busy street and guided him in the direction Bernard had taken, but she did not spy his dark hair and broad shoulders anywhere before her, no matter what street she chose. Indecision struck her as the horse just ambled on. Perhaps her lover was truly sailing to the land of those Scots Templars where they would be safe, and he was looking for her?

She must find the *quais* where the ship would be at anchor before it sailed away forever. But the streets were so clogged with uncaring humanity in their silly, stiff clothes–perhaps it was a carnival–that the horse could make little headway. She'd be better off on foot.

"What town is this, good sir?" she leaned down to a burgher with a fat paunch carrying some purchases in a basket. "Why, Collioure," the harried man grumped, looking at her askance.

She slid off the horse and with her best smile pressed the reins into his hand. "I pray you, hold this mount for me until I return?" she said and flitted away, not seeing the man's eyes go wide with astonishment or hear his indignant cry after her when she slipped through the shoppers and between the stalls. She thought she could smell the sea ahead of her.

Ferrante did not even take the time to dress down the hand-wringing Marco whose face was crumpled as if he would cry, and who had run out to find the lady but failed. "Get to the ship, dolt!" he ordered the valet and ran down to reclaim the horses before Lucco had unsaddled them. The two of them clattered out to find the addled girl, who, their host hollered at their departing backs, had commandeered his mount.

Emerging from the alley, Ferrante almost ran head-on into Germain Matz, hauling up drawn and thin on a lathered horse. Ferrante reined in. "*Jesu*, what are you doing here?" he demanded of Lyse's stubborn-jawed minion, who was hatless and agitated.

"Don Ferrante, I could not let Mademoiselle depart the country without telling her farewell, without wishing her well. God saw fit to pull me through the fever alive and I have been in a recovery. I was much wroth with la Dame for not telling me in time that you were taking my lady away, so she finally told me where and I jumped on my horse to follow. I would like to see Mademoiselle Lyse-Magdalene, Signore."

Ferrante's impatient snort was eloquent. "So would I, Matz. It seems she has wandered off from us, but we sail in an hour so we must quickly find her. Come along, if you wish, six eyes are better than four." He turned away, but remembered something and turned back. "Matz, she has suffered a fall and seems to have lost her memory, she babbles nonsense now and then. The physician says she will recover in time. Do not let it bother you if she does not recognize you."

And he swung out into the street, away from Germain's aghast look, mixed with a fit of coughing.

At the first cross street, he pointed Lucco in an opposite direction, told him to scour that district but to finally ride to the ship. He motioned Germain to stay with him.

Collioure was a quaint little port with an almost circular harbor, the town built along one arc of it and straggling back into the high, greening hills, with ships tied up all along the harbor's curve. On market day country people from all around had crammed inside the low ramparts of the town to wander the stalls and the merchandise blankets spread on every square, offering great heaps of olives in every sort of preparation, plates and spoons of polished olive wood, vegetables and poultry, thread and bolts of cheap fabric.

Lyse couldn't have ridden far in the thronged and narrow streets, Ferrante reasoned, but he was worried; time was running out and the ship's captain had made clear that he would sail with the tide, with them or without them. It was difficult pushing through the heavy bustle of people without hurting some-one, even though he had left the great Bucephalus in Italy and rode his gelding. But crane as they would in every direction from their vantage point of height, neither of them spotted the green cloak Mélline-Lyse was wearing, and no one remembered seeing her. Then, entering a crowded little square, Ferrante spotted his host's horse being watered at a trough by a bewildered looking man. Accosted, this worthy gave them over the reins gladly, afraid to be hailed as a thief.

"At least she is on foot now and can't leave the town," Ferrante said. "I feared she was going to head back to Rennes-le-Château. Let's try the *quais*, then, it might be our vessel she seeks."

They anxiously threaded through the commotion of buyers and sellers and merchants calling their wares, to the wide, cobblestone wharves edging the harbor where the riding was easier. Suddenly, as sometimes occurs for no apparent reason, the crowd before them thinned into nothing for a space and they spied, retreating from them, their quarry's green cloak and the thick, copper braid down her back.

There was the usual human babble of market day all around them and the creak of block and tackle from the loading ships, but Germain's cry rang over them all, *"Ma princesse!"* and the girl stopped abruptly, stiffened like a board, and then whirled about, shielding her eyes from the sun. On her face was an astonished smile.

Germain followed up his yell with a piercing two-tone whistle and spurred his steed into a crazy gallop down the temporarily empty length of wharf separating them, holding out his arm in a certain way. She immediately responded by turning into position, so that he swept her up clean as a broom and whirled her to plunk with a hard jolt onto his saddle. Both of them laughed wildly, although the people that had scattered before the momentum of his dash were not entertained.

He reined in and twisted around, and Lyse-Magdalene was grinning at him, her eyes a-sparkle. "Oh my dear Germain! But you have been sick! So now you are well, oh thank the Lord." She hugged him about the waist, but then she looked all about them and her exuberance collapsed into scared confusion. "But...but where are we, my dear friend? Ooh...I feel a little dizzy."

Hastily he dismounted and helped her off, peering at her worriedly. "Are you all right?"

She tried to collect herself, clasping her hands together and biting her lip. "Why yes, I am. Germain? But what are we doing in this place? How did we get here? Why don't I remember?"

Germain saw Ferrante dismount behind her and he stood back, deferring to the one with the answers.

Lyse turned around and gasped. "Ferrante!" and then launched herself into his arms. "Oh Ferrante, Ferrante, how I have missed you, I didn't even believe you were coming back. Oh, there is so much I have to tell you!"

He stood not completely embracing her, hesitant, not ready to believe that the miraculous had happened, but he was clasping her loosely. She raised her head and he saw the ingenuous, dauntless Bourbon lady looking out again from her eyes. "Lyse-Magdalene?" he ventured cautiously.

"*Mais oui*," she laughed up at him, "have I changed so much in the few months you've been gone? I have suffered a trying time, indeed, but has it turned me ugly and grey? Do I look like a little toad? Signore di Gonzaga, it is not polite to stare so and say nothing."

"Forgive me," he stammered. "I missed you too."

"But when did you return? Oh Signore, you dare not come back, didn't you hear, the king has named you one of my uncle's confederates, liable to arrest. We must hide you immediately. But–" She glanced around at the bustle of the *quais* now flowing around them, "–where are we? I don't seem to remember..."

The cloud that had shadowed Ferrante's emerald stare was dissipating, and taking its place was a relieved expression, and to her surprise he picked her up in an exuberant hug and whirled her around. "Never mind, never mind, *douce-coeur*, we are in a port called Collioure and I will explain soon, but now we must find our ship."

"Ship?" She was amazed.

"Later. Trust me." He led her to the buff horse and lifted her up into the saddle. He said to Germain, "Our vessel is out on the farther arm. Come along."

They could not ride three abreast, so Ferrante motioned Lyse ahead, content to watch her from the back, his heart feeling as if a boulder had rolled off of it. But he wanted to speak with Germain a moment.

Germain hung back and spoke first. "I don't understand, Signore. You described her as confused. She seems normal to me."

"Hah, but she *was* addled while you lay sick, innocent of her own name, and her uncle's and mine, and even of the year we live in. Neither could la Dame's potions or my own pleadings cure her. I admit, it was frightening. But the very moment she spied you she snapped out of her delusions in a second. So how do you explain that?" Ferrante was uncomfortably aware his tone was short, fostered by resentment.

"Well, we are old friends, from childhood," Germain ventured.

"So was her governess, de Dunois, from her childhood, but she did not recognize the woman's name."

"Then it was the jolt of landing in the saddle, I suppose, it always helped." At Ferrante's quizzical scowl he shrugged and explained, "Mademoiselle Lyse has always had a curious way of–of withdrawing behind her eyes, as if she saw something no one else could. It happened erratically and only in brief seconds, but she seemed unaware of it and never mentioned it, and so neither did I. But this tiny–withdrawing–when it happened, left her–" Germain searched for the word, "–disoriented a while. We liked to ride together and practice that trick mount you saw, and once I noticed, after that strange flutter of her eyes, that the jolt of our trick helped her recover herself. After what you told me, and when I saw her down the *quai,* it came back to me and I tried it."

He shook his head in self-criticism. "I should have first thought that my arm might be weak after my illness, *mon Dieu,* I might have dropped her." He glanced at Ferrante and added, "I should have asked your permission."

"There was no time. You did well, Matz, better than Lora Voisins and me together." Ferrante rubbed at his beard and decided something. "We are hastening to Italy to avoid the king's arrest warrants, sailing in an hour on the next tide. She will want you to come with her, so suit yourself. I presume the ship's master will find room for you if I put enough gold into his fist."

A painful crease cut across Germain's forehead, still with its sickroom pallor.

"Monsieur, I cannot, it is impossible for me to go to Italy and I have suffered over it ever since my princess mentioned you might take her there. I have thought long and I have decided to return home again to St. Piteu and to my father, I worry what may have happened to him, there has been no news. I am his only child."

But Ferrante was staring up at a ridge across the bay where in the distance a pennant-flying file of riders moved at a brisk pace. Grimly he raised an eyebrow; his pursuers must have ridden half the night to arrive so soon. Their ship, the Santa Teresa, was just ahead of them, but cargo was still being moved aboard. "I understand, Matz. Ride ahead then and explain it to her, and quickly make your farewell. I have a very itchy feeling. And Germain, do not return to Rennes-le-Château, it may not be safe if the same men who commandeered St. Piteu find you there and still believe you can lead them to Mademoiselle."

He dug into the purse at his side and gold flashed as he dropped heavy coins into Germain's fist. "Go home. Take care of the property that might someday be returned to Mademoiselle. Those who came there once to seek Lyse-Magdalene probably will not return."

Ferrante left Lyse and her friend to their goodbyes at the foot of the gangplank and hurried to see the ship's master, an olive-complexioned Livornese with oil glistening in the folds of his fat face, and dark, beady eyes. This worthy, supervising the loading and munching a sugary pastry bought from a dock vendor, announced that his crew was behind schedule, that they would miss the tide that would float them out of the harbor and now would have to bide until midnight.

"But we cannot wait that long, we must leave France now."

"Si, si, ye were impatient to arrive here, Signore, and now you cannot wait to get out." The master's eyes drifted to the woman on the dock bidding someone farewell, he knew she was to be a passenger. His red lips pursed. "But the five hundred wine stoups from this region of Languedoc were late and now must be carefully packed into the hold. Can't sail without my cargo."

Ferrante had the measure of the man, having spent two weeks on the voyage from Genoa gambling at cards with him and emptying skin after skin of wine. "Listen, Manzarino, there will soon be soldiers to search every corner of this ship for that lady you see there, and they will post guards to see she does not embark later. We must depart before they ride up. Leave the wine, I say."

"Ho, Signore di Gonzaga, I am not a rich man. That cargo is worth more than your passage. Impossible to leave it. Oh no, no, no."

A clatter of hooves on the *quai* and Lucco hauled up, jumped from his horse and dashed up the plank, then up the steps to the poop deck where Ferrante scowled at the Captain.

"Signore, the *duc* de Guise and a force of men have entered the town!" he panted.

"Will you take two hundred ducats in French gold for the wine, Manzarino, and I make a present of it to the town of Collioure?" Ferrante pressed.

"A tempting offer, *Visconti,* but–" he threw up his hands, "I have a merchant in Livorno who will never deal with me again if I leave behind his shipment. He is a steady and good customer patron of my services. I am a poor man."

"What will you take to cast off now? I can offer you four hundred!" Ferrante broke in.

"Impossible, sir. Pray, do not nag me. I have my work." The captain turned away, licking the last of his pastry off his fingers, to holler up orders to men clinging to the mainmast boom.

"*Immuroto!*" Ferrante snarled under his breath. "I have no time to plead." He gained the deck and strode to the gangplank, followed by Lucco. "Find Marco," he muttered to his equerry, "Mademoiselle and I will ride south towards the Spanish border immediately. Follow after us."

"The *comte* de Foix has all the Catalan border passes patrolled." Lucco reminded him.

"If we even get that far," Ferrante growled.

But they were boxed in; de Guise would soon have pickets on every gate and road and ship out of Collioure; and la Dame's nervous friend in the town would not hide them further. It was either take the risk of going over the Pyréneés or be caught by de Guise. He would not let his charge fall into Lorraine hands again if there was the least chance to take, even crossing the passes with a woman and no preparations or supplies.

"Don Ferrante, hold a moment," Manzarino's voice came from behind him as he stepped onto the gangplank.

The captain stalked over, wiping his sticky hands on his breeches and then spreading them wide in an expansive gesture. "I don't know why they want you, and I am not interested, but I despise these Frogs, they are all thieves and villains. Give me five hundred ducats and ride south to a little cove I will direct you to, and I will pick you up tonight in a dinghy, after midnight. 'Tis a promising plan, for if I sail now, before your pursuers' inspection, they may suspect you are on board and will commandeer a chase ship. *E verro?*" The red lips smiled accommodatingly. Indeed, the master had a point, and his plan seemed workable if he could be trusted, safer than heading into the treacherous spring storms in the mountains. Ferrante had not time to be choosy. "I'll give you two hundred fifty now, and the rest when we leave the ship at Genoa." He noticed an even brighter gleam creep into the captain's crafty eyes and set about damping it. "Not that I have so much gold on my person, I don't. But on reaching shore you and I will find a notary to draw you a draft on my banker in Mantua. Agreed?"

Checkmated, and because it was easy money to make, Manzarini threw up his hands and wheezed, "What can a poor sailor do? But I know this coast like the boils on my backside, so many years have I sailed along it. Come here, Signore, look beyond the harbor to that headland, where my finger is pointing. Behind the jumbled rocks along that shore south there is a path to take you around the headland and beyond it; go further a quarter hour or so and you will come to the burned shell of a chapel overhanging the beach. Hide there. Bring a lantern–" he saw one and detached it from where it hung at the rail, "–and light it, but take care 'tis only seen from the sea. About an hour before midnight we should reach your position. I will send a boat up on the beach for you."

Ferrante scowled at the rotund Livornese a moment and the man seemed to shrivel a bit under the piercing scrutiny. But Manzarino smiled weakly. "You must trust me, Senore. I am a poor man. Five hundred gold pieces is a year's profits! And it will return some of the money you won from me a fortnight past," he made a weak joke.

Ferrante unleashed his wolfish grin, one that allowed no trifling. "Of course I trust you, Manzarino. But you see my man here, Lucco Collini? He does not." Lucco folded his arms just atop the two wicked daggers in his belt. "He will sail with you, in fact like your shadow he will sit, stand and piss with you until my lady and I are aboard this ship."

The captain shrugged. "So unnecessary, Signore, since my crew could overwhelm him."

"But not before he skewered you like a rat. He's very good at spilling entrails like that. Are five hundred ducats worth abiding his amiable presence?"

The greedy eyes shifted into neutrality. The oily face wrinkled in a more sugary smile. "Of course, my good *Visconti*. I am a poor man. I will signal you with a green light."

"*Multo bene,* and I will shade the lantern to a pattern of long, long, short. Look close, see you don't miss us in the dark."

Ferrante removed gold from his pouch to slip in his pocket, then tossed the purse to the master, who nimbly caught it in his fat hands. The Mantuan whirled and strode down the plank to collect Lyse-Magdalene.

He pulled her away from Germain to help her mount her horse and there were tears on her face. Ferrante gave Germain a grudging but respectful nod. "You've done well, Matz. Should the time come when you wish to join Mademoiselle's suite again, send her a letter in the care of the duke of Mantua. It will reach her," he promised. He grabbed Lyse-Magdalene's reins and led her horse off the wharf in a quick trot.

"Stop weeping," he ordered her gruffly as they cantered towards the end of the harbor's deep crescent. "You'll soon need good eyesight to keep your mount from breaking its leg. I suspect this trail we're taking will not be any king's Royal Highway."

Chapter 30

The track was lumpy, a narrow strip of sand between cliffs and the jutting boulders some natural force had tumbled into the sea, and it was full of buried flotsam and loose rocks that wobbled under the horses hooves as they picked their way in single file. Riding around the projecting headland they could have been discerned from the wharves by a sharp eye, but the path quickly veered inland, the dried-out reeds of a spongy marsh hid them, and then a low ravine as well.

When the track emerged at the shoreline again, they had gone past the headland, well out of sight of Collioure. Ferrante drew an eased breath.

He hoped he had won the gamble that the Italian shipmaster didn't know of the arrest warrant against him plus the reward, or would be happier with five hundred gold ducats and the opportunity to thumb his nose at the 'Frogs'. He believed that otherwise pursuit would have been evident by now.

He looked back at Lyse-Magdalene as she guided her horse between obstacles in the path. Short strands of hair had come loose from her plait and blew around her face, and there was a smudge on her cheekbone. Sensing his stare, her eyes raised and her crystalline blue gaze met his, Lyse-Magdalene once more. And in spite of himself he felt—happy? That pitiable wench had run a ring through his nose!

"I must talk to you, Ferrante," she called to him.

"Shortly, *ma chère*. When we reach our shelter we will have hours to talk. And days on the ship." Her gave her a wink, for they would have time for other things beside talk, but immediately clamped down on his lascivious imagination. *Peste!* Not now.

The burned-out chapel sat brooding at the sea from a low cliff, and when the path climbed up to it they could see there was nothing in any direction from it but fields of reeds. It was only a shell of four stone walls and no roof, but at least the walls would keep the wind off them should it rise in the night. When they approached they saw to either side of the Roman-arched entry several gravemarkers, leaning and broken.

Lyse's glance stopped at one of the askew slabs and she gasped softly, for although partially scoured away by hard weather and salt spray, a splayed-arm Templar cross was discernible and part of a name, '...artin, Félix...a small' (jolt)–

she clutched the crying baby close to her breast as she trudged toward the unmarked spot where the ashes of her lover were buried in unhallowed ground. "You must remember, little one, you must keep his memory, for he belonged to us, not them," Mélline muttered fiercely. She looked up, and the sky was a fiery red-orange as the sun sank to the rim of mountains marching away from Rennes-le-Château. "Yet an hour before the old man you call father returns for us, child." Tears sprang to her eyes

"No!" Lyse cried, shouting, wrenching herself out of the memory.

Ferrante, having dismounted to make a quick reconnoitre, sprinted back to her. "What is it?"

She leaned to him and he helped her down. "No, not important. A small memory." She saw the distaste rise in his eyes, he hated the 'seeing-back'. She stammered, "B-But I have learned to control the recall, partially. Ferrante, even when Ferri and his loathsome brother made me inhale the blue smoke, I believe I didn't say everything. I tried to force my mind to hold one thought as if were frozen there, and not go ahead, not to–to put words to what my soul remembered. So they blew fresh smoke until I lost my reason, but I had guarded from them certain things I remembered."

Surprised, he said, "You can do that?"

"I–I think so. It is so hard to know for certain–"

He stopped her with a finger. "We will find some comfort inside, first. Then you will relate everything."

Inside the gaping doorway the short nave was weed-filled and open to the sky. Ferrante gestured at the empty stone frame of a window that faced to the Gulf. "When dark falls, I'll suspend the lantern from that broken tracery in the window. We can sit near it, on that fallen slab."

He unsaddled the horses, thinking he would be saddened to leave his hand-some gelding there, then propped both the saddles against the low slab so they might lean on them. Then he offered her a cloth-wrapped packet, with a surprisingly shy smile. "I was bringing you a little gift to that Coulioure house, those sugar cakes you love and a flacon of barley water. I would say the thought was prophetic of our need, right now."

"It was very sweet of you to think so kindly of me, Don Ferrante," she murmured with pleasure.

He put the packet down and took her by the shoulders. He looked deep in her eyes, then kissed the tip of her nose. "I think of you constantly," he admitted, "Lyse-Magdalene de Bourbon-Tonnière."

Her heart leaped. While they were standing on the promenade where Germain had brought back her awareness, Ferrante had not been very effusive in his greeting to her after so many months; in fact she had sensed a distance at first. She had told herself that it just seemed that way because of the danger they were in, because of his haste to leave France with her and avoid de Guise. She'd had to use strength to hold her courage together in the disarray, the mortification of not even remembering anything between being held in the Lorraine's stronghold and the Collioure wharf.

Now, even in the failing light, she could at last discern something of the once captivated lover who had reluctantly left her to return to Mantua. The dusk suddenly seemed softer, the call of birds settling into the sparse trees prettier, sweeter, the lonely stones enclosing them, more welcoming.

"Ferrante, I beg you, first tell me how we've come here together, when I remember nothing beyond being forced to breathe the *pastel* and today. It terrorizes me to have no recall of my own life. And then I will tell you of Mélline's message."

He nodded. "Sit down then, upon the saddle cloth, and I'll try to be brief." She listened carefully to his accounting of her rescue from Valmigère, of de Marques death and her own close brush with mortality, and did not interrupt.

He had asked her not to be upset that she had lost her own person so long, but the vulnerability of it made her sick inside. Unwillingly though, she was forced to plunge once more into centuries past, for she had to inform him that all was indeed lost. With resignation, sitting hunched and hugging her dark green cloak about her, she began.

"Ferrante, there is no Treasury to find. What I mean is, it can never be recovered. The Scots Templars finally entered France from an obscure Atlantic cove and made their way east to the Razès in twos and threes, wearing the garb of ordinary travelers. They converged at a camp in deep forest not far from Puivert, the coded 'key' or map to the recovery which de la Motte had sent them in their hands. But in following his directions, they found it made no sense. In desperation their leader, Brother Knight Malcolm Macpherson, came to me—I mean Mélline—for Bernard had given her name as holding a copy of the encoded 'key'."

Lyse gazed abstractedly across the clumpy weeds and grass poking through the chapel floor and into the last silver edge of daylight beyond the ruined window. Ferrante, arms folded across his chest, kept his gaze on her somberly.

She continued. "But Mélline, you see, had known for a while that the Treasury was gone forever. As the histories say, the Puivert lake of that day was dry, dead. It was stinking ground and already avoided as haunted when de la Motte's Templars in the early dark of night dug into an isolated hummock covered with small scrub and there, making a deep excavation they buried their gold and priceless treasures. They had some method of replanting the trees and vegetation so that the place would appear as undisturbed, ordinary lifeless ground, undetectable to anyone without the 'key'. They worked swiftly and through the entire pitch-black night, with only a few lights, trusting superstitious fear to keep the local dwellers away."

She gave him a brief smile. "Those lights I thought I saw from my window at Puivert? It was a memory of Mélline's, for she was visiting the château and glimpsed the diggers' lights in the distance and was the only one who knew them for what they were."

Her deep breath was a sigh. "But during the two years it took the Scotsmen to come for the horde, the unimaginable had happened, the new lord of Puivert unknowingly had shored up the banks and filled the lake! And when the Templars came, the buried trench holding the Treasury was under water so deep one can imagine no highest spire of a drowned church would touch the surface. Not even if one could be a fish would the discreet landmarks they'd left to point the way be still in place, or recognizable. The Treasury was gone, lost in a deep, drowned grave. As it still is today, and must be, forever."

Ferrante cleared his throat. Neither spoke for a few moments, weighed down by the bitter disappointment. "So," he finally said, "that is the end of our quest and Charles' wild hopes?"

"That is the end," she echoed with hopeless finality.

After another moment of silence, he leaned to take her hand and squeezed it. "And Mélline? What of her?"

"Ah, *Dieu*, you see, it was Mélline who finally betrayed Bernard's hiding place in order to save the Cathars sheltered at Le Bézu! And no matter her knight forgave her for it, she could not forgive herself! What I have always remembered was the poor woman's agonized guilt, so immense over his death. But I also know that there was a baby daughter, his child. And I think...I feel..." Lyse hesitated, knowing the next memory would reflect on her; an edge crept into her voice, "... the distraught woman went mad in the end, snapped in two by her grief. I think she poisoned herself."

He was mute. But she saw his jaw clench. Her tone became more defensive. "I have gained some control to cut off the memories, but it could be I may someday 'see-back' to Mélline's insanity. My mother died screaming with the pain of burning remembered in her mind. Am I also to end with a broken mind?" On this horror her voice, her facade cracked; she was terrified.

He stood and drew her up, grasping her cold hands in his. "No! I order you never to think that! What control you've now learned is a beginning, you will learn more. Even enough to some day be free of that damned witchcraft."

"So that is what you think it is, witchcraft! You will always view me as weird, damaged—a 'peculiar' who my uncle forced upon you." The hopelessness of her love for him, it all burst out from her. "Well now my affliction has no more value to Charles de Bourbon, nor do I, and he will certainly release you from your promise of marriage to me."

It was almost full dark, but the moon hadn't risen; she could hardly see him.

He dropped her hands and she felt him staring at her as he too grasped that his future could be given back to him. She could imagine the glint of liberation in his stark, green gaze.

And then he moved away from her. In silence he fumbled flint and striker from his pouch, set alight the two candles in the lantern and shut its glass door, then hung the lantern by its ring from the window. He covered up the sides toward them with a kerchief he drew from his doublet sleeve, but enough of a dim glow remained to illuminate his bearded face.

Lyse stood there with hands clenched at her side, feeling the spirit seeping out of her. So there was the truth, in his very silence. Ferrante did what he did for love of his cousin, her uncle, as she always thought. And when Bourbon's purpose with her was over, so was his. She was suitable enough to take to bed, but not for wife, not for chatelaine of his household and mother of his children.

Her wounded thoughts darted about in her head. He had said her little chest had been taken on board the ship, and she had the money in it her uncle had given her—no longer to take her back to St. Piteu or Moulins, for what sanctuary they had represented was vanished. But enough to buy her a place with the Ursaline sisters in Lugarno, where resided the nun who was the *marquise* de Joyeuse' daughter. She longed not to be used as an unfeeling, unnatural object any more, perhaps consigned now to who knows what man to marry, or even just ignored. She would join an Order. When they reached Genoa she would hide from this cruel Ferrante di Gonzaga, this shallow and heartless seducer, until he went on his way, and then she would travel to Switzerland.

She would learn how to pray the proper Catholic way, and pray away in the sanctity of the religious life all her grievous failures, her forebears' suspect religion and her heartbreaking love.

He turned from contemplating the darkness from the window. He stood with legs apart and fists on hips, and broke with the silence by growling, "By every Holy Martyr, it seems I do not wish to be released from you, Lyse-Magdalene! And for such folly to drive a man of my experience, there is only one answer." He walked up to her. "I must be in love with you. I know you are important to my life." Quickly he held up his hand to keep her from speaking. "But I must tell you of something, a suspicion that eats like a poison worm at my heart. So now you speak only the truth, the absolute truth, for the sake of our future."

Swept along, Lyse yet bit her lip, for she knew what he was going to ask again, and knew she must answer him. Could she find the courage to confess to dallying with the St. Piteu guard to this volatile man who had just now finally admitted he might love her? Now would he despise her, turn away from her wanton, thoughtless sinning in disgust? Would giving in to his demand for the truth be bravery or pure stupidity for her?

She stood irresolute, waiting for his question like a victim for the headsman's axe, round-eyed with dread.

"Did Charles de Bourbon ever make you lie with him? Did he ever—violate you, or teach you the ways of love when you became of age?" The words seemed ripped from his throat. "Did he–touch you in illicit lust?"

"O, *le Bon Dieu!* No!"

Her shock was completely apparent. "Of course not. I cannot believe you! What could make you think such an evil thing?"

"Your inordinate love for him," came the resolute voice.

"Certainly I love my uncle and most dearly, but almost as the father I never knew! He was affectionate and kind to a lonely orphan," she cried. "But never did he treat me with disrespect. Never."

"Hah! And your lack of virginity? Do not expect I've put much credence in that story of a riding accident."

Amazement with his blind jealousy and suspicion of Bourbon decided her answer and her shoulders squared. "Very well, if you must know, Monsieur. That was the work of a young guard at St. Piteu. He–assaulted me, and I was too shamed and afraid to tell Madame de Dunois. Fearing punishment, the villain ran away that very night and was never seen again. That was all of it. Now are you satisfied?" Rather than penitent she was furious, although there was relief that she had finally unburdened herself of her secret sin, even though truth had still not quite been served.

"Are you sure that is all?"

"Indeed, you cruel man, to force me to humiliate myself by telling such a dreadful assault I could not help." She was glowering at him, whether he could see her clearly or not. "And your vile suspicions? I thought you loved Charles de Bourbon dearly as a brother."

"I do. I would do anything for him. But somehow, the way he spoke of you, the covetous look that came into his eyes when he described you. He is a man, after all, and you were totally in his power, a beautiful innocent."

"Don Ferrante di Gonzaga, you should be heartily, deeply ashamed!"

She could see his big shoulders move uncomfortably, he was feeling chastened.

But to deflect her scorn he rumbled, "Nevertheless, I tell you, should I ever come across that pig of a man-at-arms who attacked you I will break him in two and feed his flesh to the swine. Now let us close for good and all, forever, this sour subject."

Lyse felt a smile spread across her heart, she believed she would not again hear about her missing maidenhood. There was triumph in this, although she suddenly felt weak. She sat down.

He came to sit next to her. "Are you tired?"

She did not answer, overwhelmed by her crowding thoughts.

"You could put your head in my lap and sleep. We have yet some hours to wait."

She sighed. He leaned over and nuzzled her neck. "I beg forgiveness," he muttered, "Seems I am always begging forgiveness from you."

She let this go. "But what will my uncle Bourbon do, now there is no vast fortune to save him?" she burst out. "Will he ever march back into France?"

"Funds will come, some from my brother, some from other sources. Politics change, alliances change. If the Holy Roman Emperor's campaigns against Venice and Padua are successful, that ruler will have overflowing resources to lend. Much will reach Bourbon. He still has presence as a military genius."

"And will you join my uncle now, at whatever siege he leads there in Italy?"

"I must, my hand has always been with him. But I will settle you first in Mantua, in my sister-in-law's train, and you shall have new gowns and the best professor from the University to instruct you in Italian."

She said softly, certain she had the reins now. "But I am a 'peculiar'. You even think I could be a witch."

"I think you have ensorceled me, that is all. Come here, lady."

He drew her further into the muted halo of the lantern, where he studied her face. Her eyes were in shadow, but he could see her full-lipped mouth. He asked, "But will you have me? I am a soldier and I am not noted for mincing manners or a calm disposition, although if it is your mind to persuade your uncle to annul our betrothal, you will still be safe in Mantua. It could be I shall always grit my teeth that you may be having visions of de la Motte. But I want you, 'seeing-back' or not, you are the love of my heart and I will wed with you before the summer's campaigns, and return to build us a many-windowed and cheerful abode to live in, if such will please you. If you are agreeable..."

For a moment there was only the sound of a nearby owl, hooting at them from the dark outside the old, tumbledown walls that enclosed them.

"I am agreeable, Signore," Lyse murmured, looking down, suddenly shy and awed by how true that was.

There was a green lantern that shone steadily amongst the few bobbing yellow lights hung from the galleon, standing in the calm water of a cove below them. Another wink of light below the ship showed them a boat had already been launched.

Ferrante unhooked the lantern to guide them down the slope to the beach. "Come," the *condottiere* said, and grasped his lady's hand.

But Lyse looked back into the dark shadows of the ruined church, and the stone floor where they had come together again, passionately, on the saddle-covers and his rolled-up doublet. No hardness of stone or coolness of air quenched the wild desire they had for each other, or the devotion that fueled it; it was fast but they had sweet joy of each other and all the months of separation turned to dust and blew away.

She pulled up her hood. But outside she stopped, the breeze blowing strands of hair about her face. "Ferrante?"

He turned back to her, eyebrow tilted. "*Oui, mon coeur?*"

"We already know that Mélline's era still sheltered remnants of Cathars. But I believe the Voisins here and now are somehow Cathar, mayhap even the whole village of Rennes-le-Château! I remember back to my religious education at St. Piteu, actually the very lack of it in many aspects, so I suspect my uncle Charles has such leanings too. And yet, was not the heresy stamped out finally?"

He held up the lantern to see the puzzled appeal in her eyes, begging an answer to part of her odyssey in Languedoc not addressed.

"Will you will hold your tongue, forever, on pain of causing torture and death to all whom you love?"

At her solemn nod, he continued. "There are no true Cathars remaining after almost three centuries. But there are those who prefer some of the Cathar ideals to those of the present Roman church, who are seeking a return to a simpler creed. Your uncle, yes. The Joyeuse's, Madame de Dunois, myself, some others who might surprise you."

Her eyes had pooled to wondering, darkened blue in her pale face. "Are you not a Christian?" she asked in a shaken voice.

"Yes! That is the truth! A Christian, but not altogether of Rome, just as Christ was a Jew but not of the Temple as it stood. There is a silent brotherhood of us throughout Europe, an ancient, small but very powerful alliance, deliberately unsung for safety from the Holy Office. Your uncle, Bourbon, is its current head, and we have a sign by which we recognize each other. We are sworn to keep open a path of reason, unencumbered by dogma, by which the dear prophet Jesus may truly speak to the world again. The monk Luther, who has lately broken openly with the Holy See and decried some of its strictures complicating Christ's pure vision, gives us hope."

"But what am I?"

"One of us, in the way you were raised. But after greater explanation, you may choose to continue as a devout Roman, I will respect your choice, you have my word."

"I must know more. I am at a loss, there is such a veil of mystery."

"I will tell you more, I promise, when there is time. Take my hand now, we must not keep that Livornese waiting, his ilk are not famous for their patience."

He leaned down to kiss her and she melted into him a moment, gathering strength on that embrace, and then they went on, picking their way down the slope, and they heard the creak of the approaching boat's oars.

Lyse sighed to herself in the dark, for she thought with regret that she would never see her homeland again. But she would be the mistress of Trina and although her broad-shouldered *condottiere* would often leave her to pursue the interminable wars and carry the pennant of the house of Gonzaga amongst the warrior-nobility, she would not be alone, not truly, not amongst those things and memories that together they would make theirs.

She hugged to herself what the strange hermit of the Blanchefort tomb had mentioned, that bearing a child could sometimes destroy that dreadful 'seeing-back'. With a full heart she smiled, for if deep love could make a baby, she was certain tonight had already given her freedom from Mélline. Unaware of this possibility, her lover scooped her up with a smile and stalwart strength and carried her to the boat so she would not wet her feet.

On a promontory high above the gulf, the glory of the rising sun picked out several men sitting their horses and facing out to sea, as the fresh breeze of a fine day ruffled their plumes and billowed their satin capes.

The *duc* de Guise shielded his expressionless eyes and squinted at the retreating galleon whose white wings were just descending below the horizon. "I have the feeling Ferrante di Gonzaga is on that ship," he murmured to his companions. "Yes, I know, it was thoroughly searched before it sailed, as well as the whole town, and the Mantuan and the woman might yet be found in Perpignan. But like a hound my nose sniffs out that ship."

"We could give chase," de Lugny suggested. "A fast caravel from Perpignan could catch them."

"No need. Without doubt, I will find the *condottiere* again on the battle-field, amongst the officers that support Bourbon, and now he and I will be on opposing sides. The murder of my brother Louis and the disappearance of Ferri, mayhap his murder too, will be avenged, that you can trust. That you can trust."

"And the Bourbon woman?"

"She is no longer of consequence," de Guise said dryly, ignoring the sidewise, curious looks of his followers. He turned his horse back to the road they would take north again. In Italy's Piedmont Francois Premier was waiting for him and the relief troops he was bringing to aid the besieged city of Padua, where the exiled Bourbon and a Hessian army were expected to attack.

Claude De Guise had found, inside de Marques' doublet, a letter from Ferri to de Guise by rapid courier that Louis had intercepted, divulging everything the Bourbon woman had cried out under questioning. The only treasure she knew about, the one that Bourbon was seeking, was one he'd almost forgotten, the Templar Treasury, and in her trance she had blurted out the bald truth: it was unreachable, forever drowned somewhere very deep under Puivert's lovely, turquoise lake.

Well enough, it was out of Bourbon's reach. He would consider the still missing Cathar hoard and his own grand ambitions after the summer's campaigns. For now it was sufficient that Bourbon's light would certainly fade without huge funds to buy a rebel army; and without his own troops Bourbon was merely another mercenary sword. It was the princely house of Lorraine which would now sit on the right hand of the king. And he was the house of Lorraine in France.

He looked after the ship again, but it was fast going below the horizon.

His brother's murderer and the Bourbon seer had escaped him for now, but his thin lips stretched in a false smile.

He thought the ship disappearing from France was a perfect symbol for the unalterable Bourbon eclipse.

FINIS

Author's Historical Note

Charles, Duc de Bourbon, was killed in 1527, while laying siege to the walls of the city of Rome with his troops. He was felled while mounting a scaling ladder, by a shot the goldsmith Benuto Cellini claimed to have fired. In France his title and holdings were taken over by Antoine, of the Vendôme branch of the Bourbons, whose son became King of France as Henry IV.

The beautiful valley of the Aude river with its Templar and Cathar ruins, and Rennes-le-Château in particular, have been cited as treasure locations and places of mystery by many researchers past and present. One exciting 1982 non-fiction book of speculation, *Holy Blood, Holy Grail*, by Baignent, Lincoln, Leigh, insists that an ancient, highly-secret society of lofty but mysterious purpose was at one point headed by both Charles de Bourbon and then Ferrante di Gonzaga. This society may be extant to this day, so this book claims.

If you are in Languedoc's Aude valley and can find the barely-marked road to the top of the mount, the dusty village of Rennes-le-Château, along with its old and curious history and very strange nineteenth-century church, is worth a stop.

The illustration above represents an engraved image from medieval France of two armored knights astride a charger, a symbol used at the time by the Knights-Templar.

Dear Reader

I so much hope that you have enjoyed this book and that it gave you as much pleasure in reading as I had in creating it.

I would like to invite you to write and share your thoughts on *Fire, Burn!* with me. I promise to respond, to thank you for taking the time out from your busy schedule to provide feedback that we ofttimes cloistered writers find so valuable.

With all best wishes,
Mallory Dorn Hart

Box 626
Lenox Hill Station
New York, NY 10021